BEAUTY BEHELD

A RETELLING OF HANSEL AND GRETEL

BRITTANY FICHTER

THE CLASSICAL KINGDOMS COLLECTION BOOK #3

WANT MORE FAIRY TALES?

Sign up for a free no-spam newsletter with coupons, free short stories, exclusive secret chapters, and sneak peeks at books before they're published.

Details at the end of this book.

To my littlest brother, the baby we called General. It makes me proud that even with your ridiculous number of accomplishments, you still look up whenever you hear, "Squirt!" yelled into a crowd. It's like I preconditioned you or something, which is particularly impressive considering the number of times you ~~outsmarted me~~ took advantage of my sweet and loving nature. Though I wouldn't at all be surprised to one day see the actual title of general attached to your name, you will never cease to be my baby brother. And that's not a bad thing. Even generals need older sisters who still scold, hug, and occasionally buy them gummy worms and Twizzlers.

CHAPTER 1
SICKLY SWEET

Genny, would you stop crying?"

But Henri's sister only grew louder, her sobs turning to wails. Over her noise, Henri could hear thunder beginning to rumble in the distance, and his heart beat a bit faster. The way the bare branches swayed against the ash-gray sky made him nervous, and he knew without a doubt that a storm was brewing.

"Genny!" He took her by the shoulders. "I can't focus when you're so noisy! Just stop crying and I'll find a way home!"

"But Father said he would come get us!" she protested, wiping her little nose on her arm. "If we can't go home, then why can't we go get the sweets?"

Ah, there she went about the sweets again. And Henri had been doing so well to ignore it.

For the last few weeks, the woods had smelled much like the baker's shop in town. Genny, as most children of four years would, had begged incessantly to follow the scent. And to be honest, Henri had nearly given in more than once. Unlike Genny, however, he'd lived long enough in the southern woods to have learned the hard way that imaginings, such as sweets in the woods, were always far too good to be true. As this one was sure to be, despite the draw of its delectable smell.

"Henri, we need to find it!"

With that, Genny grabbed his hand and began to pull him in the direction of the smell. One glimpse of the green mist in her eyes sent him into a full panic. If he didn't get her back to the cottage soon, she just might escape him and scamper off into the woods alone, something that wouldn't bode well for either of them. That only left him with one choice.

With the snap of his fingers, the stones that Henri had been dropping ever since they left the cottage began to flicker in the dark, little tongues of flame lapping at the quickly deepening night. His stepmother would be sure to box his ears for such a deed if she saw, but if he was ever to get Genny home, it was a punishment he would gladly endure.

He heaved a sigh of relief when the little blue flames caught Genny's attention, and she quit tugging his arm in the direction of the rapidly falling dark. Instead, she allowed him to lead her back along the path of scattered stones, giggling when he put out each flame they passed.

"Where do you think Father went?" she asked for the tenth time that night.

"I don't know." Not only did Henri not know where precisely his father had gone to cut wood, but the fact that he had never come looking for them niggled at him, like a bug beneath his skin. Genny continued to prattle on with questions about every rock and tree they passed, seemingly brave and happy now that they were walking, but Henri's thoughts were too full for him to answer her.

His father had grown up in these woods, as Henri had. How had he lost them? Surely something must have happened. Perhaps a tree had fallen on him, or he had been attacked by an animal! Henri grasped his sister's hand more tightly as he hurried them through the trees, which were still bare from the vestiges of winter. It was getting colder by the minute, and if there were a dangerous animal nearby, he needed to get Genny inside.

They followed the little trail of lighted stones, and as they walked, Henri hoped again that his stepmother wouldn't notice their path. Whether they were lost or not, she wouldn't approve of him using his *trick*, as Genny called it.

"Blasted evil," she would mutter whenever she caught him creating the flames. "Unnatural, and sure enough to send you to damnation." Henri honestly didn't know if what she said was true, or even exactly what damnation was, but on a night such as this, he could think of no other way to get himself and his sister home.

Even with the path of stones to follow, the boy was beginning to get truly worried by the time the little cottage emerged from the trees and the last flickering stone was put out. The glow of the fire lit the gaping cracks in the wood, and a shudder of cold and dread rippled through him as he pulled the large door open. He wanted to stop and fill his pockets with stones again, as was his habit before he ever went in or out, for one never knew when he might need stones to light, but he didn't have time. It was already too dark, and Genny's teeth were chattering.

"Henri!" Helaine looked up at him from the wooden table that she was setting, her mouth hanging open as though she'd seen a ghost. "What in the blazes are you doing here?"

"Something must have happened to Father," Henri said as he closed the door and began to unwind Genny's thin shawl from her shoulders. "He never came back to get us." As he spoke, the door opened again, and a gust of cold air rushed in.

"This should be enough to keep us for—" Henri's father stopped and stared at Henri with nearly the same expression that Henri's stepmother wore, his arms still full of chopped wood. They all stood there like that for a very long moment before Henri's father glanced over at Helaine. Henri's stepmother said nothing but glared as though she were about to strangle someone.

What exactly had his father been up to, leaving them out in the forest like that after dark? Frustration simmered within Henri, but the question died on his tongue. Something was definitely off. His father hadn't come back to get them. In fact, it appeared now as though he never even meant to try. Why, Henri wanted to know, would he do such a thing? And yet the way Helaine was slamming the wooden plates upon the table shut Henri's mouth for good. In his heart, he had a sinking feeling that he knew exactly why his father hadn't come back to look for them.

Supper was meager that night. Helaine had only cooked enough for two, it seemed. And though stores were running low, as winter had been long in departing this year, Henri knew there should have been enough for them all to have their fill. Genny opened her mouth to complain, but before she could, Henri dumped the rest of his food on her plate. Going hungry was better than watching his stepmother take the switch to his little sister for talking back, and, if pressed, Genny would have no reservations about doing exactly that.

"If you make so much as a peep tonight," Helaine whispered above the children as they huddled together under the single blanket on their straw pallet, "I'll get the whipping stick for both of you!" Her thin, mousy hair stuck to the sides of her face, and the anger in her eyes made her look rather like a mole rat. But these thoughts Henri kept to himself, hoping very much at the same time that his sister would keep her thoughts to herself as well. Much to his relief, however, she fell asleep almost immediately, seemingly unaware of the strange goings-on that Henri was still trying to understand.

That his stepmother and father had not expected them back was obvious. But why would they try to lose them? Henri was well aware that his stepmother didn't care a mite about his well-being or his sister's, but his father surely wasn't that cruel.

But what if he is? Henri wondered. *And what if they try again? What will I do then?*

If his parents didn't want them at the cottage, then he and Genny would need to find somewhere else to go. No one in the village would take them, of that he was sure. The township had never liked his family much to begin with. The woodcutter's family, as well as others like them, who lived outside the village, were suspected of all sorts of wrongdoings. Why else would families choose to live outside the protection of the town?

Perhaps Father Lucien would take them in. Henri was sure the holy man would at least let them sleep in the church for a night or two until Henri could find a new home. But Father Lucien hardly received enough food now. There would certainly not be enough for three. So where would a boy of nine years find food and shelter for not only himself but his sister of four?

Henri's thoughts raced in circles until they were too worn to continue. Drifting off into an aimless sleep, Henri's last thoughts were a prayer to the Maker, asking, if for nothing else, that the Maker find them a home. It didn't seem like too much of a request. And yet the task seemed much too great for Henri to carry on his shoulders alone.

For the first time in a long while, Henri, who was far too old for tears, cried himself to sleep.

"GET UP."

Henri groaned and rubbed his eyes. How had morning come so soon? A light shove to the chest from his father's boot, however, roused him enough to realize that morning had not yet come. At least, there was no sun.

"Why are we up so early?" Henri yawned, wanting nothing more than to roll over.

"Long day's work. Now get your sister. We're goin'."

At this, Henri stopped stretching and squinted up at his father. As he did, all the events from the day before returned. Immediately, he knew that whatever this errand was, it would probably have the outcome his parents had wished for the night before. "Genny doesn't need to come with us," he said in a small voice. "She's too little to carry much wood. She'll drop it when she gets cold." It was a foolish thing to say, but his foggy mind couldn't come up with any better reason to keep Genny at home and warm. Perhaps, if Henri disappeared and his trick was gone with him, Helaine and his father would be kinder to his sister.

"Nah. She's coming too. Now up, both of you, before your mother wakes up."

Henri fumbled in the darkness for his sister. Curled in a tight little ball, she was a mess of yellow curls and blanket in the thin light that came from the orange embers in the hearth. Anxiety bubbled in Henri's stomach as he gently shook her awake. "Come on, Genny. It's time to get up."

"No. It's cold."

"Genny, I mean it. Father says—" As he spoke, a brilliant flash of light briefly lit the room brighter than day. The crash that followed was loud enough to send Genny into his arms with a shriek. Henri took the opportunity to drag her out of bed and tie her shawl around her shoulders, trying to ignore the piteous whimpers she was making about getting out of bed in a lightning storm. Whenever he could, he tried to throw a glance up at his father, begging silently against hope for mercy, but the room was too dark, especially after the flash that had just blinded them all. The air was heavy, its warning thick. This storm would be bad. Why was his father so insistent on taking them out *now*? If he was so determined to lose them, as Henri feared, couldn't he at least do it when the weather was less violent?

"Here." His father shoved a loaf of bread into Henri's arms. "We'll be working a long time today."

All too soon, they were dragged outside, his father's axe upon his shoulder and Henri clutching the bread in one hand and his sister's hand in the other. "Wait!" Henri called, stooping and desperately clawing the ground for pebbles. But his father gave him no reprieve.

"We don't have time for your foolish antics, boy!" His father turned and marched back to the children, grabbing Henri so hard by the shoulder that it hurt, yanking him back up from the ground. Another flash of lightning revealed a resolve on his father's face that Henri had never seen before. The look was more like one Helaine often wore, full of loathing, than his usual grave countenance. And it frightened Henri. No, his father would not allow any more antics.

When his father seemed satisfied and assured of Henri's obedience, he turned and stalked off in a direction they didn't usually go. South, where the trees were thin and crooked, and Henri wasn't nearly as familiar with the landscape. In desperation, Henri began doing the only thing he could think of. Breaking off small chunks of the bread, he began to drop them on the ground behind them as they walked. He would have preferred stones to the bread, but it was the only way he could think to mark their trail.

For once, Genny was silent, clinging to his arm as they walked. Keeping up with their father became more difficult as the forest around them grew soggier from the rain. Genny's legs were short, and as the mud became deeper, she struggled to keep up.

"Father!" Henri called out as he paused to pull his sister's feet out of a mudhole. "Wait!" When he looked up, however, all signs of his father were gone. "Father!" Henri cried again, tears pricking his eyes, mixing with the nearly painful raindrops that were beginning to pelt them.

He had known this would happen, he tried to tell himself. That was why he'd been dropping the bread crumbs. He had known his father was going to leave them. He could see it in his face. And yet, deep down, he had hoped his father might find a shred of pity in his heart, if not for him then for his little sister. But here they were. The bread had run out a long time ago, and Henri had no idea as to where they were. Worse than that, though, he knew now what he had feared for so long.

They were unwanted.

"I want my mummy!" Genny sobbed as she began to kick and thrash against him. "I want to go home!"

"Genny, stop kicking!"

"No! I want to go home!"

"I mean it! Stop it right now! No one is coming for us! No one wants us! We don't have a mummy!"

Genny stopped struggling and looked up into his eyes, their whites lighting up more as each flash of lightning drew closer. "But you said—"

"I lied. I lied so you would think we had a mummy. But we don't, so stop screaming and let me think!"

Genny did indeed stop fighting him, but the heartbroken sobs that she now heaved hurt his heart even more. He had never been that cruel, and he hated himself for it. But the lightning was growing nearer, and he needed to get them to a safe place before the savage storm was fully upon them.

After a few minutes of turning in circles, waiting for the lightning to strike so he could see the landscape, Henri spotted a little ravine with a hidden alcove beneath it. They would be squeezed tightly inside, but it was better than being out here or beneath a tree. Henri shivered. As the son of a woodcutter, he had learned early on what lightning did to trees.

Henri took a deep breath and began to drag his still-crying sister over to the alcove. It took a few tries, but he was finally able to shove her down into it and then follow along himself. The soil that they were pressed into was slimy and thick and smelled of swamp gas, but Henri wriggled himself as deep into the bank as he could, holding his sister tightly so she couldn't escape. And none too soon, as they had only been there a moment or so before the world outside of their shelter began to explode. Genny screamed with each boom of the thunder, and Henri screamed right along with her. Never had he seen such a storm. But then, never had there been such a night.

"Henri!"

Henri moaned and tried to turn, only to realize that he was not on his straw pallet but squished up against a muddy ravine with his neck cranked uncomfortably. It took him a moment to remember where they were and how they had gotten there.

"Henri! I smell it!"

"Smell what?" Henri slowly pulled himself from the little hole in the earth to where his sister was standing, pointing with all her might to the east. The storm had finally passed, and weak sunlight made it through the thin clouds and crooked trees down to the riverbank on which they stood. Everything looked pale and tired.

"The sweets!" Genny looked at him as though their parents hadn't just lost them in the forest on purpose during a lightning storm. Instead, her pale blue eyes were alight, green shimmering ever so slightly through their depths.

Before he had a chance to ready himself, Henri was hit by the smell as well. He didn't just smell it, though. A hunger so strong it was nearly nauseating hit him like a stray kick from his father's foot, and it was hard to think of anything else but the delicacies that beckoned them to come and partake. Why had he resisted this call for so many weeks?

"Let's go find them!" Genny grinned. "Let's go find the sweets!"

CHAPTER 2
WELCOME INTERRUPTIONS

I don't think I want to go to the banquet tonight after all," Ever breathed into Isa's ear, his arms encircling her waist. "I would much rather stay up here with my wife."

Isa laughed as Ever held on to her, swaying her from side to side while giving her his most pitiful look through the mirror. "If you don't hold still, I'm going to drop this earring."

"You don't need earrings if we're staying here."

"Ah, but we cannot stay here, my love. What of our guests downstairs?"

Ever threw his head back and let out a huff before walking to the bed and falling on top of it. "I am tired of people."

"Since when do *you* tire of people?"

"Since my wife looks ravishing enough to keep to myself and away from prying eyes forever. Why don't you wear that color more often?"

Isa shook her head with a smile and walked over to the bed, where she gently pulled her husband up into a standing position. "But you look so handsome," she said as she straightened his cloak and tunic. "Don't deny me the pleasure of showing you off tonight."

Handsome was an understatement. The black tunic with silver stitching made Ever look even more imposing than usual. The strong line of his jaw and the erectness of his shoulders made her stomach warm, even after four years of marriage. A few flecks of gray peppered his golden hair here and there, much too early, Isa thought, for his thirty-one years. And yet, what could one expect with the many burdens Destin's king was forced to carry? Softly, she ran her fingers through that short hair and drew him down for a kiss. Even the gray hair she loved, for it was a constant reminder of her husband's love for his people. And his love for her.

"We need to go now," she said somewhat breathlessly, as she managed to pull out of the kiss. "They're waiting for us."

"Let them wait," Ever said in a gruff voice.

"They might not need us," she rested her forehead against his, "but the children do." Even as she spoke, Isa could feel the tension return to his shoulders, and she briefly regretted saying such a thing. Already, his storm-gray eyes had become resolute, and he leaned in for one more passionate kiss before walking to the door and holding it open for her.

"As usual, you are right," he said, his voice steeled and commanding once again. "It is time."

Once they had stepped outside, Ever offered Isa his arm, which she took most readily. Being on the arm of the most powerful, not to mention the most attractive, man in the realm still sent shivers up and down her back. Tonight, however, she felt as though she actually might match his regality, thanks to Gigi's hard work.

The red gown that Isa wore tonight was not comfortable in the slightest, its stiff material covered entirely with embroidered miniature white flowers, and it was already making her back ache with the formal posture it required. The elegance of the dress, however, made it one of her favorites. The bodice was fitted, with dozens of small ivory buttons laced up the front, a style taken from the far east, Gigi had said. The skirt was a fashion taken from their own tailors, with layers of cloth cascading in a red waterfall down her legs, much like the petals of a tight, slender rosebud just beginning to unfurl. Though intricate, the gown itself was far from soft. Its sharp angles at Isa's neck and wrists and the fierce color of the dress created an imposing combination, which was something Isa would need more tonight than ever before. This meeting of kings and queens was important, and choosing to call such an assembly had not been an easy decision to make, for they had much to ask of their neighbors.

"Your Majesties." Garin greeted them just outside the crystal balcony's doors with a smile and an appraising look. "You look ready to enthrall the world." He took Isa's right hand in one of his and placed his other hand on Ever's left shoulder. "Are you ready?"

Ever, his face set in the dutiful, vigilant expression Isa knew so well, nodded once. Garin gestured to the servants, who opened the doors to the crystal balcony.

A hush fell over the crowd as Isa and Ever cut across the spacious balcony and came to stand in its center, waiting for the music to begin. As they waited, Isa scanned the crowd. Most of the border lords were there, as well as the Tungean and Tumenian kings. A fair group of nobility who also kept lands on their borders surrounded them, along with the kings and queens of Kongretch, Pearlamar, and Anbin. But where were Launce and Olivia?

Before Isa could search more, it was time for the ceremonial dance to begin. Isa turned back to her partner to find Ever studying her face with a soft intensity, the blue fire in his eyes dancing in time to the music.

"You look breathtaking tonight," he whispered as they began the first slow spin.

"Why thank you," she murmured. Why did her cheeks still flush when he spoke to her that way? She hoped they'd never stop. "Don't get used to it, though. It took Gigi and three other servants four hours to piece me together like this."

"It's not the dress." He pulled her into a more dramatic twirl. "Your eyes sparkle when you're happy."

"And how would you know I'm happy?"

"Look." He glanced down at their feet, and Isa's heart leapt as the blue spirals of fire danced and twirled right along with them, encircling their feet as the flames rose out of the azure crystal. It didn't matter how many times they danced on this floor. The sight of the crystal's fire would never fail to steal her breath. How many dances had they shared here beneath the light of the moon?

All too soon, the dance ended, and it was time for the real work to begin. Servants ushered everyone into the grand dining hall, alight with a thousand candles hung from crystal chandeliers that reflected off pearlescent floors so that the room shone like a beacon even in the night. As soon as everyone was seated, Ever stood and gave thanks to the Maker for their bounty. Servants appeared, and platters full of steaming beef, sweet corn, honey-dripped hams, fruit so plump it was nearly bursting, and dozens of other delicacies filled the tables. The tables themselves were laid out to resemble a horse's shoe, with Ever and Isa at the front and center where they could see all of their guests before them.

Just after the first course, as the sugared rose petals were being served, a movement at the dining hall's door caught Isa's eye and she allowed herself a sigh of relief. They had made it.

"Presenting," the herald called, "Launce Armand Marchand, of Soudain, Destin, crown prince of Cobren, and his wife, Princess Olivia Edite Raquel Rocha of Cintilante Areia of Cobren."

Despite his three years in the Cobrien courts, Launce's cheeks still burned visibly as he let the servant lead them to their seats of honor at Isa and Ever's table. As they drew closer, Isa could immediately see that Olivia's face, however, was an unhealthy shade of gray. Isa's first reaction was to think the poor young woman had grown ill sometime on their journey, but as Olivia drew nearer, it became quickly apparent that no such thing had happened recently.

Olivia had never been slender like Isa but had always kept a lovely soft shape with generous curves and a wide face that was quick to share a friendly smile. But as she sat down heavily beside Isa, the sort of change that had come over Isa's sister-in-law was undeniable.

"Olivia!" Isa stood and leaned over to give her a quick, tight hug. "How... how wonderful! How long...?" Isa glanced up at Launce, who uncharacteristically ignored her as he sat beside his wife. The set of his mouth and the way he tucked into his supper made Isa realize he wasn't going to tell her anything easily tonight, so she reached out and gently probed his heart with her own. *Guilt.* He was full of guilt, as was Olivia. But at least Olivia was returning her gaze, albeit reluctantly.

"Please forgive us for our lateness." Olivia groaned as she leaned back in her chair. "I thought the carriage ride would be well enough, but I have had to stop more times than I can count."

"No, of course, we don't mind!" Isa hurried to assure her, trying not to sound as flustered as she felt. "But, Olivia, how long?"

"Five months." Olivia sent her a weak smile.

Five months. And they hadn't bothered to send word that they were expecting? That her own brother had hidden such a secret from her irked Isa more than she cared to show. She swallowed and sought to control her emotions. "But why didn't you tell us?" she asked as kindly as she could. "Mother and Father will be thrilled!"

"They know." Launce spoke for the first time, taking a deep swig of his ale.

They knew. Of course they knew. Launce might be crowned prince of Cobren, but no title would have saved him from Deline's wrath had she found out her son had hidden such a thing. Which meant Isa's parents had hidden it from her too. But why would they do such a thing?

"You are to be congratulated." Ever's deep voice rang out from behind her, and Isa was immediately grateful for the distraction as she fought to keep tears from streaming down her face. She knew exactly why they hadn't told her. It was the same reason the expecting women, servants and nobles alike, at the Fortress tended to avoid her until their babes were old enough to toddle around on their own. It was the same reason that Cerise, one of Isa's oldest friends, had suddenly taken her leave of the Fortress soon after marrying and had not returned.

The food on Isa's plate suddenly looked dry and unappetizing, and Isa wanted nothing more than to do what Ever had suggested before the banquet, to run back to their chambers and hide there for a very, very long time. But for now, she reminded herself, it was her duty, as a queen and a sister, to do what her heart wished most of all not to.

"I'm so happy for you." She turned to Olivia, hoping her voice didn't waver too much.

"Truly?" Olivia watched her through large, brown, careful eyes, so Isa nodded.

"It will be so wonderful to have a niece or nephew to play with. We need someone around here to spoil."

Just then Ever stood, much to Isa's relief, and waited for the talking to die down. When the grand hall was quiet, he looked at Isa, who rose and stood beside him. They had work to do.

"I want to begin by thanking you for coming to us," Ever began in his reverberating voice. "I know it is not an easy journey for many of you. But there is a matter of grave importance that we must discuss, and I'm afraid it is one that cannot be done through quill and parchment."

Their guests watched them silently. Even Lady Jadzia, one of Isa's least favorite people in the world, wore a look of alarm.

"We have discovered a great evil within our borders," Ever continued, "and it is stealing our children."

Gasps went up from a few in the crowd.

"In the dead of night, children from all over the kingdom have been disappearing from their beds, but when morning comes, no one can find a way or reason for their disappearance. Common children, noble children, there is no discrepancy. Boys or girls from every station of life, from three years of age up to the age of ten have gone. We have had our soldiers searching for the responsible party for weeks now. I, myself, have ventured out at least a dozen times. And yet we cannot find where the children are going, nor do we know how they are getting there. All we know is that somewhere at the core of this crime is a magic of the blackest kind."

Ever paused, Isa knew, to allow such dour news to sink in. Throughout the western kingdoms, there were little bits of magic here and there, often kept hidden by kings and lords to secretly further their own interests. But few kingdoms used the deep magics. For magic was far different from what Isa and Ever and other gifted folk wielded. Theirs was a gift from the Maker, a power that lived in their bones, and was as much a part of them as their hair color or the length of their fingers. Deep magic was conjured, dragged up from the dregs of the earth, substances and powers that no man should ever touch, according to Ever. The only kingdom to use such power in recent years had been Tumen. But even they had sworn off such power in order to promote peace within the realm.

"What is it that you could want from us, Everard?" King Leon of Lingea called out.

"I would like to position groups of my soldiers along all the borders of Destin," Ever replied. "I have the feeling that we will be smoking the offender out very soon. Should he escape, I would like my men, with your permission, of course, to have the right to chase him down, no matter which territory he crosses into."

"How do we know this isn't simply a step toward handing over our lands to you now?"

Everyone turned to see Lady Jadzia stand. Even taller than Isa and decked in emeralds that made her red hair look even redder, the woman sniffed and tilted her head with a look that made Isa want to smack her. Instead, Isa stood as straight as her own back would allow and fixed her most dangerous gaze upon the noblewoman.

"Would you prefer for the thief to run about your lands unchecked? Because I can assure you, Lady Jadzia, that such a thing would be perfectly possible."

The two women stood for another long minute, glaring at one another until Lady Jadzia finally sat down with a thump beside her snoring, portly husband. If the woman wasn't so infuriating, Isa might have felt sorry for her. To be forced to marry such a man twice her age could not have led to a pleasant life. But the sneer on Lady Jadzia's face kept Isa from feeling too sorry for her.

"Losing the guilty to a man-made border seems a complete waste of time and resources." Ever resumed his speech as Isa and Jadzia continued to glare at one another. "I would like to personally ensure that he never produces such darkness in another kingdom again."

"You have our cooperation, of course." Launce spoke up, carefully keeping his gaze directed at Ever rather than her, Isa noticed. As the other kings and nobles began to talk amongst themselves, a soldier slid through the door and approached them at a quick pace.

"Your Highnesses." He leaned in to whisper to Isa and Ever, "Another informant has been brought in. General Acelet thought you would be quite interested in this one."

"Very well," Ever nodded, "I will be down in—"

"No." Isa was already on her feet. "I will take him. You finish here."

"Are you sure?" Ever quirked a brow at her, and Isa gave him a sly grin back.

"I've been itching to get my hands on another one."

At that, Ever flashed her a knowing smile before turning back to his guests.

Isa followed the soldier as quickly as her legs could carry her, thanking the Maker all the way out of the dining hall and down to the examination room. While interrogating their newest informant would have been an intriguing task on any given day, now more than ever she was grateful for the escape. Anything to keep from having to sit beside Launce and Olivia as the object of their pity.

CHAPTER 3

SORTHILEIGE

The examination room, as it had come to be called, was located on a lower level of the Fortress. It had no windows and only one door. Ever had argued that interrogating criminals in the dungeon would have been more effective, but Isa refused to go down there. Dungeons of any sort held too many memories for her after the war with the glass wizard, even the upper dungeons that she'd never been imprisoned in. Besides, she'd told Ever, her talent didn't rely on darkness or his terrifying blue flames. She would be better able to focus in a simple room, one that allowed her to focus on the core of her victims' hearts. To that, Ever could not argue.

As Isa entered the examination room, a shiver moved across her shoulders and down her back, and she was suddenly thankful for the presence of the two soldiers that flanked her. They were two of Ever's best. *Can they feel*, Isa wondered, *the same cold blackness that surrounds their prisoner?*

Before the children had begun to disappear, Isa had had little experience involving those with the dark arts. The practitioners of Sorthileige had been well enough hunted down by earlier generations of Fortiers that there were few left in Destin. Even so, whenever word came in of Sorthileige activity, Ever had never wasted a second in tracking it down and cutting it off wherever he found it. When Isa had once asked why she should not accompany him, Ever had turned to give her a look that had chilled her to the bone.

"You will... someday. But the darkness will change you..." He'd paused, his eyes troubled. "It took me years of practice before I was ready to take the Sorthileige on without my father's guidance. One day, when I know how, then I will teach you."

Isa might have pressed harder if it hadn't been for the extreme weariness she had seen on his face every time he and his men returned from such an expedition. When she had asked Acelet, Ever's favorite general, the man had worn a haggard look very similar to Ever's.

"Such activity is not a place where we can help him. We simply clear the area so no one stumbles upon us while he is at work."

"What does he do with it?" Isa had asked.

"Burns it... all of it. Everything the Sorthileige practioner has touched or owned must be destroyed."

"Can you not set such items on fire?"

Acelet had shaken his head sorrowfully. "No mere fire burns such relics of darkness. Only the Fortier fire can engulf it."

"And the people?"

"I continue to await the day when one runs to him, begging for forgiveness, but no such thing has ever happened. They all try to escape or resist him. Every single one dies with a shriek of rage on their lips."

After that conversation, Isa had decided that Ever was right, and that she was not ready to face such an evil. Not yet. The Fortress was changing her, making her stronger to be sure, but she was still learning her own power.

That resolve had changed for both of them, however. When the children began to disappear a few weeks before, the work had become too much for Ever to handle on his own. Even then, Ever had not wanted her to touch the witnesses they were bringing in, but Garin assured him that he would be there with her as long as she needed it. Only Garin's presence convinced Ever to let her try. And to be honest, Isa hadn't really wanted to try at first, either. As always, however, in his own gentle way, Garin had guided her and protected her. Under his tutelage, her particular strength proved to be a great asset in the interrogations as they tried to track down the source of the disappearances. It had not been long before Isa was able to handle the interrogations on her own. Of course, that didn't mean she enjoyed the darkness any more than Ever had.

Still, it gave her something to do, a purpose she knew she had been made to fulfill. So now, Isa steadied herself as she faced the man who was bound to the chair in the center of the room. Chains, rather than rope, had been used, as Ever said rope was rarely effective with even the most basic of Sorthileige users.

Upon studying him, however, Isa realized that this particular man was somewhat unusual compared to their more recent prisoners. He reeked of the dark arts, as the rest of them had, but unlike the others, he wore no talismans or charmed stones. In truth, he much resembled a tavern regular, the kind one might find on its steps after having a drink too many and causing a ruckus. His stringy brown hair was long and tied poorly behind his neck. Along with the scent of darkness, his ragged clothes reeked of ale, sweat, and bodily parts that Isa preferred not to think about. As she studied him, the man stared right back at her. His dirty, matted beard covered most of his mouth, but what was visible was turned up in a cocky grin. Not that such looks bothered Isa. She had dealt with arrogance like his before, and worse.

"So," Isa began in a quiet voice as she fixed him with her most unnerving stare, "I am told you were found boasting of selling a book of the Sorthileige." She paused. "You do know that to possess such an item and not relinquish it immediately to the crown is a crime punishable by death, do you not?"

The man stuck his bottom lip out and shrugged. "I'm just a simple tradesman, Your Majesty. I don't care to make deals with the king. But you," his eyes raked her up and down, unabashed, "I might certainly be willing to make a deal with you... for the right price. We could—" The smirk melted from his face. "What are you doing to me?" He gagged.

"That is for me to know. What I need from you is the truth. Who purchased that book?"

"I don't like this!" The man shook his head violently and flexed his hands within their bindings. "Make it stop!"

"Then tell me to whom you sold the book!" Isa shouted.

"It wasn't recent! Four years ago... maybe five?"

Isa pressed harder. It was amazing how agonizing the truth could be when one had managed to suppress it for so long.

"A woman! It was a woman! She was new... I'd never seen her before that night! She simply showed up at the tavern one day."

"What tavern?"

"The one in Sansim. I don't even know how she found me. She asked if I knew where she could find a book of the Sorthileige, and I did. Picked it up off some dead hermit a few years before that. She paid me and left, and I haven't heard from her since!"

"And what, precisely, did that book detail?"

The man shrugged, his body shaking as she released him from the agony just enough for him to think. "I never read it. I told you, I'm a merchant. I have a few talents here and there, but I deal talents more than I practice them. Talismans, individual spells, even large items like the book, when I can find them." He sat up straighter. "It had something in it about fire."

"Did it never cross your mind," Isa leaned in close, "that she might use such an item poorly?"

"My lady," the man gave her a strained smile, "do you think such an object would be used in any other way?"

Frustrated, Isa stepped away to think. Of the dozens who had dabbled in Sorthileige that she had interrogated in the last three weeks, none of them had been as openly unguided or unrepentant as this fellow. Often, they would say nothing, or would try to find excuses, trying to hide their deviances in her presence. They had mistakenly seemed to believe that she would be more merciful than her husband, whom they had openly defied. They had been wrong.

Just as this man was wrong to underestimate her. He screamed as she fixed him with her most focused stare.

"You asked what I was doing, so I will tell you. I, sir, have the strength of the heart. That means that I can make you feel the truth as it is. Not the convoluted, twisted truth that you have convinced yourself exists. The real, visceral truth, the one you ignored when you sold that woman the book for enough coin to purchase a few more drinks." Isa leaned over him so that she could grab his chair and tilt it back to an uncomfortable angle. "I thought you should know that the book you sold the woman just might have aided her in luring away hundreds of children over the last few weeks, and if any of them should die, their blood will be on your head."

Isa stepped back, letting his chair crash to the floor, but she didn't release the grip she held on his heart as she sent barrage after barrage of images at the man, images of the distraught parents' faces who had come to the Fortress, begging for help. Their wails and screams and agony. This man was proving to be more difficult than most, despite his careless appearance. And yet, Isa could feel him beginning to soften as he started to quietly weep. Silently, she allowed herself a breath of relief and thanked the Fortress and the Maker.

"The southern forest," he finally said in a ragged voice, "past the Shadowed Chasm and the oak trees."

"That's nearly on the border of Kongretch!"

He nodded, still staring at the ground. "She headed south

from the tavern after we finished our deal. But I must warn you," he said hastily as Isa took a step toward him, "something is happening there, though I know not what! But the Sorthileige is even stronger there now than it was back then." He looked up at her piteously. "What will you do with me, now that you know?"

"That will be for my husband to decide," Isa said softly before turning and nodding at her guards. But as she headed for the door, the man grunted behind her. Isa's sword was out in a flash. The man's chains burst as he let out a cry of anger, but Isa was ready. He took a step back, then two as she held her sword against the flesh of his throat.

"Are you harmed, Your Majesty?" One guard wound a new set of chains even tighter around the man's wrists, while the other guard began to examine her for blood. "We need to bring you to a safer place," the guard began, but instead of answering, Isa grabbed their prisoner by the collar and tormented him in the most agonizing way she knew how.

"May the evil that you have inflicted upon others visit your soul every waking moment until you die," she whispered in his ear. "And when it does, just remember that truth is only as painful as you have made it." She looked up at the older guard. "You will have no problem with him now." Then she nodded for the other guard to walk her back up the steps and into the main hall once more.

"If I may say so," the younger guard smiled shyly at her when they were finally on their way back to the banquet, "that was quite impressive, Your Majesty." Then his face paled. "I apologize for my forwardness. I have only just begun here. I fear my mouth—"

"Your compliment is kind," Isa interrupted him with a smile. "I could not be more honored. Now," she sucked in a deep breath, "pray tell, do you know what hour it is?"

With the enthusiasm of a small child, the young man dashed

over to a passing servant, before dashing back over to her. "It is just past the ninth hour."

Isa thanked him but couldn't help the deep sigh that escaped her. She was grateful, of course, to have the information they needed. And yet she couldn't help wishing the interrogation had lasted just a bit longer.

CHAPTER 4

IN WHICH MUCH IS SAID

I must say, Your Highness." The Duke of Sud Colline leaned forward, a piece of beef sticking out of his mouth as he spoke. Ever tried to ignore it, but he had never much liked this cousin. "Either she failed miserably," his cousin continued, "or she is back very soon. If it is the latter, I am quite impressed."

Ever followed his cousin's gaze to see Isa reentering the room. A small wave of relief broke over him as she met his eyes and gave him the smallest of nods. He knew that Isa was safe within the Fortress walls, and yet the thought of his sweet wife standing within spitting distance of those who practiced darkness made his skin crawl. Not that there weren't monsters here in the dining hall as well. Ever didn't miss the way his oafish cousin studied Isa as she approached, and Ever was considering setting him straight when Isa seated herself again beside him.

"We have our heading," she announced in a small, triumphant voice. Despite her calm appearance, Ever could tell she was nearly bursting with excitement.

"You must have beat him with a weapon fierce," the duke's youngest daughter called out, her eyes bright with interest.

"Oh, of course not!" Isa smiled and smoothed her crimson

skirts. "I am a lady! Striking a man with a weapon would be highly inappropriate."

"That is not what you seemed to think this morning during swordplay," Ever teased his wife.

She blushed prettily and began to eat her meal as if nothing out of the ordinary had just taken place, and she hadn't just found a lead to their kingdom's disappearing children. In fact, Ever realized with a pang of unease, she seemed far *too* happy.

"So how do you do it?" the duke pressed. "If you don't torture them with a weapon, surely they do not give up their information on their own accord."

Isa put down her fork, having not yet gotten a bite to eat, and fixed her sweetest smile upon him. Ever nearly grinned, for he knew what treatment his cousin would now be subjected to.

"There is an undeniable truth in this world, as sure as the Maker lives. I cannot make them agree with it, but I can use the truth to make them uncomfortable, for they know deep down that they are suppressing that truth. If they are not completely on their guard, or are not very strong, the truth can twist their hearts and alter their actions."

"So you make them change their minds?"

"Oh no. That is the work of the Maker. The Fortress simply gives me the power to show them the Maker's truth. Limited insight, you could say, into the lives of those he sends my way. In this case, I just showed the man the truth about the damage he has done to so many through his selfish, careless actions."

"It must be terrible to be a weak-minded person around you," the duke chortled. "I must be grateful that such is not my lot in life."

Isa didn't answer, only frowned ever so slightly, and just as Ever had expected, the duke's face went from its usual shade of puffy red to nearly a deep purple, and his grin disappeared completely.

"You really should pay more attention to your wife, sir," Isa said. "It is a shame to waste time pining for those that the Maker did not give you."

So the duke's attentions had not been lost on her either. Ever enjoyed watching the man squirm as he looked guiltily at his wife for perhaps the first time that night. Disgusted, Ever shook his head.

After that, Isa's other admirers hurriedly found other topics of discussion. That, of course, left Isa in the same position she had been in to begin with. Ever's heart hurt as he watched her give Olivia and Launce her kindest smiles and sweetest words. When Olivia felt ill again, Isa called Gigi immediately to tend to her in the guest chambers that Isa kept prepared for her brother and his wife. Not a moment too soon did the hour eventually strike eleven, and Ever stood and thanked his guests for their cooperation and attendance before turning them over to their prospective servants to be led to their guest chambers.

Finally, he was on his own with Isa as they made their way back to their room.

"Did most of them agree to allow men to be stationed at the borders?" Isa asked as he took her arm.

"Yes. Tumen wasn't very happy about it at all, but I think even they do not relish the idea of a child thief tramping about their kingdom."

"Good," Isa nodded, "then the evening was a perfect success." She continued prattling on as Ever held the chamber door open for her, talking too fast like she always did when she was uncomfortable. "And isn't it wonderful that Olivia and Launce are having a baby! It will be a beautiful child, with her complexion, of course."

Ever folded his arms and watched her with sad eyes as she stood before her vanity and removed the piles of jewelry that Gigi had heaped upon her that afternoon.

"We'll have to get them a special gift, of course..."

The moment that Ever had been dreading all evening finally

came as Isa's voice trailed off, and she laid her head in her hands. Quiet sobs shook her thin shoulders as Ever went to her and drew her into his chest. Desperately, he tried to find words that would lift the weight off her shoulders even just a little. But no words came. For really, what could he say?

"It hurts, Ever," Isa whimpered as tears continued to stream down her face.

"I know," he whispered as he lifted her and carried her to the bed, where he laid her gently in his lap. "I know."

"My duty is to show everyone else the truth," she continued between sobs. "But that means I have to see the truth as well. And the truth is—" Her voice broke. "The truth is that the Fortress doesn't want me to have a baby." She pulled back and looked up at him with her piercing midnight eyes, reddened and wet in their grief. "Why, Ever? Why is the Fortress doing this to me?"

"I wish I knew." Ever shook his head slowly and tucked a strand of loose hair behind her ear. Upon seeing his wife in the lavish red dress earlier that evening, Ever had hoped to spend the rest of their night in a way that hadn't involved tears. But the damage had been done, and with a sigh, he knew that what she needed most right now was simply to be held. And though it had taken much heartache on her part, and even more stupidity on his, Ever had learned through the last few years that sometimes his arms were most powerful healing he could give his wife.

They lay that way for a long time, shudders and tears still occasionally shaking Isa's shoulders. Not that Ever minded, of course. But, he suggested finally, she might feel better once she was out of her stiff red dress and into some proper nightclothes. Nodding, Isa stood and went to change. Ever briefly mourned his loss as she went from the striking red gown into a shapeless night shift. But, he reminded himself, he had one duty this night, and that was to be what Isa needed. And so, after they had both shed their formal clothes, Ever drew Isa back toward him beneath the covers and carefully tucked the blankets in around her.

Let me know what to say, he asked the Fortress silently. *I do not know why you have chosen to withhold a child from her, but at least tell me what to do.*

As if in response, a little warm wind moved from the hearth over to their bed, warming them just a bit more in the cool of the early spring night. *Alright then,* Ever thought, taking a deep breath. *If this is what you wish for now, then that is what I will do.* Ever pulled her close until she was curled up perfectly into him, her head tucked beneath his chin, and he began to hum one of her favorite songs into her ear. Little by little, he could feel her begin to relax.

"Oh," she said sometime later after he thought she had fallen asleep, "I forgot to tell you about the prisoner."

"It can probably wait until morning."

"Actually," she propped herself up on her elbow and looked him, her heart-shaped face lovely in the flickering shadows of the fire, "I think we should leave tomorrow. He said the woman did indeed buy the book from him and that she left toward the southern forest."

Ever tapped her on the nose. "You mean *I* will be going in the morning. I think it would probably be for the best if you remained here."

"Ever," she grumbled pathetically, "I want to go. We've been through this how many times?"

"That's *not* what I'm referring to." He pushed himself up to face her. "I am referring to the fact that this particular case has had you rather... emotional. I don't know if it's best for you to come until you're more settled internally."

"You know you need me."

"I'm not disputing that now, nor will I ever."

"So?"

"So I just don't want you to put yourself at unnecessary risk because you're too wrapped up in the moment. I think some distance would do you good."

"I do need distance." Isa somehow managed to crawl even closer. "Launce and Olivia won't be leaving for several more days at least. Olivia's not feeling well enough. If I need distance from anyone, it's from them!"

Ever groaned as Isa watched him with her most pleading look. He knew she was using her power on him, although he was rather sure she was doing it unconsciously, as she often did when she felt strongly about something. And as much as he wanted to deny it, she spoke the truth, for he knew that her gift would be most useful in the forest if they found anyone of interest. "Very well, we'll talk to Acelet by first light."

Before he could roll over to go to sleep though, Ever found his wife's mouth suddenly on his, and immediately, all thoughts of sleep vanished. He didn't need to be asked twice.

CHAPTER 5
HIS FATHER'S EYES

Acelet," Isa called out to the general, who rode ahead of her, "how many at last count?"

As he thought, the general rubbed the back of his neck, which was probably stiff, Isa guessed, from the furious pace Ever had set since leaving the Fortress that morning. "My scouts brought in reports last night of two hundred and six, but I believe it might be higher than that."

"Why is that?" she asked.

"The woodland towns haven't reported losing any children, but I'm assuming they've had children go missing as well. They just don't like to send messengers up our way very much. The fools would rather handle their problems themselves." He looked at Ever. "And they don't much like you, Your Highness."

Ever gave him a sardonic look. "I think I shall survive."

Acelet smiled wryly before turning back to Isa. "Anyhow, I simply think there are a number of children who have probably gone missing and their parents have not come to us to tell of it. Hold now, is this it?"

They had come to a stop, and Ever was too busy studying the forest before them to answer, so the party simply waited. Isa had never been to this part of Destin before, and now that she was here, she was rather sure she hadn't missed much. The forests weren't thick and tall the way they were in the woods closer to home. Rather, the trees rose out of the ground like long, thin snakes with their heads turned toward the skies. The ground itself was wet and resembled a marsh much more than a forest. Isa was suddenly also sure that it probably hid an assortment of animals she would prefer not to meet. As she drew quick breaths in and out, the sickly, moist air clung to her lungs and made breathing more labored. No, Isa decided, she did not like the southern forest at all.

But it was better than staying at home to face Launce and Olivia's constant looks of guilt and pity.

"We'll walk slowly from here," Ever said as he dismounted and took his horse by the reins. "There is a source of power nearby. I can feel it."

"Thank the Maker," Isa heard one of the young soldiers behind her remark to one of his comrades. "I was going to puke if we ran another mile at that pace."

Isa didn't mind the speed that resulted from Ever's use of his power to hasten their travel. What should have been a three-day journey had taken place in less than one. And the view had been incredible. Isa had seen everything in one day, from their own mountain to valleys and plains to a great chasm of dark blue granite, which could only be crossed using a bridge wide enough for one horse to pass over at a time. But now that they had arrived, the sobering reminder of why they had made such a journey settled upon her once more.

"So many broken hearts," she murmured.

"What was that, Your Highness?"

"Oh," she shook her head, "only that I can feel the heartbreak." She looked up through the trees into the gray sky overhead. "Even here, the sorrow of their parents is thick in the air." Ever had been right. They were getting close.

At such a statement, an air of solemnity filled the group, and they passed on quietly, following Ever as he led them forward. Isa tried to focus, but as they moved deeper into the forest, and the despair of the many families wrapped about her like a hot, stuffy cloak, Isa's thoughts turned, as they had so often of late, to the child that by past Fortier standards she should have had by now.

If all had gone as tradition had led them to believe it would, Isa would have conceived the month they had been married. It would have been a boy, as all the Fortiers had boys first, and he would have been three years by now. She knew what he would have looked like, too. His eyes would have been the same shade of stormy gray-blue as his father's eyes, and his hair would have been darker than Ever's, probably with just a hint of her own copper red. He would have had his father's stubborn jaw and might have ended up being even a bit taller than his father.

Not that any of that mattered. What mattered was that whether he had golden, red, or even white hair, he wasn't there for Isa to kiss to sleep at night. There were no chubby arms or legs or cheeks to squeeze and no little hand to hold. And though Isa knew the Fortress made no mistakes, she couldn't help feeling that she had been robbed of something very precious, for her arms were still empty.

And so were the arms of hundreds of other parents, Isa scolded herself. Now was not the time for a good cry, though she suddenly wanted very much to have one. Even the thought of her imaginary son being stolen from her in the dark of night angered Isa to a place of danger, and if she couldn't have a child of her own to keep safe, Isa swore to herself, she was going to do everything in her power to return these children to their families. No one should have to suffer such a terrible fate as to live wondering where a child had gone and what had become of him. Then she felt it.

"Wait!"

Everyone stopped and turned to look at her, but Isa only

dismounted her horse and handed the reins to one of the soldiers nearby.

"Isa?" Ever asked warily. When she didn't respond, he drew his sword and began to follow her, but Isa didn't stop. Her fingers and toes and even her chest felt alive, humming like a hive of bees. Never had she felt such a powerful pull before, and without knowing where she was going, her feet carried her toward the source. Heartbreak. So much heartbreak. Loneliness, curiosity, and terror. The terror was thicker than any other feeling Isa could sense in the air. But this terror was different from that of the parents that she had felt earlier. Unable to utter a word, so filled was she with the need to find the children who were producing such emotions, Isa broke into a run.

"Isa, slow down!"

But Isa couldn't slow down. The feelings were too strong for her to ignore or break away from. It was as though they had stitched themselves right to her own heart and were pulling her in without her permission. Ever had been right. She was too wrapped up in this struggle. It was too personal. She should have stayed behind. And now she was letting her heart lead her rather than her head. Still, the vine-like trees continued to fly past her as she raced into the heart of the sickly wood.

Until she came to the house.

"Here," she said breathlessly as Ever came to stand beside her. "The children are here."

"All two hundred and six?" Ever cast a doubtful look at the ramshackle little cottage.

Even with the second story, there couldn't have been more than three rooms in the entire house, certainly not enough space for a quarter of so many children. And yet, the pull of terror was stronger than ever.

"Do you smell that?"

"Smell what?"

"It's sweet," she said, approaching the house. "Like... the scent of sugar." For a brief instant, a vision flashed through her mind, and instead of the crumbling stone house that stood before her, Isa saw a house made of every kind of candy imaginable. Red-and-white striped sugar stick columns supported the roof, rather than the collapsing wooden beams she had seen just a moment ago. Bright lemon drops, dark green mint drops, and even brown honey drops made up the walls, rather than gray, round stones. Roses made of chocolate, a rare delicacy Isa had only tasted after she'd come to the Fortress, lined the path up to the door, and unfamiliar blue truffles were arranged alongside them. Dozens of other sweets unknown to Isa made the house into the most lovely and inviting sight she had ever seen.

But then the vision was gone, as was the scent, and Isa was left touching one of the dirty rock walls. "Whoever did this lied to the children." She turned to Ever.

"Lied to them?" Ever frowned at her.

"I think... I think I know what they saw!" she exclaimed. "The thief used an illusion of sorts to draw them here, making them think the house was made of sweets."

Ever looked at her as though she'd lost her mind but said nothing as he moved closer to the house to examine it for himself. "Perhaps that would explain why no one saw these children leave," he said. "If the thief had the ability to create such a grand illusion, perhaps he had the ability to also cover the children with an illusion while they walked here." He turned to Isa, the blue rings of fire burning intensely in his eyes. "They must have walked for days," he said, wonder and horror mixing in his voice. "Some of the children were reported missing from near the border of Tumen, and others from the coast!"

Isa was about to respond when another wave of fear crashed through her. Again, she felt the immediate, driving need to find its source. As she began to open the cottage's door, Ever blocked her path.

"Isa, I know you are excited about this, but you need to take care," he said. When she didn't respond, he grabbed her arm. "I am serious. You need to unsheathe your sword and walk cautiously, or I will pack you up myself and send you home."

"You wouldn't—"

"I would, just as I would do to any of my soldiers unfit for duty. Something is very wrong here. Now, I need you to focus—"

"Mummy!"

The cry had come from inside the home. It was a little girl's cry, and the sorrow and fear within it touched Isa in a way no other voice had moved her before. In a moment, she had torn away from her husband's grasp and had burst through the slanted front door. She could hear Ever shouting to his men behind her, but there was no time to wait. The cry came again, and Isa darted deeper in. As she did so, however, her foot caught on a loose stone, and sent her sprawling across the dusty ground, where her head came down on the floor with a very painful crack.

CHAPTER 6
TOO CLOSE

W ell, where is she?" Acelet squinted into the darkness of the dilapidated cottage.

"Wherever the children are, I assume." Ever stood and shoved his sword back into its sheath with more force than was necessary. What had she been thinking, taking off like that?

"What do you wish us to do?" Acelet looked more than a bit unnerved, shifting his weight back and forth as he awaited Ever's answer, and Ever couldn't fault him for it. Acelet had ridden, unblinking, into every battle Ever had ever waged and had seen more than his fair share of strange goings-on in the world. But the evil in this place was nearly tangible. Though it was decently humid outside, the cabin itself was dry and chilly with the kind of cold that raised bumps on one's skin. Each strange little breeze that wafted from darkened, cobwebbed corners was one that shouldn't have been, as there was no wind outside. And just inside the horrid little cabin, the queen had disappeared.

"Set up a watch around the cabin. I want no fewer than five men surrounding it at all times. And notify me of anything that moves. I don't care if it's a chipmunk. I want to see it myself." He walked back to the entrance and gestured at a clearing just before the cabin. "Set up camp, for the time being, just a small way from the entrance. I want another look around."

Acelet hesitated, but Ever only waved him on. When he was finally alone again, Ever let out a deep breath and rubbed his face before he began to explore. It had taken all of his self-control not to explode when Isa had disappeared, just as his hands should have closed in around her waist to yank her back.

This was exactly why he hadn't wanted to bring his wife.

Since they had been married, Isa hadn't been vested in any local disturbances the way she had been in this one. From the first report of a missing child, however, Isa had poured her heart and soul into finding the girl. And then the second child, which was a boy. And then the third. And on the pursuit had gone, a piece of Isa's heart becoming further wrapped up with each child that was reported gone. Of course, it didn't help that Launce and his wife had shown up the night before with their little surprise.

"I'm not sure it's fair to be upset with them," Garin had warned him early that morning as Ever had prepared to leave. "Having a child is not a crime."

"They gave Isa no time to prepare," Ever had huffed as he'd rolled the maps they would need and placed them in a pile. "They could have at least written, instead of springing it upon her publicly."

"True," Garin had said as he'd watched Ever make his preparations. "But they are young and were obviously quite uncomfortable telling her. They weren't callous, at least."

"Have you ever wondered," Ever had turned to his mentor suddenly, forcing out the question that had been eating away at him for years now, "if it might not be my fault?"

Garin had sighed and laid a hand on Ever's shoulder, forcing him to be still. "You know there is no one to blame here. The Fortress can change your situation at any time it chooses. Apparently, it thinks that now is not the right time."

"But what happens if we never get an heir? Does the bloodline simply die?"

Garin had shrugged and begun to place Ever's maps into a saddlebag for him. "I suppose, from a human standpoint, the Fortress's holy man might try to find a distant descendant, someone from another country who had a grandparent or great-grandparent that was Fortress-born. But," he arched one of his eyebrows knowingly at Ever, "I do not think you need to be worried about such things. The Fortress knows how to care for its own. Just live in the now, Ever. Do not borrow trouble."

Now Ever walked through the cabin softly, examining all of its holes and crannies. With the number of disintegrating beams and missing stones from the walls, it was a miracle that the house hadn't collapsed yet. As he moved about the little rooms, he noticed that there was no furniture. No one had lived here for a very long time, judging by the dust that had gathered in deep layers upon the floor. There weren't even footprints, aside from his own, Isa's, and Acelet's. And yet the sensation of power was everywhere, filling the air and making it strange to breathe in and out. But where was it coming from?

Frustrated, Ever finally stomped back outside to the fire Acelet had built nearly thirty feet from the cottage's broken front door. Aware that if he continued to stew on Isa's disappearance, he would most certainly lose his composure, Ever ladled himself a bowl of meat and apple stew that someone had put on the fire.

"So how exactly did you bring that one in last night without my help?" Ever leaned forward over his cup. "I'm quite impressed, of course, but I would have thought that one with *his* abilities should have been rather dangerous." It was nearly a rebuke, for Ever hated to have his men put themselves in danger unnecessarily, particularly when the problem dealt with the Sorthileige.

But Acelet only laughed and rubbed his chin as he also took a bit of the stew. "I know what you are not saying, and you need not fret. He was so drunk when we finally tracked him down that he was unconscious on the floor of the tavern he'd been visiting that day. It was less than a day's ride back to the Fortress, so we borrowed a coffin from a nearby casket maker, nailed the top down to be safe, and carted him back." He shrugged. "Garin took him off our hands as soon as we got back to the Fortress."

"A coffin?" Ever nearly spit out his food as he laughed. Acelet was creative if nothing else. "Still," Ever tried to look stern, "what you did was dangerous. In the future I would still prefer to be called for such errands. But... thank you."

"Pardon me, Your Highness," one of the newer soldiers called out in a timid voice, "but I cannot quite understand just how this Sorthileige can do such damage, especially..." he paused, "... when it is done within the Fortress's domain."

Ever studied the young man for a moment before answering. He was one of their most recent additions, one Ever had only finished training a few weeks before. Barely old enough to have left his parents and home, Eloy had impressed Ever with his desire to serve as a soldier. Eloy still had improvements to make with his swordplay, but the young man's skill with the bow was nearly unrivaled. And though he had handpicked Eloy for this particular venture, Ever couldn't help but hate what he knew Eloy, as all of his soldiers, would eventually touch and see and experience. Such was the role of his men, but the innocence in Eloy's face now, its openness, would not always be so. And it pained Ever to know that he would be the one to steal that innocence from him.

"The Fortress with all of its power was a gift from the Maker to the people of Destin," Ever finally said. "Such power is mostly unheard of in the other kingdoms of the western realm. Of course, the Maker also gives individual gifts to people throughout the lands, common, noble, and royal alike, but only the Fortress and its monarchs have been blessed with such a concentration of enduring power throughout the generations.

"Not all powers in the world are from the Maker though." Ever stood, suddenly restless. He had never been any good at sitting still. "Many strengths are born of evil, stolen from places in the earth that should never be touched. For example, until recently, the Tumenian monarchy ruled with a dark power of their own, which was originally molded and shaped by greed, greed so intense that it began to aid the hands of its wielders. Others are gifts—or curses, rather—from the enemy of the Maker. Of course, none are as potent as those from the Maker himself, but," he stopped and looked at the young man directly, "underestimating our enemies has gotten us into trouble more times than I can tell."

"That is why we take these individual witches and sorcerers so seriously," Acelet jumped in. "Even a single person dabbling in powers he should not hold and cannot understand can do a great deal of harm."

"I've heard stories..." Eloy said. "My mother told me once of the Glass Queen as a child, before the queen's son came here. And trolls. And the Fae! Were the Fae such a people?" His eyes were huge, making their whites stand out against his skin, which was the color of dates.

"Yes and no," Ever said. "They were an imaginative people, and the Maker gave them the ability to create wondrous worlds of their own from only their minds. He even allowed their homes to be temporary, so they could continue to build and rebuild again to their hearts' delight. In addition to that, they had the ability to build temporary bridges between their home and everyone else's so that they could hop between realms and travel the world, taking new ideas with them wherever they went."

"What happened?" Eloy asked, so enraptured that he seemed to have forgotten the food he was still holding.

"They got greedy. During their first exploration of Destin, they came upon the Fortress and decided it should be their own. The Fortier line was nearly ended during the battle, and as a result, the Maker sealed the veil between worlds, and the Fae were banished to their own land."

"But it was through these forests that they were said to have made the original visit," Acelet said as he stirred the stew, his eye glinting with a wicked enjoyment as he watched the young man shiver. "Of course, they're not the only ones who have haunted this region. In the five hundred years since their disappearance, other evils have taken up residence. Witches, sorcerers, trolls." He paused and lowered his voice menacingly. "We even found a band of blood seekers here once, a group driven mad by their excess dabbling in the Sorthileige."

Ever frowned at his general, for he was enjoying Eloy's discomfort a bit too much for Ever's taste.

"But why would someone want a bunch of children?" Eloy asked, slowly taking a bite of what must have been very cold stew.

"I do not know," Ever said. "We can only guess that the thief intends to use them for a spell, to threaten the people of Destin, or to lure us into the forest."

"So this might be a trap?" The young man's dark skin seemed to pale in the thin moonlight that was now shining down through the trees.

"It probably is."

"Then why are we here?" Eloy glanced around as though he might see the abductor step out of the shadows right then.

"We need to find these children, regardless of the reason for their disappearance. Besides, the Fortress and its power are with us. Don't ever forget that this light," Ever held out his hand and a blue flame appeared suspended above his palm, "is far greater than the darkness through which we now walk." As he spoke, the blue light flooded the campsite and all of the trees around it.

"So," Eloy swallowed, "what do we do now that the queen is gone?"

"We wait."

But in truth, waiting was the last thing in the world that Ever wanted to do.

CHAPTER 7

HENRI AND GENEVIEVE

Isa groaned as she reached up and felt the tender spot on her forehead, just above her left eye. That would leave a pretty bruise. What had she been thinking, dashing off alone into the house? Guilt pricked at her conscience as she remembered Ever's warnings. When she opened her eyes, though, Isa was reminded why she had run into the broken house in the first place.

A little girl, sitting not four feet away, stared at her unashamedly with eyes the color of morning glories and hair as yellow as the sun. She couldn't have been any older than five. Behind the girl lounged a boy. His eyes and hair were the same color as the girl's, but he was a good deal older and wore an expression that was far less open.

"Well, hello there." Isa stopped rubbing her head and reached down to seat herself more properly on the ground. The sun was so bright that she had to squint, and when she was finally able to look around her, she nearly fell backward in surprise. She and the children were sitting on a small patch of sand in the middle of a great body of water. Isa had never seen the sea before, but that was all she could imagine this unending water to be as it stretched to the horizon in all directions. The sun beat down upon them, and the only shade in sight was cast by the two strange trees in the center of their little island, trees that climbed up into the blue sky with only a few wide, fan-like leaves at the top. The oddest part of the scene was that their island was not alone. Hundreds of identical islands floated around theirs, each island holding two or three children as well.

And the air that surrounded them was rife with fear.

"Where are we?" Isa whispered, more to herself than the children, but the girl answered her anyway.

"We're in the Boggart's land."

"We are not." The boy, who was leaning back against one of the trees, crossed his arms and huffed. "I told you, the Boggart isn't real."

"If he isn't real, then why does everything change when we're asleep?"

"I don't know, but it is *not* the Boggart!" He looked at Isa again. "Who are you? You've been asleep a long time."

"My name is... Miss Isa." Isa decided to forgo her title so the children wouldn't be even more hesitant to speak with her. Not that being without a title had ever bothered her.

"You're the first new grownup in the Boggart's land," the little girl said matter-of-factly. "All the other grownups just bring us food. They won't even talk with us even though I tell them I'm bored!"

"And what might your name be?"

"I'm Genny. Well, Stepmother always calls me Genevieve, but I like Genny."

"Genny it is then." Isa smiled at the girl, then looked at the boy, who still lounged against the trunk of the smaller tree. He seemed to be all elbows and knees, but there was something about him that was oddly familiar. "And what is your name?"

"That's Henri," Genny piped. "He's mad because he don't want to be here." She paused, and the smile suddenly melted from her face. "It's my fault," she whispered as she began to twist a lock of her long yellow hair around one of her fingers.

"What's your fault?"

"That we're here. We were lost, and Henri told me not to go to that house of sweets. But I did. And just when I was about to eat it, we came here."

"We weren't lost. You're gettin' it all wrong. And come here. You're mussing your hair again." With an expertise Isa had only ever seen in mothers, the boy lifted the girl and placed her in his lap, where he began to nimbly braid her hair. "Our parents sent us into the forest," he said in a quieter voice. "Actually, our father and our stepmother. She was *never* our mother." His voice grew even quieter.

"What happened?" Isa asked softly.

Henri didn't answer at first, just kept braiding. Just when Isa thought he might not answer at all, he finished the braid and sighed. "They sent us into the forest. While we were in the forest, a big lightning storm came. We smelled the sweets when it stopped. While we were out looking for the sweets, we accidentally found our way back to our house, where a tree had landed on the roof."

"That's when I asked him to come here," Genny said. "He smelled it, too, but he wanted to see the house first."

"We were already looking for the sweets," Henri mumbled, reddening a little. "We just found the house by accident along the way."

"I am so sorry," Isa managed to say. While most of the missing children had parents who had come to the Fortress begging for help, these children, it seemed, had been unwanted to begin with. How any parent, or even stepparent for that matter, could abandon children was beyond Isa. It might have been a providential thing for the horrid people that the tree had killed them, for if it hadn't, Isa would have made sure their punishment was swift and severe.

Ugh. Isa shook her head again. *Such dark thoughts!* Ever had been right. She was far too close to this problem to solve it without bias. But then again, she was too deep now to give up. Besides, Isa had absolutely no idea as to where she was or how she had come to be there. Or, most importantly, how to get out.

"How long have you been here?" Isa asked the boy, who was now tying a worn leather cord at the bottom of Genny's new braid.

"Five days," Henri said.

"Every day is different," Genny added, leaning toward Isa and getting a reprimand from her brother, who was still trying to tie her hair. "Yesterday we were in a meadow of poppies. The day before, we were next to a big puddle."

"A lake," Henri corrected her.

"A lake." Genny rolled her eyes dramatically, then she looked at Isa with a sudden intensity. "There is lots of power here. I can feel it."

Isa frowned, examining the children once again, more closely this time. How was the girl able to sense the power that surrounded them? Most humans could feel dark power in some sense, but to them, it was merely uncomfortable. Genny, however, not only felt the darkness but knew exactly what it was.

Before Isa had time to ask, a shadow rose out of the water behind her. Isa spun to face it, hand on the hilt of her sword. A woman stood before her, oddly dry though she had just risen out of the lake. She held her hands out in front of her then slowly put a finger to her lips.

"Please," she whispered, "you must come with me. Quickly!"

"What for?" Isa asked, hand still on her sword.

The woman glanced over her shoulder, though Isa could see nothing but more water and islands behind her. "They will be angry if they find out I'm helping you! Now come, before they realize I have gone!"

Isa looked back at the children. Genny looked worried and

stuck her thumb in her mouth. Even Henri seemed disconcerted. "What do you want of me?" She turned back to the woman.

"I promise you will be returned to them. I need your help, though. I am trying to get you home!" The woman glanced around again.

Still, Isa hesitated. Something felt very wrong. In fact, everything about this situation felt wrong. But, she decided, what more damage could she do by following along and seeing what this woman wanted? Finally, Isa nodded.

Without a word, the woman took her by the wrist and pulled Isa into the water. Isa fought to grab a breath before being pulled under, but to her shock, as soon as she was underwater, she sucked in a breath only to realize that she could breathe.

"How—"

But the woman held up her hand and shook her head before turning and beginning to swim. Unfortunately, Isa had never been a very good swimmer, and after only half a minute was lagging behind. Her long dress made it hard to kick, and the muscles she strengthened in the practice room were far different than the ones used to swim.

Just when Isa's arms felt like they might fall off from all the swimming, the woman stopped. Isa stopped, too, but couldn't see what the woman was looking at. The pile of sand at their feet looked just like any other. And yet when the woman touched it, a hole opened up, barely wide enough for a single person to fit through. After one more careful look around, the woman dove into the black hole.

Fortress, Isa silently prayed, *that looks like a terrible way to die. Please let me come back out alive.* Then she grabbed at the edges and pulled herself through.

As soon as she was inside, Isa heard a thumping sound. The hole was covered, and for a moment she stood in inky blackness. It didn't last long, though, for much to Isa's shock, a candle was lighted, and the woman sat upon a rock, facing her. They were in a cavern of sorts with walls made of a black rock riddled with holes.

"How are we..." But Isa couldn't finish the question as she stared at the underwater candle. It was all too much.

"I am sorry for the... unusual method of bringing you here," the woman said in a rich, low voice. "But my people will not look kindly upon an assisted escape, and that is exactly what I am trying to help you do. They won't think to look here." She stretched out a hand, palm up. "My name is Sacha."

As they briefly grasped hands, Isa realized that the woman, whom at first she had thought to be young, was quite a few years older than herself and probably even older than Ever. Her long goldenrod hair was pulled back into a convenient twist at the back of her neck, and the thinnest of lines edged her eyes and neck. Her face had a certain undeniable handsomeness to it, though, with its angular shape and even proportions. Her gray eyes watched Isa just as curiously as Isa studied her. Isa suddenly had the sensation of having seen this stranger before. It was the same feeling she'd had with Henri, although she knew without a doubt that she would have remembered someone with such specific features. Who was this woman? Or rather, what was she? Was she a human, or something else?

"I thank you," Isa said cautiously. "I must admit, though, that I am a bit confused. Where are we, and how did we all get here?"

"I will be frank with you. You and the children have stumbled into the world of the Fae."

"The Fae!" Isa gasped. "But our worlds were sealed off after—"

"After my people attempted to take control of your kingdom." The woman nodded. "Yes, I know. But somehow, the veil has been reopened."

Isa frowned. Ever had told her once that the veil between the worlds had been sealed by the fire of the Fortiers. Such a seal could not have torn easily.

"I do not know how." The woman shook her head. "All I know is that a few months ago, the children began to appear in our world. As soon as my people realized they were human, they began to capture and keep them."

Isa nodded. "But I still don't understand how we got here." She waved her hand at the underwater cave. "And Genny said something about the world changing every night?"

"I'm afraid that in order to understand that, you will need to know a little more of our world." Sacha squirmed. It was so odd to watch her hair move up and down with the currents of the water, but to be able to breathe and speak as though they were above ground was even stranger. "My people live in a world of constant change," Sacha said. "Unfortunately, it seems your human children are more sensitive to the tear than most of your human adults. That is, except for you, of course. I hope this isn't too forward, but I must ask. However did you find us?"

Isa had many, many of her own questions to ask before she wanted to answer any of Sacha's, such as how they spoke the same language when they were from such different worlds, or about the house of sweets, which Isa knew the children had seen before entering the little cottage, or how the woman appeared to be so familiar with their customs. So she decided to indulge this request as simply as possible and see what results it bought her. "I came in search of the children."

At this, the woman's gray eyes grew large. "You don't have a child of your own who—"

"No," Isa said quickly, trying to quell the pain as it grabbed at her.

"Oh," the woman said softly. "I only meant to reunite you should you have had children here. No mind then." They were quiet for a moment as Isa put herself back together. Finally, Sacha spoke, placing her hand in her hair twist absentmindedly. "The two children in your pod seemed to like you well enough. It's quite curious. None of my attendants can get the boy to speak."

"My pod?"

"At the moment, it looks like an island. But really, it's the way my people are keeping the children in their places."

"As in cages?" Isa frowned.

"I suppose you could put it that way. They look less intimidating because we can make our world look just as we want it. Islands, coves, clouds." She shrugged. "They all look better than cages. I opened yours quickly enough that my people shouldn't have noticed."

"So what do you need me for?" Isa stood and walked nonchalantly to the nearest cavern wall. She touched it. The wall was solid, but at the same time it felt as though her hand might pass right through.

"I need your help to find the tear in the veil. I want to send you all back before I try to reseal the veil once more."

Isa turned to study Sacha, trying to probe her heart as she did. But to her surprise, the woman's heart was as hard to reach as the strange hole they'd climbed down into. Was that simply because Sacha was Fae? For a brief moment, Isa closed her eyes and pressed harder, until she was nearly shaking with the effort. Finally, she felt something. It wasn't much, but Isa suddenly felt sure that whatever her reasons, Sacha truly did wish to help them find the opening in the veil.

"I'm grateful for your help. Truly. But I have to ask... why are you risking so much to help us?"

Sacha looked at Isa for a long moment. Sadness flitted through her eyes and heart. "This tear isn't new," she finally said. "I don't know why the children have begun to come just now. No one has been here for years. They aren't the first, though." She shook her head. "There was a man who moved through the veil and into our world long before the children."

"Who was he?" Isa realized she was leaning forward in anticipation.

"My father." Without another word, the woman reopened the

hole in the ceiling and swam out. Isa followed at a much slower pace. They didn't speak again until Isa was returned to the island.

"I will come get you when it's safe," Sacha told her quietly before turning and walking back into the water.

It had been such a strange meeting. Genny immediately put Isa to work shaping a baby doll out of sticks, but Isa couldn't focus the way she knew the little girl wanted her to. Somehow, she had come back from the swim with more questions than answers. The woman's heart had been heavily guarded, but Isa couldn't know for sure whether or not that was simply because she came from another world. Perhaps hearts didn't work the same way for this people. But was the woman trustworthy? And why, if the tear had been present for years, were the children only being drawn here now under the guise of a house of sweets?

Tomorrow, she thought to the Maker, she would get some answers. *But most of all,* she prayed, *let me get them home!*

CHAPTER 8

TORN WORLDS

Ow old are you?" Isa asked the little girl as she helped her skip rocks.

"Henri says I am four summers," Genny replied as she heaved another pebble out into the pond. "But Henri is more. He says he has nine summers." She stopped and looked at Isa, her clear blue eyes wide. "How many summers are you?"

Isa laughed. "More than that." For the thousandth time that day, she looked out over the rolling hills they were now occupying and wondered if Sacha would come. It was Isa's third day in the Fae world, and each day, the woman had snuck over to tell Isa that she was not yet ready to look for a way to send the children home. While they'd waited for the right time, Isa noticed at least ten more children arrive.

As Genny had predicted, each day brought new surroundings as well. The sea and islands were gone the morning after Isa stumbled into the Fae world, and instead, she and the children had awakened to find themselves atop a cliff so high that they were hidden within the clouds. Throughout the day, the wind blew enough of the clouds away to reveal the other children on little cliffs of their own. If Isa hadn't known they

63

were encaged, she might have collapsed from anxiety. The day after that had been a vast desert with yellow, blowing sand. At least today's surroundings weren't as hot as that desert had been.

Standing up, she walked casually over to the edge of their little spot where Genny played and Henri sat against a rock. It hadn't worked yesterday or the day before that, but she might as well try. Raising her hands ever so slightly, she pressed into the air that surrounded them. At first, she met no resistance. But the harder she pressed, the greater the force that came back to meet her. Even when pushing her hardest, Isa could move her hands no more than a hand's span deep into the invisible wall. Frustrated, she let her hands drop once again.

"Are you ready?"

Isa looked up to see Sacha striding down the hill toward them. She wore the same simple violet work shift she'd worn every time she had come to see Isa, but her blonde hair was pulled back tightly against her head this time. She glanced at Isa's hands, which, to Isa's embarrassment, were still in the air from her experiment.

"I've found a place we can begin searching where they shouldn't see us. Are you ready?" the woman said, a slight smile tugging at the corner of her mouth.

"Of course," Isa said as she joined the woman. Sacha paused briefly, to unlock their invisible door, Isa guessed.

"You're leaving?" Genny cried. And to Isa's satisfaction, even Henri stood up, a slight frown on his face. She hadn't been sure whether the boy had really come to trust her yet or not, as quiet as he'd been, but it seemed that perhaps he was on the way.

"She will return, I promise." Sacha smiled sadly down at the children, her gaze lingering on the girl for a long moment. Then she turned and led Isa out. Up and down hills they went, toward the edge of what looked like a distant wood. As they walked, Isa wondered at how real the grasses felt as they brushed against her legs. The sky here was blue, as skies generally were, unlike their sky of orange from the day before.

"I apologize for taking so long," Sacha called back in a low voice as they moved briskly toward a thick line of trees. "The children have continued to arrive, and I haven't been able to get away much."

"How many Fae do you have?" Isa looked around at the other little pods of children scattered over the gently rolling hills.

"Around two hundred. Our people are not numerous. Now, this is it. If you would be so kind as to feel around here for the break in the air. I've felt it here before somewhere…"

Isa froze as Sacha continued to search. How did this woman know she could feel such changes in power and worlds? In previous meetings, Isa had not told Sacha of her abilities. Her heart thumped wildly in her chest, but she decided it would be best to go on as usual and to conceal her surprise. As Ever always said, keeping her own knowledge secret might teach her more than asking many questions.

With her hands raised and her eyes closed, Sacha looked different than she had before. When her eyes were shut, it opened up her face, making it look more youthful and less austere than it had before. Slowly, Isa raised her own hands and began to feel around for a disturbance the same way Sacha was. Though she had never dealt with tears in realms before falling through the one in the cabin, she had been at the Fortress long enough to know what it felt like when power was interrupted. And as she moved along now, she could feel the ripple somewhere nearby, although where it came from exactly, she couldn't say.

"What will we do once we find the tear?" Isa asked. How glad she would be to get back to her world where oceans didn't move and invisible walls didn't keep her holed up like an animal. And what she wouldn't give for a bath.

"We'll mark it so we can find it again tomorrow. I've planned a disturbance that should keep my people occupied for a few hours. Enough time to get them out. As soon as you are all gone, I will seal the tear from this side. I'm assuming you can help them once they are returned to your world?"

"Of course," Isa said. "Actually, my husband and some of his men are waiting there now."

"Your husband?" The woman turned to look at Isa, her eyes suddenly burning with an excitement Isa hadn't yet seen in her solemn face. Then she paused. "I feel the pull a bit stronger over here to the right. Let's move that way, and perhaps you can tell me a bit more about your husband."

Isa must have looked surprised, for the woman let out a short chuckle and closed her eyes again.

"My people don't keep one partner for life, the way my father told me most humans do." She smiled, almost shyly. "Please, if you wouldn't mind, you could tell me about him while we work?"

"He's a good man," Isa began, but as she spoke, a little wind swirled around her, and Isa knew immediately that the Fortress was warning her to be careful. "He is from a long line of respected protectors of our people." She tried to sound casual. "We live together in our home on a mountain."

"Oh, surely you must have something more to say about him!" The woman pressed just a little too enthusiastically, pausing her search efforts. "Is he an avid rider? Does he enjoy executions? Come now, you can surely spare a few more details." She laughed, but Isa suddenly felt nearly queasy with angst. How did this woman know so much about their world? Had her father taken her there? And why was she so interested in Ever?

By the grace of the Maker, Isa's arm went through a hole in what should have been an ancient, gnarled tree. "I've found it!" she cried, leaning over to stick her head through to look. Before she could, however, the woman grabbed a handful of her dress and yanked her back.

"No! You must wait until we are all ready! If you go through too soon, you may cause the bridge between worlds to collapse, and you will all be stuck here!"

Isa had not appreciated the yank, but what the woman said made sense, so she held her tongue.

The woman removed a red-jeweled pin from her hair. "This," she waved at the hills behind them, "will have changed again by tomorrow morning." She drove the pin into the soft wood of the tree, a few feet below the hole. "We will use this to mark the place. It is from your world, a gift from my father. So when this wood changes, the pin will remain. Now," she turned to Isa, her gray eyes gleaming again, "would you like to help me bring the children a little treat?"

Isa needed to learn as much of this world as she could before returning to the cage, but she couldn't help but feel confused at Sacha's sudden changes in mood. For all of her trepidation and solemn words on that first day, this quick light in her eyes didn't fit with the person Isa had believed the woman to be. If only she could see into her heart more clearly!

As oddly as her host was behaving, Isa had to admit that she did enjoy their next activity. The woman, apparently, had learned to bake a little from her father, and deep in the forest in a place Sacha claimed she had created that would be hidden from the others, she had prepared mountains of cookies for the children.

"I get little chance to practice my baking," Sacha said as she handed Isa a cookie that was larger than the others. "Hopefully, it's not terrible." She chuckled to herself, then sighed. "I know my people have caused the children much fear, but I hope they will go home to happier days."

When she was finally returned to her own little spot with Genny and Henri, Isa lay back against a large stone just as Henri had been doing all day. As the children devoured their treats, Isa turned her own cookie over in her hands, wondering if it were real or just another illusion. So many illusions existed here. And though Isa still couldn't see into Sacha's heart, she could sense the presence of half-truths.

Half-truths were the worst.

Isa put the cookie in her mouth and was surprised to taste its warm, buttery sweetness. If this was an illusion, it was a masterful one. Everything about it felt and tasted perfect. And yet, so had the tree and the ocean and the desert and now the hills. How was one supposed to find truth in a land of so many false appearances? It made Isa's head hurt.

That night, when one of the Fae came to deliver their simple supper of bread and cheese, Isa dared to move closer than she had before to study the otherworldly creature. It appeared to be a woman, but as Isa searched for details in the being's face, she realized it was almost impossible to find them. When she saw the woman out of the side of her vision, the face appeared to have two eyes that slanted out, a nose, and a mouth. But every time she tried to pick out any more individual features than that, it was as impossible as focusing directly upon a star. The eyes and nose and mouth blurred into an oblong face, something vague and strange.

Finally, Isa and the children prepared to sleep. During her first night in the Fae world, Isa had awakened to find Genny burrowed into her side as though it were the most natural thing in the world. Henri had kept to himself, but as the days had gone by, he had stopped watching Isa as though she might eat his little sister. Tonight, as it was unusually cool, Isa gathered a few sticks and grasses and started a tiny fire in their circle, one that would be easy to put out should some Fae object. No one came, though, and as had become her habit, Genny happily settled herself in Isa's lap and promptly fell asleep while Isa and Henri stared into the little yellow flames.

"She calls out for her mummy at night." Isa finally broke the silence, hoping not to scare the boy off with too many questions. "Was she close to your stepmother, or does she remember your real mother?"

Henri scoffed, his thin face scowling into the growing dark. "No. Our real mother was gone before Genny reached her second summer. And Helaine never liked us. She made me learn to dress and feed Genny and brush her hair so she wouldn't have to."

Isa looked down at the little girl lying in her lap. How one could reject such a child was beyond her. No wonder Genny was so desperate for love.

"Why then," Isa croaked, trying not to cry in front of the boy, "does she cry out for her mother?"

"She thinks our mother is coming back for her one day." Henri shook his head, then brushed a patch of his yellow hair out of his eyes. "I told her that our mum was coming back one day. I only did it so she'd stop crying one night after Helaine grew angry with us. I didn't think she'd remember the next day, but she's done it ever since."

I'll need to have his hair cut when we get back to the Fortress, Isa thought to herself. Then she realized what she had just assumed, and somehow, what she had been assuming all along.

Can I take them back with me? She looked up at the false sky as she begged the Fortress, suddenly desperate for a reply. Somehow, in the last three days, she had come to assume that they were hers. Isa didn't know when it had happened or how she had begun to believe she could keep them, but now it was as plain as day. Isa had undeniably begun to think of the children as *her* responsibility. Surely it wasn't her fault, she argued with herself. No one could leave them all alone, particularly as their parents had just died. That would be irresponsible, and Isa had more than enough resources to keep them well and fed until they could find someplace else that was suitable for children.

But then again, for the truth still reigned in her heart, Isa really had no desire to find someplace suitable, either.

CHAPTER 9

OBJECTIONS

S omeone is coming!"

Ever leapt to his feet at the sound of the soldier's cry. He and his men fell into a semi-circle around the front door of the cottage.

"Hold for the signal," Ever reminded his men, looking in particular at Eloy. The young man seemed particularly jumpy today. Not that Ever could blame him. The four days they'd waited had been more than enough to try his own patience.

The shudder of power that came from the cottage was nearly enough to knock Ever off his feet. Acelet gave him a questioning look from across the half-circle, but none of the other men seemed to notice his trembling. Ever shook his head at his general and turned his attention back to the door. Some great power was moving within the old house. He only prayed that it was his wife returning, for he could allow himself to imagine possibilities no further than that.

The ripping sensation continued, and still no one appeared. What was taking so long?

"The children are coming!" Acelet called. Sure enough, dozens of children came pouring out of the little cottage, two by two. And they continued to come. Ever couldn't believe how many children there were. It seemed as though more might have been added right under their noses! *But where is she?* he asked the Fortress. Then, to his inexpressible relief, Isa appeared at the back of the great throng of children, holding the hand of a small girl. Ever sent up a prayer of thanks. Then after giving the nod to Acelet, who set the men to the task of rounding up the children, Ever ran to Isa. Before he got there, however, she stepped back and peered into the cottage.

"What is it?" he asked as he came to stand beside her.

"I was wondering if she was able to seal the tear," Isa said absentmindedly, still squinting into the dark, musty house.

"Who?"

"Sacha, the woman who helped us."

Ever strode into the dusty room once more. The shuddering he had felt was all but gone. Whatever tear Isa spoke of, it certainly wasn't there now. The feeling of evil that had pervaded the little place was entirely gone.

"Don't you ever do that to me again!" he growled, stomping back out to Isa and taking her by the shoulders. "You frightened me!"

"I'm sorry, Ever. I didn't mean to rush off like that. But..." She looked down, and Ever realized the child was still clinging to her hand. "I heard them calling for help." She looked back up into his face, her midnight eyes probing his. "I couldn't leave them like that."

"I know." He pulled her into a deep hug, only to be interrupted by a shout from one of his men. They turned to see Eloy chasing a boy no taller than his knee.

"Come back! You must stay here!"

Isa gave Ever a knowing smile and bent down to the little girl and a boy, whom Ever had not noticed earlier. "I need to help with the other children. You stay here with my husband until I come back."

The little girl looked up at him with the biggest, bluest eyes he had ever seen in such a small person. Isa smoothed the girl's hair and then smiled at Ever once more before heading off to help his men, who seemed completely inept at getting the children into any semblance of order.

"Who are you?" the boy asked, taking the girl's hand and pulling her closer to him.

"I am the king."

The boy's eyes grew even bigger before he ducked his head down and whispered something to the girl, who giggled and shook her head.

Ever looked again for Isa amidst the chaos of soldiers and children. He had brought twenty-four men with him, but even so, the children had them tremendously outnumbered. How did Isa do it, calming the children and organizing them so? And what did she expect him to do with these two?

"So," he cleared his throat, "where do your parents live?"

"They're dead," the boy said.

Well, this was going to be more difficult than he thought. "I am sorry."

"They didn't want us anyway," the boy said, watching Isa as she moved the other children into groups.

How did one respond to that? Ever sighed. Leave it to Isa to find the most pathetic, lonely children in the land. And then hand them to him to take care of.

An eternity later, Isa had not only rounded up the children, but matched their names to the lists of the missing. Then she'd placed them in groups that needed to be returned to different parts of the kingdom. There was also a number of children who were neither on the list nor did they know where they were from. That bunch would be taken back to the Fortress to be sorted out and delivered home with the help of Garin and the messengers. After instructing both the children and the soldiers on how to behave, Isa sent them in their respective directions, and finally it was just Ever, Isa, three guards, and the last batch of twelve children.

"What about—" Ever began to ask when he realized the two blue-eyed children weren't going to be grouped, but Isa stopped him.

"They're coming with us."

Ever raised his eyebrows in question, but Isa ignored him. Very soon, the smallest children had been placed on the horses with the guards, while the older children walked alongside Isa and Ever. Ever wanted to ask Isa about what had happened in the other world, as well as what exactly she was planning to do with the orphans, but he knew better than to question her when she wore that expression. Besides, it took all of their time and energy to keep even their little flock of twelve under control.

Ever couldn't push their horses back home as fast as he had before, thanks to the children. So even with the aid of a small amount of his power, they were only halfway to the Fortress by the end of the first day. Only after all of the children had been laid down and wrapped in spare blankets did Ever get to finally talk with Isa.

"So?" Ever threw his cloak over her shoulders as she stood watching the children, her arms wrapped around herself and her shoulders hunched. "What happened?"

"I'm not sure." She shook her head, still looking at the children. "I mean, I know what she told me, but I still cannot decide whether I believe it or not."

"How about you tell me, and we can choose to believe or not believe it together."

"How long has it been since the Fae world was sealed off?" She finally turned and looked up at him, the blue fire in her eyes moving in uneven bursts.

"Nearly five centuries. Why?"

"If we are to believe her, and I really can't find a reason not to…" she drew in a deep breath, "then the children and I were in the world of the Fae."

Ever was speechless. He'd known they were in some other world, but he'd never guessed it to be that one.

"I know the veil between worlds was sealed by a Fortier. So it couldn't just tear on its own." She looked up at him with frightened eyes. "Could it?"

He frowned down at her, unable to form any sort of coherent answer himself. "We need to talk to Garin," was all he could finally say. To this, Isa nodded and leaned into him. Ever wrapped his arms around her and pulled her close. "Aside from breaking every rule in the book," he said into her hair, "you did well. I would never have been able to do this without you."

"I only hope we haven't poked a hornet's nest."

Ever was hoping the exact same thing.

DESPITE THEIR SOMBER words the night before, Isa was nothing but smiles and sunshine the next day. She moved between the horses, talking to each child in turn. Little giggles would be shared with the younger girls, particularly the one with big blue eyes, whose name was Genny, Ever found out. To the boys, she would assign all sorts of tasks, such as watching for bandits and dangerous animals, which miraculously kept many of them occupied for hours. To the older children, she would move about asking more direct questions about their homes and families. Always busy, always moving, Isa seemed never to stop. And Eloy, who appeared nearly as enthralled with the children as Isa, was little better.

Part of Ever was a bit put out. He had more questions that he wanted to discuss without the children hearing them, but every time he tried to get her attention, one of the children stole it. And yet, he couldn't bring himself to be angry. She was happier with them than he had seen her in a long time. Caring for the children appeared to be the most natural calling in the world for her. Isa acted as though she had been born to mother them.

And that's when it hit him. She finally had someone to mother.

This was all well and good for the children, but it wasn't long before Ever was ready to have her back to himself. By the end of that second day, he was exhausted and felt most out of sorts. The sight of the Fortress's front steps, however, cheered his heart to no end, as did the sight of his steward, waiting with a smile to receive them.

"Garin!" Ever dismounted and clapped the older man upon the back.

"I heard reports that the outing was successful." Garin smiled, his eyes crinkling at the corners.

"The last three groups shouldn't reach their destinations for a few more days at least," Ever said, handing children down from the horses to surprised servants. "But all reported missing are accounted for. This group didn't even have time to be reported missing."

"Gigi," Isa called, "please help me find these children places to stay until their parents arrive." Immediately, Gigi, as well as a horde of servants beneath her, were out on the Fortress lawn, each taking a child and fretting over him or her and immediately dragging them back to the Fortress for what Ever guessed to be baths, new clothes, and cider. Soon only two children remained, half hidden behind Isa's skirts.

"And who are these—" Garin was staring at Genny and her brother, Henri. Before he finished his sentence, however, Garin's eyes went flat. "What are *they* doing here?"

Ever was taken aback at the poison in Garin's voice. Surely he didn't mean the two orphans. And yet, the steward was outright glaring at the children with a look that would wither any adult.

Henri's eyes grew large, and he pulled his sister as close to him as he could. Even chirpy little Genny looked frightened.

"These children have no parents," Isa said, her voice suddenly as icy as Garin's glower. "They were taken as well and need someplace to stay."

At a loss, Ever looked back and forth between Garin and Isa. For the first time in his marriage, he was stuck between his wife and his mentor. And, he decided immediately, he wanted out. "Let us take a moment and then continue this in the study," Ever said cautiously, aware that there were servants also watching the scene.

"That is a masterful idea," Isa said, her voice still hard. "I am tired, and in horrible need of a bath, as are the children." She took Genny and Henri by the shoulders. "We will talk about this after everyone has been fed, bathed, and changed. I will take Genny. Ever, would you take Henri?"

"I will take the boy," Garin grumbled. When Isa fixed him with her deadliest stare, he rolled his eyes. "I will make sure he's taken care of. You have my word."

To this, Isa finally consented, and before Ever knew it, they were all off on their own separate ways. As he walked, Ever decided that he wanted nothing more than a hard drink and his own warm bed. He had a sinking feeling, however, that those two desires would not be granted for a while, considering the daggers Isa and Garin had been sending at one another through their glares.

What had just happened?

CHAPTER 10
WHAT YOU ARE

"What is that?" Henri stared at the gigantic basin before him as the servants filled it with buckets of steaming water.

"A bath," the tall, grumpy man answered in a dry voice. "Have you never taken a bath?"

Henri scowled up at him. Of course he had bathed. But never inside the house. Instead, his father would take him to their nearby creek. Did this man expect him to undress in front of so many people?

"Where's Genny?" Henri asked, hoping the man might forget the bath if he could distract him with questions. He was to have no such fortune though.

"The queen is giving your sister her bath, but she will join you here when it is time for bed, should the king and queen decide, for the time being, to keep you. Now, I will be waiting outside this door." The grumpy man seemed to read his mind. "When you are undressed and in the tub, let me know."

Henri certainly did not intend to let him know. As soon as he was stripped and inside the warm water, which did admittedly feel rather good after their long walk, instead of calling the man,

Henri set to examining the room. It was the largest room he had ever seen, big enough that his entire cottage could have fit inside, woodpile and all. There were two tall beds, draped in thick layers of coverlets and pillows, rather than straw mattresses laid upon the floor. A fireplace nearly as tall as Henri roared not far from his tub, and tall, rectangular windows stretched all the way up to the ceiling, which must have been nearly the height of four men.

He didn't have long to enjoy the richness and splendor of the chamber, however, for just then, the door opened. The grumpy man and a plump woman with ringlets of snow-white hair waltzed in.

"Hello there, love. My name is Gigi. Now, let us get you clean!" Without hesitating, she plunged a brown, squishy blob in the water, lifted Henri's arm, and began to scrub it with the blob. "Oh now, no need to howl like that," she said with a smile.

"I can wash myself!"

"Psh, I doubt that, love. You have dirt caked behind your handsome little ears, and your face looks as though you've been rolling in it."

"You had better listen to her." The grumpy man wore an annoying grin, as though he was enjoying Henri's discomfort. "She won't stop until she's finished."

Gigi was surprisingly strong for her age. The more Henri resisted her scrubbing, the more determined she seemed to do it, humming happily the whole time. "Now, Garin, why do you look as though someone's fed you a lemon? Goodness, the king and queen come home and everyone is a wreck! There, love," she turned back to Henri, "you sparkle like a newborn babe. Here's your drying cloth."

Henri did not want to sparkle at all, particularly not like a baby, but before he knew it, she had him out of the tub and wrapped in a thick, warm cloth. As he dripped water on the brightly colored rug that had been placed in front of the fire,

Henri stared in wonder at his own arms. Had his skin always been that shade of white?

"I hope these fit you. Of course, we'll have to have some made up, but I was able to find some of the king's old clothes from when he was about your size." She stopped and pursed her lips to the side for a moment. "You do seem ever so much skinnier than he was, though. I shall have to fatten you and your sister up a bit. You look as though you haven't eaten a day in your life."

At the mention of food, Henri's evening suddenly seemed a little less dismal. If this woman wanted to feed him, surely she couldn't be so bad. As soon as she had him dressed in the brown trousers and white, long-sleeved shirt, she scurried off. Henri hoped it was to find him some food. When she was gone, however, the grumpy man, or Garin, as everyone called him, closed the door and approached him, stopping only when he was very close.

"I do not know your history," he said in a menacing voice, "nor do I know how you were raised. And for that reason, I shall abstain from making a final judgment of your character... for now, at least. But know this. The king and queen might not know what you can do, or what you are, but I know. And I will be watching you carefully."

Henri swallowed, and his hunger melted. Suddenly, he found himself wishing for Miss Isa or even Gigi. "What are you going to do to us?"

"Nothing, so long as you behave and act as any boy should who is a guest in the king's home. But if you try to hurt them, even the smallest bit, I will have you wishing you had never laid eyes on the queen. Do you understand me?"

Henri glared back at him, but worry thrashed about in his gut. Maybe he should have tried to slip away rather than allowing Miss Isa to bring them here. He hadn't realized she was the queen until they were on their way out of the forest. And how did this man know about his trick? Henri hadn't used his fire since the night he got lost. But Henri had no answers.

The man finally stood and went back to the door. "Gigi will be back soon with your supper. When you are finished, I will come and fetch you."

"Where are we going?"

"To see the king and queen. They need to know exactly what you are."

CHAPTER II

BEHIND CLOSED DOORS

Though the hot bath and clean clothes relaxed Ever's sore muscles, they did little to clear his confusion and dread. It was already growing dark outside, and if the choice had been left to him, he would have been in bed an hour ago. Instead, however, he was on his way to his study, although he got the feeling it would become less his and more Garin and Isa's domain if the evening continued the way it had begun.

Isa, Henri, Genny, and Garin were already there by the time he arrived. Garin hurried him inside and then immediately began to plug the keyholes with cotton pieces. From Isa's expression, it was clear that she was just as dumbfounded as Ever at the steward's behavior.

"Did either of you," Garin asked as he checked the windows and closed the tapestries, "see any other being leave the Fae world as the children left?"

Isa and Ever looked at one another with raised eyebrows.

"How did you know I was in the Fae world?" Isa asked. Ever wondered the same thing. They hadn't had the chance to tell Garin anything of their journey.

Garin ignored her question and asked again. "Did you see any other creatures leave that world?"

"Uh...n...no," Isa stuttered. "It was only the children and me."

Garin walked back to them. "But you swear, you saw nothing leave with you?"

"Garin, what is this about?" Ever finally broke in. Since when had the steward become so paranoid?

"What I am about to tell you has not been uttered to a soul in five hundred years."

Ever's heart nearly stopped. How he had longed to know Garin's origins! And yet, something told him this would not be the exciting adventure he'd dreamed as a boy it would be.

"Are you speaking of the Fae?" Isa asked.

Garin nodded, his silver-and-black hair glinting in the firelight. "I know that you've read what little the annals have to offer on the subject of that people." He looked at Ever. "I made sure of that myself when you were a boy. There is still much you don't know, however, because it was never written down. So few survived the battle with the Fae that no Fortress scribe was left alive to record it." He turned and faced the fire, cutting off Ever's line of sight to his face.

"The Fae were a race capable of greatness," Garin said in a low voice. "They could not only create temporary bridges between worlds, but they could also create temporary worlds within their own. When the Fae happened upon Destin in their travels, King Nel and Queen Chantal invited them to the Fortress in order to discuss new diplomatic ties." He turned to Ever. "I do not know if even you are aware of it, Ever, but the Fortress's cornerstone and inner walls are made entirely of blue crystal, rather than common stone."

"I didn't know for sure," Ever said slowly, "but I had always guessed as much."

"Well, you were right. As were the Fae. As soon as they entered the Fortress, they could sense its power."

"Did the power affect them?" Isa asked.

"No," Garin said, "they simply liked the way it felt."

"They could sense it... unaided?" Ever asked. That a whole race might feel the power of his beloved home was more than a bit unnerving. Only humans with gifts or the Sorthileige could do that.

"Without giving the king even a warning to leave, the Fae decided to claim the Fortress as their own. The slaughter began at midnight and lasted until the first rays of morning. The king's entire army was nearly wiped out, while most of the Fae remained untouched."

"How so?" Ever broke in. "Surely Nel's power would have been strong enough to defeat them."

"Oh, I'm sure it would have, had he known how to use it. The Fae's bodies are like their creations, only temporary. Every so often, they must dissolve into the mist they are and then recreate themselves in the same way they create their temporary worlds. When their emotions get the better of them, which is often, or they've waited too long to rebuild, they become a mixture of hot green light and wind.

"You can only imagine what kind of damage such an army could inflict on human soldiers. Disappearing then reappearing, the Fae moved across the soldiers in their sleep like a plague."

"And the servants and families?" Isa asked, her face taut.

Garin only shook his head sadly. "The Fae had all but taken the Fortress completely when one of the Fae soldiers found the infant prince..." Garin's voice suddenly broke.

Ever glanced at Isa, who looked very much as though she would like to go and comfort him, but neither of them moved until Garin seemed to recover himself.

"Before I go on," he said, drawing in a deep breath, "you need to know that in addition to their ability to create temporary works of beauty and intrigue in both themselves and their surroundings, they seek power of any kind, like moths to a flame. The Maker gave them the ability and physical substance to travel wherever they want, to see the world and not worry about hunger or shelter. They did not need such hindrances. For when the weather got bad or they ran out of food, they could simply transform and wander the earth as air and light until they found the next place they wanted to live."

As he continued to speak, Garin's voice began to harden, and he stood taller. "They are beautiful creatures, but when they reached the Fortress, the power here changed them, or rather, their desire for it did. Covetousness twisted their vision, and jealousy so warped their spirits that they became new creations entirely. Their innate vanity and their inability to see the world from others' points of view prevented them from living with men. Their greed rendered them incapable of love. They forgot all that they were and strove to hold what wasn't theirs to begin with."

"How do you know this, Garin?" Ever asked, dread making it suddenly hard to speak.

Garin turned and looked straight at Ever, his eyes hard like flint.

"Because I am one of them."

EVER LOOKED as though he might pass out, but to Isa, Garin's story made perfect sense. "Back in the alley," she whispered, "when you saved me from Marko..."

"Yes," Garin said as he took Ever by the arms and eased him into a chair. "Although what you saw wasn't my complete Fae form. Here, Ever. Drink this." He held a small flask out to Ever, who downed its contents in one swig.

"But you use the Fortress's power," Ever finally said when he was done, grimacing slightly as the drink went down. "How?"

"The boy prince lived, even though his father, King Nel, died.

And it wasn't for lack of trying on the part of the Fae." Garin's voice grew low again. "When I found the child all alone in his nursery, it should have been a simple solution. His mother and nanny were dead. His father, dead. I knew what I needed to do to ensure the happiness of my people. And yet, as I raised my sword, I was blinded by a barrage of images that flooded my mind. What the child could do, would do... what he would grow up to be. It was a miraculous gift of the Maker, an understanding of the situation's reality, how we were trying to take what wasn't ours. He showed me the truth, much like Isa shows others."

"What did you do?" Isa asked in a soft voice.

"I protected him from my own." Garin shrugged helplessly. "I even killed a young Fae who tried to kill the child while he lay in my arms." A darkness touched Garin's sharp features briefly then vanished, although Isa could feel the bitterness and sorrow lingering beneath his controlled expression. "Soon after that, as I held the babe in one hand and my sword in the other, the Fortress expelled the remaining Fae and pushed them back to their world. And when the boy was old enough, the Maker led both of us to the southern forest, which was much smaller back then.

"Before the Maker bid the prince to seal the Fae out of our world forever, I was given the choice of whether to return to my people or stay with the Fortress and guard the young man. 'If I return,' I told the Maker, 'I will surely be put to death. But if I stay, I am too broken in body and spirit to be a keeper of anyone.'

"'Leave your body to me,' the Maker told me. 'It is your heart I see of import. Do you trust me?' He asked."

"What did you say?" Isa asked.

"It was simple. I had tasted of the Maker's goodness for the past fifteen years as the boy had grown, and I knew I could never survive without it again. And so He made me a new body of two peoples. I no longer needed to dissipate and rebuild myself as Fae do, but I was allowed to retain a few of my Fae qualities. In addition, I was gifted certain powers of the Fortress itself. Over time, though," Garin murmured, "He did the greatest healing to my spirit." He briefly closed his eyes.

"Are all Fae five hundred years old?" Ever finally managed to choke out.

"No. We do not live that long alone. I can only assume I am still here to finish some sort of work, though how long that work should be, I do not know."

"Thank you for telling us," Isa said hesitantly. She did not wish to bring more pain upon the steward after all he had just shared with them, but she was still confused. "I still don't understand, though, what all of this has to do with the children."

Garin fixed a hard gaze upon Genny and Henri. Isa instinctively tightened her grip on their shoulders.

"These children," he said, "are no mere children." He walked back to the king's desk and pulled out the ceremonial scepter. Its sphere of blue crystal, which was fixed at the top of the golden twist handle, was as clear as water with thin, feathered lines that crisscrossed the crystal's interior like miniature spears of lightning.

"Come here," Garin told the children. Both of them looked up at Isa. Part of her wanted to take the children and dash off so she wouldn't need to see whatever Garin wanted to show her. And yet, she knew it was only right to see what he had to say, so she nodded, and they both took a hesitant step toward Garin. The steward turned the children to face Isa and Ever. Then he held the crystal out before them. "Fae are sensitive to power of any kind. Even if it is one they can't use, they can still feel it. Just as I can."

With that, he placed the crystal in Henri's hand, and to Isa's dismay, the black center of the boy's eyes began to shimmer with green.

"Just as these children can."

Isa felt sick to her stomach. The green light swirled about the boy's irises as his gaze stayed fixed on the crystal. Even worse, Isa realized, Genny was staring at it, too, a blank look on her face and the treacherous green inside her eyes as well. That's when Isa remembered Genny's claim about the Fae world being full of power.

How? Isa cried out to the Fortress, paralyzed as she watched. *How are these children Fae?* How had she managed to fall in love with the only children in the world that might be a danger to her kingdom? Her first desire was to scream. Instead, however, Isa swallowed and whispered, "How, since they were living in our world first?"

"Their bodies are too stable for them to be full Fae, which means they must only be part Fae."

"The Fae have been exiled for five centuries! So what do you mean, *part* Fae?" Ever scowled at Garin from his chair.

"I mean that someone found a way to tear the veil between worlds and sire children."

"Sacha," Isa whispered. Ever and Garin both gave her a strange look. "Sacha was the woman who helped us escape," Isa explained, looking back down at the children. "She said she wanted to help us because her father was human."

Garin began to say something, but Isa didn't hear it. Instead, she watched as Henri began turning the scepter over in his hands. And as he did, the crystal began to glow blue. It was the same light as that in Isa's ring, the one meant only for the Fortress's queens. And in Henri's hands, the scepter was glowing just as fiercely as Isa's ring ever had.

Ever pushed himself up in his chair, and even Garin seemed, for once, to be at a loss for words.

"Show them your trick, Henri," Genny said, taking her brother's arm.

But Henri just shook his head, fear filling his face as he stared at the scepter.

"Come on, Henri! Do it!"

Henri looked nervously from Isa's face to Ever's before shaking his head even more vigorously, his wide eyes making his young face look even thinner. Then he looked pointedly at Garin.

"Come on, now," Genny said, sticking her little hands on her hips. "You always do the trick for me."

Henri glanced up at Isa once more.

"You will be safe," Isa said, giving him the warmest smile she could muster. "I must admit, I am very curious to see your trick, especially if it is as wonderful as Genny says." But inside her heart thumped wildly as she prayed that his *trick* wouldn't result in something terrible.

The boy stared at her for a minute more before taking a deep breath. As he exhaled, the scepter not only continued to burn blue from within, but a tongue of blue flame rose from its surface as well.

Garin looked like his eyes might fall out of his head, and Ever, his voice flat, called out from the chair, "What is that?"

"That's his trick," Genny chirped. For a moment, no one moved. Not even Isa could bring herself to speak. Only Genny clapped delightedly. "Isn't it wonderful?" She beamed.

"Yes." Isa made herself smile reassuringly as Henri looked up at her with fearful eyes. "You can be finished now, Henri. You've worked hard enough for one day." When his fire finally went out, and Isa gently took the scepter and handed it back to Garin, however, she realized that Genny was right. It was wonderful. For though the boy's eyes certainly marked him as something other than human, his fire set him apart as well. She wasn't sure how he had miraculously received such a gift, but she did know that it just might save his life.

CHAPTER 12
FIRE OF THE FORTIERS

Ever felt numb as his wife finally left to put the children to bed. She paused briefly by his chair and gave his shoulder a squeeze before leaving. But he was going to need something stronger than a shoulder squeeze to clear his mind of what he had just learned.

"I will be needing more of that." He leaned forward and pointed to the bottle Garin had placed on his desk.

With his usual efficiency, Garin went to do as he was asked, but it felt as if Ever watched his mentor through eyes that were not his own. Never had there been a soul he trusted more, with the exception of Isa, of course. Not that he had ever known what Garin was exactly. Garin had always simply been a part of the Fortress to Ever, much like the shining white marble halls and the crystal dance floor. Garin simply belonged. And now Ever was to believe that Garin was, or had been at one time, the enemy.

"Will Isa be safe with them?" Ever managed to choke out.

"She will be fine for the time being," Garin said evenly as though he hadn't just shattered Ever's world. "I will keep a sharp eye on the children while they're here, but they seem to be innocent of schemes for the moment." Then Garin leaned back against

95

the king's desk and folded his arms. "But there is something I need to discuss with you before you go off to bed too."

Ever shrugged, out of words for the remainder of the night. Or possibly for the rest of the decade.

"Tell me everything you know about those children."

"Well," Ever pinched the bridge of his nose as he tried to recall what Isa had told him, "the children say their father was a wood-cutter not far from the cottage where we found the veil's tear, just beyond the border of the southern forest." Ever's senses returned a bit as he remembered the wretchedness on the boy's face the morning before. "Their parents turned them out and then were killed later that night during a lightning storm."

"And what led them to the Fae world?"

"Isa says that someone created an illusion of sweets in the forest. The illusion made the air smell sweet to the children, and they followed the smell. Henri and Genny followed the smell, too, and stumbled upon the house." He frowned, remembering how little Isa had whispered to him over their long journey. She'd said there was really little to tell. Most of it had been an illusion. "The woman that helped them escape told Isa that the Fae had decided to keep the children, and they would have if it hadn't been for her. The Fae must have known of the tear and used it to lure the chil-dren in. But why now," he asked Garin, "if the tear has been there for years?" It still didn't make sense.

Garin wore a pensive look on his long, thin face.

"If the Maker had King Nel's son seal the bridge between the worlds," Ever continued, "then who could have torn it? And why does that boy have the Fortress's fire?"

"Only a Fortier could have torn what a Fortier sealed," Garin said bluntly. "So one of your ancestors must have reopened the veil. At least several decades ago if an adult half-breed is running about." He raised one black-and-silver brow. "As to the boy's powers, I was going to ask you the same thing."

Ever stared at him blankly.

Garin shook his head, a look of impatience on his face. "The green you saw in those children's eyes today proved that they do have Fae blood within them. But the fire proved that the boy isn't pure Fae at all, and neither is his sister, provided they are full siblings."

"I am too tired for this, Garin. What are you getting at?"

"That fire that the boy created on the crystal? That flame can only be created by someone with the blood of the Fortiers."

Ever managed to pull himself out of the chair so he could get some fresh air. Garin didn't stop him when he unlocked the balcony doors and stepped out to feel the late spring's cool breeze upon his face.

"Isa created fire before she was a Fortier," he pointed out to Garin, who had moved to stand beside him.

"But not that easily. The boy clearly doesn't understand what a great power he holds, and yet he created a flame as easily as you ever did. What's more, the girl said he's done it before, without the crystal we can presume."

Ever turned to his mentor, too tired to guess anymore. "What are you saying, Garin?"

"How old is the boy?"

"Eight? No, nine years, Isa said. Why should that matter?"

"Nine years ago you would have been twenty-two—"

"Wait." Ever took a step back. His stomach suddenly churned. "Are you really asking if *I* fathered those children?"

"I certainly hope not. But yes, that is what I am asking you."

"No! No, how could you ask such a thing! You would have known if I had done something so audacious!" Ever began to pace the balcony, running his hand through his hair. He could hear his voice crack as he faced his mentor. "Many things I have done in my life that I regret, but never that. *Never* that!" He was shouting now, but he didn't care.

Garin sighed and rubbed his eyes. "I am sorry, Everard. You are right. I would have known—"

"No, truly! You tell me that you are...were one of the enemy, then you accuse me of sneaking out like a street urchin, finding a secret tear within the veil, then siring not one, but *two* children. Then abandoning them with a good-for-nothing woodcutter?"

"I know, I know," Garin said, his voice subdued. "Forgive me. I just... I didn't expect any of this." He looked at Ever, his eyes suddenly sad. "I haven't seen another of my kind in five centuries. I am trying to understand how this could have happened. Of all the children there with Isa, she found the two with Fae *and* Fortier blood." Garin's expression moved from one that was incredulous to one of pain. "You know what this means, though. If it was not you, that leaves only one—"

"No." Ever slammed his fist against the wall so hard he could hear the stone within it groan.

Garin stopped, but still gave him a knowing look.

"I will not even entertain that thought," Ever said, breathing hard. "My father was a good man."

"Good men can run foolish errands, my boy." Garin took a deep breath. "Isa mentioned the woman was also half human. It would seem that more than one Destinian has found the tear. There's no way of knowing how many half Fae are running about in our world or theirs."

Suddenly, this day had become more than Ever could handle. Shaking his head, he waved his hand and shuffled toward the door. "I'll dispatch men in the morning to search for reports of Fae activity in the southern forests. But now I am going to sleep."

Unfortunately, as soon as Ever took a single step out of his study he was nearly trampled by a runner. "What is it, Edgar?" Ever asked, though he was sure that he really didn't want to know.

"I apologize, sire, but there is a large group of citizens here from Soudain."

"Now? It's the middle of the night!"

Edgar bowed his head as though he had been the one banging

on the Fortress gates. "I know, sire, and I am terribly sorry. But they are insisting that you must come now. They claim," he paused before meeting Ever's unhappy gaze, "that the children you returned to them are cursed."

"Cursed?" Could this night get any worse? "How many?"

"That is just the thing, Your Majesty. All of them."

CHAPTER 13

A GOOD MAN

Whenever Ever felt as though the burdens he carried were too great, his father's voice would pop into his head with its vast number of admonishments, particularly on the topic of lazy kings. On nights like this, as Ever trudged to the throne room with Garin in tow, he sorely wished that his father's voice would sometimes just shut up.

When he stepped into the throne room, he was taken by surprise at the sheer number of villagers present. He did his best to look composed as he made his way to the throne, but inside, an uneasiness slid about in his stomach. When the runner had first come to him, Ever had hoped that a few villagers had caught a random illness, and they were only jumping to conclusions when they claimed that there was a curse. But there were far too many people for that. At least two dozen families stood in his midst and more were coming in the back.

"Alright, let us begin," Ever said, not in the mood for the usual hearing traditions. "What is it that ails you all at such a late hour?"

"Your Highness." A thin man with a graying beard and faded clothes knelt before him. "My name's Emile. I'm a baker in

Soudain. We sincerely 'pologize for comin' at this time, but the need was too great to wait until mornin'." He turned and looked at the people behind him. Some nodded. One woman in particular, however, made dramatic sweeping movements with her arms, a scowl chiseled into her bony face. He turned back to Ever. "We want to thank you and our queen for returnin' our children to us, but..." His voice quivered and faltered.

"I understand this is about the children?" Ever prodded.

"Yes. Uh... yes, Your Majesty. You see, every child in Soudain that was returned to us has been struck with maladies o' the worst sorts."

"Maladies?" Ever leaned forward. All of the children had appeared healthy to him when they'd left the forest.

The man bobbed his head. "Yes, Your Highness. They're injuries and illnesses like our healers have never seen before."

"Well then, let me see these children."

"We didn't bring them here!" the woman who had been waving her hands called out. Her tone was not nearly as respectful as the man's had been. "They're all laid up in a sick tent. You need to see them now!"

"I see," Ever said. "None have died, though?"

"No, sire. That is the strange part 'bout it," the man said, shooting the woman an irritated look over his shoulder. "Some complain o' sore aches in their arms and legs. Others've broken bones. One has lost her voice! But they all have somethin'!"

Ever sat straighter and rubbed the back of his head thoughtfully. He was greatly relieved to hear that none of the children had died, but it made no sense. Then again, his day had made little sense to begin with.

"This is what I propose." Ever stood. "As we have only just returned from the rescue, I have not yet had the time to consult with Queen Isabelle. She was the one who was with the children in the other land. Since none of the children seems to be in mortal danger, I will take this night to talk with my wife and consult with the Fortress. Perhaps the queen can shed some light on the situation. First thing tomorrow, we will visit your children ourselves."

A quiet murmur arose from the men and women present, but one voice screeched out above the rest.

"The king cares for his sleep more than our children!" It was the same woman who had interrupted them earlier.

Ever marched down the dais and over to the woman. "And would you, madam, prefer me to travel there now as I am and perhaps injure your child even further? For I can assure you, such things do happen!"

The woman still glared, but she took a step back. "I find it hard to believe the Fortress's celebrated king could be so careless," she muttered.

"Come now, Agnes." A woman with a small babe tucked snugly in her left arm gently pulled on the rude woman's hand. "You have his word. There are only six hours left until the morning light. The children will benefit more if the king is rested." She looked at Ever, her gaze similar to that which Isa wore when she looked at Genny and Henri. "Your Highness, do whatever you must to help them. I know the Maker will watch over them as we wait."

Ever's heart softened at the kindness in her voice, for he was very weary indeed. "Thank you, madam. As you have said, I will see you early on the morrow."

Garin followed Ever out of the throne room, but neither of them spoke until Ever stood outside his own chambers.

"She was right," Garin said softly. "The Maker is watching over those children tonight, and you will need your strength tomorrow. Good night, Ever."

Ever paused, his hand on the door, but as he went in, for the first time in his life, he didn't wish Garin a good night in return. He could not bring himself to pretend that everything between them was as it had been.

As he shut the door, he expected to see Isa's sleeping form in their bed, but to his surprise, she was standing out on the balcony with a blanket pulled over her slumped shoulders. He went to her and wrapped his arms around those shoulders. She leaned her head back against him, and for a long time, they stood still. If nothing else, Ever told himself, he was thankful for this. His wife had been returned to him safe and sound. For though he had told no one else at the camp, he had feared the worst when she didn't return after that first day. Only the power of the Fortress had kept him from tearing the cottage to shreds with his bare hands.

"We are needed in Soudain early tomorrow," he finally mumbled into her hair. "The children who were returned have come down with a mystery illness of sorts."

In response, Isa briefly stiffened, but then she relaxed into him again. "That is strange," she said. But something in her voice gave Ever pause. She didn't sound like it was strange, or that she was even surprised by it.

Ever wanted to ask, but instead, he decided that he had another topic he needed to discuss. It might just drive him mad if he didn't. "Garin and I spoke after you left," he began, suddenly very afraid of what she might think. Should he even be telling her this? "It's about the veil."

She finally turned to look at him. "What about it?"

"Garin says that because a Fortier sealed the veil between the two worlds, only a Fortier could have torn it again." He took a deep breath. "He also thinks that a Fortier must have fathered those children."

Isa's eyes widened a little, but she turned them on the darkened mountain. "He thinks it was you."

"Well, at first, yes," Ever hurried to explain. "But he would have known if I had done such a thing. I swear Isa, those children are not mine!"

Instead of crying or looking suspicious or even studying him as Ever had expected her to do, Isa gently took his face in her hands and gave him a tired smile. "I know."

"You know?"

She smiled and lightly touched his chest, sending ripples of warm relief through the rest of his body. "I will admit that Henri does have moments when he reminds me of you. I thought that the day I met him. But," she turned her lovely moonlit face up to him, her pink lips parting softly, "four years have passed, and you still forget my gift sometimes. Ever, I know that you have only ever been faithful, even before you knew me." She gave him a meaningful look before taking his hand and leading him over to the bed. "I don't need my gift to know that."

"But how?" He wanted so desperately to believe her, but it seemed too good to be true.

She pulled the covers over herself and leaned back into the pillows, looking suddenly as exhausted as he felt. "Because I know who I married. And you, Everard Fortier, are a good man."

Tired or not, Ever leaned over to give her the kiss she deserved. How he had survived without her, keeping any semblance of sanity, he would never know. For though the world was falling to pieces around him, the look his wife was giving him now made him feel as though somehow, everything would be made right.

CHAPTER 14
PANIC

Although she'd lived in Soudain her entire life, it occurred to Isa that she had never visited this quarter of the capital city before. The houses were small and cruder than those in the main city blocks, patched up with straw thatch and mud. The people looked haggard as well. Such an area was no place for a young lady on her own, her father had sternly warned her once when she was seven. And now she understood why as she glared back at some of the men who were making not-so-subtle examinations of her person.

"Why would they put the tent here?" Ever asked her as he stopped his horse before a flimsy canvas structure. "The children were taken from all over the city, not just the outskirts."

"Because the well-off said they were too good for such commons." A scowling skinny woman appeared before them, wiping her hands on her apron. Her wiry hair was pulled back beneath a dirty rag. "Said they would keep their children in their own homes and buildings, rather than have them mingle with the *riffraff*. It took you long enough, Your Highness."

Isa stared, shocked at the woman's audacity, but Ever just shook his head ever so slightly.

"Sires," a man hustled out of the tent and stepped in front of the rude woman, "we're so thankful you've come. Please, follow me." Ever helped Isa dismount before nodding at his guards, three of whom followed them into the tent. The other two stayed outside with the horses to ask questions of those who lingered outside.

As Isa's eyes adjusted from the brightness of the morning sun to the dark of the tent, she made out ten little mattresses lined up in a row, each with a child lying upon it. When she drew closer she was surprised to find that none of the children shared symptoms as she had expected to find. One child had large brown boils covering his face, neck, arms, and legs. The next little girl had a broken arm. The boy after her appeared fine, but his parents stood over him looking anxious.

Isa knelt down beside the mattress closest to the door and laid her hand upon the boy's forehead.

"I remember you," she whispered to the little boy, forcing a smile upon her face. The little boy gave her an ornery little smirk. He had given the guards particular trouble before returning home. "Tell me, does this hurt?" She pressed gently against the child's arm, just above a boil.

He gave her a slight nod.

"Poor baby," she murmured. "You're burning up. Do you feel hot?"

At this, he shook his head and gave her another grin. "Only my skin hurts. I feel good enough to climb a tree, but Mummy says I must stay in bed." He crossed his skinny arms, a disgruntled look coming to his face.

Isa smiled. "I am thankful you feel well, but I think your mother is right. You need to stay in bed until your skin stops hurting."

"My papa is a healer," he said as she continued to examine him. "But he can't heal me. Can you?" The hopeful look he gave her made Isa's heart ache.

"We'll do our best." Isa felt her smile falter just a bit. "Now, I have a question for you. Did you talk to anyone while you were in that strange world? Anyone besides your friends?"

The boy immediately shook his head.

"Are you sure? I need you to think very hard and really try to remember."

He bit his lip for a moment, then his face lit up. "I talked to that woman with the yellow hair before she brought us cookies. She asked me about my mummy and papa."

Isa's heart sank as she looked up at his parents. "You say that this began after the soldiers brought them home?" His mother and father stood behind the bed with pinched faces and clasped hands.

"Not even an hour after," the mother said, her eyes never leaving her son. "We sent for help immediately. The fever came so fast. I didn't think he'd make it through the night..." Her voice broke as she leaned down and gathered the little boy in her arms, who promptly began to squirm.

"But after we were told your husband was otherwise occupied last night," the father dared a fierce glance at Ever before turning back to Isa, "we realized that he wasn't being affected by the sickness. At least, not in the way such fevers usually go."

"And he has remained like this since then?"

"Aye."

Isa thanked the parents and ruffled the little boy's hair once more before moving on to the next mattress, and then the next. Before long, she had talked to the parents of every child. Determined to leave no stone unturned, she then went to visit the eight families who were keeping their own children at home. Each story was essentially the same, but Isa grew wearier with each home she visited. The weight of helplessness was in each parents' heart, and as a result, in hers as well. The skinny woman, Agatha, whose daughter had blisters covering her hands, at one point accused Isa of being apathetic. If only she knew. If anyone understood their plight, it was Isa. Not only because of her gift but because Isa had a story like theirs all her own.

Something deep down, possibly the Fortress, warned her that theirs might not be a plight Ever's fire could easily fix. For there was a new power here that she felt slipping through the blood of each child. The strength was foreign but also familiar. It was the same power she had felt back at the torn veil, and the same strength that now moved through her blood as well. Ever hadn't been able to feel the tear in the veil as she had. And now she wondered if he would be able to heal a malady that seemed to come from the same source. And yet he had to try.

"I need her away from the other children," she told the father of the girl on the last mattress. Ever sent her a questioning look, but she gave him the slightest shake of her head. If this didn't work, she didn't want it to incite panic among the people.

As soon as they had the girl by herself in a corner, Ever took the child's throat gently in his hands. Her voice had disappeared, her parents had told them. She couldn't even whisper. Isa relaxed a little as her husband's familiar blue light moved from his hands into the child. The Fortress's fire was always comforting. They stayed that way for a few minutes, Ever kneeling before the girl's pallet with his eyes closed in concentration, and the child watching the ceiling with wide eyes as she waited.

But something is wrong, a voice inside her whispered as Ever's face tightened infinitesimally. *He should be done by now. Please, Fortress, let him heal her!* But as seconds stretched to minutes, Isa could see the parents beginning to shift nervously as well, and she could feel Ever becoming agitated. Finally, he let go, but she could see from the tightness in his eyes that he was not at all confident in the work he'd done.

"Well?" the father asked his daughter. "Did it work?"

The girl opened her mouth, but to Isa's dismay, nothing came out.

"I need to speak with you." Without waiting for the parents to respond, Isa took Ever by the hand and led him over to another corner of the tent.

"I don't understand," Ever said, looking at his hands. "I had hoped it was simply an effect of spending time in the Fae world..."

Isa shook her head, looking at her feet. This was not a conversation she'd planned on having here in front of their subjects, but she needed to tell him.

"Last night, when you were talking with Garin..." She stopped and drew a deep breath, willing her voice to stay steady. "While you were talking to Garin, I fell asleep and had a dream."

"A dream?" He raised an eyebrow, and she nodded.

"I dreamed that everything in me was emptied. I felt dry, parched, as though I'd walked for miles in a desert. Then I realized I *was* in a desert. I came upon an old orchard, where trees grew in the sand. But none of them bore any fruit. I woke up then and had the most terrible pain." She closed her eyes.

"Where?" Ever's voice was strained.

"Here." Without thinking, she placed her hand in the same spot that had kept her doubled her over the evening before. "Ever, I know I haven't conceived yet, but there was always the possibility. I could feel it. But now..." She shook her head. "I'm barren."

Ever's heart was more unreadable than usual. He opened and closed his mouth twice before simply staring outside the tent for a long minute and rubbing the back of his neck the way he did when he was unsure of what to do.

"It was her," Isa continued before she lost her nerve and her self-control. "It was Sacha. It had to be!"

"But how?" Ever finally looked at her, his eyes still indecipherable.

Isa had asked herself the same question the night before. "There is only one answer I can come up with. She baked us all cookies. I couldn't feel anything at the time, but there was just so much power everywhere... I can only guess that she used some sort of Sorthileige."

"Couldn't it have been the other food?"

Isa shook her head. "According to the children, she spoke with every child, asking them their parents' occupations before giving them their treats." Now that she thought of it, why hadn't Sacha talked to Genny or Henri? Perhaps she had but did nothing to them because they were orphans. They had no parents to affect.

"But why all the different maladies?" Ever looked back at the children over her shoulder.

"She chose what she knew would hurt each family the most. The boy with sores is the son of a healer. Who would visit a healer who can't heal his own son? The girl without a voice is from a family of minstrels. The one with blisters comes from a family of bakers."

"But what about you? Did you tell her you were the queen?" Ever looked incredulous.

"I know better than that," Isa huffed. "I told her you and I protect the region." Isa sighed. "Still, any wife would have one overarching duty for such an important calling."

"Which would be?"

"Produce an heir to follow in our footsteps."

Ever's jaw tightened as he closed his eyes again. "When were you planning to tell me this?" he asked in a low, dangerous voice.

"I wanted to! Last night, when you came to me and the dream and pain had passed, but then you told me about the children and I didn't want to worry you even more!" She took one of his large, calloused hands in her own. "I didn't understand the connection until this morning. I am sorry, Ever. Truly!"

"One might think," he pulled his hand free, "that our ability to have children could actually be my concern as well, worry or no." He stalked toward the tent door and motioned to his soldiers. Isa followed more slowly, trying desperately to keep her tears at bay. It hurt to hear, but he was right. Her pain was his business, and by hiding it from him she had only muddled things further.

"Get the med packs," Ever was quietly telling his men when

she caught up to him. "We're going to do what we can for these children before heading back up the mountain."

The men exchanged looks of confusion, but they knew better than to question him. Soon they were all attending to the children. Isa helped one of them set the little boy's broken arm, but her attention remained on Ever, who was furiously mixing a salve for the boils and blisters. All around her, Isa could sense the confusion and frustration of the parents and the others who had come to watch the king work his miracles. Why hadn't the mute girl's voice been restored by his fire, and why wasn't he using that fire on any of the others?

And sensing the state of Ever's heart was even worse. Though it was vague, as usual, she could still feel pangs of panic. Fear. Frustration. Self-doubt.

And sorrow. One wouldn't know it by looking at him, ferocious as he appeared, but inside, he was mourning, just as Isa had done the night before.

When they were all done, Ever and his men quickly gathered their supplies before reloading their horses, and they were just about ready to go when the skinny woman ran after them.

"Wait, Agnes!" A man named Emile ran after her, but she shook him off before jabbing her finger up at Ever.

"What now? Are we too lowly for your precious fire? Are you that much high and mightier than us peasants? You won't even have mercy on our children?"

Since the night before, Isa had felt like a piece of string being wound tighter and tighter. Now, that string snapped. Dismounting her horse, Isa strode back to the woman and stopped when their noses were less than a hand's breadth apart. "You would dare to speak to your king this way?" she hissed. "The king comes all the way from the Fortress to your home, and you attempt to shame him so?" She took a step forward. "If the Maker does not deem it the proper time for your daughter to be healed, do you think anything my husband does shall change that?" She grabbed the woman's wrist and gripped it tightly, despite the woman's protests.

Isa focused all of her energy on the truth that she had just spoken. As she continued to hold Agnes's wrist, the woman's pulling and thrashing stopped, and she fell to her knees in the mud.

"Forgive me," she sobbed. "My husband passed last year." She looked up at Isa through red, glassy eyes. "She's all I got left!"

Isa's anger dissipated at the woman's pleas. "We will pray for guidance and continue to search for answers," she said, letting go of the woman's wrist. "Perhaps the Maker has another way in mind." After helping the woman stand, Isa mounted her horse once again, and they set off to the Fortress.

As they went, though, Isa could still feel the tension they were leaving behind. Agnes's change of heart wasn't reflected in all of those who had witnessed Ever's failure. Or even many of them. Most of the crowd still consisted of confused, angry parents, grandparents, and friends. Isa got the feeling she would be using her gift more than ever before in the coming days, and she prayed she would be up to the task.

As soon as they were at the foot of the mountain, Ever turned to one of his men. "Hamon, show me the gash you received two days ago in training."

The red-haired man looked startled but did as Ever said, removing his glove to reveal a puckered scar above his fourth knuckle. Ever placed his hand above it. As the fire burned brightly for a brief moment, Isa wondered whether or not it would work. But to her relief, when Ever pulled his hand away, all signs of the man's scar had disappeared.

"Thank you, sire," Hamon said, bowing his head.

Ever looked up at his men. "I want the rest of you to return to the Fortress. Hamon, report to Garin what happened here today. I need to speak with my wife alone." He dismounted, then held his hands up for Isa to do the same.

Isa's stomach did a flip as she dismounted and turned to face him, and she suddenly felt like a little girl when her father would call her to his chair to admonish her for some wrong she had committed.

Rather than rebuking, however, Ever only took her hand in his and began to run his fingers over her knuckles, a nameless expression upon his face. Isa tried to read his heart, but it was too muddled.

"I am not angry," he finally said in a soft voice. "I only wish you had come to me sooner." He met her gaze, the fiery rings capturing her in their depths. "You of all people should know by now that we must do this *together*. You've never wanted me to leave you behind." He arched an eyebrow, inviting her to challenge him. But of course, she couldn't. "Now I have this request of my own. You cannot try to shoulder your burdens alone." He clasped her hand tightly in his own, and Isa reveled in its warmth and strength. "Are we agreed?"

Isa nodded, despite the tears that were running freely down her face. Ever gave her a sad smile and reached up to wipe them away. Was it possible for her to love him any more than she did now?

"Now, though I am afraid of the outcome, let me see what I can do for you." Gently, he laid his right hand over her belly while he held her arm with his left. "I will be using a much stronger fire than usual," he warned her. "This may hurt a bit." And with that, he pressed in.

At first, it was just a flicker of warmth, the way it felt when one sat too close to the hearth on a cold day. But the longer he pressed, the hotter the flames became, and it took everything in Isa not to leap away. *Please let this work!* she begged the Fortress, gritting her teeth and mashing her eyes closed as hard as they would go. She could vaguely feel Ever stroking her hair as he continued to work, but it was of little comfort. The pain was too severe. If it could heal her though, she could survive anything.

Finally, however, the fire was simply too hot, and Isa let out a cry of pain. Immediately, Ever stopped and grabbed her arms so she wouldn't fall. Isa hobbled over to a large, flat rock and lay down. Ever sat beside her, drawing her close until she was recovered enough to breathe and take stock of herself.

"Well?" he asked, hope rising up within him even though Isa could feel him trying to quell it.

"No," she whispered. "It's still there."

CHAPTER 15
A BOY'S TOUCH

Where is Miss Isa?" Henri asked the servant tending to the garden.

"The *queen*," the servant woman gently corrected him, "is with King Everard in the Tower of Annals."

Henri sighed. Exactly where they had been for the past three weeks. Did the king and queen ever do anything besides sit up in that tower?

If it had been up to him, he and Genny would have been spending the day differently as well, *in* kitchens, rather than outside of them. But Genny had insisted on coming outside to chase butterflies. One of these days, he swore to himself, he was going to stop letting his little sister always have her way. Butterflies were fine, but Cook's bread was delicious.

It wasn't Genny's fault that he was in a bad mood, Henri reminded himself as he munched on the tomato he'd snatched when the servant wasn't looking. It was King Ever's fault. Or perhaps it truly was his. He wasn't sure anymore.

During their second week at the Fortress, long after the other children had been returned to their parents, the king had taken to reading books at the table while they ate. Henri could tell that

Miss Isa didn't approve of the king's habit much, judging by the little frowns she would send him and his books every few minutes. But she said little about it, often spending her time talking with the children instead. And Henri didn't at all mind missing out on the king's company. The king frightened him.

Though Henri had seen taller men, King Ever had arms and legs thicker than both of Henri's legs put together. The king's voice boomed, and his ability to fight would have put Henri's brawny father to shame. The king was generally in a rather short mood, and though he would make attempts to talk to the children now and then about little details such as the weather, Henri simply preferred to stay out of his way completely.

The night before, however, which had marked three weeks since he and Genny came to the Fortress, Henri made a grave mistake. As they sat down to supper, something that seemed a nightly tradition at the Fortress, Cook brought out a new frothy drink, one with foam and bubbles that nearly spilled over the sides of the cups.

"Madame Gigi told me you two might enjoy a new kind of treat," he had said, a twinkle in his narrow brown eyes. Henri had immediately taken a sip, and to his delight, had found it the sweetest thing he'd ever consumed. Genny, on the other hand, seemed to have plans other than actually drinking her treat. As soon as Miss Isa stepped away from the table, the little girl had giggled then blown a few pieces of foam onto her brother's plate. Without thinking, Henri had returned the favor with his own foam. Unfortunately, he blew much harder than he'd meant to, and to his horror, a large bit of the foam flopped down right on the ancient text the king was reading.

Henri's face had flushed with embarrassment as King Ever fixed his steely blue eyes upon him, and the look the king had given Henri had made him want to run upstairs and hide in his new room forever.

"This text is over four hundred years old." The king's voice reverberated in Henri's chest in its low, menacing tone. "I do not think blowing our drinks across the table is appropriate supper behavior."

Henri's horror had only grown when Genny piped up without hesitation, "But Miss Isa says readin' at the table is not *app-er-o-piate* supper behavior either!"

The king had stared at them for so long that Henri thought he might toss them outside right then and there. Finally, however, he only slammed the book shut and stomped out of the room, probably, Henri guessed, to head back up the tall tower, taking his supper with him.

Now, as he watched his sister chase the butterflies, Henri wondered again what he would do if the king and queen threw them out. He couldn't deny that he had quickly grown accustomed to a warm bed and full stomach. It was nice to see Genny happy, and no one, not even the king, had raised a hand against either of them since they'd arrived. Though he was far from trusting that the situation could last, for it seemed quite too good to be true, Henri wished to the Maker desperately that it might. Being rejected by parents who had never truly loved them had been bad enough. He didn't know if he could stand being rejected by someone as kind as the queen.

Henri had never known a woman like Miss Isa. He remembered little of his own mother, and whenever Helaine had turned to address him directly, it was usually to bark out an order or to make sure he remembered his place, often with the backside of her hand. Miss Isa, though he would never admit that he liked it, was full of hugs and kisses. She reprimanded them enough, but her words were never cruel. And she made Genny happy.

Henri stood and walked out to where his sister had collapsed on the ground, breathing hard after nearly an hour of running in circles and jumping up and down. Plopping down on the grass beside her, he asked, "Do you think Miss Isa looks more tired today?"

"No." Genny shook her head as she kept her eyes trained on the robin-egg blue sky above them. "Miss Isa always looks beautiful."

"I don't mean that she doesn't look beautiful," Henri scoffed. "I mean I think she looks tired. Her eyes are dark, and I think she seems... sad."

"No," Genny chirped again, still unperturbed.

"I don't know why I even bother asking you." He stood and brushed himself off before heading for the kitchens. Sometimes he wished Genny were just a few years older. Having a conversation with a four-year-old could be nearly impossible. If she was so determined not to talk sensibly, then she could lie there by herself. He was going to get some of Cook's sweet bread.

Just before he made it back to the vegetable plot, the door was blocked by Gigi, the older servant who fussed over the king as though he were Genny's age and not thirty-one, as Miss Isa said he was.

"There you are!" She smiled at him, though he thought her smile looked strained. "The queen is sorry she cannot have the midday meal with you today. She's very busy. But Master Garin has informed me that he would like to speak with you over the meal instead. He's sent for a picnic so you can all eat out on the Fortress's front lawns."

She said something else, but Henri didn't hear. All he could think about as he looked at the size of the basket Gigi carried was the loaf of bread his parents had given him before leaving them in the forest.

The king was sending them away. If it had been the queen who had suggested the idea herself, he might have thought otherwise. But the horrible memory of the foam-stained page from the night before was suddenly all he could think about.

They were being rejected again.

"I don't think so," Henri said in a small voice, shaking his head vehemently as he fell back a step. "I think I will just wait for Miss Isa."

"Nonsense." Gigi *tisked* as she reached for his hand.

Henri panicked, and before he knew what he was doing, a thin blue flame had not only engulfed his hand but hers as well. With a cry, Gigi fell back, clutching her hand to her chest. Henri couldn't move. He stood frozen in place as he watched her cradle the hand, already red and swollen.

Like a rabid wolf the king was suddenly there, although Henri had not the slightest idea as to where he had come from or how he had known what had happened, as there were no other servants about. The king gently took the older woman's hand and rubbed his own hand over it. He was asking her something, but Henri couldn't hear it for the sudden roar in his ears. Then the king grabbed Henri's arm so tightly it felt like it might break. Without pause, he dragged Henri all the way up to the children's room, where the king practically flung him onto the bed and slammed the door behind him.

Trembling, Henri hugged his knees to his chest as he rocked himself back and forth on his bed. He had never hurt anyone before with his trick. He'd only used it to provide light at night or for Genny's amusement. In fact, he hadn't even known that his fire *could* burn someone. He truly hadn't meant to hurt the old woman. His flame had been instinctive, as though it had a will of its own. Shame and fear took turns riding the tide of dread within him.

At best, he and Genny would merely be cast out of the Fortress. At worst... Henri shivered. He didn't even want to think about the worst that King Ever could to do him.

Miss Isa had spoken before about the power of the Fortress, how it heard her thoughts and created power within her. She had also said that the Fortress knew one's heart, even when others couldn't see it. *Well,* he thought feverishly, *if that's true, Fortress, I need you now!*

CHAPTER 16

STORY ABOUT A BOY

Isa let herself fall into bed, allowing her weary limbs to relax one at a time in its feathery depths. How many times had she tried to hide away in her room like this, just to be thwarted by another knock at the door? It seemed there was always a needy servant or a desperate parent begging her to return to Soudain to see to a child whose condition hadn't changed in weeks. Not that she wished to shirk her duties, but rather, Isa simply longed to have an hour to herself to pause and breathe.

Just one hour.

As if on cue, Isa could hear her husband's heavy, quick foot-steps fast approaching their door. She sighed up at the red canopy above their bed, counting down the seconds until he burst through the door with some new emergency, no doubt, that simply could not be remedied without her.

Sure enough, the door banged open. "Come here." His voice had an edge to it that Isa hadn't heard in a long time.

She sat up. "What is it?"

Ever's face was an alarming shade of red, and the anger

within him was nearly palpable. "I need you to see what he's done."

"Who?"

"That boy of yours. Come with me."

Scrambling out of the bed, Isa was immediately alert, all memory of exhaustion gone as her heart pounded away. She considered asking him what he'd meant by *her boy* but decided against it. She had learned long ago that nothing good came of arguing with her husband when he was in a mood like this. Better to let him calm down and then discuss whatever had roused his ire. But, she wondered, how long would that take this time, for she had not seen him in this kind of temper for a long, long while.

While Ever hadn't exactly been taken with the children as Isa had been, he had tolerated their antics rather well, even venturing cautiously to speak with them now and then. To his credit, he'd tried, considering he'd never spent much time around children even when he was a child himself. But the way he walked now frightened Isa, and she hurried even faster as they headed downstairs and rounded the corner to the first sick room.

"Gigi, what happened?" Isa ran to the older woman's side and gently lifted the hand that the healer had just cleaned. Bright red puffs of skin covered her hand, wrapping around it the way another hand might. Though Isa was no healer, she knew a bad burn when she saw one.

"Your boy did that," Ever fumed.

"Please, Ever," Gigi stuttered, seeming close to tears. "It was an accident. I only frightened him, that was all!" From the way her voice trembled, though, and the paleness of her round face, it was obvious that Gigi had been shaken by the incident.

"I wanted you to see this before I healed it," Ever said, still fuming, "so you would know exactly what he is capable of!"

Isa didn't answer him. Instead, she gently lifted Gigi's burned hand and placed it in Ever's hands before squeezing Gigi's shoulder. She focused on what Gigi had told her, that the boy had meant no harm. As that truth flowed from Isa's hands into Gigi, Isa could feel the older woman relax. Her white curls ceased to shake, and color returned to her cheeks. Hopefully Ever could do his part now. Isa held her breath.

Just then, Isa noticed Garin standing in the corner of the room, a tight, intense look on his face.

"Where are the children now?" Isa asked as Ever set to healing.

"Locked in their room," Ever said. "Where I told them they would stay unless they wished for the direst of consequences to befall them."

Isa closed her eyes and said a quick prayer. It was very possible that Ever had just done more damage than good, but she would need to talk him into a calmer mood before she took any drastic measures. As she opened her eyes, Ever let go of Gigi's hand. Isa sighed with relief as Gigi moved her fingers. It seemed that at least for this ailment, Ever's powers were still effective.

Ever gave Garin a meaningful look. Garin nodded, and the two of them stepped out into the hall. As their footsteps faded, Gigi looked up into Isa's face, her eyes imploring.

"Please, Isa!" she said, her voice hitching again, "don't let him be too hard on the boy! I should have known better, given their... circumstances. I know Henri didn't mean anything by it. You should have seen the look on his face when he realized what he'd done!"

"I promise," Isa said, leaning over to place a kiss on Gigi's soft cheek. "We will get this all sorted out." As she spoke, an idea came to her, an answer to the prayer she had uttered only a moment before. She knew exactly what she needed to say. But first, she had to catch Ever.

Isa broke into a sprint, but as she ran, she wondered with annoyance at how quickly the exercise was tiring her. When was the last time she'd gotten more than four hours of sleep uninterrupted? Her tired mind couldn't recall. What she wouldn't give for a nap right now. Thankfully, she didn't have to run far before overtaking Ever and Garin, for they had been stopped by one of Ever's soldiers. Isa stopped, too, but waited just close enough that she could hear what the man was saying.

"... healing people in the southern woods. The parents who have brought their children to her claim they've shown no symptoms since."

"How many people know about this?" Ever asked.

"Enough. Bartholomew says there is a line every time she appears, and that she never heals every single one. Mostly the woods people are those who have been going to her thus far, but news is spreading fast."

Ever stood perfectly still for a long moment. Finally, he told the soldier in words nearly too quiet for Isa to hear, "We'll set out tomorrow before first light."

Isa wanted to groan.

"How many days should we prepare for, sire?"

"It's a three-day ride to the town." He paused. "We will travel without speed this time. I will need to save my strength for the meeting, should it go badly." He glanced up at Isa, then told the man that he would be down to discuss logistics with him soon enough but for him to relay the plans to Acelet in the meantime. Isa took that as her signal.

"Please." She approached her husband and took hold of his arm, keeping her voice low so the passing servants wouldn't hear. "Let me talk to the children."

"I think not."

"Ever," Isa said, "you are angry right now. I know how much Gigi means to you. But how much good will it do for you to frighten Henri more? That is how this mess began in the first place."

Ever glared at her for a long time, but to her relief, Isa could feel him beginning to soften. She hated using her gift on him but sometimes it was necessary when he refused to see sense. Thankfully, however, she did not have to use it this time, for he finally let his head droop to his chest as he let out a gusty breath.

"Take Garin. I don't want you alone with them until I know what the boy is capable of."

"Actually," Isa leaned in, "I was hoping you would both accompany me. I believe this is something you need to be a part of."

Ever hesitated, casting one last look of longing in the direction of the soldier he had just sent away, then nodded reluctantly. Isa sent him the most confident, peaceful smile she could muster, praying all the while for her plan to have success. For if it didn't, this could end very, very badly.

By the time Isa and Ever arrived at the children's door, Garin had unlocked it and was standing by the hearth with his arms folded. Genny seemed oblivious to the fact that her brother was curled into a little heap on his bed, or that there was a problem at all as she pulled at Garin's trousers and begged for him to tell her a story. The little girl's blue eyes lit up as she spotted Isa, but as soon as she spotted Ever, she wilted like a flower in the dead heat of summer. Ever must have noticed, too, for Isa felt a flash of guilt move through him as she wrapped the little girl up in her arms. Good. He hadn't needed to scare Genny too.

"Are you ready for bed?" Isa asked the little girl as she plopped her upon her bed and began to braid the child's hair. Genny gave her a big grin.

"But it's early! Cook only just brought us supper! Plus, we still need a story." Then she turned her little face to where Ever stood and drew her lips up into a pinched frown. "Except from him. I don't want a story from him."

"Well, I have a special story tonight for both of you." Isa tucked Genny in, then went over to Henri and began to unfold him from his little ball. "In fact, it is one of my very favorites because it's a *true* story." As soon as the children were both beneath their covers, she sat down beside Henri.

"Long ago, there was a boy, a prince, who had special powers from the Fortress."

"This Fortress?" Genny sat up, her eyes wide.

Isa laughed. "Yes, this Fortress. You see, the prince was very strong. Even as a boy he could best grown men with the sword, and with only his hands he could create a power so strong that it was like the lightning from the sky." As she spoke, Isa watched Henri. He still looked terrified, but the more she spoke, the less he hid his face beneath the blankets.

"When he was thirteen, the prince was in a royal procession with his parents. Many people came to see the prince, for news had traveled far and wide of the young prince's power *and*," she added, "his kind heart. And his heart was indeed kind. For when a girl fell into the street, he climbed off his horse and helped her stand."

"That was nice." Genny nodded matter-of-factly.

"Yes, it was nice," Isa said with a sad smile, flicking her gaze over to where Garin and Ever stood by the door. Garin's arms were still folded in front of him, but his eyes were closed now. Ever's face was slightly twisted in a way that made Isa's heart ache. But, she reminded herself, bones needed to be broken before they could be reset. Ever needed to hear this before he allowed his anger to carry him away.

"Unfortunately," she turned back to the children, "the prince also had a temper that often got him into trouble. And on that day, it did just that. You see, the girl didn't know she wasn't supposed to touch the prince, so when she ran up and grabbed his sleeve, hoping to thank him for his kindness, he lost his temper and accidentally hurt her with his power."

"Was it fire power?"

"Yes." Isa nodded, thankful Henri was finally talking again.

"What happened?" The boy studied his hands thoroughly as he spoke, still either unwilling or unable to look her in the eyes.

"He had to realize that the Maker still loved him, as did the Fortress and all of his friends who lived there with him. But that didn't mean there were no consequences. You see, his power hurt the girl badly, and it changed her life. She couldn't walk well, nor could she use her hand the way she once had. It took her many years to heal." Without looking at him, Isa could feel the shame burn through Ever as it always did when her old injury was brought up. Directing her next words to him, Isa lifted her gaze, wishing he would meet it.

"But the Fortress would not allow the prince to go on in sadness and loneliness."

"What happened?" Genny asked, somehow more out of the blankets than under them once again.

Isa smiled and tucked her back in. "The Fortress and the Maker brought the prince and the girl together so that neither of them could go on until she forgave him and he learned how to say he was sorry. In that forgiveness, they fell in love." Isa smiled to herself as the joy of that forgiveness filled her even now.

"Did they get married?" Genny asked.

"They did." Isa grinned as she leaned over to kiss Genny, then Henri. "They were soon married, and are *now* living happily." She stood to leave, but Henri's words brought her to a halt.

"I didn't mean to do it." Henri's voice was quiet. The way it cracked broke Isa's heart. "I never even asked for the fire. I just have it."

"None of us did." Isa sat back down and took Henri's hands. "But the Fortress has a purpose for everyone it gives strength to." She lifted his chin. "Including you. The hard part is waiting to see what our purposes are. Patience is a lesson we must learn." She looked up at Ever. "All of us."

Henri sighed and nodded before lying back down. "Fine. I'll think about it. But I'm not marrying Gigi!"

Isa laughed, and even Garin smiled, but Ever's face remained grim.

AFTER ISA HAD SNUFFED out the candles and made sure the fire in the hearth had enough wood, for it was still chilly in the evenings despite the coming of spring, she, Ever, and Garin filed out quietly.

Before going his own way, Garin turned to Isa in the hall and gave her a wry smile. "Five hundred years I've spent in this place and yet you still manage to surprise me. If I ever need more humility, I shall be sure to come to you in the future."

"Does that mean they've won you over yet?" Isa asked.

"Perhaps," Garin said thoughtfully, "I am beginning to see that dealings with my own people are not as black and white as I remember them to be." Isa returned his grin, and Garin excused himself, leaving her alone with Ever.

"Come," she said, taking her husband's hand and leading him down the hall. "Let's get some air."

As they walked, she tried again to read him, to see into the depths of his soul. What was it about the children that bothered him so? But, as usual, she was shut out.

Isa had once asked Garin why it was sometimes so difficult for her to read Ever's heart. Others came more easily to her, but for some reason, Ever could close himself off like a bear in its den.

"You were privy only to the last few months of Ever and Nevina's rivalry," Garin had told her.

This mention of Ever's old enemy had surprised Isa. She'd been sure Garin would talk about Ever's father and all of his infamous lessons in denying his feelings.

"Nevina knew how to use Ever's feelings against him, and she did so until the day she died." Garin had given Isa a wry smile when she'd stared in surprise. "I know what you're thinking, and yes, King Rodrigue *did* have a great hand in teaching Ever to keep his emotions hidden, but much of that training is gone now. You, my dear, have worn it away. The shield Ever places over his heart at this time is one born of need. He placed it there to keep Nevina out."

"But she's long dead. How do I get past it?"

"I helped him build it for his own safety, but I'm really not sure how to break it now, to be honest. He was still building it even up until her death." Garin had shrugged. "I don't know how long it will be before he knows how to take it down, or if he'll ever even have the ability to do so himself."

Now Ever's defenses were up in full as he followed her out to the crystal balcony. No musicians were there, as the hour had grown late, but Isa pulled him to the center of the blue floor and began to lead him in a slow, simple dance. That her story to the children had touched him was sure, for his eyebrows were drawn into a thoughtful, somewhat pained frown, but to what extent she had really reached him was still a mystery.

"Ever, what's troubling you?"

In response, he drew her in for a kiss. It was gentle and sweet, but there was no passion in it tonight. Rather, his lips seemed to match the expression on his face, reserved and unsettled.

"What was that for?" she asked.

"For showing me the truth," he said slowly. "You were right. I reacted far too quickly with the children. My anger was out of place." He gave her another soft kiss on the cheek. "Now, you need to go to bed. You've been staying up entirely too much lately."

That was quick. Isa had hoped to talk more. Although, since he had mentioned it, bed did sound wonderful. "We all need reminders." Isa smiled up at him.

Ever gave her a tired smile of his own, then turned and began to walk away.

"Wait!" Isa called out.

He turned, raising his eyebrows in question, and Isa's blood suddenly raced, for she knew what she was about to say couldn't be taken back.

"It... It will take a while for the children to find their places here." She gave him the most hopeful smile she could muster. "They'll need time."

The blue flames that were always dancing around the pupils of Ever's eyes changed direction, and Isa knew immediately what he thought of her suggestion as his face settled into its most guarded mask. "Isa," he said softly, "I don't know if—"

"Your Majesty!" A young soldier, Eloy, burst through the door of the dining hall, stopping so fast he nearly fell over when he laid eyes on Isa. "My Queen!" He bowed, breathing hard. "I am sorry. I didn't know you were both here."

"What is it?" Ever stepped forward.

"We have found where the woman appears every day. She comes from..." He hesitated, looking at Ever and then Isa as though unsure whether or not they would believe him. "A tree. There is no door, no way to enter or exit, but she still comes from the inside of the tree every day. She melts through it, like a mist."

"Where?" Ever asked.

"Just outside the small forest village of Sansim where she does her daily healings. And not only that," Eloy still breathed heavily, the white of his dark eyes standing out in the low light of the moon, "the people are beginning to talk. Not just the forest villages either."

"What are they saying?" Ever asked, and Isa held her breath.

"Forgive me for uttering their words, Your Highnesses... but they are saying that you have failed them one time too many." Eloy's voice fell to a whisper. "They wish to make her queen."

CHAPTER 17
TIES OF BLOOD

One day, Isa thought ruefully as she donned her bow and quiver, she would get a full night's sleep again. But this was not that night. For as soon as the mention of an uprising had fallen from the soldier's lips, Isa knew they were leaving. And though her exhaustion was great, she didn't dare mention it to Ever. Mentioning a weakness of any kind would only send him into a worried tizzy that would land her in bed. If she was lucky, he might let her out again in another decade.

So instead of complaining, she allowed the servant to help her mount her horse. She would sleep again, she told herself.

Eventually.

"Tell Henri that I will teach him to read his new book when we return," Isa said to Garin as the steward adjusted one of her saddlebags. "And please ask Gigi to tell Genny a story every night before she tucks them in."

"I think that by the time you return," Garin said with a sly smile, "Gigi will have spoiled them so rotten they care for nothing but sweets."

Isa had to smile at this, for she knew it was true. Despite

Henri's incident, Isa knew that Gigi would spare no expense in making sure the children were cared for and happy.

"Let us go," Ever announced. The horde of servants that had come to help them prepare stood back as their king, queen, and five handpicked soldiers set out into the blackness of the early morning.

Isa tried unsuccessfully to quell the fluttering in her stomach as they began to make their way down the mountain road. If there was truly an uprising, there would most likely be blood shed at some point. And though no one could equal the strength or ability of her husband, Isa knew his reluctance to take up arms against any of his citizens. For all his hard exterior, Ever loved his people. And just as it had nearly killed him when the evil enchanter had tried to take the Fortress three years before, Isa worried that his compassion might lead to his injury now, or even worse.

She must not think of these things, Isa admonished herself. They had a three-day ride ahead of them. Ever did not wish to spend his strength on speed but rather wanted to save it in case there was a confrontation. Instead of worrying the entire time, Isa decided to focus on what she wanted to say to Ever about the children. What she *needed* to say to Ever about the children. They had been on the cusp of such a conversation before Eloy had interrupted them, and whether Isa wanted to or not, they would need to finish their discussion sometime. They might as well get it done sooner rather than later.

Her chance did not come that first night, however, for they rode straight through the rest of the night and then on through the following day, stopping only to rest their horses. Isa slept each time they paused, managing to get an hour of sleep here and there, but it was never enough. On the second evening when they finally did stop for the entire night, Isa fell asleep before supper was cooked. It was only on the third night that she finally got the chance to speak with Ever. The rest she had taken the night before had strengthened her some, and she felt as though she might burst if she did not speak to Ever soon.

Her prayers were answered when Ever took the first watch. Isa waited on her sleeping roll until she could hear the steady breathing of the three men who were not on duty, and Ever had walked far enough away that whispers wouldn't wake them. She wrapped her blanket around her shoulders and slipped out of the camp to stand beside him as he studied the moonlit landscape before them.

"I've never much liked these open valleys," he said softly without looking at her. "They make me feel vulnerable. I would much rather travel along those bluffs in the distance." He nodded at the tall shadows along the horizon. "But they're too far out of the way for where we are going."

Not sure what to say to that, Isa simply waited for her courage to catch up to the moment, her breaths coming too fast and making her feel almost dizzy. But this was her chance.

"Ever, I've been thinking," she began, suddenly unable to look at his face. "When this is all over," she gestured back at the camp, "with the children, I mean..." Despite her nearly incoherent words, she could sense him stiffen in the dark, and his heart began to seal itself up again.

"Before you fall in love with them," he said, his voice kind but firm, "have you considered the repercussions of such an action?"

"Giving two orphans a home?" Isa's voice was suddenly too loud and one of the men stirred. "Yes, I have considered that. I've concluded that taking them in permanently would mean we would have two fewer children in the streets!"

"Isa, I know you want a child. And I understand—"

"No, Everard! You do not understand!"

"Then please enlighten me!" He finally turned toward her.

"You want an heir! Someone who will follow the rules and take the kingdom and do exactly as he's told. But I want a child... children! Soft, warm children who make mistakes and make messes and say the wrong things at the wrong times. I want to hold a girl in my arms and whisper that all will be well when she cries, and to straighten her braids and have the tailor make her a dress that twirls when she spins! I want a son who is honest to the point of offending an odious supper guest because he is only saying what everyone else is thinking." Isa leaned forward. "I want us to be *needed*, Ever, and those children need someone to love and hold them, to undo all the hurt their parents inflicted upon them."

"I am sure they have family somewhere," Ever said, his voice growing stiffer. "Your parents have a wide range of influence in Soudain. Surely they would know someone who could take them."

"Henri has power. Genny might very well, too," Isa said. "Other homes wouldn't be prepared for such children. Genny told me that their stepmother didn't like Henri's fire. That might very well be why they were abandoned!"

"But you haven't considered the long-term effects!" The fire in Ever's eyes leapt wildly. "Suppose we do keep them! What happens if we die without an heir? Who do you think the people will crown?"

"Does it make a difference?" Isa's voice was as cold as Ever's. "You know that those children were sired by someone in the Fortier line, and we *both* know who that was!"

"Don't," Ever growled, but Isa ignored him.

"Those children are your blood! Your sister and brother! They deserve love from you before they deserve it from anyone else!"

"You think I don't know that?" Ever took a step closer, his voice dark. "You think I haven't considered that in all the weeks they've spent with us? Every time I look at that boy, I see myself! But they are also Fae, Isa." He stopped and took a deep breath. When he spoke again, his voice was resigned as he reached up to pinch the bridge of his nose. "I cannot afford to consider the fates of only a few. Once we are gone, Destin will lie in the hands of the crown prince. I can see that there is Fortier blood within them, but I do not know how strong the Fae blood runs either. I cannot be blind to what they are, whether I want to see it or not. I cannot be blind to the truth of their origins. You, of all people, should understand that."

He turned and began to walk away, but Isa followed him, ignoring the jabbing weight of his words.

"You are so blind that love could hit you on the nose and you'd never be the wiser!" She turned and stomped back to her sleeping roll as tears blurred her vision. Unfortunately, though, as soon as her head was quiet enough to think, she was struck with the truth of his claims that she had suppressed during their argument. What he had said about the children had verity. But her argument did as well. The children were Fortier *and* Fae, and though Isa could see the truth in their need, she could not see the future. If their natures were eventually to war within them, she could not confidently say which side would win.

For the first time since she had realized her power, the truths within Isa seemed to collide, and she could make no sense of them. Every time she shut her eyes, the world began to spin.

CHAPTER 18
SOMETHING FAMILIAR

The next morning, Ever's mouth was still set in a tight line, and Isa was feeling no less frustrated. But as much as she wished to continue their argument, doing so now would only be detrimental to their mission. They had come to gather knowledge about a possible enemy and nothing else. Ever then planned to return immediately and consult with Acelet and Garin before making any far-reaching decisions.

Thankfully, it was cool enough for everyone to wear their cloaks without seeming out of place. Before entering the village, Isa and Ever donned their hoods. People from the smaller outlying villages generally stayed put, rarely visiting Soudain or the Fortress. This gave Ever and Isa the advantage of more anonymity, but it was still best to take precautions. Being recognized would jeopardize their entire mission.

Before leaving the Fortress, Isa had asked Ever if he couldn't use his power to disguise their faces.

"I've heard there are some with the ability to make things appear as they are not, and I do not mean the way the Fae do it," he'd said, "but that particular gift is not in my range of skill."

So now, as they made their way to the little village of Sansim that bordered the woods, Isa did her best to push all thoughts of the argument out of her head and focus on blending in. That would be more difficult, however, as long as they were riding their horses. In most of the outlying villages, few individuals could afford to keep a horse. As their little party made its way through Sansim, Isa realized theirs were the only horses in sight. And it made her more than uncomfortable.

Ever, however, looked completely unruffled, as usual. The only sign Isa could find of his restlessness was in the way the blue flames in his eyes continued to jump and turn in short, agitated bursts.

The mysterious woman would not be healing until that afternoon, according to his men, but Ever had announced that morning that he wished to hide the horses before most of the people were milling about to see them. Without the royal crest on the soldiers' breastplates or Ever's ceremonial armor, they would be given only as much respect as their weapons could buy them. Isa had even removed her blue crystal ring for the event, something she had only done a handful of times since Ever had placed it on her finger.

The ride to the church seemed to take much longer than it should have for such a small town, but the streets were hardly straight, and they began to fill more quickly than Isa had expected. Rickety carts and stubborn mules moved at painfully slow paces, and many children seemed to prefer watching the goings-on from the middle of the street rather than the side. The roads here were naught but mud and the houses were hovels pieced together with sticks, mud, and straw.

The early risers who were out now in the pearlescent pink light carried axes, baskets, flax, and bundles of firewood. They watched the company of seven ride past with open resentment in their eyes. Isa shivered. By the time they finally reached the church, even Ever was flexing his jaw regularly, making his face seem even more angular and immovable than usual.

Degare, the eldest of their guards, dismounted and went to knock on the church door. As they waited for the holy man's answer, Isa studied the church itself. It seemed to be the only building in the town that was made of stone rather than mud and sticks, and the entire building could have fit within her own personal chambers at home. Three small square windows were carved into the church's right side. They did not have real glass panes, as most buildings in Soudain had, but instead were covered with thick animal skins stretched at an angle to keep the rain out.

Finally, the door was opened and the priest appeared. He must have been at least fifty years of age, probably more, his head completely devoid of hair. Bags hugged his eyes. His round face, however, wasn't unpleasant as he spoke to Degare. Isa couldn't hear what was being said, but Degare scratched his red beard thoughtfully as he considered whatever it was that the priest said. Eventually, he glanced up at Ever then Isa before turning back to the priest and nodding once.

"We'll go around the back," Degare said as he rejoined them, taking his horse's reins and leading them toward the left side of the church between the building and the edge of the wood. "He says it would have been best if we'd come sooner before anyone was awake, but he will do his best to keep the horses safe for us until nightfall."

As they rounded the corner, Isa felt very doubtful that the horses would be well hidden at all. A little covering stood upon four poles that stuck out of the ground, its roof made of the same straw thatch that covered most of the cottages around them. All she could do was thank the Maker that the church was at the edge of town. Perhaps there would not be so many people passing by who might see the seven great horses resting beneath the small shelter. If their horses were stolen, king and queen or not, it would be a very long walk to the next place they could purchase replacements.

The priest appeared at the church's back door and quickly motioned for them to follow him inside. Isa wondered at the urgency in his face, for Degare had been instructed not to mention their true identities to anyone. Did this priest guess at their purpose in being there? Or was he simply concerned for the group that was very obviously not from anywhere nearby?

They entered the church quickly in single file, as the door was too narrow for anything else. The small chamber they found themselves in was apparently not part of the church's main chamber, the one with the leather-covered windows. Instead, it was a windowless room with a small fireplace and just enough space for a few pieces of rough furniture. A small cot was pushed into a corner, and a little wooden chest beside it had clothing spilling out. Was this hovel where the man of the Maker lived?

"Your Highnesses!" The holy man quickly closed the door and turned around, the light from the flames dancing across his face. "It is not safe for you here!"

Isa didn't miss the rebuking look that Ever sent to Degare, but the priest only shook his head. "I've been to the capital. I know who you are. Now, pray tell, why are Your Highnesses here? I told your spies only last week that this region is full of traitorous whispers and schemes!"

"And for that, we are indebted to you," Isa said quickly, hoping to soothe the man's anxiety.

"We have come to see this woman for ourselves," Ever said, his face dark even in the light of the hearty fire. "She is dabbling in a magic blacker than I have seen before."

"Oh, she does more than dabble!" The priest squeezed through the group to lift a stack of parchments from a crooked little table in the corner. They were covered with ink scribbles, though Isa couldn't make out the words from where she stood. The holy man handed one to Ever, who squinted at the paper as he tried to read it.

"I have lived in this region since I was accepted to the

church, and I have been making notes of the goings-on in these woods since I began." He looked at Isa, his round face scrunched into a troubled frown. "Dark arts are not so uncommon here, more common than even you would know, Your Highness, if I may say so." He nodded at Ever. "But in the last nine years, I have begun to see an inexplicable rise in the evil that sometimes pervades these woods. At first, the disturbances were only small, as if someone was testing himself, learning the tricks of wickedness and practicing them as one might practice smithing or sewing."

"Why was I not notified?" Ever frowned as he reached for another paper. "Father..."

"Oh, Lucien, Your Highness. And please forgive my boldness, but though it is a good deed done when you expel this or that bit of darkness as you always do, there are a dozen more for every one that is cast out. You would never have time to do anything else if you chased after every single one." The man looked at Isa desperately, as if hoping she would understand better than her husband. "But it stopped, you see, about five years ago. Then it began again last year."

He turned back to the table and pulled out a map that Isa guessed he had made himself. The drawings seemed to depict the region Sansim was in, encompassing the town as well as the southern woods to the east, direct south, and west of the church. The details were more intricate than any map of the southern forests Isa had ever seen at the Fortress.

"Last year, children began to disappear from our village, as well as the three or four nearest by," the priest said, pointing as he spoke. "Then they would be returned only a few days later. It frightened the parents at first, especially when the children returned speaking nonsense about mystical places and houses made of sweets. But when the children always returned no worse for wear, people eventually stopped worrying." The priest glanced up at Isa. "Again, my apologies, Your Majesty, but the people around here haven't much trust for the crown. I urged them to go to you, but they wanted to fend for themselves."

"That's why no children were reported missing from the southernmost villages," one of the guards murmured.

The priest nodded. "It happened often enough that the people began to talk of spirits in the forest who took the children to drink of their youth before sending them home again. Utter rubbish, of course." The holy man shook his head. "But that there was an evil at work, I had no doubt. Still, that was nothing compared to the sicknesses and injuries that began to shake the people a few months ago."

"Sicknesses?" Isa asked.

"Yes, my queen. People began to experience all sorts of strange maladies, but no matter how many healers saw them, they could not be healed. I, myself, went to pray for them often. Soon they began to despair, though, and brought in the dabblers of the Sorthileige to attempt their charms and incantations." The priest shuddered so hard his faded blue robe shook. "Of course, that in itself brewed a new pot of problems, but to say the least, nothing worked."

"Tell me," Ever said, his voice suddenly lifting the way it always did when he was excited. "No one died from these ailments, did they?"

There was a long pause. "No, Your Highness," the priest said slowly. "They are all still alive. They were even cured... all of them, about two months ago."

"What do you know of this woman?" Isa asked, suddenly fighting the urge to track down the woman then and there.

"Little," the priest said. "I went to see her for myself when she first appeared last week, and when she emerged from her tree, I knew immediately that darkness came from within her. I confronted her, but she mocked me in front of the people, and I was nearly driven out of the town."

Isa closed her eyes briefly and pressed her hand to her belly.

The ache caused by the curse had left long ago. Still, her middle hurt from time to time, and her womanly cycle had never returned. Whatever force it was that had stolen her chance at natural motherhood could not be allowed to continue roaming like this. She wouldn't allow it. Though she had never killed another human with her own hands, nor had she any desire to do so, Isa felt a sudden fire flame within her. She would do whatever she must to remove this monster from the people.

The priest's sigh broke through her thoughts. "I know this village is not much to look at. Its people are rough, and they often lack in decorum." He lifted his shoulders in a helpless shrug. "But I love them. They are not all as you have seen. Many are simply trying to survive."

"We are indebted to you," Ever's voice rumbled as he finally looked up from the stack of papers that he had been reading. "You have done the Fortress and the kingdom a great service." The priest began to utter protests, but Ever held up a gloved hand. "When we are done with this debacle, I will return and you will accompany me to the Fortress. We will see what we can do to help your village and others like it."

"I would love nothing more, Your Highness." The priest's shrill voice quivered as he spoke. "But first, you must survive the day." He ran to the hearth and stooped at its edge, gathering ashes in his hands. "You are far too clean to look like you belong here." With that, he ran between each of his guests and began to smear the ashes upon their hair and faces. Isa didn't particularly relish the idea of being covered in ashes until they reached the Fortress again, but she didn't argue as he dirtied her face.

"Now," he brushed his hands off over the hearth and placed his fists on his hips, "after you finish watching her this afternoon, I would like you all to return here. It is the safest place you will find in this town." He gave a sardonic chuckle. "It is also the only place you will find to stay. Since word spread of the woman's healing, families have been flocking here from all over with their sick children. She emerges from her cursed tomb of a tree and heals at the third hour every day, but for one hour only. Then she returns and everyone waits until the next afternoon."

The way he ordered the royal party around made Isa smile. Few men or women were bold enough to tell the king and queen what to do. But Isa liked it. This man truly cared for their welfare and for the welfare of his little village. She would like to know him better if she ever got the time.

They spent the remainder of the morning and the early after-noon in the priest's cramped quarters. Isa found his stories and knowledge fascinating, and she discovered that he had been born in a part of Soudain not far from where her parents lived. Soon, however, the priest reluctantly told them that if they wished to get close enough to the woman to see her, they would need to leave and find a place in the crowd, despite it being only the first hour of the afternoon.

As they donned their hoods to leave, Isa was reminded of a comment Henri had made once about going to the church in his little village.

"Father." She turned back to the little man. "When we came to these woods and found the children in the Fae land, there were two without a home to return to. The boy, Henri, is nine years of age, and he once lived nearby, in the forest, I believe. He has mentioned several times that he used to come to the church and talk with the priest." She was suddenly praying that this man might be able to shed light on Henri and Genny's shadowy past. "He has a little sister named Genevieve."

A sad smile came to the priest's face. "Ah, yes. Young Henri and Genny."

Ever gave her a look of impatience as he ducked out the door, but Isa tarried just a moment longer. She needed to hear what this man had to say about her peculiar little charges.

"Henri is a special boy. He sees things differently from other children. He also has unusual... talents." The priest frowned slightly before giving her a more reassuring smile. "But I never found a child so desperate to belong. I am glad to know they have found a safe place where they can finally rest."

"Take these." Isa pressed two gold coins into his hand. "Buy glass panes for the church. No one should have to pray in the cold." She gripped his hand briefly, squeezing the coins so the man couldn't return them. Then, as she followed her husband and their men, she tried to steel herself for whatever revelations lay ahead.

As they found the crowd and moved toward the center, the guards began to separate, each one taking a particular position in the crowd where they would all have a different vantage point to watch and listen.

While Isa now partook in most of Ever's defense schemes and even made some of her own, military strategy was one area that held little appeal for her. So she simply allowed her husband to do as he wished, and she did as she was told. For this plan, she was to stand near Ever with her hood drawn, an arrow nocked and held low where the people pressing in around them wouldn't see it. Ever and the guards had more close-range weapons at hand, swords and knives ready and waiting. Isa prayed they wouldn't have to use them in a crowd so dense and so full of sick children. Families were already beginning to shove to the front.

Just as Isa was about to whisper to Ever that the number of people present had far surpassed her expectations, the crowd roared. Isa was tall, but even she had to stand on her toes and crane her neck to see what the cheers were about. She could only just make out a large tree near the edge of the clearing that was beginning to shimmer. Isa was reminded of her time in the strange world of the Fae and the way the surroundings constantly changed. And though she had somewhat expected it, Isa was still somewhat surprised when the woman that she had known as Sacha stepped forward and smiled sweetly at the people, holding out her arms and dropping a little curtsy.

"That's her," Isa whispered to Ever. "Sacha is the one who helped us escape."

Only now she wasn't wearing the simple purple gown that she'd worn in the Fae world. This dress was made of rich yellow tones and had much fuller skirts. Her ears, neck, wrists, and fingers dripped with jewels. She had also chopped off most of her hair so that it only reached the edge of her jaw. With her hair down and near her eyes, the woman suddenly looked very much like Genny. One glance at Ever and Isa knew he was thinking the same thing.

"Dear ones," Sacha clasped her hands in front of her and bowed her head once more, "I am honored to see that so many have come today. Since you are great in number and I can only heal for one hour, I will try to see each one of your loved ones as quickly as possible. Now." She held out her hand to a small girl in the front, one Isa immediately recognized as one of the children from Soudain. The one with the missing voice.

Green mist began to envelop the woman's hands. Gently, she tilted the girl's head back with one hand, and with the other she grasped at the girl's neck. The green continued to swirl until the woman let go of the girl's head.

"Now sing for them," she commanded. The little girl looked back at her parents, who nodded cautiously. Then she turned to the crowd and opened her mouth. Immediately, a lovely little melody danced on the air, inviting hushed tones of awe from the people and a feeling of icy dread from Isa.

"My lady!" a familiar voice called out. Isa quickly spotted the skinny, red-haired woman from Soudain, the one who had rebuked Ever in front of the tent. "Why is it," Agnes asked in her shrill voice, "that you can heal our children while the king cannot?"

"Ah yes," Sacha said, nodding her head. "I am asked that question often. But the time had not yet come to answer... until now."

Suddenly, Isa felt a fierce hatred emanating from Sacha. Before, she had been secretive and hidden, pushing Isa's abilities to their limits to read some sort of emotion in her. But now Sacha hid nothing in either her heart or her eyes.

"It was not time because my little brother was not present to hear what I have to say. But now he is here, so I can tell all of you." Sacha turned and looked directly at Ever. "Isn't that right, little brother?"

CHAPTER 19

REMINDERS

Henri skidded to a stop when he saw the Fortress steward leaning intently over a book, a new candle upon his writing desk. Perhaps this was not the morning to visit the Fortress library after all. Despite his inability to read, Henri loved the books with their beautiful leather spines and their spidery words on each page. Miss Isa had told him that she'd added the room herself after she'd married, for she thought all Fortress inhabitants should have access to books. But looking at books was not worth another run-in with the steward.

Before Henri could fully retreat, however, Garin called his name. Henri looked up at the distant ceiling, just as he had often seen Miss Isa do. "I thought you liked me!" he whispered to the Fortress.

"Henri."

"Coming."

Slowly, Henri trudged back to the steward, staring at the ground as he waited to hear what new rule he had broken. Once he was standing before the steward, however, Garin was simply quiet. In fact, he was quiet for so long that Henri's curiosity finally got the best of him, and he sneaked a peek up at the older man.

The steward did not look young nor did he look old. Rather, his age seemed to change depending on whatever he was doing at that moment. There were deep lines at the corners of his eyes, and strands of silver glinted against the long, straight black hair that was tied neatly behind the man's neck with a leather thong. Henri had rarely seen the steward's thin face in anything but a scowl, particularly when the topic of conversation had to do with him and his sister. But today he was surprised to find only a thoughtful look on Garin's face as Garin tilted his head and rested his chin on his thumb and index fingers.

"You seem to have quite an attachment to these books." He glanced up at the three stories of shelves that vaulted up around them. "This is your third visit this week. Had you ever seen a book before coming to the Fortress?"

Henri swallowed hard before answering. "Yes, Master Garin."

"Where?"

Henri hesitated. Few people had ever known about his excursions to see the holy man in the Sansim, and he had tried hard to keep it that way. His father wouldn't have approved. "I would visit with our priest," he finally said, keeping his voice as low as he could make it. Perhaps Garin would become tired of hearing his quiet words and let him go.

But instead, the steward only leaned forward. "And what would you do while you were there?"

Henri shrugged. "Sometimes I swept the church floor. Sometimes he showed me the Holy Writ." Would the steward be angry that he had seen something so sacred? Would Father Lucien be punished?

"Why did you go to the church? Was it the one your parents attended?"

"My father and Helaine did not attend the church."

"Then how did you come to find it?"

Henri balked. This was a part of the story he did not wish the steward to know. Who knew if he would bring it up later to Miss Isa or King Ever? And yet, when the steward raised his eyebrows, Henri knew he had no choice. "There wasn't much food in the house. Genny kept crying because she was hungry, so I..." He paused, studying his foot. "I might have borrowed an apple from Father Lucien's storehouse."

"An apple?"

"And maybe some bread and cheese." Henri looked up at Garin, wishing desperately that the questions would end soon. "I meant to pay it back! But—"

But Garin held out his hands. "No need to go into all of that. I understand."

He did? Henri studied the steward's face again, searching for a sign of anger or disappointment. But to his surprise, there was none, only a slight frown. And for once, it wasn't directed at him, but rather, the floor.

"Surely your mother—"

"She was *not* my mother," Henri snapped. "My father only married Helaine because he didn't know what to do with Genny." He crossed his arms, suddenly not caring whether or not he was being impertinent. "Not that she ever took care of her."

"What do you remember of your real mother?" The steward's voice was surprisingly gentle.

Henri paused. What did he remember? "Not much," he finally admitted after a moment of thought. "She didn't hate my trick the way Helaine always did. Father said she was killed in a hunting accident nearby." He shrugged. "That's all I remember."

It was a long time before either of them spoke. Garin's eyes were distant, focused on someplace behind Henri, though Henri didn't know what. The silence was so long, in fact, that Henri began itching to move. He hated standing too still. It was tempting to roll a bit of flame across his fingers, but he didn't dare do so in front of the steward.

Just when standing still was becoming nearly impossible, Garin's eyes softened as they refocused on the boy. "You remind me very much of a small boy I knew once." He placed a hand on Henri's shoulder, then knelt to look Henri in the eye. "I fear I must ask your forgiveness in misjudging you and your sister. I believe... I can only guess that you know little of the Fae?"

Henri shook his head, and Garin nodded.

"Let it suffice to say that our mutual relatives are not a people you should ever wish to meet. It is not your fault that their blood flows in your veins any more than it is my fault that I suffer the same fate. But the day will come, I fear, when you will be made to choose one side over the other."

"How do you know that?" Henri didn't like that idea in the slightest. How could he be forced to choose between things he didn't understand?

"I don't. It is only a feeling I have. But if one day you are told to choose either the side of King Everard and Queen Isabelle or the side of the Fae, remember the goodness the Maker has shown you in bringing you and Genny here. And if you understand nothing else, know that a strength lies in your blood that is of the Fortress, and thus, of the Maker. You may be young, Henri, but that strength is not dormant. It was given to you for a purpose."

With that, the steward began to stand and gather his belongings from the desk.

"Wait," Henri said. A question inside had been nagging him for weeks. He might as well ask it now while the steward was, for once, not angry with him. "When the king and Miss—Queen Isa return, what do you think they will do with us?" As soon as the question had left his lips, he immediately regretted asking. He didn't know if he could really handle a dismissal now, not when they'd come so far.

Surprisingly, however, a small smile lifted the steward's thin lips. "I do not know for sure, but the king and queen have very pressing matters to attend to currently, and will, it seems, for some time. I wouldn't go worrying about your place anytime soon. Now," he turned and began to walk toward the door, "would you and your sister like something to eat? I believe I smell blueberry tarts."

Never one to turn down food, Henri trailed after Garin, and for the first time, he didn't feel afraid.

CHAPTER 20

AT WHAT COST

Years of practice kept Ever's face as unflinching as always on the outside. But inside, he felt as though he had just shattered into a million pieces. Though he had known deep in his heart that his father must have been unfaithful, Henri and Genny's ignorance about their own past had allowed him to at least pretend another explanation existed. But now, in front of hundreds of his subjects and even his own wife and guards, this woman was proof that Rodrigue had broken his word to the Fortress, to Queen Louise, and to his people. To his son.

Though Ever had always favored his father in appearance, looking at Sacha was too much like looking in a mirror. Her gray eyes, the shape of her neck, and the strong shoulders, though most definitely feminine, were all too familiar.

"So the tear between worlds," Isa called out, her voice much stronger than Ever's would have been at that moment, "was only a ruse."

"A test," the woman said, looking at Isa as though her presence was just a minor annoyance. "I was testing my brother to see if the great Fortress our father always spoke about was really with him. But when he failed to find the tear and you did instead,

I realized that I had been right all along." She turned and raised her voice to the people, addressing them now instead of Isa or Ever. "Perhaps the Fortress has tired of these men that forever go on playing their games of war and self-righteousness!" Her low voice rang clear in the perfect silence of the crowd as everyone looked back and forth between their king and his sister. "And," she fixed her eyes back on Ever, "when you failed, Brother, I knew that it was the Maker declaring a new era. It's my turn now."

"You blaspheme the king!"

In one smooth motion, Degare had thrown back his cloak and drawn his sword. People stumbled over one another as they pushed out to give him space, trying to get away from the weapon.

"Degare," Ever called softly. Degare was one of his favorite guards and loyal to a fault. His temper, however, matched the color of his flaming beard, and if Ever wasn't careful, the man would take on the entire crowd to honor Ever's name.

Before Degare could take the hint, however, two dozen other members of the crowd raised their own hidden weapons, long skinny pikes with a bundle of thick green leaves tied together and hanging just behind the sharp pike heads. Hemlock, Ever realized, to poison the victim after breaking the flesh. By plunging the pike even deeper into the wound, the hemlock leaves would be dragged into the body behind the sharp head. They were crude weapons, but their damage could certainly be deadly. Ever guessed that there were more enemies hanging in mist form nearby.

Despite his men's skill in battle, Ever knew that there were far too many Fae for any sort of fair fight. Besides, the citizens that surrounded them would surely get in the way and be killed themselves.

"Admit it, Everard," the woman called out to him. "Four years ago, you brought a curse upon your great Fortress, and now, it seems, you have brought a blight upon these people as well. You are too much like our father."

"You think I did this?"

"I've been watching you, and the evidence is too great to ignore. Look around at the proof. Could you heal the Fortress four years ago? Answer me honestly."

"The Maker had to heal the Fortress. That was the point," Ever said, "to prove that I was not able to do so on my own..." Ever's words trailed off as he realized that he was digging himself into an even deeper hole. Arguing was not kingly, and by the sudden look of horror on Isa's face, Ever knew that true or not, his words had just spelled out his judgment in the eyes of the people.

"And if the Fortress is so intent on keeping your line upon the throne, why is it that your wife," she gestured to Isa, "has not yet conceived a child?"

Ever's mouth was suddenly bitter. Who was this woman to think she could insult his wife? To his surprise, however, even his anger was eclipsed by that which he felt coming from Isa. So great was her anger, it seemed, that he could feel her power for once instead of the other way around. And yet, Isa was not simply angry. He could feel her familiar power working on the woman's heart, trying hard to impress the truth of the Fortress's love upon her. But some hearts were stiffer and more hidden than others, and for all of Isa's glares and hard work, Ever's sister only smiled.

Whispers broke out around the crowd. But as the three continued to stare one another down, the whispers began to lose their whisper quality, and even without Isa's gift, Ever could feel the frustration rise within the air.

This had been a terrible plan.

Just as the first Fae soldier began to step forward, shimmering slightly as he went, and Ever drew his own sword in response, a blur of gray robes darted between them.

"Please!" Father Lucien held up his hands, gasping between words. "I know you are all confused, but please do not turn our home into a village of blood!" He turned in agitation from side to side in short, jerky movements. "Certainly there must be a more legal, civilized way to go about deciding this!"

To Ever's surprise, his sister spoke up, her voice suddenly gentle. "You are right, Lucien. There must be another way to bring these people what is rightfully theirs without fighting around their children." She turned to the Fae, her golden hair bouncing as she began to step backward in the direction of the tree from which she had first appeared. "We are done here today. I will heal again tomorrow."

The people began to groan, but she held her hands up. "There are children here. Do you wish violence upon them?"

Before Ever had time to hear their responses, the priest lurched at Isa and grabbed her hand, before fairly dragging her back toward the town with him. Immediately, Isa disappeared. She wouldn't be able to hold her invisibility for long, though. It was a skill she still struggled with. Ever used his power to project his own invisibility onto the holy man, something he had only tried once or twice before. The invisibility wasn't perfect, but it did the job of mostly hiding the priest as they raced toward the church.

As they rounded the back of the church building, Ever could hear footsteps in the distance behind them. Despite his sister's words of peace, the people hadn't listened, it seemed. They wouldn't have long to hide. Without a word, Father Lucien, Isa, Ever, and their men darted into the priest's hovel. There was no light inside this time, not even a fire. They did their best to crouch in the corners, but Ever knew it wouldn't do them much good if the door was broken in.

"We will have to fight," Olivier, their knife master, murmured.

"No." Isa's voice was quiet but commanding. "There are too many children."

"If we die," Degare pointed out, "then all of the children of Destin will be at risk from that witch!"

Ever felt a soft hand work its way into his. "I can do this, Ever." Her voice was quiet but resolved.

"It's too dangerous." He knew he wasn't fooling anyone, though. Even Ever knew this was a losing battle. Too many innocents would die if fighting ensued.

"This is my gift," she said in the same soothing voice. "Trust the Fortress. Pray for me, and let me talk to them."

Ever squeezed her hand so hard that it must have hurt. But she was using her gift on him even now, and as much as he abhorred it, Isa was right, as usual. She was their only chance of escaping without the shedding of blood.

"This will draw more strength from you than you have ever expended," he said in a voice that shook far too much. "You've been pushing yourself too hard."

He was interrupted by more shouts outside the door, but Isa simply squeezed his hand again, and in the dark, leaned forward to kiss him on the cheek.

"I love you."

With that, her hand was pulled from his, and he could hear her rise and walk to the door. Immediately, he made himself invisible and went to stand just beside her. She might be their only hope for peace, but he was not about to allow his wife to face the crowd alone.

Isa opened the door, the light of the fading sun touching her hair and making its copper strands shine almost blindingly. The crowd that stood just outside the door was mostly void of children, but there were still enough present to make a fight difficult.

Fortress, he prayed as he lifted his weapon, *give her strength.*

"Where is the king?" someone called out. Ever suddenly felt like a louse for hiding beside her. He nearly revealed himself, except for the slight flick of Isa's hand that reminded him to leave her be.

"Does it matter?" she asked evenly, her dark blue eyes searching each of the faces before her. "For you have seemed to forget that the throne was rightfully mine before it was King Everard's."

"And a fine job you've done then, as well," another man sneered, his bushy black hair streaked with mud and oil. Ever itched to teach the man a lesson for speaking so rudely to his wife, but another slight wave of Isa's hand kept him at bay.

"I understand your frustration," she said quietly, and the calm of her voice seemed to quiet the crowd somewhat. "You are worried for your little girl. Cyrille, was it? I remember her." Isa smiled in that gentle way of hers. "She has pretty green eyes." How did she recall these details? Ever could hardly remember what he had eaten for supper the night before.

"Yes," the man said in a more subdued tone, his eyes moving to his boots. "That's 'er."

Ever could feel Isa beginning to work the crowd. She had never tried to influence so many people at once. Even now, he could see the tiny bead of sweat that was forming on her temple. How much longer could she last?

Please, Fortress! he begged. *Just a bit more!*

"I can see in your face that you love your daughter, that you would do anything for her," Isa continued.

"That's what I'm doin' now!"

"Then would you want her to see you tear a person limb from limb, as you have been contemplating doing to me?"

The man froze, his eyes wide and full of terror.

But Isa didn't stop. "Would you be proud to tell her what kind of deed you had committed?"

For all of the mob's jeering and shouting just a few minutes before, the crowd had grown nearly silent and still in the quickly falling light of dusk. All the while, Isa maintained her calm and steady gaze. Only Ever could see her wrist as it trembled with the effort she must be expending. She couldn't have much strength left.

"No." The man finally swallowed and bowed his head.

Without another word, he turned and began to walk away. Slowly, one by one, the rest of the crowd followed his example. Men and women dropped sticks, axes, and whatever makeshift weapons they had managed to grab on their way to the church. Finally, the last woman left, and Isa turned to them, a slight smile on her face.

"We will be safe tonight. But Ever?"

"Yes?"

"Catch me."

CHAPTER 21

SHORT WORDS AND DIRE PLANS

Though she never lost consciousness completely, Ever could feel Isa's utter exhaustion when her knees buckled and he caught her in his arms. He wanted nothing more than to let her sleep the night away in the church. Father Lucien advised leaving Sansim as quickly as possible, however, so Ever was forced to place her before him in his saddle so she wouldn't fall off her own horse. It would put a strain on his mount, but they would be at the Cobrien border by the next day. Surely she would be stronger by then.

The group was quiet that evening and then the next day as they rode. Ever was grateful for their silence. They had been by his side long enough to know his ways and when he did and did not wish to speak. Still, he could feel their curiosity and pity in the sidelong looks they cast him. But he didn't want pity. He wanted a solution.

"We're approaching a stream up ahead, sire," Leroy called from the group's point. "Do you wish to stop there and rest the horses?"

"That sounds wise. Is there shade?"

"Yes, sire. A grove of trees lies a little way to the north. We'll be mostly hidden."

They turned their horses off the rough road, and within minutes, Ever spotted the trees peeking up from a ravine. It would be the perfect place to examine Isa again, shielded from the heat of the late morning sun.

As they rode, Ever scolded himself once more for his negligence. Isa had not only worked tirelessly alongside him for the last month as they'd visited the sick children in Soudain, and searched every scroll and book in the Tower of Annals, but she had also continued to manage many of the Fortress's comings and goings that had nothing to do with their current problems. And as if she hadn't been busy enough, she'd spent every spare second with Henri and Genny. Last night had been the breaking point. Never had she tried to work so many minds at once, and now she was paying for it.

Ever wanted to kick himself.

When they had all moved down into the little ravine, Ever gently handed his wife down to Degare before jumping off the horse himself. Then, taking her back, he carried her to the edge of the stream and knelt so that he could fill his waterskin while holding her in his lap. As he poured a little stream of water into her mouth, Isa's eyes opened, and a deep sigh of relief escaped him. She hadn't looked so awake in hours.

"Why hello there." He put the waterskin down and propped her up a little higher, drinking in the alertness of her beautiful blue eyes like a man dying of thirst. "How are you feeling?"

"Better." She squinted and blinked a few times before pushing herself into a sitting position. Ever let her but kept his arm behind her back in case she collapsed again. "How long was I asleep? Where are we?"

"I don't know if you remember, but we left Sansim last night. You've been sleeping on and off since. We'll reach your brother at the border in just a few hours."

"Launce? Oh, right." She rubbed her eyes. "Why are we seeing him again?"

Ever spoke slowly, hoping his words wouldn't startle her into a true fainting spell. "I need to plan with him for the possibility that we'll need to relocate our troops. I sent a message the night that we left. I supposed you wouldn't mind?" Actually, he had worried very much that she would mind, particularly after her initial reaction to Launce's last little "revelation" at the party.

But Isa only gave him a tired smile. "I will be glad to see him." She looked around. "Do we have anything to eat?"

Ever leaned her against the bank then leapt up to dig a hunk of dried beef, bread, and a few pieces of fruit out of his pack. It was good to see her eat. She did so almost ravenously, as though she'd skipped two days of food rather than only two meals. Perhaps her strength would return sooner than he'd first thought.

"Can you walk?" he asked.

She smiled and nodded, and he helped her to her feet, keeping her hand tucked into his as they walked a bit away from the men. After riding through the night, their men deserved some sleep.

"Leroy, keep watch for a few minutes," Ever called over his shoulder. "I will take it when I'm done."

"You need sleep too," Isa said softly, but Ever only shook his head. Even if he had the time for it, his mind wouldn't allow him to rest now.

When they had walked around a little bend in the stream and were hidden from the sight of their men, Ever eased Isa down onto a large flat rock then sat beside her. "Isa," he started, "I must ask forgiveness for my poor judgment last night. I wasn't thinking clearly. If you hadn't been there to stop them..." Ever shuddered.

"You might be a gifted king," Isa said quietly, leaning her head on his shoulder, "but you are still human. Learning a secret of that magnitude would have shocked anyone."

"I have to wonder, though," Ever said slowly, staring into the stream as it bubbled up continuously around a boulder, "if perhaps she is right. I *was* the one who cursed the—"

"Everard!" Isa's voice and eyes were suddenly fierce as she grabbed his face with both hands and turned to face him. "You know that her words were lies, and I never want to hear you utter such blatant nonsense again! Do you understand me? Your father's infidelity says nothing about you, nor does it make you an unfit king." She loosened her grip, and her face relaxed slightly, but she didn't let go. "The Fortress loves you, and it has proven that time and again. I do not know why the Fortress has not allowed you to chase this evil from Destin's borders. But somehow we will. Together." The blue fire in her eyes blazed wildly, and the thin set of her lips told Ever that his wife was deadly serious. And as she held him there, he could feel her using her gift on him with all she had. All he could do was nod.

Before she began to tremble too hard with the effort, Ever gently removed her hands from his face and held them in his lap. "I believe you," he promised her. "No need to collapse on me again. Your brother might have my head if he finds you in such a state."

For an immeasurable time, they sat there together staring at the brook and its shallow sandy shores as she leaned heavily against his shoulder. For how long they sat, Ever didn't really know. "Leroy," he finally called out. "I'll take watch. You get some rest."

But there was no response. A nasty feeling settled in Ever's gut. Isa stared up at him, concern etched on her face. After another second of brittle silence, Ever grabbed Isa and pushed her back against the ravine then wedged himself beside her. When they were both flat against the bank, he prepared to peer out from behind the bend. Before he could, however, a change in the water caught his eye. Where the stream had run crystal clear moments before, a thick red now flowed down.

Glancing back at his wife, Ever swallowed hard. Usually he

could count on Isa's sword just as well as he might Acelet's. Isa had spent many long hours training to ensure that. But the ghost-like color of her face worried him. She couldn't fight today. "Stay here," he mouthed at her, praying that for once, she would listen.

Finally, he leaned around the corner. Leroy was lying half in the water and half out, a long pike sticking out of his gut. To Ever's shock and relief, however, the other men were still only sleeping. It was as if there had been no fight, not even a scuffle. The only sign that Leroy had even tried to fight back was that he had drawn his weapon. Unfortunately, it looked as though he'd never had the chance to even use it.

A movement caught Ever's eye. Though the young man looked to be asleep, Eloy was gripping his sword so hard that his brown knuckles were turning white. But where was the enemy?

A cloud of something humid and warm flashed across Ever's face and yanked him forward. Ever found himself on the ground beside Eloy, his head dangling out over the stream and his sword hand pinned to the ground. In the blink of an eye, the mist had shifted from its cloud form into a man. And that man was trying very hard to push his head under the water.

With his other hand, Ever grabbed the Fae by the neck. With a yank, he had it off his chest and on the ground. Just as his sword should have bitten the creature's flesh, however, it was gone, the green mist rising instead. The mist darted up near his face, then brushed behind him. Ever tried to flip but was too late, and his sword was too slow to block the man's shove to his back. He fell forward, clipping the side of his face on a boulder.

Eloy leapt up with a cry, only to be knocked back down by another quick appearance of their attacker. Not wanting the boy to get himself killed, Ever tried to stand. But as he did, his vision doubled. Sensing a presence to his right, he rolled over to face his attacker head on, but it was impossible to tell which was the true opponent, for there were suddenly two identical Fae that raised pikes above him. Just as the pikes began to make their way down, a flash of silver knocked the pike out of the attacker's hands. As the world came back into focus, Ever realized that the only reason he hadn't been run through was the head of copper hair that had distracted his opponent.

Whether fueled by the Fortress or his anger, Ever didn't know, but immediately his vision was restored, and he leapt up in a rage, blue flame building dangerously in each of his fists. Just as the thin man raised his pike against Isa, he turned back to see Ever, and his slitted eyes went blank. Isa didn't hesitate, knocking the pike away, thin blue flame exploding from her hands. Then Ever's sword was in his heart.

Where their enemy should have slumped onto the sandy bank of the stream, however, he only dissolved into a heap of ash.

"Their lips!" Isa cried, drawing his attention back to his men. They rushed to the three guards lying limply on the ground. Eloy was able to sit, but his face looked unwell, too. Isa's eyes widened as she took in Leroy, but Ever was proud of her as she gritted her teeth and focused back on the men that still breathed.

"Hemlock poisoning," Ever said as he lifted Degare's head. "They've not been stabbed, but it's been rubbed all over them. Hold him in your lap for me. I will have to heal him, but it will hurt, and he'll thrash."

Isa nodded stiffly, and Ever was grateful that she didn't give voice to the fears that swirled inside of him. Would he be able to heal them? So many times, he'd failed... No. He couldn't afford to think that way now.

Please, he prayed to the Fortress, *let me help them!* The skin was already beginning to bubble around the man's mouth. If Ever didn't act soon, his throat might swell shut and the man would surely die. With Ever's heart in his stomach, he gently took hold of Degare's pale face, resting his fingers above the mouth and below the chin. After taking a deep breath, Ever exhaled. And then they waited.

The seconds turned to years, it seemed, before the man began to thrash just as Ever had predicted. But Isa held on tight, and to Ever's joy, Degare's eyes opened, and his flaming red skin began to recede.

"To Olivier!" Ever told her. By the time the noontime sun was directly overhead, all of their men had been healed.

All except for Leroy. It pained Ever that they could only do a short battlefield service in honor of his friend. Leroy had saved his life on more than one occasion in battle, and in the few times he'd been willing to share his opinion it had always been worth its weight in gold. Their small party watched solemnly as his friend's ashes were gathered and placed in a small bottle for the man's poor wife. *Let him know,* Ever asked the Maker, *that he shall be missed, and that I look forward to seeing him again when my night comes.*

"Why would only one Fae follow us?" Jori Blanc, the group's navigator, asked when they were back on their horses and a respectful distance from the ceremonial pyre. "Any why not kill us all?"

"It was a warning," Ever said as he glared at the road ahead of him. "She means to let us know that we are being watched."

"She can watch all she wants."

The ferocity in Isa's voice took Ever by surprise and he turned to look at her. With her copper hair swept back into a tight braid and her leather riding trousers sticking out from beneath her slitted skirt, his wife was a fierce sight to behold. But even more intimidating than her combat attire, or even the sword and bow she wore, were her eyes. Isa's eyes flamed in agitation as they fixed themselves upon Jori with dangerous care, like a panther ready to strike.

"Because if it is Destin that she desires, then she will have to pry it from my stiff, lifeless hands."

CHAPTER 22

TAKING CARE

"What is she doing here?" Ever growled.

"They aren't aware of the gravity of the situation," Isa murmured, ever the peacemaker. Despite her gentle words, however, her stress was evident in the taut muscles of her face.

Ever grunted in response as they approached the border. White canvas tents were stretched out along the river that ran between the two kingdoms. Servants walked between them carrying food and other supplies.

"Does he think we're here for a festival?" Ever muttered, to which Isa shot him a frown. "It looks like a bloody carnival." The message he'd sent Launce had been short. *Meet me at the northern border near the crooked river. Bring men.* He hadn't expected Cobren's new prince to bring half of the royal court. Or his pregnant wife, for that matter. "Stay with her," Ever said to Isa. Guilt gnawed at him. "Keep within sight of my tent. I hate asking you to protect her, but—"

"Ever," she said gently, a tired smile on her pretty face, "I didn't spend all those hours on the practice floor getting bruised up for nothing."

Ever nodded, but it didn't make him feel any better. The Fae had killed one of his men and nearly him as well. Only between the two of them had the monster died. And yet, he didn't want Olivia to hear what he was about to tell her husband. A pregnant woman didn't need that kind of stress, and Isa was the best protection he could think to offer her. But that didn't mean he had to like it.

"Everard." Launce strode forward to greet him as they crossed the river over a thin stone bridge. Before they could grasp hands, however, Isa ran up and threw her arms around her brother. As he tried to hug her in return, she pulled back and gave him her fiercest glare and then punched him in the arm. Ever smothered a smile. Her punches hurt. He had seen to that.

"*That* is for not telling me you were expecting," Isa said. "Now where can I find her?"

"She's in that tent," Launce said, rubbing his arm. With an indignant flip of her hair, Isa turned and marched off.

"You really shouldn't have your wife here at all," Ever said as Launce turned back to him, still massaging his arm.

"She felt badly about making Isa uncomfortable last time we met. She wanted to apologize and make things right."

"Is there a place we can talk?"

"Yes. Behind me." Launce turned and led Ever into the smallest tent. "Out," he ordered the men that were gathered to talk inside.

As he watched the young man take control of the room, Ever had to admit that he had indeed grown since taking his place as prince of Cobren. When Ever had first met Launce, he'd been a skinny, angry young man with a hatred for much of the world. He'd hated Everard in particular. But his most redeeming quality had been his care for his sister. Before Ever had loved her, Launce had been there watching over Isa to the best of his limited abilities.

"I will put this as simply as I can," Ever said when the room was clear. "Before I was born, and then again after, my father opened an ancient barrier and had an affair with a woman of the Fae people."

"The Fae?" Launce's mouth fell open, but Ever held up his hand.

"Let me finish. There are two children back at the Fortress that Isa found among the missing that were lured into the Fae realm. They are, it would seem, my younger brother and sister, part Fae and part Fortier. My older sister, however..." Ever took a deep breath. No matter how many times he remembered the events from the day before, they still seemed surreal.

"My older sister has decided that it is her duty to claim the crown for herself using her own personal army of Fae to do so. On our way to meet with you, we were attacked by a Fae who killed one of my most trusted personal guards. That is why this is no place for your expecting wife."

Launce stared at him for a long moment before finally giving his head the slightest shake. "I... I'll send her home immediately." Then his eyes grew large, and he ran to the tent's opening and began to look around wildly. "Where is she?" he asked as if Ever had been keeping track.

Perhaps the young man had not grown up quite as much as Ever had first thought.

"Isa is with her," Ever said, wishing very much instead to let Launce wallow in his fear for a moment. It would be a good lesson to him, but Isa wouldn't approve of such a sentiment. "The reason I called you here was to make a plan."

"Did you know someone was after your throne?"

"Not for sure," Ever shook his head, "until she revealed it to me yesterday. But I had a hunch that someone was planning an invasion. The veil between the two worlds could never have torn by itself. When Isa discovered the Fae realm where the children were being taken, and my younger sister and brother showed up, I knew something was wrong." He paused and looked at one of the maps spread out on the table. It depicted the Fortress's mountain as well as the desert mountains and valleys directly to its north and the thick forests to its south.

"What do you want from me, Everard? Ask and it will be done."

"I do not yet know how to defeat the Fae."

Launce's eyes widened, but he said nothing.

"I will talk to Garin when we return. Hopefully he knows something."

"But why would Garin—?"

"A long story for another day. But if we are attacked before I can correctly train my men, I will need a place for the army to go until I've learned to fight the Fae properly. And when I do, I will call my men back with this." Ever took off his signet ring and placed it on the table. Launce picked it up and examined it.

"I may be the prince of Cobren now," Launce said in a soft voice, "but this wolf will always be in my heart." He handed the ring back to Ever. As Ever slipped it back onto his finger, the jewel-eyed wolf stared back at him with the same piercing look Rodrigue had given him often in his boyhood. At least the wolf had always been faithful.

"What I need is a place for my men to camp on your side of the border, just at the foot of the mountain. At a fast pace, it would take them only a day to make it up the back side of the mountain and to the Fortress."

"And what of the people?" Launce gave him a wary look, and Ever knew he was thinking of his parents and sister.

"Sacha is using the people to gain her the throne, manipulating them through a magic I do not understand nor am I familiar with. They are her path to the crown. She won't jeopardize their trust, for it is their good graces she is relying on." Ever shook his head. "They would be in more danger if I sent my men to find her. The war would be fought in the streets." He fingered the hilt of his sword idly. "I'll have to draw her out like poison."

"Consider it done," Launce said, still frowning down at the map. "I'll wait for them here with a number of our men as well. I assume you'll send a bird?"

"I will send whatever messenger is at hand," Ever said, his mouth suddenly feeling dry as he considered such a dire situation. "For if we are that far gone, I will consider it a blessing to find a drunkard in need of coin."

The two men stood there quietly. Would it really come to such things? Ever wondered. As if reading his thoughts, Launce gave him a weak smile and clapped him on the shoulder. "Let us pray we never find such a day, and that you will defeat her quickly." He glanced outside. "I assume you will be leaving soon?"

"We'll head out in the morning. Isa has been pushing her powers further than she should. She needs a good night's rest before we set out again."

"Let her go back with Olivia!"

The sudden fervor in Launce's voice took Ever by surprise.

"She can protect Olivia," Launce continued, "and they will both be safer with Olivia's father. Besides, if something should happen to me, someone should be there when..." his voice trailed off, and Ever's heart went out to the young man. He was willing to sacrifice his life for Ever's cause. Ever briefly imagined Isa bringing a child into the world without him, and it twisted his heart.

"As you said," Ever sighed, "we shall pray that nothing comes to fruition. Besides," his voice softened, "I need her. She has been gifted by the Maker in ways I will never even hope to understand."

"Surely you could spare her somehow."

"You know as well as I do that she would never go, even if I tried to force her."

Launce studied him for a moment. "Much has changed in the last three years." Then he looked down at his own golden ring, the one his father-in-law had given him on his wedding day, the promise of Cobren's crown. "Though I still don't agree with everything you do," Launce threw Ever a wry grin, "I must admit that I now better understand your decisions far more than I once did. And I thank you for being patient and trying to teach me. Just..." Launce hesitated, "you know I trust you, but as a younger brother..." He cast a look of longing outside again before looking Ever in the eye. "Please take care of my sister."

"Oh... Oh dear!" Olivia's face went so white that Isa nearly ran to fetch Ever, but Olivia just shook her head and lowered herself onto a large boulder. "I'm fine. I just need a moment to think." She looked out over the water, rubbing her belly as she did. Isa felt a stab of guilt over having to tell her sister-in-law about their newfound danger in such a disorganized fashion. If she hadn't, though, Olivia would have continued to insist that they take a long walk by the river. Isa didn't want her to take a walk at all, but at least Olivia had stopped now just at the edge of the camp. Isa kept her hand on the hilt of her sword, but all seemed peaceful for the moment. If only it could stay that way.

"How are you both doing?" Isa forced a smile and nodded pointedly at Olivia's burgeoning belly.

"Huh?" Olivia looked up. "Oh, thank you. The sickness has abated, it seems, but now I can never get enough to eat." She looked down at her belly and grinned. "The little thing is always hungry, and if I don't eat enough, likes to kick me in the ribs. My nurse says this is good, though, since it means the child is strong." She sighed and placed her hands behind her, leaning back and closing her eyes as the sunlight washed over them. "But some-times, what I wouldn't give to be a tad less round." She laughed then, her warm brown eyes opening to meet Isa's. "There are days when I fear I will always be this large. And I still have a long way to go!"

"You look beautiful," Isa assured her. And truly, she was. Olivia's fine olive skin had always glowed as though she'd rubbed a sunbeam all over her skin. But now her eyes were alight with excitement whenever she talked of her baby, and though she had filled out quite a bit, it wasn't unbecoming. The loose yellow and orange wool dress that Olivia wore flowed over her soft curves, giving her the look of an ancient queen. Many of the old queens had once worn dresses like Olivia's, according to the paintings in the Tower of Annals. As much as Olivia might be tired of her new size, it made Isa happy, for it meant her niece or nephew would be healthy and strong.

"Isa."

Isa squirmed under Olivia's gaze. She'd thought she'd been concealing her feelings decently, but the concern in Olivia's warm eyes told her otherwise. "Are you well?"

"To be honest..." Isa hesitated. It was not considered queenly to share one's entire burden, for the weights of the monarchs were theirs alone to bear. Or so her etiquette instructor had told her. But Olivia was also a royal. And more importantly, she was Isa's sister now. "I know Ever is only being practical. He always is." Isa stared into the river as it flashed by, wishing she could toss her burdens into it and watch them be carried away. "We had an argument a few nights back about the children I told you about, Henri and Genny."

"Let me guess, you want to keep them."

"They're his blood!" Isa turned to face Olivia again. "Henri's already shown the Fortress's power. Who better to care for them than us? Besides," she pouted, "I want them."

"And you're sure they're his younger brother and sister?"

Isa shrugged. "They're not Ever's children. I know that for sure. But whenever I try to discuss their future with us, he's too worried about tainting the bloodline with Fae blood, particularly now that we've seen what his older sister has become."

"Does he say as much?"

"Some yes, and some no. But I can see it in his eyes. Our division is to the point where he has become wary every time I've spoken with him since we left the Fortress."

"Does she know about them?" Olivia shifted on the rock, frowning thoughtfully.

"I don't know. She saw them when they came to the Fae world with all of the other children. She even put me in their holding chamber. But she treated them no differently than the other children. Except..." She turned to Olivia, her heart suddenly racing. "All of the other children who were kidnapped were cursed with an injury or illness after they returned! I thought at first that Henri and Genny weren't cursed because they were orphans. But... she never even spoke with them! She *couldn't* have known they were orphans!" How had Isa not seen this?

"Isa," Olivia said in a grave voice, "I have no gifts as you do, nor am I familiar with the ways of your enemy, but it would seem to me that she knows exactly who those children are."

"I must tell Ever!" Isa took one stride forward, but Olivia managed to grab her wrist and pull her back.

"Before you go, I need you to hear two things," she said.

Isa stared down at Olivia's serious face, wondering what on earth she could mean.

"Rodrigue Fortier and my father were close enough that I have known Everard all of my life. I know he can be gruff and stubborn. Even as a young man, he was never good at having fun. His father didn't allow him to. But never in his life did he do anything out of spite. If he says he is concerned about taking these children in permanently, then he is genuinely worried. Your husband is a good man. Don't forget that."

Isa took a deep breath as she stared into her sister's sweet face, and a part of her couldn't help but soften. Olivia was right.

That didn't mean that she agreed with Ever by any stretch. But as Olivia had pointed out, his intentions were always honorable. Isa couldn't deny him that. He was simply afraid.

If only Isa understood what moved through the minds of men to make them think as they did.

"What was the second thing you wished to say?" Isa asked softly, to which Olivia gave an ornery grin.

"I only wished to say that if you are intent on dashing off to talk to your husband this instant, I would be much obliged if you could first put me to rights and on my feet. For if I try to get off this rock by myself, I will end up in the water."

Isa laughed as she bent to help her sister stand. For all Launce's faults, he had chosen a wonderful wife.

CHAPTER 23

THE WEIGHT OF SIN

A celet's not going to like this," Isa said as they neared the Fortress gates.

"Let me handle him." Ever clucked to his tired horse.

Isa's smile grew mischievous. "Oh, I plan to. I have two children to visit with. The monotonous business is yours today."

Ever laughed, but inwardly, he allowed himself a deep sigh of relief. His conversation with Launce had only served to reawaken his worries about Isa's health. Launce was right to be concerned. They were traveling far too much and she was getting far too little sleep. Their run-in with the village mob had only made things worse. And though Isa was far healthier and fit than his own mother had ever been, Ever suddenly recalled the way Queen Louise's face had been pale and drawn in the final days before her death. He couldn't allow the same thing to happen to Isa. Visiting the children wouldn't allow any sort of real rest, but at least it meant she wouldn't be gallivanting about the Fortress grounds on official business.

The rest of the afternoon passed in a blur. As soon as Ever had given his horse to a groom, he changed clothes and immediately called General Acelet to his study. Isa's prediction about Acelet proved true. The general was not pleased with Ever's emergency defense plan, to say the least. But Ever wasn't in the mood to argue, and in the end, he won simply because he was the king. He didn't find such victories satisfying, as he much preferred to be in agreement with his general. But Ever had a more pressing conversation on his mind, one he'd been dreading since meeting his sister back in the forest. For there was only one person in the world who could shed light on such a situation. And Ever had been avoiding him as much as possible since the arrival of their two little guests.

True to his nature, however, Garin didn't even need to be summoned. As soon as Acelet walked out of the king's study and closed the door, Ever could hear the two men's muted voices outside. He caught something about "beyond trusting" and "not enough time" from Acelet, but as he responded to Acelet's agitation, Garin's voice was indecipherable in its usual maddening calm. Finally the door opened, and Ever could see Acelet shaking his head and stomping away as Garin glided in.

"He seems less than enthusiastic about your plan." Garin placed a tray of tea and biscuits on Ever's desk. "I must say, I understand his frustration." His eyes darkened a shade. "While I don't think your foe is yet ready to take the Fortress, I doubt we'll have the time to properly train the men before she is."

Ever ignored the tea and instead stood and went out to the northern balcony. "So I take it you've heard then, that she is my sister?"

"I had guessed as much."

Ever turned and gave his steward an icy stare, but Garin just shrugged.

"Word has been spreading that the Fae woman is a Fortier. I didn't want to jump to conclusions without talking to you, but I had my suspicions."

"You mean you suspected it even before I met her."

Garin looked at the ground. When he spoke, his voice was soft. "Don't be mistaken in thinking that I enjoy being right, Ever. This was one prediction that I was loathe to make." He looked back up at Ever. "Five hundred years is a long time to study man and his tendencies." Garin went back to the tray and poured himself a cup. "Nevertheless, the people are beginning to believe her now as the word spreads throughout the kingdom. Enough for a number of factions to have started forming."

"Factions?"

"Many in the streets are calling for her coronation. It's not a majority by any means, but the number is far greater than any rebellion I've seen."

In five hundred years this was the greatest? Ever swallowed hard. "But she created the sicknesses! I'm sure of it! Even Isa..." Ever's voice trailed off as he remembered that they weren't only blaming him for the sickness, but also his inability to wipe it out. Suddenly he needed to sit. "What do I do, Garin?" he groaned as he fell into one of the deep red leather chairs.

"Do you really want my advice?" Garin's words were annoyingly patient.

"What choice do I have?"

"How much time do you believe we have before she makes her move for the Fortress?"

Ever shook his head helplessly and shrugged. "I don't know. A week at least? Maybe two?"

"Then this is my advice." Garin placed a firm hand on Ever's arm and leaned over so that Ever had to meet his eyes. "Your people need you now more than ever. The best way to convince them that she is not their savior is by showing them that you still care. Heal them." Ever tried to protest, but Garin only held his hand up, then continued. "Heal the everyday maladies and illnesses as you usually do. Hear their needs. Attend the Seasons Ball. The guests will be arriving in a week. Don't worry about the army, for I will work with them myself. And Ever?"

Ever glared up at him, his head spinning with all of the reasons not to follow Garin's advice.

"Take care of Isa."

This last piece of advice took Ever off guard. His shoulders slumped, and he knew he couldn't argue with such logic.

A long silence ensued, interrupted only by the crackling of the fire. The biscuits smelled intoxicating, as Ever hadn't eaten for hours, but he couldn't bring himself to bridge the gap and get them from his desk.

"I was Fae on the night you were born, Ever." Garin's voice was almost too quiet to hear. "And I was Fae on the day I met your wife when she was a little girl. Has such a revelation altered everything I've done for you in the past?"

Of course it didn't. But, as Isa was fond of saying, truth often felt much like a surgeon's blade. Ever stared out at the Fortress's mountain through the balcony's open doors, still unable to look at the man who stood before him. Finally, Garin stood to go, and Ever's gaze didn't waver.

"You know where to find me," Garin called out, a raw undertone in his voice that Ever hadn't heard before. Just as the door clicked open, however, Ever turned.

"Wait."

Garin stopped and looked at him expectantly.

"How... How were the children?"

The ghost of a strange smile touched Garin's eyes. "You would be surprised at how much young Henri is like you."

"Actually, I wouldn't. Considering that he is none other than my brother." The anger that had been building within him warred with his morbid curiosity. Suddenly, the need to know burned so heavily in Ever's stomach that he stood and walked to Garin without hesitating as he had done for the last five weeks. The time for petulance was over.

"How did this happen?" he asked, choking as he spoke. "After all the lectures about duty and self-denial and selflessness, how could he treat my mother and me like this?" Rodrigue and Louise had never been close in the slightest, but it still irked Ever that his father could have been so unfaithful. "And the Fortiers always sire boys first," he bellowed on. "Why was she a girl?" It didn't matter, of course, but Ever was tired of mysteries and riddles.

"Walk with me," Garin said, holding the door open. Ever complied, and soon they were walking in the direction of the tower.

"As to why Sacha is a woman," Garin said, seemingly unfazed by Ever's childish temper tantrum, "that is easy. Whatever Fae woman birthed Sacha was not the crowned Fortress queen. Therefore, the Fortress traditions did not apply to her. As to your father, I've been thinking about that." He pulled out a key and unlocked the heavy door that led into the tower. After their run-in with the glass prince three years before, the door had been completely remade and now was three times heavier than before, thanks to its triple iron casings.

"Your father would take off on personal missions of sorts," Garin continued as he locked the door behind them. "I recall one such mission about two years before he was married to your mother. A bear touched by the Sorthileige was rumored to be running about the southern forest, and your father went to deal with it. He was gone an exceptionally long time, though, for the kind of errand it should have been, two weeks at least. When questioned upon his return by your grandfather, he simply said he had discovered more pockets of the dark power and had worked to rid the countryside of them. As this was in line with his character and dedication, we didn't think twice. After that he continued to claim that he was receiving messages from other individuals dealing with the darkness in the same vicinity, and he continued to return there, even after he was married and you were born."

"He was gone so much," Ever said as he began to thumb through a book, only to slam it shut in frustration. "I never questioned his intentions on such campaigns. His constant absence from Mother and from me was only duty, he said." And Ever had believed him, never considering that his father was absent because he might be finding familial fulfillment elsewhere. Ever had been an idiot.

"Your father loved you," Garin said in a gentle voice. "He was often at a loss as to how to show it, but for all of his pains, look at what you have become."

"An arrogant fool who knows how to shed blood better than he knows his own people," Ever said, the words tasting sour as he spoke them.

"A strong, vigilant leader," Garin corrected him, placing a hand on Ever's shoulder. This time Ever didn't shake it off. "Yes, you have sinned. But do not forget the first lesson you learned from the Fortress. Because it is one that many of your forefathers never learned. The Fortress loves you and uses you in spite of your shortcomings, even through them! Just look at the wife you were given, despite your doing everything in your power to push her away at first. You have been willing to learn and grow, and you have been forgiven. You are not the same man you were four years ago, Ever, nor will you be the same man you are now in another four years."

"Perhaps," Ever stared at the ground, "that is why I am not yet a father. The Fortress knows how I could still ruin the life of a child."

"Now whatever would make you say such a thing?" The shock in Garin's voice made Ever look up.

"My father, despite his best intentions, ruined so much in me. And look what he did or didn't do for this... sister of mine. He was with me often enough that he couldn't have given much time to her. Maybe the Fortress knows I'm enough like my father that I would do the same."

"Nonsense."

But Ever shook his head. "You said yourself that Henri is much like me. Such waywardness would devastate him. What if I do to him what my father did to me?" Ever could just imagine himself pushing the boy to his limits, forcing him into a role that allowed him no choices.

"What happens if no one loves him?" Garin asked, fixing two steely eyes upon Ever. "You maintained pieces of your natural self because I was here, and because of Gigi and the servants, and sometimes even your father. Because of the Fortress. Now, imagine yourself as a boy and ask yourself what ultimate rejection would have done to you."

Ever held Garin's gaze unhappily. He didn't want to even contemplate that outcome. It would have been disastrous for the entire kingdom.

"Because," Garin continued, folding his arms defiantly, "that is exactly what is happening to that boy right now. I can see it in his eyes. He's desperate to find a place for himself and his sister. And if he cannot find it through natural means, he will look in places that no child or adult should even consider."

Ever stood still for a long time. Part of him, the part that often sounded a lot like Isa, knew what he should do. The other part, which sounded more like his father, much to Ever's disgust, was very, very afraid.

"Isa has been asking," he began slowly, "about what we plan to do with the children." He took a deep breath. "What do you know of Blood Sealing?"

Garin frowned but didn't seem completely taken by surprise. "That is a serious matter indeed. I am not surprised Isa wishes to know, but how do *you* feel about such an undertaking?"

"They have no one." Ever shrugged. "The girl seems harmless enough right now, but the boy needs someone to teach him how to use his power correctly before he accidentally obliterates an entire village. And Genny has become Isa's shadow..." He looked at his feet, suddenly frightened of what he might see in his mentor's eyes. That the children were part Fae still concerned him, and he fully expected Garin to capitalize on such a glaring risk.

Instead, however, Garin simply said, "Follow me," and turned. Curious, Ever followed him to the northern side of the tower. Garin knelt beside an ancient chest that sat against the window wall, and then opened the lock with a large, rusty key Ever did not recognize. Ever wondered how he had never noticed this particular chest before. It was so old that the blue paint had all but peeled off completely. With a creak and a good deal of encouragement, the lid finally came up and Garin reached inside. Ever peeked over his shoulder to see a few dozen scrolls on yellowed, cracking paper inside. What on earth could those contain?

"Here it is." Garin's voice was muffled from inside the trunk as he rummaged around. Finally, he stood and pulled out a scroll that had been rolled and tied carefully with a ribbon. The ribbon was so thin that its crimson color was all but gone. Reverently, Garin took the scroll back out to the large wooden table and slowly unrolled it. It took Ever a moment to make out the faint markings on the page.

"This is in the old language!"

Garin nodded. "This oath is as old as the Fortress itself."

"Has it ever been used?" Ever leaned closer and squinted to make out some of the smaller words.

"No. There has never been a Fortier to go childless. Even when the first son was killed, there was always a younger brother or sister to take his place."

Until now, Ever thought unhappily.

"I will not try to persuade you one way or another," Garin said. "This decision is for you and Isa alone. But," he leaned forward, "should the two of you complete the covenant, the oath will be binding. The children will be your own flesh and blood in the eyes of the Fortress and the Maker. There is no going back."

"Thank you, Garin." Ever took the scroll and carefully rolled it up once again. Despite his love for his steward, he needed some-place where he could be alone. He needed to speak with the Fortress.

As Ever began the long walk down the stairs, he shook his head. It was all too confusing. *I need guidance!* He stopped and leaned against the wall. *I want to do what is right. But my fear is crippling me.* Ever sat on the step, placing his head in his hands. *Tell me what to do!*

"Your Majesty"

Ever's prayers were interrupted by a panicked shout that echoed up the tower, and with it, the prickling sensation that something was wrong. "What is it?" He stood as the breathless chambermaid paused just steps below him.

"A demon has come... in Master Henri and Miss Genny's rooms!" She doubled over as though she might faint. "Queen Isabelle is holding it off, but—"

Ever didn't hear the rest of the woman's words, for he was already halfway down the tower steps.

CHAPTER 24

DECISIONS

Ever burst into the children's chambers. When he stopped he should have been between the hearth and the two large canopied beds, but instead, Ever found himself in a swamp. Stinking gas bubbles rose and popped at the surface of a rancid pond, and chirps, grunts, and all sorts of other sounds assaulted his ears. Only the sounds of the children's screams drew him forward.

Only then did Ever remember what Garin had said about the Fae creating illusions. Isa, too, had said the candy house was only an illusion for the children. Was this how the Fae had killed Leroy so easily, blinding him first? Ever inched forward. "Isa!"

"We're here!" Isa called back, much to his relief. The Fae must not have been strong enough to block their senses completely. "We're by the window!"

"I can't see you. You'll have to keep talking!" He needed to follow the sound of her voice through the mist that surrounded him. But as he was looking for Isa and the children, where was the Fae? Were there more than one? "What happened?"

"It was hiding under the bed when I arrived," Isa called back.

Her voice was strong, but Ever could detect a tremble. "I was able to graze its arm with my sword, but nothing else."

"Where is it now?" Knowing the creature was there in the room with them somewhere, Ever felt like his skin was crawling. He still only felt the oppressive wet air of the swamp upon his skin and saw strange ripples in the stagnant water as he walked upon the moss-covered log that spanned the frightening, gray depths.

"I think it's in the hearth."

"Henri, Genny," Ever said, praying the children would listen, "grab onto Miss Isa's skirts. Isa, hold out your hand. I'm going to pull you back toward the door. Then, Isa, I want you to find Garin, and keep the children with him until I kill this miscreant."

"Miscreant?" A thin voice warbled.

Ever froze, his left hand outstretched toward Isa. The voice had come from his right.

A hazy figure stepped out from behind one of the swamp trees, and two slitted green eyes glowed at him. "You are hasty to judge a creature you've never met, Your Majesty."

Ever's title was said like a curse word, and Ever gripped his sword more tightly as he stepped away from Isa and the children and toward the creature. "I *see* that you are in my home, uninvited. Hiding in the children's room is hardly a way to get in my good graces. Now that you have my attention, would you like to tell me why you're here?"

It didn't answer, though. In a second, the swamp was gone, and the room was blacker than any darkness Ever had experienced before.

"It's got me, Henri! It's got me!"

The little girl's shrieks awakened a new kind of anger in Ever. A ball of flame appeared upon his left fist. In the light of the blue flame, he could see Isa with her sword held out protectively before Henri, who clung to her skirts. But Genny was gone.

"Ever!" Isa shrieked, her eyes wide. Following her eyes, Ever turned to his right to see green mist materialize into the thin form once again. Its new form was more like a human than the reptilian creature that had appeared only moments before. But the slitted eyes were still too far apart, and its mouth was far too wide. And it was staring at his flame as though in a trance, even as it held Genny pinned to its side.

Henri let out a shout, then, and Ever kept his fire lit as he turned to see a second creature holding one of Henri's legs, trying to loosen the boy's grip on Isa's skirts. This creature was suddenly staring at his fire, though, too.

Isa met Ever's eyes and gave the slightest nod before yanking Henri back and pinning the creature to the ground with her sword. Ever whirled and threw all of his weight against the first Fae. It dropped Genny's arm as Ever slammed into it. The fire disappeared from his hand, but a few sparks fell into the hearth, and the tinder within it began to catch, giving light to the room. With a shout, Ever thrust his sword through where the Fae's chest should have been.

But before his blade could draw a single drop of blood, the creature dissipated into the green whorl of light drops, which swung around and wrapped themselves around Ever's throat. Invisible fingers began to materialize, crushing his airway.

"Isa!" Ever rasped. "Go!"

With the flame gone from Ever's hand, the creature that Isa had pinned looked back up at her and dissolved. Isa didn't wait for the Fae to materialize again. She darted past Ever and his foe and grabbed Genny by the arm, but just as she threw the door open, Henri let go of her hand and took a step back toward Ever. As Ever fought for air, he tried to motion to the boy to go and leave him be, but a determined look came into Henri's eyes.

"No," Ever tried to yell, but he was too late. Henri held up a hand, and immediately, a little blue flame appeared inside his palm. The Fae stopped squeezing Ever's throat. Instead of watching the little blaze as it had done with Ever's ball of flame, however, the Fae disappeared and then shimmered into being right in front of Henri. It reached out and grabbed his hand that held the flame, and with its other hand, it grabbed Henri's throat. But before it could squeeze, Ever threw himself upon the creature, blade down. And this time, his sword hit its mark.

A sharp cry rang out behind Ever. He turned to see the second Fae, horror in its eyes as it stared down at its dead brother. Ever sprang at the living Fae and grabbed it by its scrawny neck before it could escape. This time, he kept his flame burning as he pinned it to the ground. And no matter how it squirmed and fought him, it couldn't quite tear its focus from the flames that leapt from Ever's hand.

"Why are you here?" Ever growled as he pressed the Fae hard into the rug. But the Fae only spat on him. Ever lowered his hand until the flames began to singe the edge of the creature's human-like hair. It screamed, and Ever pushed down with even more force. "Why have you come?" he bellowed.

"It matters not," the Fae hissed as it glared up at the flame with its slitted eyes. Its form shimmered, but it managed to stay solid. "She is coming, and she will avenge us." It flicked a trembling finger at the dead Fae, which was now a pile of ash. "You think you have the right to—"

"I have the right to protect the children within my home. And I will rid that home of vermin like you and your brother." He squeezed the Fae's neck once more, bringing his flaming fist just inches from its face. "Now, when will she be here?"

"She already is." With those words, the creature tried to kick Ever in the stomach, but Ever was faster, plunging his sword into its heart.

The dark mist disappeared, allowing the light of day through the windows once again. As the light returned, Ever could see that the body at his feet was indeed human in shape, but only just. Lines that should have appeared around the eyes, mouth, palms, and fingers were nonexistent. The skin had no variations or spots of any kind but was one continuous color. Seconds later, it, too, dissolved into ash.

"These must have been young." Garin's voice came from behind Ever. "They weren't very good at imitating other forms yet."

Ever wiped the sweat from his eyes. "Thank you for keeping the door."

"I would have interfered, but you appeared to have it quite well under control."

Ever nodded. "Unfortunately, it seems you won't have time to work with the men after all." He finally tore his gaze from the pile of ash and met Garin's eyes. "She's here."

Garin's eyes began to fill with something that, if Ever hadn't known better, looked very akin to hate. "Shall I tell Acelet to take his leave then?"

Ever took a deep breath. "I'm only beginning to understand how to defeat them," he said softly. "The men wouldn't stand a chance right now."

As Garin nodded and headed off, Genny began to cry.

"Get her calmed down," Ever told Isa. "When they're better, give them to Gigi. I... I need to speak with you."

Isa looked at him curiously before picking the little girl up in one arm and taking Henri's shoulder in the other. As soon as she was gone, Ever looked down once more at the pile of ash beneath his feet and shuddered. He had a decision to make and much less time than he had expected to make it.

"Wait," he called out, catching them in the hall. They stopped as Ever knelt before Henri. "Do you like it here?" he asked, knowing that he must look like the biggest fool in the world to the child. After weeks of stomping around the Fortress and muttering about the children's antics, would Henri trust him enough to answer honestly?

Henri studied him for a long time, his blue eyes wary in his thin face.

The more Ever looked at the boy, the more he saw himself. From the golden hair to the angle of his chin, the boy was his spitting image. But Ever had spent so long trying to push him away that he suddenly wondered if he was too late.

"Why?" Henri finally asked.

"I fear..." Ever took a deep breath. Admitting his errors had never been one of his strengths. "I fear I have not been entirely fair to you. You are of the Fae and the Fortress because the Maker created you so, and I allowed my fears to blind me to that. For that, I am sorry. But now, I wish to know what you think of this place. If," Ever swallowed hard, "you could ever think of it as home."

"When I lived with my father and stepmother," Henri spoke slowly, "I never felt like I belonged. The cottage was there, and my family was there. I only cared about Genny, though. But here," he took a deep breath and looked at his feet. "I don't know how to say it..." He shook his messy golden hair, a look of frustration on his face. "Here I feel like there's someone watching out for me. For both of us. Like when those things came." He nodded at the bedroom. "Genny's been saying there was a monster beneath her bed for four days. But it didn't come out until—" He stopped and looked up in wonder. "Until you and Miss Isa were back to protect us."

Ever felt his heart stop. The Fortress had answered his prayers, even as he had uttered them on the tower steps less than an hour before.

"Meet me in the Tower," he said to Isa. "There is something urgent we must do."

CHAPTER 25
SEALING WORDS

Forgive me for taking so long," Isa said as she shut the tower's heavy door, her copper hair falling prettily out of place. When she turned, her eyes were wet with tears. "Genny was still upset, and it was nearly impossible to get them to go down the mountain without—" She stopped when she saw Ever and Garin standing at the heavy wooden table. Garin stood by the fire and Ever stood across from him. Between them on the table were laid two parchments. One was the ancient scroll that Garin had removed from the chest earlier that afternoon. The other was a new parchment, which had been written out by Garin himself upon Ever's request.

"What is this?" she asked breathlessly, looking back and forth between the parchments and the men standing before her. Finally, her gaze came to rest on Ever. Ever went to her, feeling suddenly as nervous as he had the moment he'd asked her to marry him. There were dark bags under her eyes, the same ones Ever wore constantly now, too. But in that moment, the flush of her cheeks and the slight parting of her lips was the most beautiful sight he'd ever seen. Gently he leaned down for a kiss, which she gladly gave him. Then he placed his forehead against hers.

"Garin has found the vow for Blood Sealing," he said in a voice that didn't sound at all like his own. Ever's voice was always confident, nearly always loud, and never betrayed any uncertainty. But now it wavered like an adolescent youth's.

"Blood Sealing?"

"You were right." Ever stepped back to search her midnight eyes. "Those children are creations of the Maker, just the same as you and I. They need love, and they need a home." He took her right hand and drew it up to his mouth, kissing each finger softly in turn. "I was stubborn and foolish—"

An amused snort sounded from behind him, but Ever ignored the steward and continued.

"As always, I wanted to protect the kingdom in my own way. But the Fortress has opened my eyes."

Isa's eyes grew wide. "Really?" she whispered.

"If you are willing, then we will complete the Blood Sealing now," Ever said. At this, a radiant smile began to form, but Ever held up his hand. "Before you make a decision, you need to know that should we ever have a child, he will be third in line for the throne. There will be no distinction between my siblings and our children, for they will be sealed as our own bone and blood. I have read the text, and there is no way out of the covenant once it is made." He drew her closer. "Are you prepared for that?" he whispered.

"Absolutely." She didn't even blink. When Ever gave her a wary look, her smile became fierce, and she clutched his hands tightly. "These children were given to us for a purpose, Ever! I don't know why or how, but I *know* these children need our love. And," she paused, reaching up to touch his face, "we need theirs, you as much as I. Only," she paused, looking down the mountain through the window wall, "do we have time? Sacha could be here any moment!"

"I have word that Sacha has been spotted hiding in the forest west of Soudain. We have at least two hours. But even if she comes sooner," he took her hands in his, "I believe the Fortress desires this, what we are doing now. It will provide us the time we need."

Isa responded with an even brighter smile.

"Then," Garin said, "let us begin." Clearing his throat, he began to read from the ancient scroll that he had translated earlier that afternoon. Though Ever didn't need the translation, Isa had not learned the old tongue, so it was for her that Garin read. Ever wanted her to know what they were doing through and through.

"The almighty Maker has seen it fit that man and woman should be joined in marriage, and they should beget children," Garin began in a low, clear voice. "At times, Darkness shall interrupt this sacred order, and such Darkness will work its contrivances, disease, illness, and evil to separate parent from child and child from parent. In the event that such harm should infiltrate man's native familial roles and interrupt such circles of devotion, the Maker has also seen it fit to bring new life to a man's empty home and new love to a desolate woman's arms."

A tear rolled down Isa's face, but when Garin paused, she quickly brushed it away and just shook her head. Garin continued.

"For the Maker finds it pleasing to confuse the schemes of evil, making it his desire and plan for evil's personal wiles to ultimately submit and serve the purposes of good. For this covenant such good will be borne by joining bone to bone, blood to blood, and flesh to flesh. Parents and children who were parted will become one, and there will be no difference between begetting and vowing. What is vowed once will never be broken, for such a forged bond cannot be severed in the Maker's sight."

Garin looked up over his spectacles at Ever and then Isa. "If you are ready, my queen, you will take your vows first. Please present your ring."

Isa looked surprised but held out her left hand. The heavy

blue crystal in her ring and its swirling silver filigree flashed in the light of the hearth's fire and bounced off the glass walls, which were now orange with the sunset's glow. Garin poured a little pool of silver wax upon the new parchment. Then he took Isa's hand and guided her ring into the wax, and as he held it there, he instructed her to repeat after him.

"Mortal bodies, precious ways..." he said.

"Mortal bodies, precious ways," she echoed.

"I will love you all my days. There in sorrow, there in joy, heartache e're will be destroyed."

As she followed Garin through the vows, Isa's voice became stronger and more resolute. Her chin lifted, and for the first time in a long time, she looked neither tired nor sad.

"Now it is your turn, Your Highness," Garin said, nodding to Ever. Again, he poured more wax, and guided Ever's signet ring to it, holding it there for the duration of the vow.

"Repeat after me. Holy vows and lonely kin, never will you be again. Fighting as with sword and bow, in my heart you'll stay and grow."

As Ever said the words, he wondered at how such beautiful words had never been used. Surely some king or queen had seen and pitied an orphaned child sometime in the last thousand years, even making it only a third or fourth born. And yet, here they were once again, doing what no king or queen had ever done before. But then, since they'd met and married, he and Isa had never been the sort to follow tradition's path.

"In the eyes of the Maker, the Fortress, and I, your witness," Garin said, letting go of Ever's hand, "you have completed the blood seal. The children are now yours."

Ever turned to look at his wife, then back at his steward. Such a short ceremony to reap such large consequences. He was a father now. And his wife, a mother. And yet, he didn't feel any differently. Was he supposed to?

"What now?" Isa asked. Before Garin could answer, a knock sounded at the door.

"Please forgive my intrusion," one of their personal guards called out, "but I could not delay. Sacha is approaching the Fortress, sire. She and her followers should be here within the hour."

"Thank you." Ever was already headed downstairs, clutching Isa's hand tightly when the guard caught them and spoke again.

"There is one more thing you should know, Your Highness. She is spreading the word as to what she is planning."

"And that would be?"

The guard paused and looked at the floor.

"She's telling the people, Your Highness, that the Fortress has abandoned you this night. She will be made queen. And you will die."

CHAPTER 26

SACRIFICE

Isa couldn't help crying as they sent off the last of the servants. She would have cried even harder had they not sent the children down to Soudain already. The tears didn't absorb into her sleeves, though, as she was now in her battle dress. The leather leggings beneath her gown and the long leather sleeves that covered her arms and the tops of her hands were meant to keep water out. Well, that was fine then, Isa thought. If she was meant to let the tears dry on her face, then so be it. It only served to stoke the fire within her.

By the time Isa returned from dismissing the rest of the servants, Ever was already in the throne room. Isa marveled, in spite of her sorrow, at the warrior sitting in the throne beside hers. Ever wore his full battle armor as well. His large shoulders looked even more massive, as did his chest, beneath their steel coverings. Chain mail covered his sides and the lower part of his neck. Whether for ceremony or intimidation, she wasn't sure, Ever had donned his crown, a piece he rarely touched. But now, as it sat upon his brow, it only served to make him look even more fearsome with its blue gems glinting in the bright light of the thousands of candles that lit the throne room.

As she drew near, Ever stood and walked to her, holding Isa's own diadem. Thinner than his, with silver ivy upon the gold that matched her blue crystal ring, the queen's crown was the loveliest creation Isa had ever seen, and as such, she was rather hesitant to wear it except for ceremony. But now he gently placed it upon her head.

"This is so we remember who we are," he said softly, "no matter what she says."

Isa's throat tightened, and she had the sudden urge to kiss her husband as she never had before, a desperate, urgent kiss that would have done dangerous things to her concentration. Instead, however, she merely took his hand and held it as tightly as she could. His return grip was just as fierce.

"She's coming!" a guard called out from the hall. Isa closed her eyes. *I don't understand, Fortress. Why?*

Warm, familiar fingers placed themselves under her chin, and when she opened her eyes, Ever was inches from her face. "Together," he said.

Isa nodded, and then he led her up the steps of the dais. Once she was on her throne, he sat in his. The wait felt like eternity as the approaching party made a ruckus in their attempt to open the great doors of the Fortress's front hall. Wordlessly, four of their five remaining guards appeared beside them. The Fortress's holy man, and finally Garin, joined them last. As he often did during ceremonies, Garin stood just behind the two thrones where he could be quickly consulted should the need arise.

The air was heavy, as though someone had placed a giant boulder upon the earth itself, pressing everything down beneath it. Isa reached out and tested the hearts of her little group. Fear was the overwhelming emotion, but the guards bore it well. Garin was angry more than anything else and had a good deal of dread as well, something Isa could only guess would come from seeing one's people for the first time in five centuries. Ever's heart, as usual, was more hidden. Trying to read it was like trying to see the bottom of a pond while the water was being splashed about. His face was like granite. Once again, Isa wanted nothing more than to lean over and kiss it, melting away the man of stone into the gentle, kind husband she knew so well. But now was not the time. Now was the time to wait. And pray.

If only the Fortress would listen.

"Your Highness," the fifth guard called out, his voice dripping with sarcasm. "A woman is here demanding entrance. She claims to be the rightful queen."

"Let her in," Ever said in a voice so calm it surprised even Isa. And it was a good thing, too. Isa's response would have included words not fit for a lady, much less a queen. As they waited, she squeezed the silver-veined marble arms of her throne until her fingers hurt. At first, when she'd heard that Sacha was in Soudain, Isa had been filled with fear like their guards. But with each passing moment, the fear began to flee, and raw determination took its place. Ever's sister or not, this woman had much to answer for.

And Isa was determined to make her do just that.

Sacha did not carry herself like a queen as she stalked past the guard into the throne room. Her long, exaggerated strides reminded Isa instead of a dog's gait when it was warning others to keep off its territory.

People crowded in behind her, their dark rags and garments standing out vividly against the pristine white of the marble walls that surrounded them. Most of them were poor and many were dirty, no doubt from their long trek if they had followed Sacha all the way up from the south. Isa wondered how Sacha's gaudy golden dress had stayed so clean after traveling such a distance. Even on a horse, Isa's clothes had never stayed so spotless. The size of her puffed sleeves and the hundreds of jewels that bedecked the bodice of her gown were so numerous that Isa was sure they must be illusions as well. She was tempted to use her power to see, but then decided against it. She was likely to need all of her strength very soon. So instead, Isa sat up even straighter, pressing her spine up against the hard back of the throne. Jewels did not make a queen.

Sacha came to a stop just at the foot of the dais. A number of hooded figures, probably three dozen at least, came to surround her. Nasty hemlock leaves swayed gently from leather thongs tied beneath the pointed ends of their crudely hewn staffs. The citizens that accompanied the party filled in behind and around them, their whispers and tittles creating a low buzzing sound like many bees in a hive.

Isa closed her eyes briefly and tested the hearts before her. Fear. Anger. Hate. Uncertainty. There were hundreds of souls present, too many to count. And, to Isa's disappointment, there were at least a few dozen children in their midst as well. Would these people ever stop bringing their children to dangerous gatherings?

"Brother. I have come to stake my claim to the throne."

At the sound of Sacha's voice, the crowd went silent, looking back and forth between their monarchs and the usurper.

Isa chafed inside. Could no one remember *her* place in all of this? "Actually," she called out, lifting her chin and making certain her voice didn't wobble, "it is *me* that you should be addressing." Sacha gave her a strange look, at which Isa allowed herself a small, victorious smile. "The throne was mine first."

Sacha looked momentarily taken aback, and Isa allowed her half-grin to grow, reveling in the woman's temporary confusion. Sacha had hidden her feelings from Isa very well during that first meeting, but with each encounter since, Isa had become more convinced that the woman was loathe to do so. In fact, she seemed to struggle greatly with not giving wind to her whims now as her emotions wreaked havoc with her carefully laid plans. Even without her gift, Isa would have been able to tell such from the woman's stunned expression.

There were a few moments of silence before Sacha brought

her face under control once more. "But you are a Fortier now, are you not?" she asked impatiently.

"I am."

"Well, I am, too." Sacha turned to the crowd and raised her voice. "Your late King Rodrigue was my father first before he sired Everard." She turned back to Isa and Ever. "And therefore, I challenge you for this throne."

"And how do you propose to do such a thing?"

Isa was amazed at Ever's calm as he spoke. For all the vague turmoil she could feel within him, his face was completely impassive, his voice unshaken. Meanwhile, Isa was boiling. "As my holy man and many of these citizens here can attest to," Ever swept his arm out over the throng of hundreds that had gathered before them, "we took the sacred vows. The Fortress has accepted us as its servants."

Sacha stared at them, and all at once, Isa could see what Garin had meant about the Fae changing so very quickly. The speed at which Sacha, who was only half Fae, changed her mood reminded Isa of the way a storm cloud might change its shape, tossed about and remolded continuously by the winds. Simply being near her was giving Isa a headache.

Just then, the woman's eyes focused on something behind Isa. "It can't be," she muttered.

"Oh," Garin said in a dry voice, stepping forward so he was standing between the two thrones, "but it is."

"How did the traitor live?" she bellowed, turning to some of her hooded cohorts. "It has been nearly five hundred years!" She looked back at Garin. "Stories are told of your treachery!"

"Then how do you know I am he?" Garin's voice was taunting now.

"I would know a Fae when I see one, particularly one who is the king's lapdog!"

Isa heard the holy man gasp, as did a fair number of the citizens in their midst. Isa and Ever hadn't made that bit of Garin's past known to the public, but it was too late to care now. Isa kept her eyes forward.

"It would seem the Maker still has a purpose for me then, wouldn't it?" Garin snapped. "Or I wouldn't be here."

Sacha stood silent for so long that Isa wondered if she might faint. Isa could sense her heart racing in frantic, stilted bursts. Finally, however, she merely tucked a single piece of straight golden hair behind her ear before shouting at someone behind her, "Get the child!"

Isa's mouth tasted sour as a little boy was brought forward. He looked to be around five years of age, just a bit older than Genny, and Isa vaguely remembered seeing him as one among the kidnapped. A surge of dismay hit her from the right, and Isa turned to see Ever staring at the child as well. Not a muscle moved in his stony face, but he paled infinitesimally.

"Before you make this challenge," Isa spoke, hoping to give Ever time to recover, "you should all know that this woman is the one who took your children and grandchildren in the first place. It was she that I met in the *otherland* beyond the veil. *She* was the one who stole your children and cursed them before returning them to you."

A murmur began to spread among the people, but Sacha turned to the crowd and raised her hands. "Deep claims, your queen makes!" She turned back to Isa, her eyes narrowing. "I would like to see you prove it."

Isa narrowed her own eyes in return. Oh, she would most definitely do that. *But...* she glanced up at the crowd. *If only the crowd weren't so very big.* Convincing the crowd in Sansim had taken nearly every ounce of strength she had. This crowd was more than ten times that size.

"I have a question," Ever's voice rumbled down to the people. Thankfully, he seemed to have recovered himself well, for there was no trace of hesitancy now as he spoke. "Have you not lived in peace and prosperity in these past few years? What claims have you brought to me that I have not addressed? And considering that, what in this woman's history has proved to you that she should rule this kingdom? What does she know of stewardship, of keeping a treasury full or settling land disputes?" He stood slowly, and the people standing nearest him at the foot of the dais scrambled to step back. Relief nibbled at Isa as she felt the first wave of guilt work its way through the crowd. But just as people began to talk amongst themselves, a familiar mop of red hair appeared and began to push its way toward the front.

Agnes. How could one baker cause so much mischief?

"You have not healed our children, sire." The skinny woman spat out Ever's title. Then she looked at Isa. "And before you go saying such, Your Highness, I was patient! I was patient like you told me to be! I prayed without end that my daughter's hands would heal. And yet, this woman here was the one who healed her!"

With that, Agnes nodded to the two men who had brought the boy forward. Normally, Ever would not have allowed such flagrant disrespect to continue in a throne room hearing. But the only guards present were those who surrounded them, and losing any of them to wrestle away an unruly peasant would not only cost them bodies, but would show the crowd and Sacha that their numbers were indeed low. Better to let them think Ever was simply being unusually patient.

"Do you think then," Ever asked in the same calm voice, "it would be better to bring her on as a healer?" He looked back to Sacha, his eyes suddenly kind. "I would very much like to know the sister who was denied to me."

And, Isa could feel, he was being completely honest. One of the few areas in which Ever and Isa had never understood one another had been on the subject of siblings. As an only child, he'd never had the chance to enjoy the inexplicable bond that forms between brother and sister, older and younger. Isa had, of course, experienced such a bond with both Launce and little Megane. And as Ever continued to stare at Sacha with a sudden expression of longing, Isa was hit by the strength of his desire for a sister. In four years of marriage, Isa had never known that such a desire burned so strongly within him.

"You would make me another servant. How kind. No, I think you have been tested by this Fortress enough... and failed! And the people of this kingdom deserve new blood, not the line that has grievously injured them over and over and over again."

It took all of Isa's willpower to keep her eyes trained on Sacha's quick, angry movements. For beside her, she could feel the pain of transgressions remembered beginning to eat away at her husband. Again. Somehow, his sister had found the chink in his armor. If Ever doubted anything in the Fortress or Destin, it was himself.

Truly, Isa wondered as she scanned the crowd, how had so many come to join Sacha? What illusions had the Fae shown the people that they might believe what she was telling them about Ever? About her?

Ever turned to the holy man who stood trembling to his right. "What is there in the Holy Writ or the ancient texts that might suggest a legal path for what my sister demands?" He was stalling. Isa knew there was nothing in the texts that could justify ripping two monarchs from the throne who had sworn their lives to and been accepted by the Fortress. But it might buy them time. Though to what end, Isa wasn't sure. With so many children present, how could they fight?

Please, Fortress. Show us the way.

"There is no path to the throne," the holy man stuttered. "You have made a covenant with your lifeblood to serve it all of your days. The only way to fulfill such a promise is..."

Sacha smiled. Her smile should have looked like Ever's, as her face mirrored so many of the Fortier features. But rather, her smile was cold and hard. The people behind and around her began to hiss and boo, displeased with the holy man's answer, obviously missing what Sacha had not.

"See how little he cares for your children? I cannot heal this many without the power from this holy place. And though he cannot do it himself, he *still* denies you that healing!"

The shouts of outrage began to grow louder, and the crowd began to move like a creature being awakened from its slumber. Sucking in a deep breath, Isa pushed the truth out into the crowd, straining to cut through the lies they must have been fed. But every time she got one group calmed down, another began to rail against them even more loudly, and the effort quickly drained her. Yet she continued, straining until she shook with the effort. Until a warm hand gave her shoulder a gentle squeeze.

Isa opened her eyes and looked up to see Garin standing over her. A soft blue light shone from beneath his hand even though it was gloved, and Isa felt a rush of healing take her body.

"What can I do to appease you?" Ever stood. "For it seems your minds are made up no matter what the truth."

Taking the boy by the shoulders, whom Isa had nearly forgotten in the throng of angry people, Sacha led him up the dais until he stood before Ever. "Then show us the truth," she said, holding a hand up behind her. The people quieted but not as completely as the time before. "Heal this boy, and we will all know whom the Fortress wishes to sit upon its throne."

Ever stared at his sister for a long time. Then he placed his hand on the boy's head and closed his eyes.

A blue flame began to spiral above them, dancing in slow swirls as it radiated from his hand into the child. As it grew in intensity, the fire began to move up into the air before cascading back down around them like a fountain. The amount of power Ever summoned was immense, and caught Isa's breath in her throat. She had never seen him use so much power before. Never had he been so strong. When the boy opened his eyes, they glowed with the intensity of a full moon, large and luminous in his little face. Isa could hear exclamations as the people pressed forward to see. And yet, Ever's power continued to build until it swirled above their heads, nearly touching the ceiling in its reach.

Slowly the fire began to sink, slowly, slowly returning to Ever until the room no longer glowed blue, and the fire was gone.

"Well, son?" A man pushed forward, breaking away from the throng. "What do you see?"

The boy hesitated before answering, his eyes moving back and forth cautiously. Finally, he turned to face his father.

"Nothing, Father."

Isa's heart plunged. The boy was still blind. All that power and the boy was still blind.

Without a word, Sacha took the child's hand, and a blue light began to move down her arm and into his hand. But it wasn't the deep, pure blue of the Fortier power. Rather, it was tinted with green. Garin's grip on Isa's shoulder tightened ever so slightly as they watched the far less impressive display, Sacha's strange fire making a faint buzz as it moved through the boy. Finally, she let go, and the boy opened his eyes and turned toward the crowd once more.

"Papa!" he cried, looking directly at the man who had called to him moments before.

"Take them," Sacha ordered. "But I want *him* alive."

Isa's hand was on her sword in an instant, but Ever was faster. The two Fae that climbed the dais with their pikes in hand got their weapons sent clattering to the ground. Isa felt a movement to her left, turning just in time to block the strike from a third Fae.

Isa had spent countless hours with Ever in the training room and had even progressed enough to begin practicing swordplay with multiple enemies. She was growing proficient, he'd told her. But her best efforts had only included opponents of twos or threes, and they had been human. Now, as she and Ever fought back to back, Isa felt perspiration building quickly on her skin and running down her back and temples as she moved faster and faster to block the attacks of the spirit men. She could see now why Ever hadn't wanted his soldiers fighting an army of this. The creatures would lose their bodies in one location just to materialize in another. She heard her crown's clang as it fell to the floor. A quick glimpse told her that Ever had lost his as well.

Just as she began to lose her balance, a deafening roar filled the air. Fae screams mixed with the cries of the people as a great wall of black rose around them. As it shot up, the Fae disappeared along with Sacha and the mob. In an instant, the throne room with its towering rectangular windows and its glittering white walls disappeared, and there was only a single light from above, though Isa couldn't tell its source. Black surrounded them in every other direction. But it was not an oppressive black. Rather, it felt like the darkness of a gentle summer evening just before the stars began to appear. And it was quiet. Nothing stirred, save for the sounds of their own ragged breathing.

"Garin," Ever said, gasping for breath, "what is this place?"

Garin simply cupped their faces in his hands in the same way Isa's father had caressed her face as a little girl. Without a word, he pulled Isa toward him and softly placed a kiss on her forehead. And then Ever's.

"The Maker saw it fit for me to defend this sacred ground from the bloodied hands of my own son," he whispered. "But He gave me two new children in my boy's place. Now, my children, go!"

Garin placed his hands upon their shoulders and shoved them backward. As Isa felt herself hit the floor the black curtain disappeared, and they were once again on the throne room dais. The irate crowd still shouted, but this time, neither the people nor the Fae were looking at them. The people were looking at Garin as he walked toward them with the utmost calm.

Then Garin changed. As he removed his gloves and tossed them off to the side, his skin began to blaze so brightly that looking at his skin was like looking at sunlit snow. Silver wings unfolded from behind his shoulders. Once spread, the wings were wide enough that they spread all the way across the dais.

Even Sacha stood immobile, her mouth open as Isa felt the horror pulsate from her nearly as strongly as her hate.

With one final step to the edge of the dais, Garin turned once more, his eyes smoldering, a blue-white glow as they locked with Isa's. His silver wings began to shimmer like metal that was being put to the flame. "Go!" he ordered in a voice that shook the Fortress walls.

The Maker had indeed made him a being completely *other*.

Isa stumbled forward but turned when she realized that Ever was not at her side. Instead, he was still on the floor, lying exactly where Garin had pushed him. Crawling back, Isa took his arm and pulled him to his feet. She had to drag him all the way down the front lawn, down to the edge of the forest. Only when they were safely hidden within its sheltering trees did she allow herself a short sigh of relief.

But as they began the trek down the mountain, Isa still guiding Ever, a familiar voice gave a cry so loud that it escaped the Fortress's walls and echoed into the night. And Isa couldn't tell whether it was the cry of a warrior or a cry of pain.

CHAPTER 27

GO

S o..." Isa's father shook his head as if to clear it of the horrible events Isa had just related, the lines in his face suddenly looking much deeper in the light of the single candle. "What do you need?"

Though Ever sat beside Isa in body, Ansel had eventually stopped directing any questions his way, as they could draw little from him except grunts.

"We'll need at least three horses and supplies for a week's journey," Isa said softly as she stroked Genny's golden hair. "The Fae can sense our power, so we won't be able to use our fire to speed the horses. It will take the full three days to get to the southern forest. I can only guess we'll spend a day or so there. Then it will take another two days to reach Launce."

"You can't go straight to Launce?" Deline pursed her lips tightly. "He could offer you shelter at least."

Shelter wasn't exactly what they were seeking. Rather, their rendezvous with her brother would be in preparation for war. But Isa didn't correct her mother, for doing so would have only brought on more worry. Instead, she continued to brush the little girl's golden locks with her fingers. Genny stirred in her sleep, but didn't awaken.

Henri slept, too, though his head was on a cushion Deline had provided rather than Isa's lap. Still, he was close enough that his knees were pushed up against her, something he wouldn't have allowed even a few weeks before. In the midst of all the dreadful goings-on, Isa took comfort in this little victory.

"And what of the children?" Ansel asked in a wary voice.

"Megane," Isa murmured, turning to her sister. "Take Genny for me?"

Megane nodded eagerly, taking Genny in her arms so quickly that Isa guessed she had wanted to do so all night. As soon as the little girl was resettled, Isa motioned her father up out of the cellar. They took no light, leaving the single candle behind them with the others.

"Ever and I were going to... actually, we took the blood joining oath just before his sister arrived." Isa was glad she couldn't see his face through the dark. "They're ours now. They don't know it yet, but they will be coming with us."

Ansel paused for a moment. It must have been a strange night for him, Isa thought wryly. Not only was he sheltering his children on the run, but he was learning that he had suddenly become a grandfather as well.

"Wouldn't it be safer to leave them here?" Ansel finally asked, his voice trembling just slightly.

"No. We're not sure what she wants with them, but we're sure she has something planned. Unlike all of the other children, they were never cursed. And then she sent a Fae after them in the Fortress."

"Do you think she knows of their relation to her?"

"We believe so, but we would prefer not to find out."

"Huh," Ansel said. Isa nearly cringed as she waited for her father to warn her against the dangers of taking two children halfway across the kingdom while they were being pursued. But to her surprise, he only sighed. "And what of your steward?"

"He's in the Fortress's hands now. He ensured our escape when Sacha arrived."

One of the floorboards was lifted, interrupting whatever Ansel was about to say. Megane peeked through the crack, then emerged from the cellar.

"Where are you going at this hour?" Ansel asked with a frown.

"It's almost dawn," Megane said, nodding at the window. And to Isa's surprise, it was. The gray light was beginning to seep beneath their drawn curtains. "Mum says she wants me to get some salve and bandages for Isa and Ever on the off-chance they should need it. I'm also to ask Mr. Sager if we can borrow his spare horse."

"Be careful, Megs," Isa said. "I will not have you getting hurt over this."

Megane laughed, her blue eyes twinkling. "Are you in earnest? This is the first adventure I've gotten a part in. You and Launce have all the fun!" And before Isa could warn her anymore, she grabbed her basket and flounced into the street.

"That one is going to give me more gray hairs than you and your brother combined." Ansel shook his head as he frowned at the slamming door.

Isa wished she could argue, but Megane indeed possessed a flair for the dramatics. And it didn't help that she was still a few years too young to enjoy the court lives of her brother and sister. Granted, growing up as a merchant's daughter when one's brother was a prince and one's sister was a queen would be sure to rub anyone a little in the wrong direction. Hopefully, Isa thought, this taste of adventure would suffice for her until Megane was of age and a little more discerning.

As time passed, Isa prayed that her sister would keep her head. The errand that should have taken only twenty minutes turned into forty and then into an hour. Ever continued to brood in the basement, but the children eventually woke up and were kept quiet with cookies. Isa and Deline continued to exchange looks of worry as the sun grew higher and there was no Megane to be found.

Finally, just as Ansel was ready to grab his coat and go looking for his daughter, Megane came skipping in. "Mrs. Sager says they'll bring the horse over this afternoon. Mr. Sager has him out in the fields."

Instead of smiling at the girl's enthusiasm, Isa grabbed Megane by the arm and dragged her up to the attic. She didn't want her new children to hear the chewing-out she had planned for her sister. For judging by the look on Megane's face, she'd been up to no good. As soon as they were alone, Isa slammed the door shut and turned to glare at her sister. "What took you so long? We were so worried!"

"I was hurrying, I promise! But then Margot caught me just outside the Pottens's shop."

Isa groaned. Would that old busybody *ever* learn to mind her own business?

"She asked me where I was going in such a hurry, so I had to think up a story on the spot!"

"What did you tell her?" Isa almost didn't want to know.

Megane turned a light shade of pink and giggled. "I told her that Davin Crowley and I were going to be kissing on the old bridge, and that I was late so I had to hurry!"

Isa was horrified. "Megane, you are to be telling no such stories to people from now on! Do you understand me?"

"I had to think of *something* unless you wanted me to share your real whereabouts!" Megane smirked, then made a sour face. "Is that an order from my *queen*?"

"That's an order from your *sister*, and I have a good mind to tell Father what sort of mischief you've been up to!" She looked hard at her little sister. "You haven't been kissing Davin Crowley, have you?"

"No!" Megane's face had gone from pink to a near gray. "Oh, please don't tell Papa! I was only trying to help!"

"Yes, and you wanted your bit of fun while you were at it, didn't you? Now Mother and Father are going to have to listen to the whole town whisper of nothing but your upcoming nuptials, and possibly worse." Isa pursed her lips then sighed and drew her sister in for a hug. "Megane, what am I going to do with you? You are to tell no more such falsehoods, understand?"

Megane nodded miserably into Isa's chest. "I'm eleven now, Isa. You don't have to worry so much about me. I'm not a baby."

"And you sometimes think you're fifteen." She pulled back to study her little sister's face. "Part of growing up means doing what is responsible, rather than what sounds fun." Suddenly, something caught in Isa's throat, and it was difficult to speak around it without croaking. "Father and Mother are going to need you now more than ever. Launce and I can't be around to take care of them all the time, as much as we would like to."

"Isa." Tears began to run down the girl's face. "You will be coming back, won't you?" She wiped her face with her sleeve and tried to smile. "You promised you would take me to my first ball! You can't go breaking it on me now."

"I'll do my best, Megs."

"Wait now." Megane pulled back and gave a shaky laugh. "You'd better stop crying before your face gets all blotchy and ugly like it does when you cry."

Isa was about to smack her sister with her glove, but a flash caught her attention through the attic window that faced north. In one movement, Isa had shoved her sister down on the bed before running to the window. At first, there was nothing, only the rooftops of the city's northern quarter looking just as they should on any early summer day. But just as her fingers touched the open window, a swish of green fog appeared before her.

With a shriek, Isa jumped back then regretted it immediately.

She had shown the Fae exactly what it was looking for. Who knew how many more were out there looking for them?

"Ever!" Isa grabbed Megane by the wrist and turned to drag her downstairs again, but the sound of breaking glass made her pause. A green wisp flew past them. Then a man with a vague, flat face and slitted green eyes materialized at the bottom of the attic steps.

CHAPTER 28

SON

"You've been quiet," Ansel said, shooting Ever a sidelong glance.

Ever continued brushing the horse. It was disrespectful not to answer his father-in-law, and Garin would have given him a withering look for such behavior. But today, as with the night before, no words came. Ever simply had none left.

"I built this stable soon after we realized Isa would always struggle with walking," Ansel spoke again. If he was trying to make Ever feel better he wasn't doing a very good job. The last thing Ever wanted to think about was Isa's accident. But Ansel kept talking anyway. "Before that, we'd only ever needed one horse, so our old horse had made do with a lean-to that attached to the house. After her accident, though, I knew two horses wouldn't fit into the tiny space, and since I figured we would always have more than one horse after that, I thought I might as well build a decent stable."

Ansel stopped fiddling with the saddle he'd been mending and gave a distant smile. "You should have seen the look on her face when I brought her to the horse breeder. She immediately fell in love with this hulking midnight-black fellow, a giant of a horse.

233

But when we asked the owner how much, we found that we couldn't afford him, and I realized very quickly that bringing her along had been a mistake. I'd raised her hopes only to break her heart again." He sighed. "I cannot tell you how ashamed I felt the next day when I brought home the most pathetic, half-starved beast you'd ever seen. An acquaintance had offered him for less than a third of what the black steed would have cost.

"I felt like a failure as I finally presented her with that sad excuse for a horse." Ansel went back to the saddle he'd been working on. "Isa was not a begging child. There was only one thing in the world she had ever truly asked of me, and it killed me that I couldn't get it for her."

"What happened?" There were few topics in the world that could generally entice Ever from his worries, and stories of Isa's childhood were one of them.

Ansel smiled as he placed the saddle on one of the horses. "It is funny how the Maker uses our failures. Isa was disappointed to be sure. But that pathetic creature was in such poor condition that it was only a matter of minutes before she was fawning all over the poor beast, brushing out the snarls in its mane, bringing it carrots, and doing everything in her power to restore it to health." He paused. "I think that's when she truly began to heal... when she had another creature that needed her. And the Maker knew she would never find that with such a fine horse as the first fellow she saw.

"You know," he said, placing a calloused hand on Ever's work, forcing him to stop. With resignation, Ever turned to look Ansel in the face. The wrinkles around his mouth and eyes had deepened considerably in the last few years, and the hair that had been peppered gray and black when Ever had first met him was now mostly gray. He stood a tad shorter than Ever remembered, and his midsection was a good bit rounder. But the intensity in Ansel's gaze held Ever to the spot. "I see the fear in your eyes," Ansel said, "when you look at those children."

"I don't see why I shouldn't." Ever snorted. "The first thing everyone mentions is how much I am like my father. And the older I get, the more I see it in myself. Now I'm taking children into my home, and I find I have no home to take them to." He looked at Ansel, suddenly desperate for the older man to understand, though he really wasn't sure why. "What if I slip?" He went back to filling the saddlebags. "What if I can't protect them? How could they even want me for their father after what happened last night?"

"Are you regretting your decision then?"

"Of course not. I just pray to the Maker that I don't fail them as my father failed me."

"Oh, you will fail them. There is no question about that," Ansel said. Ever gave him a skeptical look, but the older man just shook his head. "Every father fails his children. And he does it again and again. What I have found, if you wish to take my humble experience, is that asking forgiveness ... and speaking *with* them instead of *at* them can strengthen our ties to our children far more than the best gifts ever could."

Ever chuckled without humor. "Now you sound like Garin."

"Good. At least one of us is—"

But before he could finish, Ever's skin prickled, and a scream sounded from the house. Ever dashed to the stable door. It was midday, and the sun nearly blinded him after being in the dark cool of the stable. After a second of squinting, he made out a broken window in the upper attic. Another scream sounded.

"Megane!" Ansel cried, but Ever was faster, his sword already drawn as he sprinted to the house. Before he could reach the back door, however, the house disappeared. Sand bit his eyes and tried to burrow into his skin, and the friendly noon sun became cruel and blisteringly hot. And there was nothing. Nothing for miles and miles except for dunes of loose sand and gales of wind blowing it around like walls of biting insects.

"What is this?" Ansel cried out.

"Don't believe what you see," Ever called back. "The Fae are here." But even as he spoke the words another shriek came from the direction that the house had been. It was Genny this time. Drawn by the scream, Ever began to push forward again, but just as he should have reached the house, a green whorl stood in his path. Ever stabbed at it, but the blade sliced through the cloud-like creature as though it weren't there at all. The green mist darted behind him, and Ever realized it was heading for his father-in-law who was still protesting, demanding to know where they were.

As the green mist began to whip around Ansel in circles, the older man stumbled and fell, fear filling his eyes as he beheld the ghostly creature. The green mist began to materialize into the shape of a woman, but before she could finish, her legs still invisible, she flipped her head and her strange green eyes widened as she looked at Ever.

What is she staring at? Ever looked down at his hand to see a ball of blue flame floating just above his palm. Then he remembered the Fae in the children's bedroom, as well as Garin's words.

Fae are sensitive to power of any kind. Even if it is one they can't use, they can still feel it.

"Cover your face!" Ever yelled to his father-in-law. "This might hurt!" As he spoke, Ever ran through the risks in his head. It was dangerous to gather too much power in a place as closely contained as the little city neighborhood. In his throne room, he had used the Fortress as his aid, and he had known exactly how well the great room could contain his strength. But here, with houses crowded beside one another and people still in the streets, there was always the chance his power would touch someone unintended.

Another scream sounded, but Ever couldn't tell whose it was. "Isa!" he shouted, hoping desperately that she could hear him. "I need to find the stable. I need to see!" He waited, holding just enough power to keep the Fae's attention. As he did, more Fae began to appear around him.

It wasn't fair of him to ask her to break their illusion. She hadn't been able to do it the day before, and there had been only two Fae in the children's room. But as the seconds ticked by, Ever knew he couldn't wait much longer. He began to inch his way to where the stable should have been. Each time he moved the Fae shimmered as though trying to awaken themselves from the spell he held them captive in, and he was forced to increase the fire just that much more. If he wasn't careful, the stable or house could go up in flames, and he wouldn't even be able to see it.

Just as he was about to give up that she'd heard him or that she was capable of breaking the vision, her familiar power pushed its way through, and the vision the Fae had cast cleared just enough for him to dart into the stable and leap upon one of the horses.

Much to his relief, the Fae gave chase. The faster he pushed, the more the vision faded, and Ever could once again make out Soudain's neat cobblestone streets. One glance back, however, told him that even more Fae had begun following him. Now that he was safely in the middle of the road and he could see, Ever increased the brightness of his fire, hoping it would draw Sacha's entire search party, however many that was.

But he hadn't expected the Fae to be quite so fast. Whether it was their desire to stay near his power or their rage at his escape, they began to gain on him. Ever pressed the horse harder, adding his strength to aid the beast's speed, all the while holding his left hand high to keep the Fae's attention. Once he was out of the city, he could lead them to a private place where he might take advantage of their obsession with his fire and pick them off one at a time. Then Isa and the children could make their escape.

But that, he realized as he glanced back again, was all contingent on getting the Fae out of the city's borders. Their green eyes glowed and their teeth gnashed as their horde continued to near

Ever's horse. He would need more than just a flat piece of farmland to fight them in. He would need someplace with obstacles where they couldn't all descend on him at once. Twice now he had clashed with the Fae, and twice he had nearly been killed in the process. He would need to do more than simply get out of the town.

He would need a miracle.

CHAPTER 29

DIVERSION

*P*lease, Ever begged the Fortress as he left the city, *I don't know what you wish me to do. But for their sakes, show me where to go even if it leads to my death!*

Just then, Ever remembered an underground cave five miles east of Soudain. The immediacy of the answer to his prayer was both relieving and a discomfort at the same time. Would this fight be his doom?

Ever nudged his horse off the main road and into a vineyard. He could barely see the raised lip of the cave over the edge of the vines. *Just a little longer*, he thought. But his arm shook with the effort of staying raised, and Ever gritted his teeth. *Just a little closer*. The cave would provide him some much-needed respite for his poor horse. And it would make the fight even.

Somehow he made it through the vineyard with his arm still up and then plummeted into the belly of the cave. His horse resisted, but Ever pushed him on into the dark, keeping to the walls of the cave as they skirted the pool of water that filled most of the cave. His blue fire threw strange shadows against the stone walls and the stalactites, which sparkled like knives hanging perilously from the ceiling. As he reached the back of the cave,

Ever extinguished his fire, leapt from his horse, and rolled behind a pillar of rock. The horse pounded back through the entrance, leaving Ever alone to face the beings which he could now hear entering the cave.

His confidence in the plan wavered as he counted the green mists floating in. He had expected perhaps six or seven, including those that had first sought out Isa and the children, but not fourteen. Still, he was too deep into his plan to back out now.

The mists floated cautiously above the pool, pausing hesitantly beneath the glow worm colonies that hung between the stalactites like stars in the dark of night. Ever began to inch his way back toward the entrance of the cave along the outer wall. It was highly tempting to break into a sprint every time a green mist drifted near him. But Ever forced himself to breathe through his nose and take his time.

Finally, he reached the entrance of the cave. Mild regret filled him as he placed his hands against the largest white sandstone pillar and began to push. He had loved visiting this cave as a child. Cracking sounds filled the air as Ever continued to press against the sandstone, sending the whorls into blurs of green agitation. By the time they seemed to realize what was afoot, however, it was too late. Ever rolled out of the way as the pillar crumbled and the entrance collapsed with a deafening crash.

Except for the light blue glow of the worms on the ceiling, the cave went completely dark. The water of the pool lapped up against its edges, the only sound to follow the great crash, until, for the first time, one of the Fae spoke.

"What do you plan for us here, oh son of Cassiel?" a thick voice called out, taking Ever by surprise. How did the Fae know of the Fortress's first king? "You know there are many more of us back at the castle."

Ever didn't answer, but instead squinted through the darkness as he moved to his hands and knees again and began to crawl toward the center of the cave. A change in the lapping of the water and that one of them had spoken with human words told Ever that at least some of the Fae had transformed into their more solid bodies. *Good.*

Ever continued to crawl as his fingers touched the water's edge, regretting that he couldn't first take off his boots. Wet feet would be miserable, but cutting his foot on unseen rocks at the bottom of the pool would be even more miserable. He could heal himself, of course, but that would take time and power, neither of which he had any to waste.

Ever had nearly reached the pool's center when a green mist that had been hovering above him began to take its more human form. Suddenly a leg appeared right where there had been none before. And he had run right into it.

"He's here!" a female voice cried.

Ever jumped up and punched his announcer right in what he guessed to be the nose. It must not have seen him, he realized, for rather than driving his hand through a shapeless green mist, his knuckles made a satisfying crunch as the creature went down. Buoyed, Ever lifted both his hands into the air. A ball of blue fire blazed between them, and this time, Ever didn't hold back. Hotter and hotter, the flames grew between his palms until the ball began to lift of its own accord into the air. Sweating with the effort of keeping it raised, Ever left one hand in the air to guide the fireball and unsheathed his sword with the other.

Just as he'd hoped, the remaining whorls changed into their human forms. With their mouths agape, they walked toward the fire. Ever retreated slowly to give them more room. He would have only one chance at this.

In the dance of blood that he knew only too well, Ever began to meet his enemies. One by one, they were felled. Garin had been right. Their thirst for the power, their draw to it would be their undoing. And Ever would have felt much worse about exploiting such a weakness if it hadn't been for the fearful cries of his new children still ringing in his ears.

And Garin's cry.

It wasn't long before Ever had taken out ten of the fourteen Fae. But as he continued to fight, relying more on his senses than his eyes in the blackness of the cave, he began to struggle. He wouldn't be able to hold the flaming globe aloft much longer. As he decided that his power would hold for four more minutes, the sound of splintering rock above him broke his concentration. Just before the blue flame fizzled out, Ever had time to witness a great crack running through the ceiling. As the crack continued to grow, he could hear the thousands of stone icicles above him began their own chorus of snaps and cracks.

A sharp pain in his left shoulder made him cry out. Warm blood began to seep down his arm as his globe of flame fell out of the air and died in the water. Before he had time to resume the fight, however, he was thrown to the ground by a body, and he choked on the water as he went down. Hot hands pressed down on his chest, keeping his face beneath the surface.

Ever did his best to lift his throbbing left arm up out of the water, but the pain made it nearly impossible. With a garbled shout, he torqued his body until his hand was free enough to reach up into the air. It fizzled as the blue fire struggled to light on his wet fingers. Just before he should have passed out, however, the fire grew strong, then fizzled out again. The distraction was short, but just long enough for Ever to shove the Fae off his chest with his sword.

Leaping to his feet, Ever realized the three remaining Fae had returned to their mist bodies. He wrapped the blue fire around his hand once again, but this time, it didn't burn as brightly or as blue. He was tiring and wouldn't last much longer. Never in his dozens of previous battles had he faced opponents like this.

Unfortunately, the remaining Fae seemed to have more self-control than their brothers and sisters that lay at Ever's feet, for the fire did not bring them to their bodies as it had the others.

Instead, they began to circle around him. As they did, however, more cracking sounded from above. Ever looked up just in time to see the cave ceiling begin its collapse. Rocks started to rain down upon them, small at first, but then growing in size and weight. Glow worms fell into the pool with the rocks, taking even more of the light with them. Ever was forced to duck and cover his head. For unlike the mists, he could be crushed.

Another loud tearing sound echoed throughout the round cave, and again, Ever was underwater. A large boulder pinned his left knee to the ground. He couldn't breathe. Gurgled laughs sounded as the three whorls morphed into distorted bodies that walked toward him.

Ever had never been burned by his own fire before, but as the desperate idea entered his head he wondered if this trick might just be his last one. His mind was made up, though, when a foot delivered a kick to his ribs. Ever dropped his sword and stretched his hands out before him. *Once more*, he told the Fortress.

Hesitation did not hold him back this time as it often did. There was no wondering about whether his power would be too much for his surroundings. Ever dug down to his core and mined every bit of strength he had left.

Placing his hands beneath the water, he let all of his power go. The wave of flame left his fingertips with a hiss, and the water that surrounded him sizzled as it cut through the air. The three Fae screamed as the scalding water hit, so hot it turned into its own mist.

Then all was quiet.

CHAPTER 30

THE HARD QUESTIONS

I'm cold," Genny moaned.

"We only have two blankets, and you've got one of them," Henri reminded her, less patient with his sister's demands than usual. The hot, dusty three-day ride had made him grumpy, and the hard floor beneath him now only made it worse.

"How about you snuggle with me?" Miss Isa reached over and drew the little girl close before wrapping her cloak around them both.

"I still don't understand why I can't use my fire," Henri mumbled.

"The Fae can sense power the way you do. If you use your power, they have a better chance of finding us. We need to stay quiet and hidden until we rejoin King Ever."

"When is King Ever coming?" Genny asked as Miss Isa rearranged their blankets.

"Soon, I hope," Miss Isa said as she leaned back against the hard wooden bench, but Henri could see the strain in her smile this time. After the king had dashed away with the Fae trailing him, Miss Isa and the children had bolted with what little supplies had already been packed upon the two remaining horses.

For who knew, Miss Isa had said, when more Fae would be sent? With tears and prayers, Miss Isa's family had sent them off, Miss Isa on one horse and Genny and Henri on the other.

The first day hadn't been so bad. On the contrary, Henri had felt like a warrior on a quest as they'd ridden through the countryside. But as they'd begun to draw closer to the southern forests, the pleasure had fled, and it was all Henri could do to keep from turning the horse around and racing right back to Miss Isa's family instead.

What he wouldn't give for a few more of Mrs. Marchand's cookies.

"I don't see why we have to stay here," Henri grumbled as he moved back up to the bench. Perhaps it would be more comfortable on the bench than the floor, though it hadn't been the last three times he'd tried. "Father Lucien is gone."

"Father Lucien must have been needed elsewhere," Miss Isa said. "But I know he would wish for us to rest within the church if he were here."

Henri frowned at the queen. The church had been locked up when they'd arrived, but she had shown no hesitancy in loosening one of the animal skins that covered the windows and climbing inside.

Breaking into the church wasn't exactly the kind of behavior Henri would have expected from the queen. He and Genny were the ones who were expected to break the rules, not her. It seemed wrong. But as the air had grown colder and dark had begun to fall, Henri had stopped objecting. Staying in the church seemed better than freezing out in the night.

They sat quietly for a long time as Genny's breathing became deep and even against Miss Isa's chest. They had no fire, as the church had no hearth, and it truly was beginning to grow chilly despite the fact that summer would soon be upon them. The dark of the night and the thin blanket Henri had wrapped around himself reminded him that he was tired as well, but he wasn't yet ready for sleep. They were too close to his old home, the cottage with the tree-smashed roof and nine years of memories that Henri would rather not possess. So instead, he decided to ask more questions.

"Why does that woman want us?"

Miss Isa looked at him, and even in the weak silvery light leaking in from the outside, Henri could see her look of surprise. They hadn't told him or his sister much about their enemy, but Henri had done enough eavesdropping to know that this mysterious woman was not a gentle spirit.

"I do not know," Miss Isa finally said. "I can only guess that she knows you are part Fae as well and thinks you should be within her ranks instead."

Huh. That was certainly not an outcome Henri desired. All his Fae blood ever seemed to do was get him in trouble. Living with people like him was the last thing he wanted. "If she's at the Fortress, then where are all of the soldiers? Shouldn't they have stopped her?"

"The king sent them to a secret place to wait until the time is right to retake the Fortress."

A brief silence lapsed before Henri decided to do something daring. It was the question he'd been dying to ask for weeks but hadn't had the courage. "Why have you kept us for so long?"

At this, Miss Isa frowned. And with each passing second of silence, Henri was sure she was searching for a way to tell him that they didn't want the children anymore, and that he and Genny would be sent off on their own as soon as possible. He and his sister had not been easy guests, he knew. They were too noisy and ate too much food. Genny was always whining for Miss Isa, and Henri seemed to be incapable of staying out of the king's way. So when Miss Isa finally answered him, he was taken completely by surprise.

"You need someone to love you." She paused before adding, "And we need someone to love us, too."

Henri gulped. Could she be saying what he hoped she was? There was only one way to find out.

"That boy from the story... Was he ever lonely?"

"Yes," Miss Isa murmured, sounding tired. "He had no brothers or sisters to play with, and most of the other children his age were afraid of what he could do."

"Does *he* want me?"

"Why do you ask?" Even in the muted light, Miss Isa looked weary as she held Genny and leaned back against the church bench, but Henri had to know. Because he was dangerously close to letting himself fall in love with a family who might not want to love him.

"I don't think he wants me," Henri continued. "I'm too much like him. And he doesn't like himself sometimes."

"He saved you, didn't he?"

Henri didn't answer. As though able to read his silence, Miss Isa pushed herself back up into a sitting position and reached out to take his hand. Henri tried to wiggle it free but the queen held firm.

"King Everard shows his love in a different way from many other people. He does things for others, keeping them safe and cared for. His father taught him to use a sword to show love instead of words. King Everard is learning to show his love in other ways now, but learning takes time." She smiled a bit. "Like the way you are learning to control your powers. Now," she yawned, "tomorrow will have its own troubles, but I think those troubles will be easier if we get some sleep tonight. Goodnight, Henri."

With a sigh, Henri obeyed. The queen's voice was sadder than he'd ever heard it. And though the king still made Henri nervous, Henri decided that he did indeed want the king to come back soon. For he could see how sad Miss Isa was without him. And the queen was too kind to be kept sad.

HENRI WAS AWAKENED some time later by the murmur of two voices. Stiffly, he rolled over to see a hulking form standing above the queen. Panic seized Henri as he tried to see her. Was she still breathing? Had the stranger hurt his sister?

"How is your knee?" Miss Isa's voice was quiet.

Relief made his limbs feel wobbly when he heard the king answer.

"It's a little sore, but it will be fine in a few days."

"You didn't *walk* here, did you?" She sounded alarmed.

"I had no choice. Your father's horse ran when I ducked into the cave. Hopefully, he went home. And don't worry, I healed it enough that I could run some."

There was a pause, and Henri guessed that the queen did not like that answer. Finally, she asked, "How long do you think until we reach them?"

The king groaned. "Four days at best. Maybe longer."

"Could you send Acelet a message, now that you know how to fight the Fae?"

Henri did his best to look like he was asleep. He didn't know why, but excitement tickled his chest when he realized they were talking about standing up to the enemy. He tried to peek at them from beneath his eyelids.

To his relief, the king had turned so that Henri could see what he was doing. He held up the ring he always wore, the one with the image of a wolf on the top. Its gold gleamed even in the low light.

"Launce knows not to accept any summons except this. I wasn't sure if my sister could create the illusion of me well enough to fool him, so he is not to follow a single word I say or send until he can hold this ring in his hand. Unfortunately," the king put the ring back on and ran his hand through his hair, "I couldn't find any birds when I arrived here."

"It was that way when we got here," Miss Isa said quietly.

Henri shivered at the memory. For as long as Henri could remember, Father Lucien had lived in the little windowless room behind the church. But when they had arrived that afternoon, Henri had nearly been sick at the sight of the blackened, torched hovel. The main room of the church had been left alone, but it didn't make him feel much better. Father Lucien, the one friend he'd had before the king and queen had come along, was gone, and the holy man hadn't left a clue behind as to where he went.

"How did you all fare?" the king asked.

"We did well enough. My father had at least packed us two blankets and enough food and water for a day. Yesterday we found a stream that had some apples nearby." She paused. "You would have been proud of Henri. A single Fae began to chase us after you left, but Henri was able to throw wads of his fire backward until it no longer followed us."

Henri nearly jumped when the king turned to look at him, the rings of fire burning into his eyes as though he'd known Henri was awake the entire time. Henri cringed, ready for the lecture. Instead, however, the king only stood and walked over to the bench where he lay. Laying a hand on Henri's arm, the king said quietly,

"You did well. I'm proud of you."

As the king then walked to the front of the church and lay on the bench closest to the door, Henri felt an immense wave of peace wash through him. For nearly a week, he had gone to sleep with the feeling of being chased. Even at the Fortress he'd slept poorly. But, for the first time in what felt like a long time, Henri let himself drift off to sleep. He felt safe.

CHAPTER 31

HOLD THEM TIGHT

Isa studied the set of Ever's shoulders as his horse led the way into the woods. Because they had only two horses instead of three, Isa and Ever had redistributed their weight by placing Genny with Ever on his horse and Henri on Isa's. Now as he held Genny in front of him, he appeared confident enough, his back straight and shoulders high. There were even moments during their trek when Isa believed him. But whenever she tried to peer into his heart, to reach out and touch the man inside, there was too much turmoil. Confidence, yes. But pain, too. Duty. Abandonment. Longing.

"I don't like that tree." Genny's little voice interrupted Isa's musings.

"And why is that?" Despite his volatile mood, Ever sounded amused.

"It dropped me."

"You mean you fell out of it." Henri smirked.

Isa laughed, a strange sound in the midst of the skinny, crooked trees and the sickly yellow light that filtered through them. How she longed to be free of these oppressive woods. Heavy rains had kept them inside the church for the majority of the morning. Ever had gone out to inspect the tree from which Sacha had made her appearances, but nothing had been revealed. He had more faith, however, that they would find answers back at the cottage Sacha had lured the children to, which was still a day's ride away. That, he felt, was where the original tear between realms would be.

They found a place to spend the night just before the sun set. By then they had traveled deep enough into the woods that the light was weak, and Ever didn't want to be caught unawares in the dark without a fire. As soon as the horses had been watered, Ever made a little fire no larger than the size of his fist, though he used natural means so as not to attract any wandering Fae's attention. Then Henri showed him how to set a trap to catch a hare. Isa couldn't help giggling to herself as she watched that unfold, for Ever's annoyance at not knowing how to carry out the simple skill was expressed through his continually deepening scowl. Before long, however, two hares were caught, and everyone settled down to a hot supper.

"King Ever, I have a question."

Ever froze, his wide eyes meeting Isa's. Isa was just as surprised. Since arriving at the Fortress, Henri had done his best to avoid Ever, answering his questions in as few words as possible. And he had never spoken to Ever voluntarily.

"When you heal," Henri continued, "does your fire burn the people you touch?"

"No," Ever said slowly. "Why?"

"I have fire, but I can't heal people. I only burn them." Henri frowned and held out his hands. "My gift doesn't seem very useful."

"You might be surprised," Ever said, taking another piece of meat from their makeshift spit. "With the proper training, you could learn to use your fire in many ways."

"Do you have fire?" Genny asked Isa.

"A little, when I need it. My gift is different than King

Ever's, but I can use the Fortress's fire for small things." Isa hated calling Ever by his title in front of the children. After all, he was their father now. But there hadn't yet been a time that felt right to tell the children about their adoption. It was not the kind of information one could spring on a child right before bed.

"I wish I had a gift." Genny pouted. "Henri can at least make fire. I can't do anything!"

"Now, Genny, your smile alone is full of magic." Isa tickled the little girl.

But Henri wasn't looking at them. He was still staring at Ever. "How do you make your fire heal?"

"Give me your hand," Ever said. Henri stared at him for a long moment before ever so slowly raising his right hand. Ever reached over and took it, placing it inside his own large hand. Henri looked nervous as Ever closed his hand over the boy's. "Do you feel that?" Blue fire engulfed both their hands.

Henri nodded.

"Good. That is my fire as it comes to me, raw and undisciplined as yours is."

"I can control it," Henri grumbled.

"Somewhat. But now feel the difference." The flame began to dance. Most humans wouldn't have been able to feel it, but Isa could, and even Genny's eyes grew rounder as Ever's fire changed its rhythmic pulsing. "It has taken me years of practice to achieve such, but I have trained my fire to do more than burn air. Instead, it can move through substances as well as people. I recently healed a man who struggled with fits of coughing."

"How?"

"Ever," Isa murmured, hating to break the moment, "the Fae might sense you."

Ever let go of the boy's hand and the fire disappeared. "I sent my fire into his blood. As it traveled his body, it purged him of the illness that resided within it. As fire takes away dross from gold, so can my fire do with sicknesses. It can also speed healing of skin and bones."

"That sounds impossible." Henri rubbed his hand.

"It is not my place to judge what is or is not impossible," Ever said, returning to his food. "Only to trust that the Fortress will do as the Maker wishes it to. I must be willing to serve as a vessel for those choices, whether that be in humility or victory."

Henri looked thoughtful but said no more. After supper, Isa wrapped each child in one of the blankets. Within a few minutes, Henri fell asleep, his head resting against one of Isa's legs. Genny, however, had other plans. Without a word, she marched up to Ever before turning and plopping herself in his lap. Ever looked at Isa with panic in his eyes, but Isa only smiled. So many times she'd imagined her husband cradling a child in his lap. And now he was, albeit involuntarily.

Still, as the little girl curled up in his arms, wonder filled Ever's eyes. Softly, so softly, he reached up and stroked her hair, and for the first time that day, Isa felt peace ripple through her husband like a little stone in a pond.

It seemed that Isa had no sooner closed her eyes than a distant explosion jolted her awake. Lightning filled the sky's holes in the forest canopy above them, lighting up the trees like daggers in the night. Isa turned to pull Henri to his feet, but Ever was already ahead of her and had both children off the ground. In no time, both the children were on the horses, and Ever and Isa were leading them on foot, though where they were going Isa had not the slightest idea. She thought she heard Ever saying something about ruining the horse's feet in a forest as this. But their progress on foot was slow at best, and the storm continued to build as it chased them deeper into the heart of the woods.

"Will we make it to the cottage?" Isa yelled over the wind.

"No!" Ever shouted back, squinting through the rain that was beginning to pelt them more steadily. "It's too far!"

"We can't stay out in this!"

As if to agree, a bolt of lightning struck a tree just behind them, and as it fell, Isa and Ever had to swerve dangerously, making their horses squeal in protest. Isa prayed the children would hold on.

"Wait!" Henri's call was so frantic that Isa slowed just a hair to look back at him. "I know where we are!" he shouted. "My old cottage is just that way!" Henri pointed south. "A tree fell on it, but we'll be out of the rain!"

Immediately, Ever turned and began to lead his charges south. As they ran, Isa prayed that the children's parents had not died in the cottage as Henri thought they had. *For the children's sakes,* she begged the Maker, *let someone have come and taken the bodies!*

But as they continued to push on, Isa made out what looked like a light up ahead of them, a faint yellow glow against the black of the forest. It was a lantern, she realized, which hung in the window of a fully functional little cottage. She thought about asking Henri if this was a different cottage, but a bolt of lightning struck so close that a tree not thirty feet away caught fire.

Moments later, they reached the cottage. Ever dragged both children off the horses and pushed them under the eaves with Isa, then he practically shoved the horses into the pathetic little lean-to that stood beside the house. "In!" he ordered, throwing the door open.

None too soon, either, for as soon as the door was closed, another tree even closer to the cottage burst into flames behind them.

"That was close," Isa murmured as she looked at her little band. They were all dripping and looked quite disheveled. They were also all staring in the same direction. Ever's face was drawn into a tight frown, and Genny's was one of timidity. Henri looked as though he might faint. When Isa turned to see what they were looking at, she found herself staring at two commoners, a man and a woman.

The man was stocky and short with a scraggly brown beard, and the woman was lean with a pinched face. They had been eating at the little wooden table just to the left of a glowing hearth, but now they both stood, looking as though they wanted to run.

Isa had thought at one point that her heart couldn't break any further. In the last few months, she had lost her home, her friends, Garin, her kingdom, and her hope of ever bearing a child. But she had been wrong. For the single word that Henri uttered caused her more pain than she could have known possible.

"Father."

CHAPTER 32

A LUCKY THING

The king looked down at Henri. "I thought you said your father was dead."

"But a tree fell on the roof..." Henri trailed off, looking back at his father. It was wrong, but he somehow felt more bothered by Claude's life than he had been by his death. Henri had seen the tree and the smashed roof. But as he looked around now, Henri realized that the house had been completely repaired. New glass windows were in place, unfamiliar stones strengthened the walls, and the roof was even higher than it had been before.

"Your Highnesses!" his father sputtered, finally seeming to awaken from his initial stupor before turning to his wife. "Don't jus' stand there gapin' like a fish, woman! Get 'em something to eat!"

Helaine blinked a few times before nodding blankly at Henri's father. But the look she sent Henri and Genny over her shoulder made Henri cringe. *That* look often came with an ear boxing.

"Forgive us for intruding," King Ever said in a tight voice. "I am King Everard Fortier, and this is my wife, Queen Isabelle. We were out in the forest when the storm hit. I appreciate your hospitality."

"Of ... of course, Your Majesties. I seen you before. In the town, I mean. Allow me to introduce m'self." Henri's father gulped. "My name is Claude Biscoup. This here is my wife, Helaine. And you, boy," he looked down at Henri, "go get some more firewood for our guests."

Henri swallowed the storm of feelings that raged inside him as he prepared to face the storm again, but a hand placed itself firmly on his shoulder, pinning him to the spot. Henri looked up to see the king glaring at Claude.

"He will do no such thing," the king's voice rumbled. "It is dangerous."

Henri could have hugged him.

"I want to go home," Genny whimpered, turning to Miss Isa and wrapping her arms around Miss Isa's legs. But the queen was distracted, too, staring furiously at Helaine much in the way King Ever was doing with Claude. A long, awkward silence stretched between the four adults.

"Thank ye for bringing our children back," the woodcutter finally mumbled, looking at his feet as he spoke. "We was looking for them for quite some time now."

"The boy says they became lost in the woods. Twice." The king's reply was icy. "They even found their way back once to find the cottage destroyed."

"Storm did that while we was out looking for the little buggers," Claude muttered.

"Of course." But the king's face was dark, and his mouth was in a tight line.

"I'm sure once you've eaten and warmed and the storm is over," Claude nodded at the window, "that you and Her Majesty will wish to be on your ways?"

Henri's chest suddenly tightened, and he silently begged the Fortress not to let the king push his father too far. Once the king and queen had gone, he and Genny would be all alone again. And who knew what kind of punishment Claude and Helaine would pour upon them for their subsequent humiliation?

Henri hadn't realized just how much he wanted to stay with the king and queen until he had seen his father and Helaine again. His stomach twisted into a knot. The king had moods, to be sure, but so did Claude. And at least the king's moods had a purpose. Claude's moods, and worse, Helaine's, could come at any time, often ending in purple and blue marks on his and Genny's skin. And for all of King Ever's stern words and expectant looks, never once had he struck either Henri or Genny in anger. Of course, this thought only made Henri shake harder.

"Actually," the king said, his grip tightening on Henri's shoulder, "we are in need of a place to pass the night. I am sure it will not be an imposition to stay here with you."

"As you wish, sire." Claude bowed his head and turned to throw another log into the fire.

"You two!" Helaine's grating voice snapped. "To bed with you. It is late, and you will be worthless in the morn if you get no sleep now."

Henri knew Helaine would make him regret it later, but he dared a glance up at the king, wishing suddenly with all of his heart that the king would carry them away again just as quickly as they'd come. Henri would never run in the Fortress halls again or spill the king's wine, and he would keep a tighter rein upon Genny. But King Ever only gave him one slow nod.

Surprisingly, Genny did as she was told, something Henri gave silent thanks for. But in spite of that miracle, wretched tears threatened to escape from his eyes as he slumped forward to obey his stepmother. It felt strange to lie upon the scratchy straw mat with Genny, now that he was used to sleeping in nightclothes and in the palace bed all his own. But the itchy straw pallet and lack of bedclothes were the least of Henri's worries.

Witch or no witch in the Fortress, Henri knew that under no

circumstance could he live in this house again. Never again could he watch his stepmother lay a hand on his sister, nor could he endure his father's cruel words. After the king and queen left them, they would run to Soudain. He didn't know how, as they had no horse, nor did they have any food, but he would get them there somehow. Perhaps Miss Isa's parents would allow him to work in their store. They seemed nice enough. Anything was better than living unwanted and despised.

A lone tear rolled down his cheek.

"It's a lucky thing you're getting rid of these ones," Helaine was saying in a sour voice. "They're no innocents like other children their age."

"How did they come to wander in the forest alone?" Miss Isa asked, ignoring Helaine's comment. Henri wanted badly to see her face as she asked such a bold question, but he didn't dare. Helaine would double his punishment in the morning.

"They were out in a storm," Helaine said uneasily. "My husband had been cutting wood in the deeper parts of the forest. Some parts of the woods is more confusing than others. Anyhows, Claude here turned to find them when the storm got closer, and that's when he found they were gone. None too convenient, either. The lightning just got so close he had to come home. Nearly killed us it did." She paused. "The witch got them the next day when we went looking for them again."

The queen said something else, but Henri didn't hear what it was. Instead, his heart began to pound, and he began to shiver all over. Helaine was lying. Her story hadn't at all been how he and Genny had become lost. Such, though, he had expected from her.

But how did she know that Henri and Genny had been captured by the witch?

CHAPTER 33

HALF-TRUTHS AND QUANDRIES

You're lying." Isa interrupted whatever gibberish the pale, stinking woman was spewing. Ever had been considering interjecting with some objection of his own, but Isa's quiet tone promised danger. Claude and Helaine stared back at her blankly.

"What happened? In truth." Isa leveled a dark look at them, Helaine in particular. Her voice was perfectly calm, like a lake of ice. But Ever knew that deep inside her heart must be breaking.

What Ever couldn't understand was how Henri and Genny had come under the care of this worthless man and his awful wife in the first place. Despite the fact that his world was falling apart back at the Fortress, Ever suddenly needed to know. It made sense, of course, that Rodrigue's mistress, the children's true mother, might not have wanted to raise the children in the Fae world. But if this couple disliked the children as much as they obviously did, then why had they kept the children for so many years before getting rid of them? Did they know where the mistress was? Did they know that the children had royal blood? Fortunately for Ever, he didn't have to ask many questions to get his answers. It seemed Isa would do all of that and more for him.

She was still glaring at the silent couple across the rough wooden table.

"I would answer her," Ever warned them.

"I am not their mother!" Helaine blurted out.

"So the children have told us," Isa said.

"They belong to my first wife," the woodcutter added.

"Well," Isa asked after a moment of silence, "do you care to explain? Or shall I make you?" She raised an eyebrow, daring him to refuse.

"She was an odd little thing," Claude sighed. "Half starved 'n half mad when I found her in the gutter of a village not far from here. Kept mutterin' that the king was her father. I thought it was the hunger 'twas driving her mad, so I brought her back to the village church and asked her to marry me. Told her I'd feed her 'n give her a home." He paused. "Never thought the madness would stay after she was fed and rested," he then added with a grumble.

His first wife? Ever was reeling. Sacha was the children's *mother?*

"Her mouth was so dry she could barely say the vows—"

"You didn't have the decency to get her to her right mind before wedding her?" Ever interrupted in disgust. "You couldn't even wet her tongue?" His voice was louder than he'd meant it to be, and the man shrank back like a frightened rat. *Good.* When Ever glanced at Isa, however, he realized she didn't seem nearly as surprised by this sham of a marriage as he was. Only angry. How common was this kind of marriage, where one could carry the other away and the holy man would oversee the vows without question?

"I didn't want nobody to think I was bein' indecent with 'er." Claude swallowed loudly.

"Continue," Isa said.

"We... We gets home, and she has a fit. 'I can't find the veil,' she says over and over again. It was a few weeks with me before she stopped talking so much nonsense. Liked to take long walks in the woods, though. And never got terribly fond of me."

"Did she ever find anything on her walks?" Isa asked.

"Not for a long while. Another few months and she was too heavy with the boy to walk far anymore." The woodcutter frowned, scratching his wide chin for a moment. "I didn't know what she was until after the boy came, though." He glanced at Henri, who now snored quietly in the corner beside his sister. "I soon found that she an' him could do things... Came in one day to see them playing with fire!"

"What were they doing?" Ever leaned forward. He had an idea as to what Claude meant, but he wanted to hear more about Sacha's abilities. And Henri's.

The woodcutter held up a rough, meaty hand. "The boy was makin' some sort of fire with his fingers, rolling it and bouncing it upon them, and she was watchin'." Claude shivered. "When I saw th' look on her face as she watched our son, I figured for the first time that she was no ordinary woman. An' she was different after that. Like another creature. Somethin' had changed her. Somethin' like," he leaned forward and whispered, "the Sorthileige."

"What did you do after that?" Ever asked.

The woodcutter just shrugged. "What could I do? She was short-tempered and did as she pleased. Still went on walks every day. Left the boy with me most hours."

Would it kill him, Ever wondered, *to ever use his son's name?*

"Few years later we had Genevieve. As soon as she saw the child, she insisted on walking again, though she was dirty and still breathing hard from the birthing bed. Still didn't find nothin'. Began to get even more ill-tempered. It became that if I displeased her, something unpleasant would happen the next day. She all but stopped talking t'the boy. Would come back from her walks with books and such. I can't read, but they gave me shivers enough whenever I looked at 'em."

Ever was beginning to see why Henri had spent so many hours at the church instead of at home.

Claude sighed. "I knew that it wouldn't be long then from the look she got in her eyes whenever she looked at the children. Sure enough, soon as the girl was weaned, barely over a year, Sacha went for her usual morning walk. Never came back. After she left, I had the holy man come and bless the house." Claude's voice cracked as he stared hard at the table. "'Twas a house of darkness."

Ever glanced at Isa, but her face gave nothing away. "Is that why you remarried?" she asked.

Poor Isa. She must have been dying on the inside to hear how these children she loved so much had been cast off. And, Ever found, it angered him too.

Claude nodded hesitantly, the silver in his beard glinting slightly in the firelight as he mumbled something about not being able to care for two young ones on his own.

"And I tried!" Helaine squawked. "But soon it was obvious that boy had witch powers in him. He would set things on fire! The house, the woodpile, even—"

As she prattled on, Ever couldn't help but think that it was a wonder Henri hadn't caused any more accidents than he already had, especially with someone like her around to make him doubt and hate himself so much.

"You still," Isa snapped, "haven't explained how the children got lost in a place where they had lived all their lives. Why would they get lost here? And why now?"

Claude didn't answer. Instead he turned to his wife and slightly lifted a brow. Her gaze flitted back and forth between her husband and Isa before finally nodding and making a subtle noise with her throat.

"Before the children were lost, unlucky things started to happen. Accidents befell us. Common and uncommon sicknesses, fire... even more than the boy's usual upsets," Claude whispered. "I knew it was her, calling them. I could feel her near."

"So you *gave* them to her?" Ever stood so fast his chair flipped backward with a bang, but he didn't care. "You are their *father*!"

"What could I do against her?" Claude blanched, holding his hairy arms out before him. "With all due respect, Your Majesty, you have never been in my place, nor do y'know what you would've done, what with Her Majesty not being able—"

"I would never have traded them for mere peace and quiet! I can promise you that." Ever spoke through clenched teeth, leaning over the table so that his nose nearly touched the large man's face.

"Hold on," Isa said. "You say you heard her *calling* for the children?"

"More or less."

Isa stared at Claude. Her dark blue eyes flashed as Ever felt her reach out with her power and wrench the man's soul out from its hiding place. And she didn't do it gently, for which he was glad.

"Oh, just tell them!" Helaine crossed her arms and rolled her eyes.

Claude made a gagging sound as Ever felt Isa release him from her stronghold. "She came to us, and we made a deal."

Ever had a mouthful of words that he wanted to shout at the man, including a few words in particular that he rarely uttered. Before he could, though, Isa turned to him with fear in her eyes.

"She was the one who placed us together!"

"What?"

Isa shook her head impatiently. "When I hit my head and fell through the tear, Sacha was the one who placed me with the children! They weren't there by accident. And neither was I. She *wanted* me to fall in love with them! Ever!" Isa covered her mouth. "She's planned this from the very start!"

Ever stared back into her eyes as the words sank in. The whole thing had been a trap.

"Get the children."

Isa scrambled to do as he said, but Claude protested.

"You can't just take my children! You just brought 'em back!"

"You said yourself that you cannot protect them." Ever grabbed the stocky man by the arm, satisfied when he heard something snap. "I'm not about to leave them with someone who would use them again to purchase peace of mind." With that, he turned and stormed over to where Isa had awakened Henri and was trying to rouse Genny. Ever scooped the little girl up in his arms and strode toward the door. "We're going. Now."

CHAPTER 34

THE RIGHT THING

"Ever," Isa called softly as he placed Henri in front of her and then lifted Genny up onto his horse with him. Henri stirred in her arms but quickly settled into another doze. Ever didn't answer her, so she called his name again and finally moved her horse in front of his to make him stop. When his eyes met hers, they were full of a kind of pain Isa had never seen before. And yet, she had to ask. "What are we doing?"

"We're going to meet your brother. You and the children will stay with him, and I will come back and look for the veil's tear."

"But, Ever, these aren't our children," she said, her voice breaking.

"We can't simply leave them with him—"

"I know that." She prayed for the right words. "But I just need to be sure we're doing the right thing." Isa paused. "They're hers, too," she whispered.

"Well, what do you propose we do?" he demanded. "Leave them with the father who gave them up to his wife of darkness? Or should we leave them to the Fae when she sends another creature to chase them?"

A tear slipped down Isa's cheek in the dark. That hurt. "Of course not," she said. She wanted them so badly it hurt. Every moment she held Henri's sleeping form close it broke her heart just a little more. They had said the vows. For one fleeting moment, she had been a mother.

They sat silently, not looking at one another as the sounds of the forest echoed around them. Thank the Maker the storm had abated, although thunder would have been a welcomed alternative to the brittle quiet now. Finally, in the thin light of the moon Isa could see Ever rub his face with his hand, the stubble of his untrimmed beard making a scratching sound as he did. "We need to keep going."

Isa nodded and nudged her horse forward.

Hours slipped by as they passed through the forest. Isa could feel tingles run up and down her bones, some stronger than others, as they went. The darkness that seeped out of nooks and crannies beneath stones and in the shadows of the trees was cold and wet and made her shiver. Never had she felt the Sorthileige in so many places. How had they been so naive as to think the dark magic had been nearly banished from their land? But then again, they had been blind enough to miss the children's true connection to Sacha. It seemed so obvious now.

"Where are we?" Henri raised his head and rubbed his eyes.

"You won't be staying with them after all," Isa said into his hair, not answering his question.

"Is it because they lost us on purpose?"

How much did he know?

"Some of it, yes," Isa said cautiously, wishing she could see his face better, rather than sitting behind him.

"Why would my father do that?" Henri asked then, his voice suddenly angrier than Isa had ever heard it.

"Because some men are just bastards," Ever growled. Isa shot him a pointed look, but Ever just ignored it.

Another silence stretched until the fuzzy gray of morning began to break through the trees. Finally, Isa worked up enough courage to ask Henri a question she knew might hurt him. But it had to be asked.

"Henri, did you recognize the woman who tended to us in the Fae world? The one who brought me to you, and who gave you cookies?"

"No." To Isa's great relief, Henri shook his head. "Why? Are you going to give us to her?"

"We will be doing no such thing," Ever said in a stern voice. "It's still early. You need to go back to sleep."

To Isa's surprise, the boy only gave Ever a long look before nodding slightly and leaning back against her. In only a few minutes he was snoring lightly.

"I'm sorry," Ever said. When Isa looked over at him, his gray, fire-ringed eyes were burning into hers.

"For what?"

"For how I spoke with you earlier." He sighed. "It was just ... In the moment the bastard admitted to giving them up, I finally understood the pain you must have been feeling for so long. I ... I *wanted* them."

Isa's eyes must have been ridiculously wide as she listened, but she was too enthralled to care.

"I've always wanted an heir," he continued. "It was expected, just a part of life. But now... now I want children. *These* children. And it kills me that I cannot change the life they've had to live when I have been only a short distance away. And the things that monster did to my sister?" He shrugged helplessly. "Maybe I could have prevented all of this long ago. Or at least much of it."

Isa sighed as he spoke. Once again, her husband had managed to hide a world of pain from even her. And yet her heart soared as it dawned on her that she was no longer alone in such longing. That he felt it too.

"There's no use in such thinking," she finally whispered. "You had no way of knowing what your father had done."

Ever moved his horse closer so he could reach out and gently squeeze her arm. "You asked if we were doing the right thing in taking them from their old home. They might not be my siblings, but they are still my father's grandchildren, which makes them children of the Fortress. Let us content ourselves for now knowing that we are still protecting them. And that's what matters." He paused. "We will sort it all out when things are better and the danger is not so high."

In the early morning light, Isa wondered again at just how incredibly striking her husband was. The sharp angles of his face and the way the gray light reflected off his armor made him look fierce. But the vulnerable, gentle way he was looking into her eyes now made her want to melt. Suddenly, her tired muscles felt loose and relaxed, and Isa felt a serenity that she hadn't felt in a very, very long time. It was with a sudden intensity that she longed to draw him close and kiss him as she never had before, to hold his face in her hands and to run her hand through his short golden hair. Had she ever loved him so much? Had she ever needed him so much?

"How are you feeling?" he asked, the kindness still on his face as he searched hers.

"I might have been helping the children sleep, so a bit more tired than I would have been otherwise, but," she paused and smiled, "I don't think I have ever been better or happier in my life."

The look Ever gave her was a reward itself, for just then the sun rose and set his golden hair aflame, and his smile was like its own beam of light.

Oh, why did they have to be running for their life just at this moment? She would much rather have spent it with her lips on his, holding him tightly against her away from harm and sorrow.

Just as she began to say as much, Henri startled awake, and then Genny. The brother and sister briefly looked at one another before Henri twisted around to look at Isa, his eyes troubled. Green mist floated through his irises as he gazed up at her.

"Someone's coming."

CHAPTER 35
MOTHER

Isa tightened her grip on Henri as dozens of blank-faced men and women with pikes made a half circle about them. Sacha rode to the center of the semicircle and stood before Isa and Ever on her own horse. Isa wanted to scream in frustration. How had she found them? Then she remembered the two miserable creatures back in the cottage they had just left.

"You." Sacha turned to a nearby male. Wordlessly, he came and helped her down from her horse, where she stood and stretched for a moment before speaking. From the way she moved, Isa guessed Sacha was not used to riding horses for long distances. Isa hoped the witch's behind would bruise. She also wished bruises upon the two degenerates they had just left behind. Sacha must have been just on their trail the whole time.

"Henri."

Isa tensed as Sacha turned to her son.

The woman's voice was gentler than Isa had ever heard it. "Do you remember me?"

Henri leaned back into Isa as he studied the woman before him. "No." He paused. "Wait. You were the woman in the other world, the one who gave us cookies."

"Yes, that was me. But do you not remember me from before?"

Henri shook his head, and a brief flash of pain lit the woman's face before she smiled again.

"I'm your mum. Your *real* mum." When Henri didn't respond, she picked up a nearby stone and set it flat in her palm. With the snap of her fingers, she set the stone on fire and began to roll it along her fingers. "Do you remember," she whispered, "when we used to do this together?"

"That's Henri's trick!" Genny said, pointing.

But Henri stiffened beneath Isa's arm. "You look different from her."

She smiled wryly. "I look like the queen I am now, if that's what you mean." She eyed him up and down. "Just as you have come to look like the prince you truly are."

Isa closed her eyes briefly and tried to test the woman's heart. What was she up to, trying to contact the children she had abandoned? And why now? But unfortunately, it seemed that Sacha could be just as skilled at masking her feelings and intentions as her brother. What little Isa could taste was fear. But what was Sacha afraid of?

Sacha walked a few steps closer, and Isa clutched the boy more tightly to her until Henri turned and looked at Isa directly, his blue eyes full of questions.

"You knew she was my mother?"

"Your father only told us last night," Isa said, her throat tight.

Sacha's face was beginning to redden, and she had taken one more step toward them when Genny spoke up.

"King Ever, who's that?"

"My darling!" Sacha turned to the little girl as though just remembering that she had a daughter too.

Ever's eyes burned more brightly, and like Isa, he squeezed the little girl closer to his broad chest.

"You don't remember me," Sacha stretched her hand out, "but I'm your mummy!" Genny leaned back into Ever and frowned, but

Sacha continued to stretch both arms out. "Give me my daughter," she said in a strained voice. "I have not held her since she was a babe."

"An injustice that is your fault entirely. If you think I am going to willingly hand over a child that you sent a violent Fae to fetch *after* you abandoned her twice, then you are sorely mistaken." Ever drew his sword with the arm not holding Genny. "Either of these children, for that matter."

In response, Isa drew her own sword, and the soldiers began to thin into green mists, staying just solid enough to hold their pikes. Sacha drew her sword as well.

In one swift move, Ever was off his horse and had wedged Genny in the little space between Isa and Henri. He slapped her horse on the rump. "Go!" he shouted. Just as her horse turned, however, it stopped and reared. Pain shot through Isa as she was slammed to the ground. Genny landed on her chest and Henri on her legs.

She wasn't allowed to recover her breath, though, for the Fae were upon them immediately. Green mists faded in and out as the Fae moved between forms like dozens of green snowflakes melting and then freezing once again. Isa leapt to her feet as well as she could, still holding Genny against her legs as Henri scrambled up to stand beside her.

Fortress, she cried out inside, *I will not pretend to know what you are about here, but please protect your children, just as you promised!*

Bringing her sword up, Isa could feel the Fortress's power move out of her like rain bursting forth from a storm cloud, heavy and dark. It was not the heart power that she usually felt, but rather the same fiery strength that Ever possessed. And today, it was hers.

Genny shrieked as the first Fae made its attack, thickening again and grabbing its pike from the ground as it moved toward them. But Isa met his attack easily. As more and more Fae, male and female, tried to touch Isa with the poisonous pikes, Isa could feel the power of the Fortress pulsing around and through her. The Fae gnashed the teeth in their blank, simple faces, but no matter how many seemed to pile in around them, only one at a time could step through the blue whirlwind of fire that surrounded her and the children. And Isa was more than ready, all thoughts of exhaustion gone as Genny pressed in at her legs and Henri at her side. The attacks continued to come, but each only further ignited Isa's raw determination to keep them safe.

Ever seemed to have received no such respite. The flash of his sword against his sister's was blinding, lightning striking repeatedly as they clashed. Isa peeked at them between her opponents' attacks and was dismayed to see that Sacha seemed to be just as skilled with the sword as Ever. Even her twists and turns were familiar as they battled over the rocky, pinecone-littered terrain. For the first time in her life, Isa wondered if Ever would defeat his opponent. His sister's power was palpable and her moves swift and deadly. His many times in battle should have given him the edge. But the rage Isa could feel radiating from Sacha's heart was vicious.

A shriek from Genny snapped Ever's head toward them and reminded Isa of her own fight. She had become lazy in her defenses. A female Fae had edged closer to them, despite the fire wind's blanket of safety. Isa quickly knocked the pike from the woman's hands, but the damage had been done. Ever's distraction had given Sacha the chance to spring at him and knock his sword out of his hand. Ever immediately grabbed Sacha's wrist, the one that held her sword. Back and forth the sword went, first closer to one face and then to the other. Ever cried out, though, when Sacha delivered a kick to his bad knee.

The Fae stopped attacking Isa, also watching their leader face off with Destin's king. The longer the siblings fought, however, for control of the sword, the more Ever began to lose his ground. The angle at which he gripped the sword was awkward, and Sacha had the higher ground.

"Stop!"

Everyone, even Sacha and Ever, turned to look at Henri. Before Isa could stop him, he broke away from her, darting through the dying fire wind and changing green mists, throwing himself between Ever and Sacha. "We're going with my mother. Genny and me."

Isa turned to resume her fight, for there was no way she and Ever would allow such a thing. But for the second time that day, she was tossed to the ground so hard her vision spun. A blurry figure pulled Genny from Isa's arms and carried her away. Not far off, Ever cried out. Then all went black.

CHAPTER 36

NOT HERS

Two whole days of travel passed before Henri could gather the courage to talk to his mother.

His mother. What a strange thing to say.

It seemed wrong to call her *Mother* when she was the one who had sentenced King Ever and Miss Isa to ride behind them as captives even after his sacrifice.

He had hoped that upon giving himself up and going with the new woman, the king and queen would be allowed to run to her brother as they had planned to do. Then they could return to the Fortress and save them all. He had never expected the Fae to strike Miss Isa upon the head, or worse, for another to stab the king. The pike head had gone so far into the king's shoulder that the two leaves tied to it had also been buried in the flesh. Now as they rode the king's face was deathly pale, and his body shuddered from time to time. He might have fallen off his horse if they hadn't tied him to it.

Perhaps, if Henri were brave enough, he might convince his mother to be kinder to them. Maybe, at the very least, she might let the king have some water.

Henri swallowed hard, clutching Genny tightly to his chest,

before riding up beside his mother's horse. As he did, he was thankful again that Miss Isa had taught him to ride a horse so he didn't have to ride with one of the blank-faced Fae that surrounded them.

"How do you know him?" he asked.

"Hm, what?" His mother shook her head as though awakening from a daydream.

He repeated his question.

"Henri, that man is my younger brother, your uncle."

"Our uncle? Then why didn't we meet him before?"

"Oh, he was too busy guarding his riches and wealth and training his precious army." Her eyes glinted the way Genny's did when she was about to throw a fit. Henri would have to tread carefully.

"Is he why you left?" he asked.

She turned to look down at him, and her eyes softened. "In a way, I suppose."

"Because you wanted to see him?"

At this, her eyes bulged. "Why would I do that?" Henri looked down at the ground that passed beneath them, but his mother continued. "Why would I visit the man who lived only days away and let his nephew and niece nearly starve to death? That man is dangerous, cruel, and selfish, not at all the man he's tricked you into thinking he is. Never doubt for a moment that Everard Fortier is an instrument of evil." Her frown deepened. "Just as my father was." She stopped talking for a moment and studied Henri for the first time since she'd met them in the forest two days before. "Out of curiosity, why do you ask?"

Henri had to take a deep breath as he struggled to hold her gaze. What he wanted to say seemed very much like it would make her angry. That the things she and her people had done to the king and queen were cruel and nothing like what he could ever do to Genny, even if he were very angry with her. "I... I don't remember you much," he finally said in a low voice. Not a true answer to her question, but it seemed to appease her, for the intense glare once again softened on her face.

"What do you remember?"

"You taught me my trick." He held up his hand and briefly rolled a little ball of blue flame between his fingers.

She nodded. "What else?"

Henri looked back down at his sister's curly yellow hair. She hadn't said a word since the king and queen had been tied up. Not even their mother's best pleading and promises of treats had gotten her to speak. And, Henri realized with annoyance, she really didn't have any reason to. He might have vague memories of his mother's face, the way her chin had a handsome tilt to it, or how she rolled the fire around her fingers. But when it came to Genny, Henri had done it all. His mother had done nothing. He could feel the heat rise to his face, and before thinking better of it, he snapped.

"I remember teaching Genny to walk. And talk. And Stepmother made me learn to braid her hair so she wouldn't have to. And you didn't say anything when we were in that other world, even though you knew it was us!" He was suddenly shouting. "Miss Isa and King Ever talked to us and spent time with us. More than you ever did!"

His mother held her fingers up and snapped them, uttering something under her breath that Henri couldn't hear. His mouth immediately shut, though he wasn't done talking.

"Hold!" his mother called up to the front before moving her horse over to his until she was close enough to reach over and grab his chin roughly. Henri tried to jerk his face free, but she was too strong. As she leaned in, her short, golden hair swayed back and forth along her jawline. "I don't care what your uncle did with or for you before I was here. Everything I've done, including leaving, was for you and your sister. I wanted to give the world to you. *This* world! But I couldn't do that with your worthless father around, so I had to go! I even sent you with *her*," she jerked her chin back in Miss Isa's direction, "so you could live in the palace until I came. But from now on, you will respect and obey me, or you will be very sorry you didn't. Understand?"

Henri could feel Genny shrink into him, but something within him, a fire from deep down, would not allow him to look away. He nodded, but only because his chin was beginning to hurt.

As she let go and yelled for the group to continue, he felt the familiar flash of warmth move through him as he always did when he sensed someone about to use their power. His mother barked out orders and their horses began to pick up speed.

Something strong was stirring within his mother. She claimed that all she did was for him, but Henri sensed that whatever power she was harnessing was volatile and barely restrained. In fact, it didn't feel like it belonged to her at all.

Suddenly, Henri wanted nothing more than to hide in Miss Isa's arms once again. For that, he would happily trade having a mother.

CHAPTER 37

THE OTHER ONE

"Take her to the dungeon and my children to their rooms," Sacha announced as they marched through the Fortress's grand entrance. "I want to speak with my brother." She turned and glared at her companions. "Alone."

Ever glanced at Isa, who gave him a weak smile and a nod as the Fae began to pull her toward the main dungeon. At least, it seemed, they didn't know about the outer dungeons. Not that either was highly desirable. His heart ached when the children also turned and looked at him, their eyes wide with fear. It killed him that he could do nothing. But the poison from the hemlock was thick in his blood by now. And even if he could fight, he couldn't best all of her men. They'd already proven that. Isa or one of the children might be hurt.

As he turned and began to follow his sister, he noticed that new banners already hung from the walls. A sickly mixture of green and yellow, it appeared, but his headache was painful enough that he couldn't really trust his eyes.

Ever's heart sank even deeper as they descended into one of the lowest levels of the Fortress. He didn't have to look up from the floor to realize they were headed toward the practice room. As they neared it, to his surprise, she fell back a step to walk beside him. When she did, he couldn't help but study her in the dim light of the torches hung on the walls. Seeing his father's familiar features in a female's face was strange. She wasn't what he would call beautiful, but handsome would have been a better word if his view of her hadn't been so skewed by her evil.

"So, little brother," Sacha said pleasantly, "I want to get to know you. Tell me about yourself."

"What is it you wish to know?"

"Did our father love you?"

Ever studied her for a moment longer, a bit surprised at the question. Her tone was friendly enough, but she was blinking too rapidly to be as calm as she appeared. "In his own way," Ever said slowly.

"How so?"

"He trained me."

"Ha," she scoffed. "He trained me too. What else?"

"Tell me where Garin is and I'll answer you."

"How about you tell me what I want to know, and I'll not kill him right at this moment."

Ever bowed his head in concession, but inside he was rejoicing. His mentor was still alive. For now, at least.

"Our father taught me to control my temper, a hot one that runs in the family, I'm afraid."

"Maybe," she said, not looking at him this time, "if you hear my side of the story, it will loosen your tongue a bit."

Ever was all for that. The long walk was beginning to strain him. It was far too much like the time he was cursed, for his breaths were beginning to come hard and fast, and sweat trickled down his temples and back.

"Rodrigue never lived with me and my mother in the Fae world. He couldn't, he said. It shifted too much. Nothing lasted, he would rant, and that was not his way. But he visited quite a bit, and always with gifts." Her gray eyes became distant. "He had the best presents. Toys, dolls, and as I got older, gowns, jewels, and weapons." The small smile that lit her face as she spoke looked strange in the flickering light of the torches.

"When I was six, he decided to train me. He would bring a new weapon every few months. A sword, a bow, a knife, and so on. I was good, he told me. I had a gift! Then about the time I was eight, he began to teach me how to use my special powers. Powers, he said, that came from a long line of strong warriors."

Her voice had become dreamy, but then she shook her head and lifted her chin slightly higher as she spoke. "I always begged him to take me with him whenever he left. Enough of his human blood was inside me for me to hate the Fae world. There is no continuity, and the older I got, the more I could see why he disliked being there. My mother cared little, for she had other men. Fae are not monogamous, you know."

Ever didn't know, nor did he really want to.

"But *I* was half human, and though my peers shared little care for their parents' affection one way or another, I did care. Still, he never let me go with him. He said his world was not the place for me, and mine not for him."

Finally, they reached the large wooden door that opened up into the great room of stone and walls covered in weapons.

"Choose," Sacha said once they were inside. Ever stared back at her until she rolled her eyes and gestured at the hanging weapons. "Choose one, or I shall choose one for you."

Ever trudged slowly over to the wall. The larger weapons were tempting. After the sword, he was quite comfortable with the short-handled mace or even one of the staffs. But his strength was waning quickly, and he needed something small and light that would allow him to fight without being hindered by its size.

"You're stalling," Sacha said.

Ever walked slowly to the wall and pulled down the claw blade, a knife no larger than his hand with a hilt and blade that curved up like a crescent moon.

"Interesting choice. Now it's my turn." Sacha went over to another wall across the room and pulled down one of the daggers. "This way we will be even, little brother."

"And what exactly are we fighting for?"

"I want to see how our father did with you."

"Didn't we just do that?"

"You were distracted by the others. This time if you are distracted, you have no one to blame but yourself." She backed up and began to walk a wide arc around him. He had no doubt his father had trained her as she melted into the stance of a great cat. It was his stance.

"He said nothing to me of you," Ever said quietly. "I swear."

"I'm sure he didn't." Her voice was bitter. "No king would want to admit his illegitimate child to his heir." She kept circling but regarded him with an unreadable expression. "I heard someone say one time that you grew up a lonely boy. But even *you* can't empathize with a half-human who grew up in the world of Fae."

Ever stood still as she circled him, trying to regain the energy he lost on the walk to the weapons room. "We reproduce," she continued, "but there are few family ties. There were once, I heard, but that hasn't been since ... well, since your precious steward betrayed us all. It was decided that loyalty to the people should be chosen over that of the family. Children are kept alive by their parents when they are young, but most simply fend for themselves within a few years of birth. Parents do little in the lives of their children now among my people. Keeping to the Fae people as a whole is more important."

"That makes little sense." Ever crouched but found his joints stiff.

"Does it?" She began to close the distance between them. "I don't know what your steward told you, but the young Fae that he killed to save the Fortier line? That was his son."

Ever stared at her, and Garin's last words came back to him from that awful night.

The Maker saw it fit for me to defend this sacred ground from the bloodied hands of my own son.

In one brilliant leap, Sacha crossed the distance between them. Ever ducked and rolled, but his shoulder screamed with pain, and the swift movement made him dizzy. Before he could orient himself, a thin line of blood rolled down his left arm, breaking, Ever was sure, the quick stitches Isa had been forced to give him the night before as they'd camped. Sacha hopped back a few feet.

"Too many died in the Fortress's final scourge because of your steward. After that day, the remainder of our people, thanks to the traitor, decided that families should not be tightly knit. Rather, children would learn from all. That way, there would be no particular ties to one individual or another. Along with families, monogamous bonds disappeared as well." She flipped her short blonde hair as she began to circle him once again. "It couldn't have been a difficult transition, I suppose. Our natures are transient enough."

"You don't sound convinced," Ever said as he pushed himself to his feet again, praying suddenly for some way, *any* way to reach her. The pain and loneliness on her face were clear. If only he could use that to show her what she could have if she joined him. Them. Everyone Ever held dear. A curious, childlike voice inside him wondered what it would truly be like to have a sister.

Sacha shrugged. "It's how the Fae are, and I have seen the efficiency of their methods now. But there was a long time before that when I didn't." She pranced forward again. This time, Ever was able to block her first strike. He leapt forward to grab her wrist and twist it. She grunted as he wrapped her arm around her back and stole the dagger. The fast movements were making his head spin, however, giving her the time to elbow him with enough force to bloody his nose and loose the dagger from his hands. In a second, it was hers once again.

"I always saw myself as lesser," she said, hopping back, "because I couldn't disappear completely as my peers could do. I longed for our father the way none of them had ever yearned for their parents. When he was around I could be proud, for he was able to show me what I was capable of. He even taught me how to use the power from *both* of my heritages. One day, I vowed, I would be like him."

"When did he stop coming?" Ever asked, trying to ignore the violent throbbing in his nose as he wiped the blood on his shoulder. A shudder passed through him, and for a second, his hand and wrist seized from the poison. He needed to keep her talking so he could catch his breath.

"As I grew older, he visited less and less, but when I was seventeen, he finally told me he wouldn't be returning again. He was needed elsewhere." She stopped moving for a moment, her face suddenly hard. "You wouldn't happen to know anything about that, would you?"

Ever didn't know how old his sister was, but a whisper in his head told him he knew exactly what period of time she was referring to. And from the cutting look in her gray eyes, a look his father had worn often, Ever knew he had just forfeited his chance of winning his sister over. Or rather, his father had.

"When he told me," she whispered, "I clung to him, begged and wept that he would take me with him. I couldn't stand living in that wretched world forever. But to no avail. The last time he touched me in my world was when he brushed me aside so he could return through his precious veil."

"I am sorry," Ever said, unable to think of any words more adequate. As harsh as Rodrigue had sometimes been with him, it now seemed incomparable to what his sister had lived with.

A small smile touched Sacha's thin lips. "He thought he'd sealed up the veil behind him, but I was able to use my powers to place a foothold as one does with a door to keep it from closing. I bided my time until I could hoard enough food for some sort of journey. Then, when I was eighteen, I slipped through the veil and set out in search of our father."

"How did you find him?"

"Sometimes people took me in. I looked and acted human enough not to raise too much suspicion. Other times I slept in the forest or on the road. I knew that I would probably find him near the beloved Fortress he'd told me so much about."

She stopped and held up her weapon, testing its edge on her finger. Ever didn't miss the hint. "It took me weeks, but eventually I did find him. When I did, he was making a speech at Soudain's edge, just at the foot of the mountain." She looked at Ever, tilting her head slightly and placing a finger on her cheek.

"You were there by his side. He had never told me I had a brother, but you looked so much like him that I knew immediately who you were. Still, I was so excited to see him, and I was so sure he had missed me, too, that I shouted out in the middle of his speech and ran to him as fast as I could."

"I wish I remembered." Ever shook his head, trying to clear the cobwebs inside that the hemlock was weaving in his mind.

Sacha gave him a sour smile then began to creep forward again. Ever tried to stand ready, but his strength was leaking like water from a cracked pitcher. His knee felt like it was shattered.

"It was probably no more than a nuisance to you. And you were young. I'm sure a more unacceptable sight could never be seen by a father, though. His unwanted daughter was running toward him with her hands burning blue and green, wearing a dirty dress some peasant woman had offered me along the way when my own gown had become too torn to continue properly.

"To this day," Sacha's voice was suddenly dead as she raised her knife, "I don't know what he did to me, but I could not use my power after that for a very long time. None of it, not even my Fae abilities. He personally dragged me to the edge of the crowd, and I'm sure would have gone farther, except that you ran up to him to ask him what he was doing."

Ever tried hard to recall that day, but he couldn't. How old would he have been? Had he truly seen his sister years before? Before he could remember, he was on the ground again. This time, the dagger traced his collarbone down one side and then up the other. Pain followed each slice. With a shout, he was able to shove his body over enough to knock her off his chest. As soon as she was off, he rolled backward until he could pull himself up to his knees. But no higher.

"He stopped to tell you to stay where you were." Her wry smile was gone, and in her eyes was only hatred. "I took that moment to run."

"Where did you go?" he rasped.

She lunged forward again, this time leading with her fists. He blocked her first flurry of punches, and even managed to hook his little knife around her neck, but he wasn't strong enough to hold her there. She shrugged out and danced away again. When would she tire of playing with him? *I can't hold out much longer,* he told the Fortress. In response, a tiny breeze fluttered around him, only strong enough to tickle the nape of his neck. Ever almost smiled. *If this is what you wish, then I will continue to wait,* he thought. His cuts screamed and his head throbbed and his vision was most definitely blurred, but the Fortress was there with him. For this reason, Ever would hang on.

"I wandered," Sacha said, "doing odd jobs here and there. I wasn't much use to most. Few people want a half-starved woman who knows how to use the sword. But eventually I learned how to feed slop to the pigs and corn to the chickens. Seven years of wandering will teach you that, you know. Then, after a particularly bad beating by my most recent employer, my *husband* found me in a gutter, filled me with wine, and dragged me down to some holy man not worth his cloth who married me to a stranger without as much as noting my sobriety."

Ah. This was why the Fortress had told him to wait. "You could have told me who you were," he said.

"You wouldn't have believed—"

"I would have felt your power, and so would Garin," he cut her off sharply. "Father might have denied you, but I never would." He leaned forward on one hand, begging the Fortress to let her *see*. If only Isa were here. "I always wanted a sister. I would have protected you! The Fortress would have protected you!"

She lowered her weapon and studied him with her too-bright gray eyes. For a moment, Ever saw the vulnerable, injured girl she must have been. Her eyes were wide, and despite the thin lines around them, she suddenly looked very young. And lonely. It was a look he had seen on Henri's face many times.

"You would have been sheltered," he whispered, stumbling to his feet, "just as your children were."

The open expression was suddenly gone, and her mouth twisted into a smirk. "And how well were they received by your steward? After all, he killed his own son."

"I still don't understand why you wouldn't come to me," Ever said again, ignoring the bait. "You could have at least tried."

"Let me put this clearly." She melted down into her cat-like stance again. "You were his spitting image, down to that quirked brow you hold now. I knew better than to place my hope in a man."

"I have changed," Ever said quietly. "I am not that man anymore."

"You're right. You aren't that man anymore." Sacha began to stalk forward, and Ever sensed she wouldn't be toying with him for much longer. Warily, he raised his own weapon one more time, trying to ignore the way his back and shoulders seized up.

"I might not have been in the Fortress courts," Sacha said, "but I have kept watch on you and your little wife since the beginning. She's changed you. Made you soft. If it hadn't been for her effect on you," Sacha crouched low, "I wouldn't have gained my foothold in your door. It took me five years, but I *did* find the veil's tear. And when I did, I returned to a people who had mocked me for too long. But unlike *your* people, we hold on to our legends. They do not become a thing of myth. There are few direct ties between kin, but as a people, we are strong! And when I told them that I had found the man whose ancestor banished us to our realm, they were thirsty for blood."

"Why are you telling me all of this?"

Instead of answering, she pounced. Ever's head hit the stone floor. His already queasy stomach nearly convulsed as she planted a knee in it. Her dagger was to his throat, and her face was so close he could feel the heat of her breath.

This was it then. *Take care of them,* he begged the Fortress. His fever was raging, and he began to shake violently, though from the head injury or the poison, he couldn't be sure. He'd been using his power to hold off the worst symptoms, but now there was little left to fight with.

"I told you so you would know," she said, "that I am not a complete monster. You see, I cannot blame you wholly for what our father did or did not do for us. I also, however, believe that I *am* the rightful heir since I came first." She moved the dagger down over his heart. When she spoke again, her voice was surprisingly soft. "I am going to give you this one chance to live and take my mercy. I'm sure by now your wife has informed you that her ability to grow her own child has been removed?"

Ever's anger that had subsided returned to him like a flood. With a roar, he shoved her off his chest and leapt to his feet, but she easily knocked the knife from his hand and had him at her dagger's point once again.

"Here's my offer. I remove the curse which I placed upon her if you swear to leave Destin and never return." Her voice grew nearly inaudible. "Find a quiet place and settle down. Have a family." She leaned back a bit and searched his eyes. "Be happy."

"And leave you with my people and the two children whom you sent two Fae after?" he growled.

"Oh, that. I wanted to know your strength. When the messengers didn't return, I knew more about you, and that you were willing to do what you thought was necessary to protect your hold on the kingdom."

"And had I failed," he ground his teeth through another round of shaking, "what would you have done if the Fae had killed your children?"

"They wouldn't have—"

"I know bloodlust in a creature's eyes when I see it!" he shouted.

"But you didn't let them hurt the children, did you?"

"So you sent your own people into my home to die? Life is quite cheap to you, isn't it?"

"And I would do it again!" she shouted back. Her hand shook as she held the dagger against him. Green mist rippled through her gray eyes. "If there was one thing I learned from Father, it is that I will do what I must for the better of my people."

"And so will I."

"So," she stepped back, "you would refuse your wife the one thing she desires, to save your own crown?"

For once, Ever had no answer. The pain in his chest was too tight. *Why,* he cried out to the Fortress, *are you allowing her to do this? How has she grown so powerful as to defeat even the power you have placed in me?* But there was no answer. Only that nagging sensation to be patient. So he said nothing.

"Then you may expect no other such offers from me," she said in a low voice. With that, she reeled back and smacked the butt of her dagger across his head. "Put him with the others. But I want them in separate cells."

Two Fae, a male and a female, came in and began to drag him

toward the door by his arms. Ever thrashed, trying to break free, but it was no use. The hemlock's venom was sending his body into convulsions, and his efforts only brought him a severe bout of pain as he was dragged back to the hall.

"Oh," Sacha said, turning just before they led him out. "I will take this first, though." She lifted his left hand and slipped the signet ring from his finger.

CHAPTER 38

RELEASE

The poison had kept Ever's heart beating at an erratic pace for hours, sometimes slowing it dangerously and other times speeding it so fast he felt lightheaded. But he felt his heart come to a complete stop when his eyes adjusted to the dark enough to make out the limp body hanging in the stocks.

Before he could run to the body, however, one of the Fae delivered a sharp kick to his shoulder. Pain seared down his arm and even his chest and sides as he clutched at the bloodied hole the Fae's pike had left three days before. Through stinging tears, Ever raised his shaking head to look at the man in the stocks again. But before he could speak or reach out, both Fae guards picked him up and tossed him into an empty cell, sending yet another wave of pain through his body.

"Ever!" His wife's voice came from somewhere else in the dark room. There, in the faint light of the single candle, Isa knelt on the other side of Ever's bars in the cell adjacent to his. "You need to heal yourself now!" Her voice was strained. "The poison will kill you if you don't stop it."

"I don't have time for that," Ever panted as he rolled slowly to his knees. "Takes too long." He began to crawl toward the bars but was interrupted by a violent twitching in his right arm. The smell of mildew assaulted him, and odd lights briefly danced before his eyes. The poison was spreading, but all Ever could do was grind his teeth as he waited for his vision to return to normal and his arm to stop moving. He'd had brief sensations like this over the past four days, but this was by far the worst. With Garin on the other side of the bars, however, Ever hadn't the time to pay heed to his wound. As soon as he was able to sit up straight, he crawled over to the bars in stiff, awkward movements. "Garin?"

At first, Ever feared the man in the stocks wouldn't move at all, but finally, his head rolled to the side just enough for Ever to see that Garin was still there. Ever grabbed the bars in front of him and began to pull. Isa protested and scolded away about his health, but Ever didn't listen. The bars gave way a little, but much less than they should have. His strength was almost gone.

A sharp object was thrust through the bars, just inches from his face, and Ever looked up to see the Fae woman guard standing just outside his cell, her face taut. Ever grabbed the pike's end and was about to loose the rest of his strength into this evil, mystical creature, when he heard a soft voice to his left.

"Slow down," Isa said softly. "Let me handle this."

Ever wanted to retort that he didn't need her help in tearing this monster limb from limb, but as he opened his mouth, the Fae's face smoothed, losing what little emotion it had held before. Ever turned to see Isa closing her eyes, one hand on the bars and the other outstretched palm up to the Fae woman.

"We need time alone," Isa whispered. "We will not be escaping tonight." Normally, it would have bothered Ever to have his wife promise a guard they wouldn't try to escape, but this time he knew she was right. Garin wasn't moving anywhere in such a poor state, and Ever was not going to leave him again.

It took longer than usual for Isa to convince their captor to see the truth, so long that Ever thought it might not work. But finally, the Fae woman nodded once before returning her pike to its upright position. To Ever's surprise, she even took out a key and unlocked both his and Isa's cell doors. She shut the prison door behind her as she left.

Isa let out a sigh but didn't open her eyes. "Go on," she said. "Let him loose."

Ever nearly passed out in his attempt to lift Garin out of the stocks, and when he finally did, the older man's body dragged along like Genny's rag doll.

"Garin," he started, but he could say nothing else. Dried blood matted Garin's face and his long gray hair, and even in the dark his skin seemed nearly transparent. Ever delicately lifted the steward's head and shoulders into his lap, and Isa, seeming to have recovered herself, scrambled to sit on Garin's other side.

"There you are." Garin's eyes opened a slit, and though his breathing was labored, he gave Ever a ghost of a smile. "I wondered what was taking so long."

"Forgive me!" Ever pulled him closer and laid his head on the steward's shoulder. "I shouldn't have gone! I should have come back for you."

"You did exactly as I told you." Garin burst into a fit of coughing. The spell lasted so long that Isa also placed her hand under Garin's head, her face puckering with worry as she wiped the beads of sweat off his forehead with the end of her skirt.

"What did they do to you?" Ever whispered. But even as he asked, he knew what he needed to do. Closing his eyes, Ever gathered what little remained of his strength, taking the steward's hand in his own. The moment felt eerily familiar.

And like his father, the steward pulled his hand free. "No, Ever," the steward said.

But Ever wouldn't lose another this way. Not again. Determined, he firmly placed his hands over Garin's heart, and the blue light began to drip from his battered body into his friend, a light blue glow emanating from Garin's chest.

"Ever." Isa placed her hand on his. "This isn't going to work."

But Ever only shoved her hand off. Why wouldn't they just let him focus? Again, he pressed, and again, the blue light began to trickle out, but it was getting harder by the second, and Ever began to shake with the effort.

"Everard!" Isa took him by the arms and shook him hard, briefly reigniting the pain in his shoulder. "You need to stop! You're killing yourself!"

"What if I want to die?" he shouted back. The words were out before he had time to consider them. He didn't miss the look of pain on Isa's face. "I can't do it." He hung his head as tears began to drip from his eyes. "First she'll take Garin. Then she'll take you. I cannot keep watching this death." Sobs racked his body.

"No need to be so dramatic, Ever." Garin's voice was surprisingly mild, as though he were actually smiling. "We all die."

"Why, Garin?" He stared hard into his mentor's face, trying to memorize its features in the dim light. "Why would the Fortress allow this? Why must so much evil abound?" His words were hard and cold as he spoke them. There was no excuse for this, no reason that the evil should have its way so easily.

"That is simple. Because my duty is now fulfilled."

"It can't be. I still need you. I need you more than ever now, to tell me what to do!" Another spasm tried to take him, but Ever fought it with all his might. As he did, though, something inside warned him that his ability to ignore the poison's effects would soon be gone.

Garin reached up with a shaking hand and gently touched Ever's face. "You helped heal a heart that had been broken for centuries. I lost my son to the evil of my people, but the Maker has kept me here for so many years, waiting until I found another."

"But I'm not your son. And I brought the curse! I have pained you again and again with my folly. And yet you bore it with patience! I cannot have been the good son you deserved to have!"

"You may not be my son by blood, but you became my life. From the moment I looked into your eyes, I knew I would love you in a way I hadn't loved anyone in five hundred years." He chuckled softly, which sent him into another coughing spell. "There were moments, to be sure, when you tried my patience. For example, all those times salt magically appeared in my tea." He squeezed Ever's hand. "But you are a man now. And I couldn't be more proud."

"But—"

"That's what a father is, Ever. You watch your children fall, and you help them get back up. And you love them through it all." Garin turned to Isa, his breath becoming fainter each time he spoke. Still, he managed to reach up with a shaking hand and touch her cheek as well, wiping at the tears that were rolling silently down her face.

"Be patient with him, my dear. And never lose that heart of yours. I knew you were special the moment I saw you as a little girl, with your bouncing braids and bright eyes. In the last four years, you have far exceeded even my expectations. Now that I will be gone, it will be your duty to take care of Ever." His eyes twinkled even in the dim light. "Someone has to do it."

Isa wiped her tears on her sleeve and nodded, still crying as she leaned down to plant a kiss on the older man's forehead.

How dare she nod? Agreeing with Garin was admitting defeat.

"I need to know, though," she said in a shaky voice, "why couldn't Ever heal them?"

"Because they were never sick."

"What?"

Garin let out a raspy sigh. "I should have seen it before, but I've spent a long time away from my people. I happened to see one of the children more closely as they prepared to punish me for my crimes."

Ever burned with rage as he listened, but he let Garin continue uninterrupted.

"I realized that the children's symptoms, like so much else, were only illusions."

"But the pain!" Isa said. "They were in pain!"

"My people are skilled deceivers."

"Then why couldn't I see through it?" Isa sounded indignant.

Garin laughed again, his chuckle hardly more than a whisper. "You are strong, but there is still much of your power that you haven't even tapped." He broke into his worst coughing fit yet, and when he lowered his hand, Ever could see drops of blood on his palm.

"So it was all a ruse," Isa whispered. "Just like the house."

"Don't you see why we need you?" Ever leaned closer. "We cannot defeat her on our own!"

Garin let out another rattling sigh, the gleam no longer in his eye. "I have been working for over five centuries, Ever. I am tired, and the Maker has seen fit to finally bring me to my eternal rest."

Ever shook his head at this, tears beginning once again to fall, but in the dark, Garin smiled. "You will see me again when it is your time." He wheezed out a chuckle. "That, of course, gives you no right to try and see me sooner than you must. You have a family to care for now. Your wife needs you, the kingdom needs you ... and those children need you."

"They cannot be ours. Both of their parents live." Ever's voice came out more bitter than he'd expected.

"That does not mean they need you any less. You, of all people, know what woman you leave them to if you allow her to keep them. Now, promise me, Ever, that you will not give up." Garin suddenly jerked forward, grabbing Ever by the collar and pulling his face down. "Promise!"

But Ever could only shake his head. "I don't believe it," he whispered. "The Fortress *will* restore you. It always does." It had to. Ever had never needed Garin so much in his life as he did now.

Yet Garin closed his eyes, a small smile on his lips. "Not this time, son. But," he squeezed Ever's hand once more, trembling as he did, "the Maker has left me enough life that I may finish this final task."

"No!" Ever cried out. He tried to pull his hand out of Garin's trembling grasp, but it was too late. Garin's hand seemed to be sewn to his. Blue whorls of light began to ebb out of the steward's body and into Ever's. The waves of light looked like water flowing out of a crystal pool. Ever could feel the power entering his body, and he begged the Fortress to make it stop. But the power continued to come until it slowed to a drip. Finally, it grew so thin that Ever didn't know whether it was still coming or not. He clung to Garin's body, praying until he broke into a cold sweat. *No,* he told the Fortress. *Not now. If you love me, you won't take him from me. If you truly love me, you'll leave him for just a while longer.*

How many hours passed, Ever didn't know, nor did he care. And finally there came a moment when Garin let out one breath and did not draw in another. For a brief moment, the room grew as bright as day in the flash of a blinding light. Azure fire glowed, lighting the edges of Garin's body, the protector of kings that Ever held in his lap. Fierce wings exploded upward, and in that short moment, Garin himself shone like a star in the night skies. Then the light went out, and the man Ever had cradled was gone.

CHAPTER 39

REASONS

As the Fae led him up to the Tower of Annals, Henri was suddenly very glad his sister hadn't been allowed to come. He had always been curious about this room, but the king had insisted that it was sacred and not a place for the children. Now as he entered, the large room with its circular wall of windows would have been a pleasant sight had it not been for the sickly warmth that wriggled through his arms and legs and into his chest.

His mother was bending over a large book on the sturdy rectangular table near the hearth that stood in the center of the room, her short blonde hair falling in front of her eyes. The sick chill, however, wasn't coming from her but from the black cauldron hanging over the fire.

"There you are." She looked up from her book and beckoned him forward. "Help me with this bundle before we stir it in." She held out a little bundle of twigs, herbs, and flowers all tied together, about as long as the palm of her hand.

"What is it?"

She tilted her head and studied him. "What do you know about your power?"

"I can still make fire in my hands."

She nodded, as though she had expected such. "You, as I do, have not one but two sources of power that flow through your blood. Did you know that your blue fire was given to you by the Fortress?"

"What do you mean?" He frowned.

"You have the blood of the Fortiers who get their power from this very place." She gestured around her at the tower they stood in. "And you also have the power of the Fae."

Henri shuddered. He had never questioned his ability to feel power, to sense it when it was nearby. It had always been a part of who he was, something he thought everyone felt until Father Lucien told him otherwise. But he wanted nothing to do with these green misted beings that floated about.

"You know," she said, eyeing him as she stirred the cauldron of sickly bubbling brown goo, "you shouldn't be ashamed of your Fae blood."

But Henri didn't answer, studying the herbs on the table instead. As he did, a sparkle caught his eye, and his heart fell as he recognized the king's ring on the table beside her knife. Now King Ever couldn't even send for help.

"Come here, son."

Henri took a step forward but stumbled backward when he felt the wave of raw force surge from the cauldron. "What is that?" he whispered.

"Your uncle is very strong, and so is his wife. In fact, she's much stronger than I would have ever expected, considering the pampered wench that your grandfather picked for *his* wife." Henri's mother sniffed. "I am strong, too. Even with my Fae power and Fortier fire, though, I'm not sure it will be enough to best both of them. So this," she gave the cauldron a stir, "will be our third source. I had to work long and hard to find the recipe. But," she added, looking thoughtfully at him once more, "it will be even more potent with another's assistance. Stand here. You're going to help me."

Henri hesitated, suddenly wanting very much to run and hide behind the many shelves of books that filled the room.

"Henri," she said, lowering her voice, her eyes pleading, "I'm not strong enough to do this on my own. I need your help."

And yet Henri couldn't move his feet. Whatever was in that cauldron, boiling, bubbling, and snapping as it was, smelled so sour it made him want to retch on the ground at her feet.

"Then let me put it this way." His mother's affectionate tone melted. "If you won't help, I suppose I will just have to fetch your sister to come up and do as I say instead."

Henri's feet suddenly had the ability to move once again. Trembling, he went to stand beside his mother as the roaring heat of the fire scalded his ears and eyes from being so close. With a cry, he jumped back once again.

"What is the matter now?"

He stared at her. How could she not feel that? His skin felt as though it might dissolve if he stood near the cauldron for more than a few seconds. "It's too strong." He shook his head.

"I told you, it will take an enormous amount of power to defeat my brother. That's why it is so important that you do exactly as I say. One wrong move and this entire castle could go up in flames."

Henri's breaths came in and out too fast, but he did as she told him, creating a fire in his palm and holding it out as she picked up the bundle of herbs once again. A pungent odor wafted from the bundle as she held it over his flame. It was not a friendly smell. Henri grimaced, but his mother acted as if she were used to such a scent.

Her calm disappeared, however, when sparks began to fly from the herbs. His mother leapt back with a yelp, and Henri gaped at his hand. His flames had never done *that* before.

"What did you do?" she cried, holding up the charred bundle

of twigs. After examining it closely she looked back at Henri. Henri wondered what she saw, for something in her face changed, though he couldn't exactly say what it was.

With the slightest shake of her head, she dropped the burned herbs on the table and began to cut more. "That is enough for today," she finally said. "You may go back to your room now."

Henri was out the door in a flash, gasping for fresh air as he fled down the winding stone steps. The air he sucked in as he descended was stuffy, but anything was better than the scent of that vile concoction his mother was brewing upstairs.

As Henri reached the bottom of the steps, though, he realized that his original escort had fled. Whether he, too, had gone up in a puff of green mist, or whether his mother knew Henri would never try to escape without Genny, Henri was free for a few precious moments. Before he knew exactly what he was doing, Henri found himself on the way to the dungeons.

He hadn't been to the dungeons before, but he'd once watched Garin accompany a drunk down with one of the guards. He had watched them for long enough to know that it was in the northern wing of the Fortress. Henri kept to the shadows when he could and darted from corner to corner where there were none. Though he'd come to love the Fortress in his short time there, the building now seemed eerie without its bustling servants and constant stream of visitors. Every so often a green mist would float by, or a blank-faced Fae with a pike would walk past, but to Henri's relief, there were very few to witness his four failed attempts at finding the dungeon door. Two storage rooms, one room with nothing in it, and one sick room later, Henri finally opened a door that reeked of dank soil and mildewy rock.

The room was so dark that Henri nearly tumbled down face first. He caught himself, however, on the second step and crouched there until his eyes adjusted to the dimness, for the room was lit only by one candle.

A nudge to his arm nearly sent him screaming until he saw

that it was only a Fae guard poking him with the butt of his pike, a thin frown on his flat face.

"I'm just sitting here," Henri grumbled. After looking at him a moment longer, the Fae shrugged and dissolved before floating back outside the door. Henri peeked around the corner to see Miss Isa and King Ever kneeling on the ground, a limp body stretched out between them, its head resting on the king's lap. Henri squinted, trying to think of who it might be. Then he heard the steward's voice.

Henri couldn't hear what Garin said, but whatever it was, the king responded by choking out a sob that made Henri's heart hurt as the king cradled the older man in his arms. King Ever was brusque and often stern, but Henri had long ago stopped questioning his motives. Seeing the king's body shiver with tears and jerk back and forth at random was more frightening than his mother's concoction upstairs.

Suddenly, Henri understood why the king hadn't fought back after that initial meeting with his mother. It was the same reason Henri hadn't fought his mother in the tower. Henri had Genny, and the king had Miss Isa, Garin, and the rest of the kingdom. And his mother was using them all.

Henri wandered slowly back up to the main level. *Fortress,* he thought, *I don't know if you're listening to me. I know I'm not the king or anyone important like that. But ... I want to stop her. For my sister ... and for them.* Henri stopped where he was and looked up at the glistening white molded ceilings that vaulted above him. He strained to hear an answer the way he had seen the king and queen do on many occasions. But no words came. There was no sign that anyone or anything had heard him.

Annoyed, Henri kicked at a corner as he headed toward the kitchens. Well, if the Fortress wasn't going to help him, he would just have to find something to eat, as he and Genny hadn't eaten since noon. There was no soft, warm bread waiting for him as there always had been before, but after a bit of scrounging through the cabinets Henri found some dried salted pork and a few cold biscuits. With his arms loaded up he was about to start walking back to his room when a movement caught his attention. What was that?

Henri turned back and walked to the window. To his disappointment, he realized it was just a bird picking a berries out of the garden, blue ones, almost the color of the stones in the king's ring.

Henri nearly dropped his food.

After stuffing his pockets with as much meat and biscuits as he could carry, Henri dashed out of the kitchens and back to the stairs. Once he made sure no one was near, he skittered up the steps, taking them two at a time. Only when he reached the door to the annals did he realize he had no idea as to how he would explain his entrance to his mother. To his joy, however, the room was unlocked, and upon peeking inside, he found that his mother was nowhere in sight. The ring, however, was still on the table.

Henri sprinted over and snatched the ring up, only to hear voices coming from the other side of the room. His mother's and the flat, disinterested voice of one of the Fae. Henri raced back out of the room and down the stairs, not stopping until he reached the bottom, panting. His first thought had been to simply get the ring. But now what should he do with it? How was he supposed to get it to the soldiers at the bottom of the mountain that King Ever had spoken about?

The birds. King Ever had wanted to find Father Lucien's birds! Once again, Henri took off. As he tried to recall where the animals were kept, he begged the Fortress for the bird boy to still be there.

"You!" he shouted as soon as he was through the door of the bird coop. But there was no one there. Henri's heart sank as he found himself in the empty stall. He threw himself down on an empty cage and ran his hands through his hair.

"It's not fair, Fortress," he mumbled. "If you love them so much, why don't you save them?" His voice cracked, and Henri felt a lone, traitorous tear slide down his face. He was so tired. Suddenly, all he wanted to do was go back to his room and sleep for a hundred years.

Something nudged his elbow. Henri jumped up, but there was no one there, not even a Fae. Then again he felt a nudge, this time toward the door. Henri continued to find himself pushed along until he was standing before the cage closest to the door.

"I don't know what you want me to do," he grumbled, staring at the bird inside. "I think King Ever was going to use his power to make it go to the right place. I don't have his power."

Once again he felt the nudge at his hand. This time, however, a trickle of peace began to flow through him. "Fine," Henri sighed. "If this is what you want me to do." Henri opened the cage and gently pulled the bird out. It fluffed its warm feathers against his hand and tilted its head. "The bird boy told me you only fly home," Henri frowned at the bird, "but if the Fortress thinks you'll go to the right place, then I guess I'll send you."

Henri found one of the little packs hung on the wall, took it down, and tied it securely to the bird's back. It looked crooked, but it should stay on at least, he thought. The ring itself seemed nearly too heavy when he dropped it inside the pack, but once again, he felt the gentle push.

Shouting jarred Henri from his focus. Panic struck as he looked out the door to see his mother and a dozen green mists charging straight for him. "Go!" he shouted at the bird, tossing it in the air. Then he turned and began opening the other cages. He'd only succeeded in freeing three by the time his mother caught his arm and threw him to the ground. As he fell, more cages fell open and more birds were set free.

"Where is it?" she shouted. "Where is the ring?"

Henri didn't answer her. Instead, he scrunched his eyes up and tried to put his arms over his face as he curled up in the hay and dirt.

"Bring them down," his mother yelled. Henri's heart sank as

he saw one of the Fae pull a bow from his back. As his mother began to drag him away, he could hear one soft thud after the other as the little bodies hit the ground.

"The Fae want you dead, just so you know," she said through gritted teeth as she dragged him back into the Fortress. "Because you are my son, and only because you are my son, I will give you this one last warning. But if you fail me again, your sister will take over your responsibilities!"

"But she's too little!" Henri protested, trying to keep up as his mother marched him toward his room. "She doesn't have the fire like I do!"

"Then if something happens to her, you can take comfort in knowing that it was your fault."

CHAPTER 40

A SCORE TO SETTLE

Ever?"

But Ever didn't answer her. Not so much as a muscle moved. Instead, he stayed curled up as though he still held Garin's empty body and it hadn't disappeared with the steward's soul.

She tried again. "You heard Garin. We need a plan. Sacha won't wait much longer."

Still nothing. Isa felt a flash of irritation. It wouldn't be long before another set of spasms took him, shaking his body until it seemed it would burst. If he were an average man without his great power, the poison surely would have killed him by now. "I need you to heal yourself," she said, making her voice as severe as she dared. "You will die if the poison stays inside you much longer. You need to fight it!"

But there was no response. Dismay threatened to make her panic as Isa prodded at his heart. Usually she could sense other emotions there, even if she wasn't wholly aware of his exact sentiments. This time, however, there was nothing. No anger, no rage, no fear, no sorrow. Not even longing. Sacha had done what no other creature had done before.

She had broken him.

Before Isa could think of anything to say, a convulsion shook Ever so hard that he slumped to the ground when it was done, his eyes closed.

"No!" Isa rolled him over and smashed her ear against his chest, listening, praying for the heartbeat. Seconds felt like hours, but finally, she heard it. The sound was faint and uneven. And yet ... Isa stopped listening and focused instead on what she felt. Beneath Ever's skin was the smallest of vibrations. Garin's gift, it seemed, was still present. *Don't let Garin's sacrifice be in vain,* Isa prayed.

After a long stretch of waiting, Isa was sure Garin's power was working. Ever's heart was slightly less erratic. It seemed that the miracle would simply take time. Well, that suited her just fine. Isa laid his head and shoulders gently on the ground and stood. Sacha had managed to break her husband's heart. But Sacha had not broken her.

She had a score to settle with Sacha.

Isa closed her eyes and leaned back against the bars of the prison cell. She was tired, but her exhaustion was incomparable to her determination. She would not lose Ever so senselessly, not after all they had survived together. Isa wouldn't let Sacha have him in either body or mind. So in her own mind, Isa traveled the length of the Fortress, searching the halls, the chambers, the king's study, the kitchen, even the gardens until she located Sacha's heart. It was in the tower.

A few minutes later, a new Fae appeared. Instead of merely replacing the Fae Isa had sent away earlier, however, he motioned for her to follow him. Isa laid a soft kiss on Ever's cheek before straightening and following the Fae, holding her head up high as she did. She might be a prisoner, but she was still the chosen daughter of the Fortress. This was her home, and she was queen.

"I thought that tugging sensation might be you." Sacha didn't even turn away from the fire as Isa followed the guard into the annals. "What do you want?"

Isa was surprised to see that the sun was fading once again over the mountain. Had they already been here a whole day?

"I must admit," Sacha continued, "I'm rather curious to know the woman who changed my brother so." Sacha had changed clothes since Isa had seen her last and was now wearing Isa's new red dress, the one Ever had liked so much. Did this woman have no end to the ways she could aggravate her? Isa shoved that thought aside and focused on what she had come to do.

"I am here to discuss the current state of affairs."

Sacha motioned to a chair near the fire, but Isa stayed put. "I know about the children," she continued, "and that they were never sick at all."

"There is something you should know that I did not tell my brother, for I feared it would only puff him up more than he already is." Sacha spoke as though Isa hadn't said anything at all, finally turning to face Isa, her gray eyes sweeping up and down the mess Isa must look. But Isa only stood her ground. She wouldn't be intimidated by such paltry judgments.

"I never wielded my fire as easily as Henri does, but," Sacha said, her eyes growing distant, "the first time I showed my father how I could make a flame, Rodrigue promised me that one day he would take me away from the Fae world and that I would be queen." She turned to stir whatever was inside the black cauldron upon the fire, though Isa could not see what. "I would be loved by all, he promised. And revered. I can only assume this was before Everard was born, for I was quite young. But," her face hardened, "he chose Everard."

"It matters not whom he chose to be king," Isa said, "for I was chosen to be queen of the Fortress before your brother was ever coronated. In fact, he only became king because he married me." How did *no one* remember this? She took a step closer to the woman, her arms crossed. "So if you're here to squabble over titles, it is *me* you should be dealing with."

"I want what is mine by right!" Sacha exploded, hurling a little glass bottle to the floor. It shattered, and Isa wondered what had been inside. "I deserve this! My children deserve this! We will be loved by the Fortress and its people forever!"

Isa wanted to spit every vile word that she knew at the woman, but something held her back. *Tell her*, it said, *what it means to be my daughter.*

Isa wanted to groan. *Now* the Fortress was telling her what to do? Yet she knew better than to ignore its instruction. That never ended well. Taking a deep breath, Isa sought to calm herself.

"If you truly wish to be a daughter of the Fortress, you must be willing to be molded and wrought into a creature of compassion and sacrifice."

Sacha rolled her eyes before turning back to the strange cauldron that hung over the hearth, but Isa continued.

"It is a hard, painful path, and your brother has been melted down and recast time and time again upon it. But if you want to know true love," Isa took a step closer, her heart pounding, "then surely it is a lesson you could learn. We all do in time."

Sacha didn't respond, only continued stirring whatever was in the pot. For the first time, Isa picked up a whiff of something sour, like rotten cabbages. She also felt a strange twinge ripple through her body as she stepped closer to the hearth. What was in the cauldron?

"You think your husband would be willing to allow me to stay by his side to learn such a lesson?" Sacha's voice was petulant, but Isa answered anyway.

"Ever has always wanted a sibling! I know he would open his arms with joy if you would only join us and give up this darkness." She eyed the pot. "You could live with us, and we could rule together! But you must be willing to withstand crippling blows for the sake of your duty to this place. For the Fortress shapes those it loves."

"You seem so confident of your place in this great castle." Sacha turned once again to glare at her, and Isa could feel the hatred in the woman's heart begin to coalesce. "Feather beds, full bellies every night ... This hardly feels like sacrifice and destitution to me! I *know* sacrifice and hardship!" Her words moved to a high pitch. "You cannot speak to me about hardship until you have been shunned by your people and your father abandons you, and then he casts you out and you are taken advantage of by a greedy man with even lesser means than he has compassion!"

"There are many kinds of suffering," Isa said quietly.

"You know what? You are right! And since you seem so intent on belittling mine, I shall prove to you how set I am in my ways, and that you shan't dissuade me." She jerked her head in the direction of the hearth. "Come here!"

Hesitantly, Isa did as she was bid. The Fortress had brought her here. It would not abandon her now. But that didn't stop her from trembling. The closer she drew to the cauldron itself, the more suffocating the air seemed to get. Isa's skin prickled as though unseen eyes watched her, and the heaviness in the air was suddenly so intense it was dizzying.

"Tomorrow morning," Sacha said, "you will stand before your kingdom. I've already summoned as many people from Soudain as will fit in your courtyard and down the mountain road. They will bear witness to the change of crown. I will finish this spell, and you will burn from the inside out. And after they watch you die, they will know who their queen is!"

"You do not have the power for something so dark." Isa fought to stay upright as she stood beside the bubbling mixture of evil. "I can feel your heart, and it is dark, but it is only so strong."

"Perhaps you are correct, and I do not have the power necessary. But my son does."

Immediately, Isa's vision adjusted and she could see more

clearly. That this woman would dabble in the dark arts was bad enough. But to involve Henri? Isa clenched her fists, wishing with all her heart to knock the woman into oblivion. And then it occurred to her. A question that no one should have to ask a mother, but one that might allow Isa a peek into her heavily guarded heart.

"Do you love your children?"

"What?" Sacha had bent over a thick book on the large wooden table. In it were all sorts of drawings of circles and stars and herbs.

"Do you love your children?" Isa demanded more loudly this time. And as she did, she was suddenly caught up in a vision.

Generally, Isa could sense the temperature of the hearts of those around her, sensing both their version of truth and showing them the real truth at the same time. But this vision was much stronger than any she had ever experienced before. It wasn't just a feeling. Isa saw into the woman's very soul.

"You're afraid of them!" she gasped. She could feel Sacha grab a handful of her dress and shove her up against a wall, but the vision was still too strong to escape.

"I fear no one!"

"You're going to kill them!" Isa watched in horror as all the woman's plans and imaginings came to life before her eyes. Repeatedly and in different ways, she watched the children die.

As her sight returned to her, she realized that Sacha had placed her elbow across Isa's chest and shoulders, pinning her hard against the wall. Sacha clapped her other hand over Isa's mouth and leaned in close. Isa bit her fingers hard. Sacha leapt back with a shriek, cradling her hand.

"You hate them," Isa continued in a rush, "because they're too familiar for your comfort! You thought you wanted them until you came back and found them just as you were once, unwanted half-breeds. Henri especially! He frightens you with his power. It's growing quickly, and it leans far more to the Fortress side than the Fae!" Isa felt like she could sing for joy. It was a fierce joy.

Sacha dashed over to the cauldron. Lifting a large ladleful of the brown liquid up to her lips, she began to whisper into it. Immediately, a sharp burning, like holding a candle too close to the skin, began to eat its way through Isa's insides. Isa's knees hit the ground with a sharp crack, but it was nothing compared to the scorching inside.

Sacha said something, but Isa couldn't hear it over the pain. Two sets of hands grabbed Isa by the shoulders, but just after they lifted her, Isa felt someone take hold of her hair and yank it back.

"For all that talk of being the Fortress's chosen queen, the Fortress doesn't seem to care much about you now. Does it?" Sacha whispered. And with that, Isa was dragged all the way back to the dungeon.

CHAPTER 41

THE CONDEMNED

The Fae guards tossed Isa down into the dungeon, worsening the pain that already racked her body. The fire still burned inside, so hot that Isa couldn't seem to find her voice to cry. Whether or not Ever was still on the ground Isa couldn't tell, nor did she have the strength to look. She could only draw her knees to her chest and silently beg the Maker to extinguish the fire inside her, to kill her if He must, but to just end the pain.

One arm was slipped beneath her knees and another behind her back. "I tried to go after you," Ever whispered hoarsely, "but I'm not strong enough—"

"Heal me!" she gasped into the darkness.

"What did she do?"

"Just do it!" she tried to scream, the fire clawing its way up her throat. "It's burning me!"

"I can't heal you if I don't know what she did!"

"Sorthileige, Ever!"

One hand was placed on her head and the other on her stomach. A weak blue glow began to move into her. But the longer she waited, the more scorched her insides felt. No relief trickled in like the cool stream Isa had expected. She moaned, and tears streamed down her face as he tried again and again. But he couldn't seem to manage a fire greater than anything Henri might have produced.

Ever finally shook his head. "It's too strong. It's the sick tent, all over again."

The fire inside her continued to burn, but his words cleared a hole in the cloud of smoke that filled her mind. Isa clenched her teeth and fought to slow her breathing. She focused on what little precious truth she knew.

Sacha was terrified. Though Isa couldn't see exactly what she feared, the woman's fear was nearly visceral. In her fear, Isa was sure that Sacha would use no less than all the powers she could summon. And though that meant she was using her Fortress fire as well as the Sorthileige, it also meant that she would be using her Fae powers, too.

And the Fae power was only a lie.

Slowly, ever so slowly, drops of release began to dribble through her. And though the pain was still there, Isa could finally breathe again. Wearily she let herself droop against her husband. For a long time they lay that way, Ever against the wall and Isa against Ever.

"I tried to go after you," he said again into her hair. "As soon as Garin's power began to clear my mind, I fought them, but I wasn't strong enough yet."

Isa didn't think she'd ever heard so much shame in his voice. "Shhh." Her throat was so parched that she broke into a coughing. "You did nothing wrong," she rasped when it was done. "I went on my own accord." She twitched as a tongue of flame licked her chest.

"This is my fault," he said into her hair. Isa wanted to ask how that was so, but talking was still hard. "Sacha offered to heal you," he continued. "She said that if I was willing to leave Destin and never return, she would lift the curse on you. We could go somewhere quiet and alone." His voice moved to a whisper. "She gave us the chance to be happy. And I threw that chance away."

Isa squeezed his hand. "I've seen enough of her heart," she croaked. "She would have chased us down eventually. There's," she paused to swallow, her mouth still unbelievably dry, "no way she would have allowed us to live. She's too frightened."

"I feel as though I've asked the Fortress a hundred times in the last hour, a thousand times in the last month, why it would let this happen." He began to rub his hand up and down her back, and though it didn't help quench the fire, the touch was at least soothing.

"All I can imagine is this." She pulled back to look up at him. Even in the weak light of the candle, the sheen of sweat on his face was easily visible, as was its unusual pallor. "We have asked the Fortress *why* in all of our darkest hours. When the curse was cast. When Nevina attacked. When Bronkendol nearly killed my brother." Isa drew a deep breath. The more she spoke, the less power the fire seemed to possess. "But we never question the Fortress when the good happens. Why were we brought together, despite our hatred for one another? Why did the Fortress use my kidnapping to show me my true strength? Why were Henri and Genny pushed into our lives? For every *why* there has been a gift ... one that neither of us deserved." She gave a shaky laugh. "I may have little strength left in me, but in my heart ... I feel peace."

Whether the burning was truly beginning to dull, or whether she was just beginning to go numb, Isa didn't know, but she was immensely grateful for whichever was bringing her relief. And with it, clarity of mind. "We need to fight this. She's going to execute us at dawn."

"And just how do you propose we do that?" His burning eyes locked onto hers. "I'm improving, but I'm not exactly battle fit. And please do not take offense, my love, but you are hardly looking well-rested and ready yourself."

"Ever, she's going to kill the children."

He stiffened beneath her. "She wouldn't dare." His voice was deadly. "They're her *children*."

"I think she always meant to be reunited with them, but Henri threatens her. He's far more powerful than she expected." She paused. "And I think you are right in that we cannot defeat her. But," she brushed a piece of hair from his eyes, "the Fortress can. And as for me, I've seen too much *not* to trust the Fortress. And I will not be taken quietly."

They were silent for a long time. Ever stroked her hair as Isa snuggled beneath his chin. Her stomach, chest, and even her arms and legs still hurt as though she'd left them uncovered in the summer sun for hours. But she was well enough to think and pray and hope.

Ever, as usual, was closed off. She could still feel the pain and shame flowing from him like a river cresting during a storm, but his exact emotions were hidden. *Please, Fortress,* she thought, yearning overtaking her as it never had before. *Let me know his heart. Before we die, break down his walls and let me know him!*

Then it hit her. For weeks, they had studied the ancient writings in the Tower of Annals. They had hunted for their enemy, and they had tried to take the kingdom back by force. In the same way, Isa had been trying to shove the truth in her husband's face whenever she thought he needed it. Then when it didn't work, she'd allowed frustration to take her every time he'd failed to see the light. Isa had been wielding the truth like a hammer to prove to everyone that she was right. And yet, the peace she felt now was anything but a weapon. Instead, it was gentle and quiet, a rain on a summer's day.

And it was the most potent peace she had ever felt in her life.

She moved in stilted, slow motions until she was kneeling before him. With shaking hands, she took hold of his shoulders. "Kiss me."

Ever leaned forward. The kiss he gave her wasn't nearly the passionate, exuberant, wild kiss she'd been wishing for back in the southern forest. But it was real. As his lips softly molded to her own, Isa breathed out the peace that was within her. For her peace was the truth. Whatever the Fortress had planned for them, it would be for the best. Perhaps they would be saved or perhaps they would join Garin in eternal bliss. If that happened, maybe Henri would one day become the great king the people deserved, despite his mother's intentions. Then when it was their time, Henri and Genny would join them in eternity as well. The pain for Isa and Ever would be only a moment in comparison to eternity. But for the short seconds they might suffer here, the Fortress would be with them through whatever fire they might walk. The Fortress had never failed them before. It would not fail them now.

As she poured the truth of her own heart into the kiss, Ever's own kiss grew eager and even desperate. Gripping her arms, he pulled her tightly against him. He trembled, but she could sense that his shaking wasn't from fear or even from the poison. His mouth was hungry, kissing her lips, her temples, her neck in turn. His fingers wove themselves into her hair, and Isa closed her eyes as she thanked the Fortress for bringing him back not just from death's door, but also from despair. Pain still lived in his heart as it did in hers. But his determination was quickly beginning to eclipse that pain.

And then, as if the heavens had exploded above her, Isa saw into Ever's soul. Resentment for his father, like the color of dried blood. White-hot mourning for the loss of his mentor. Sunbeam-yellow streaks of pride for his men and the kingdom he loved so much. A brilliant violet surprised her with its intensity, mourning the child they'd never had and the children they were losing now. The black of a bottomless pit for his sister and the pain she'd caused them. A wave of silver thanksgiving and devotion to the Maker and the Fortress. In that instant, though, his overwhelming flood of emotion was his desire for her.

Until that moment, Isa had never understood just how deeply her husband needed her. Memories of their early days were a deep hue of twilight blue, interwoven with more recent memories of emerald green the color of grass. But most of all, Ever's heart was red like spring's first rose. Isa sighed into his kiss, her pain suddenly overshadowed by her bliss. His heart was marvelous.

How long they lingered in that kiss, Isa couldn't say. Again and again, his hands explored her face and her neck before sliding down to the small of her back. In turn, she also memorized his features, the curve of his stubbled jaw, the straight lines of his neck, the way his arms felt as he wrapped them around her.

"I am greatly curious to see," she finally leaned back and let out a short breathless chuckle, "how we might find our way out of this predicament. I think I should like more nights like this, rather than letting this one be our last. The last time we were in prison, Garin had the plan."

"First of all," Ever nuzzled her jaw with his nose, "I think this getting thrown into prison is a terrible habit that we ought to break. It sets a bad example for our children."

Isa giggled. *Our children.* How her heart soared when he uttered those words.

"Second," Ever said, "whatever my sister has planned for us we will face with dignity and faith." He took her face between his hands, and with his thumbs he traced circles beneath her eyes. "Do you forgive me, Isa?"

"For what?"

"Despairing." He shook his head. "If I have learned anything, it is never to underestimate this Fortress." He softly turned her head to place a lingering kiss on her cheek. "Or you." Then his lips were on hers again, and he hugged her so tightly to him that Isa's ribs hurt. "I do not know what destiny is ours," he whispered in her ear. "So for now, in this moment we have been given, I will no longer ask why."

"What will you do then?" Isa's heart beat fast.

"I am going to give thanks and enjoy these beautiful moments with my wife." His voice was suddenly gravelly and breathless once again.

In spite of their dingy, dark surroundings and their pending executions, Isa's happiness became one she had never known before.

CHAPTER 42

WHAT LITTLE STRENGTH

Isa woke with a start as the dungeon door banged open. It took her a few hard blinks in the light of the torch before she could clearly make out the Fae who seemed to be holding the door open for them. Her determination to fight was still there, of course, but Isa wouldn't have minded just a few more hours of sleep before they faced whatever nightmare Sacha had prepared for them.

When Isa tried to get up, though, Ever's arms stayed tightly wrapped around her, holding her to him. "I am afraid you shall have to tell us what exactly you want us to do," Ever said, shrugging helplessly. Isa glanced up to see his face full of innocence. He was taunting them. "That lovely hemlock did a lovely job of addling my mind, you know."

"Her majesty wants you," was the Fae's terse reply.

"Do you hear that, my dear?" Ever looked down at her, his smile polite and his eyes gleaming mischievously. "We have a queen calling for us!" He looked back up at the guards, still smiling pleasantly. "Send our regards, and please apologize for our absence. But as you can see, we are quite busy and cannot spare a second. Perhaps," he wiggled his eyebrows at Isa, "we should send a gift to make up for our absence. Do you suppose a stuffed pig would be to her liking?"

The Fae didn't respond, but Isa felt something in the creature's heart flutter. She wiggled out of her husband's arms and stepped through the open cell door. The Fae's eyes widened as she approached, but he stayed still.

"Isa?" Ever's voice was no longer mocking.

Isa placed her hand on the Fae's arm and looked into his green misty eyes. What she felt from his heart surprised her. "You were not meant for this world," she whispered.

The Fae didn't answer, only stared sadly back at her. His attitude was very different from that of the Fae Isa had encountered earlier.

"Why do you follow her?"

"Because ... we deserve more?" it said slowly.

Isa studied him, reaching deep within his heart. And while she couldn't put her finger on any one emotion, she could suddenly see why the Maker had created such a realm for them, one that was pliable and ready for shaping again and again. They were too changing, too fluid to live in a world with rules and hard structure. They were meant to wander. If they continued to reside in Destin, it would not only injure the Destinians. The Fae would die as well.

"You need to go home," she whispered.

The Fae only continued looking at her with his large frightened eyes, shivering slightly every few moments. Suddenly, he tilted his head as if listening. "Come."

When Ever joined her he no longer wore his obnoxious smirk. Instead, he allowed the Fae to bind his hands behind his back, slipping Isa a wry smile as he did. The plan they'd pieced together the night before wasn't as glamorous as anything Garin would have come up with, but it rested on the Fortress's faithfulness and on Isa's revelation about Ever's heart.

They were herded across the Fortress and up the tower steps.

During their long walk, Isa was relieved to see that her husband's gait was once again strong and sure. Garin's gift seemed to have restored at least most of Ever's health. Now if only Isa, too, could survive whatever horrors Sacha had planned for them. Her whole body ached, and she felt as though she might drop into a deep sleep at any moment. If she was still able to stand by the time they climbed all the way up to the annals, Isa would count it as a miracle.

When they finally entered the tower, Sacha and her Fae waited out on the balcony in the fuzzy gray of early morning. The tower's balcony was wide enough to hold at least a dozen men between the window wall and the ledge, but crossing it felt to Isa like a lifetime of its own. She knew what awaited her. Her heart still caught in her throat, though, as she got close enough to the edge to see below.

Just as Sacha had promised, the Fortress's front lawn and the road down the mountain were filled with hundreds of people. Fathers, mothers, and children, old and young alike were there to witness their demise. From the crowd, however, there was none of the bravado or excitement she'd felt from the mob on the day the Fortress was taken. Instead, Isa sensed overwhelming fear rising like a storm cloud nearly full to bursting. These people didn't want Isa or Ever to die, she realized. They'd only come because they were summoned, like her. Were her parents there? She hoped not.

"You look well." Isa turned to see Sacha eyeing Ever suspiciously. "No matter, though." She waved her hand dismissively and walked to the balcony's edge.

"Destin!" Sacha's voice echoed down from the tower to the people below. "My name is Sacha Fortier. I am the firstborn of the late King Rodrigue, and I have come to take my place." She began to list all the ways Ever had failed the Fortress and its people, but Isa didn't listen. Instead, she stared into the beautiful gray eyes of the man beside her. At any time now they would need to set their plan into motion, but oh, how she wanted to linger in the stormy depths of his gaze.

"So you don't think me heartless, I will offer my brother mercy one more time," Sacha said, turning back to Ever and Isa. "Do you renounce your claim to the throne and swear never to enter this kingdom again?"

Ever turned to look at his sister straight on. "I swore to serve this Fortress until death. Doing anything less would be dishonorable," his voice boomed. "So no. I will not surrender what I have sworn to protect."

"And you?" Sacha turned to Isa, her eyes hard. "Do you renounce your title?"

"I took the same oath as my husband. Honor will be for us both."

"Fools," Sacha muttered before turning back to the people. "Since they won't renounce their claims to the throne, even though the Maker has clearly delivered the Fortress into my hands, it is my duty to take it from them. By fire they have lived, and by fire they will die. Henri."

Only then did Isa realize Henri and Genny had been brought out onto the balcony as well. Henri whispered something in Genny's ear before letting go of her hand and trudging out to join his mother. Genny screamed as she fought to free herself from the Fae, but Henri only walked forward. Behind him, two of the Fae carried the boiling cauldron out, placing it between Sacha and Ever. Despite her resolve to stay calm, Isa fought the urge to lunge at Sacha. Whom had Sacha threatened to coerce the boy into such evil? Isa could guess only too well.

"Henri," Isa called out softly. "You don't need to do this. Trust the Fortress! She cannot touch you without its permission—"

Sacha's hand was sharp and fast, and it made Isa's face sting. Ever looked as though he might tear his sister to pieces, but Isa bumped into his arm and shook her head. They needed to wait for the right moment. She needed to get to Henri. If she couldn't convince Henri, they were all doomed.

Sacha walked back to the cauldron and held her hands out, then she looked expectantly at Henri.

"Henri, no," Isa whispered, but Henri raised his hands as well, refusing to look at Isa as he stared stubbornly into the cauldron's brown bubbles. Thin gloves of blue and green fire wrapped themselves around his hands, and he placed them on the side of the cauldron.

Sacha began the incantation, and as her voice rose the burning began again, this time in Isa's feet. The sensation reminded her of walking barefoot on Soudain's cobblestone streets after they'd been too long in the sun.

"Isa." Ever had leaned down, his eyes burning brightly. Knowing it might be her last, Isa craned her neck up and met him for a brief, beautiful goodbye. His lips were feverishly hot, and she knew he was feeling the Sorthileige's heat as well. Still, it was a strong kiss. One that made Isa smile. As they said goodbye, Isa felt the rope around her wrist burn off with his fire. They were ready.

In one instant, Isa was kissing her husband. In the next, he was gone. Ever jerked around and threw himself at the nearest Fae. It disintegrated, and he fell hard on the ground. In another second he was up, swinging the Fae's pike around in the air like a staff, his fire flaming from it at both ends.

Sacha's surprise showed on her face, and for a moment she forgot to chant. Isa took that moment to throw herself down at Henri's feet. She considered pushing his arms down, but the green and blue fire that encircled them convinced her that was a bad idea. Instead, she placed one hand on his face. "You don't have to do this," she whispered.

"Get away from him!" Sacha screeched, but Isa ignored her. If her hands hadn't been held out above the cauldron, Isa was sure Sacha would have killed her in that moment. As it was, the burning not only intensified in her feet but moved up to her ankles as well. Isa stifled a short cry. Sweat began to roll down her temples, and Isa clenched her muscles tightly to try and repel the burn as she forced herself to look back up at Henri.

"She said she would hurt Genny," Henri whimpered.

Sacha's incantations became a shout, sending another wave of pain over Isa.

"Do you remember all those times," she gasped, "when I told you we needed to trust the Fortress?"

"Yes."

"This is the most important time of all."

"Shut up!" Sacha screamed at her, but Isa kept talking. Whenever the woman became distracted, the burning that now had risen to her calves would lessen for just a moment. Behind her, Isa could hear the sound of fighting as Ever shielded her from the Fae. She needed to move quickly.

"Your mother needs you for this because she is not strong enough to unhand us on her own. If you stop helping her, she will not be able to continue." Isa sucked a quick breath in. The fire was now at her waist, and the world was beginning to tilt. Shaking her head to clear it, Isa continued. "Did you know that before we met your father and mother, King Ever and I decided to keep you as our own—"

Isa's words broke off in another bout of pain, but Henri's fire flickered.

Drawing in air was becoming more and more difficult. The burning was now up to her lungs, and Isa had to place a hand on the ground to remain upright where she knelt. *Please, Fortress,* she begged. *Just a little longer!*

"We love you, Henri," she gasped. "If... If we hadn't been attacked that night, you and Genny..." But she couldn't continue. The pain was too much. Clawing its way up her throat, her world exploded into one burning chasm of fire. The ground began to rise again, and Isa hit the balcony floor.

"No!" Henri cried out.

"Henri! Get back here!" Sacha shouted, but instead, Isa felt a small hand clutching her arm. Somehow, she pried her eyes open one last time.

"You were going to keep us?" Henri whimpered, his golden hair falling in his eyes as tears began to stream down his face. He still held one hand against the cauldron, but the other hand was holding her.

Isa smiled, reaching up to caress his face with a trembling hand. "We love you and Genny so much..." she sucked another breath in, "... that we vowed to go to the ends of the world for you. And this is me doing just that." Isa's body felt as though it should imitate the Fae and fall into a pile of ashes. But in slow agonizing movements, she pushed herself up on her knees and wrapped him in an embrace. As she held him tight, Isa gathered all the love in her heart and impressed it upon his.

Just as she'd opened Ever's heart the night before, now Isa wrapped the truth around Henri. There was no more hammering away at the walls he'd erected around himself. Instead, she wove the truth of their love in and out of his soul as one might weave a ribbon of silk. She showed him the way she felt when the children entered a room. She let him feel Ever's anger at their father's carelessness. She sang to him of the tears of joy she'd cried as they'd sealed the blood vow.

Slowly, ever so slowly Isa felt Henri's heart begin to open. His fear began to melt away, and his breathing grew deeper. And Isa thanked the Maker as Sacha's screams sent waves of fire up her arms and face. He had answered her prayers. And though Sacha's fire was great, the fire of the Fortress within Isa was greater. Sacha might burn her body to nothingness, but Isa's soul could not be conquered.

Isa would have gone on hugging Henri forever, but eventually she could hold on no longer. Briefly she saw the blurry form of a boy reaching out for her as she let herself fall. As the fire ravaged her body from the inside, her strength melted like wax.

People shouted from all around her. Men's voices in particular began to drown out the others. She could feel Henri still battling with himself over whether to continue aiding his mother or to let go of the cauldron completely. He longed to let go, but there was just enough fear left to keep him from it.

"Henri," Isa whispered. She could vaguely make out the sound of weeping, and a small hand found its way into hers. Sacha was screaming something again but Isa didn't care. The pain was so great she was nearly numb. "The truth is that you are loved. You need no longer fear." As soon as the words had left her lips, Isa felt herself slip away.

Her life at the Fortress had not been long. But Isa's four years had been good. Oh, how good they had been! Her journey, which had begun with a broken body and broken heart, had brought her the purpose she had so long craved. Ever, once the hated prince who had ruined her life, had become the friend who valued her life above his own. And even if it was only for a brief time, the Fortress had brought Isa children as well. Not a detail would she change in the life she had been given.

Take care of them, she silently asked the Fortress as she pushed the last of her strength into the boy's heart. *He's seen the truth. Now let him believe.*

CHAPTER 43
INTO THE FLAMES

Ever wondered how much longer he would be able to hold up. The burning was more painful than the hemlock's poison had been, but at least it didn't send his body into convulsions. Still, both hurt more than Ever had once thought possible. Only by the Fortress's mercy was he still fighting.

At least he didn't have to think much about his fighting tactics. With each Fae it was the same.

Burn the fire brightly on the pike.

Wait for the Fae to come, like moths to a flame.

Wait for the Fae to materialize while drawing close to the flame.

But just as he would kill one Fae, another would come. Then he would have to mesmerize that one, too. How many had Isa said there were? Over two hundred? Still, Ever wondered, where were the others? He'd witnessed at least four dozen Fae with them when they'd first arrived at the balcony. Though his opponents here were still coming fast and steady, there weren't nearly as many as there should have been. And that made him uneasy.

Unfortunately, another bout of burning punched him in the gut, and Ever hit the ground. A swift crack to the head from his latest foe's pike sent his vision spinning as well. Ever swept his left arm back blindly and managed to knock the Fae over. She quickly rematerialized on her feet, this time with four more Fae at her side, but he couldn't seem to rise again. Without his fiery torch to distract them, the Fae crouched back ready to spring, with more joining them by the second. Ever did the first thing he could think of and threw a little ball of blue fire high above their heads, just as he had in the cave. The Fae stopped advancing to watch it as it rose. But where was his pike?

Panicked, Ever searched the ground for his weapon only to realize it had rolled away. Just as the Fae began to look back down from the sky, their eyes once again focusing on him, two of them gave a rasping sound and collapsed before turning into a pile of ash. Ever looked up to find the last person he had expected to see.

"Acelet!"

"Keep drawing them!" his general said, crouching low to meet another. "We'll pick them off!"

Ever didn't stop to ask how his general had known to come, but in his heart, he was in awe. The Fortress had answered his pleas. Somehow, the fire continued to build in his hands, though his body felt like it should collapse at any minute. And yet, he felt at least temporarily invigorated as his men flooded the balcony around him. As they tried their first attempts at fighting the airy creatures, Ever had an idea. *I can't do this without you*, he told the Fortress. *I'll need more fire than I've ever wielded before.* Then he balled his fists and raised them up to the sky.

In response, each of his soldier's weapons burned bright blue with his flame. Ever was so surprised that he nearly forgot to focus. It was an incredible sight, the glowing green eyes of the Fae meeting the blazing blue weapons of his men. As the men fought, different flames would go out here and there, and Ever had to rebuild each. Every ball of blue flame was harder to make than the last, as was the glow of each sword. If he could just hold on, though, his weariness wouldn't matter in a few minutes, for Acelet's men would have won the day and Ever would be free to face his sister. And with that in mind, Ever was able to push out the pain just enough to continue the fight.

A cry interrupted his focus on the balls of fire, however, and immediately, the burning lessened.

There was no celebration, though, when he turned and saw Henri staring in horror at the ground. Henri clutched at Isa's arm with the hand that wasn't touching the cauldron, tears slipping down his thin cheeks.

The world stopped. Ever stumbled then found his feet, only to fall again. Pushing, shoving, crawling, and running, he might as well have been wading through tar. The way her eyes were closed and the absence of color in her skin were too real. They looked too much like death. But Isa couldn't be dead. He wouldn't allow it.

Finally, Ever broke through the battle raging around them to collapse at Isa's side. He could hear his men's dismay as their fires went out, but he didn't care. Lifting her head up, Ever placed his ear on her chest. It wasn't moving up and down.

"Henri," Sacha screeched, "if you stop now, the Sorthileige will kill you!"

"That's not what Miss Isa said!" Henri took a step closer to where Ever cradled Isa. The boy touched the edge of the cauldron with only a few fingers.

"You will die!" Sacha's voice was hysterical.

"No!" Henri shouted. "You're lying!"

"Henri, I will kill you myself if you don't finish this!"

Rage took Ever as it hadn't before. This woman must die.

Before he could intervene, however, Henri turned to his mother. "No," he said, his young voice suddenly as calm as a pond.

"No, what?" Sacha's shoulders heaved as she threw even more green flame into the cauldron. The pain took Ever by surprise, and a cry slipped out against his will. "You worthless piece of—"

"I am not worthless! Miss Isa and King Ever were going to keep me and Genny because they loved us. And the Fortress loves us. So I don't need you." Henri looked from his mother to his hand. "And I don't need this."

An inhuman shriek tore itself from Sacha's lips as Henri let go of the cauldron. Genny screamed from another part of the balcony, but Ever couldn't see her.

"Get down!" he shouted, praying desperately that Genny was out of the way. Ever grabbed Henri and threw himself over the boy and his wife. As he did, the dark swell of Sorthileige that Ever had felt building inside the cauldron broke. Sacha was enveloped in one quick burst of green flame that burned brighter than the sun.

Then she was gone.

The remaining Fae that had battled around them collapsed into the familiar piles of ash, their pikes making clacking sounds as they hit the ground. In awe, the soldiers watched their enemies' remains float away on a sudden wind.

A cry of victory was raised from one soldier, and soon they were all shouting, as were the people on the ground below them. But not Ever.

Now that the burning was gone and Sacha was dead, he lifted Isa's lifeless body into his lap. "No," he whispered. *It can't be true, Fortress! She's not gone. She can't be!* Tears began to run down his face, and before he knew it, sobs racked his body more violently than the poison ever had. An emptiness filled him, one as black as ashes and even more suffocating. His world was devoid of light, of air. It was a thing of nothingness and death.

"Everard?" Launce called from somewhere behind him, but Ever ignored him.

This woman was his beacon. She was the voice of purity when the siren call of his own demons haunted him. No one else had been able to reach him when he had been in his darkest days. Not even Garin had touched his soul like she had. The memory of the night before floated before his eyes. It had only been hours ago that her arms had held him, her slender hands tracing the contours of his face as she whispered, "I love you," over and over again. He could have ... should have loved her more. Four years wasn't enough, not with all of the wrongs he still had to right. He still needed to tell her he loved her one more time.

If only Sacha had killed him too.

"Let's give your father a few minutes alone," Ever heard Launce say in a low voice. He felt Henri rise, as if being pulled.

"But she's not dead!"

Ever looked up to see the boy frowning at Isa. "Henri." He tried to speak through his tears, as he knew Isa would want him to do. "She's not breathing." It felt like death to say that.

"But there's power still inside her. I can feel it!" And before Launce could grab him again, Henri had shrugged out of Launce's grip and threw himself down beside Isa's body. "We just need to pull her out." He stretched his hand out over Isa's heart, then looked at Ever, his thin face falling a bit. "I still don't know how to control my fire like you do."

Ever stared at Henri in disbelief. Was the boy telling him he'd missed his wife's spark? Ever wanted to retort to the boy that this was foolishness, and that he was just holding on to a dangerous, damning hope. But just as he was about to say as much, Henri touched Isa's hand, and a green mist filled the boy's eyes.

Ever moved so quickly he nearly toppled. Shaking, he held his hand over her heart. At first he felt nothing. But reassured by Henri's eyes, he pressed harder.

Sure enough, after an immeasurable moment, the slightest ember still burned within her. "Take her hand!" Ever ordered the boy as he scrambled to lift her head up. "On my command, press your fire into the palm of her hand!"

"Genny!" Henri waved her over. "Come here!"

Ever wanted to point out that as the little girl didn't have the Fortress's fire yet, she would be of little help to them. But the way she tore herself from Eloy's grasp and threw herself down next to Isa kept him quiet. That was fine then, as long as she didn't get in the way.

"Now, on the count of three!" Ever closed his eyes and began to focus all his efforts on reigniting the spark inside her heart. "One, two—"

"Genny, what are you doing?" Henri cried.

Ever opened his eyes to see Genny leaning over Isa.

"Wake up, Mummy." With those soft words, Genny placed a little kiss right on Isa's lips.

Isa's eyelids fluttered.

EPILOGUE

JUST WAIT

You certainly act as though your tummy is feeling better," Isa said, smiling wryly as Genny bounced on her bed.

"My tummy has been better for a long time!"

"Then why did you tell Cook that you needed cake for supper because greens made you feel sick?" Isa quirked an eyebrow.

Genny sighed dramatically, falling back on her bed like a rag doll. "I was just making sure it was better. But as you can see, it is!"

Isa shook her head and proceeded to tuck her wiggly daughter into bed. *Her daughter*. The words felt so wonderful to even think.

"When is Daddy getting back?"

"You ask that every night." Henri frowned as he walked in. "And I thought you were still sick."

Isa stepped back and watched, amused, as Henri began to tuck his sister in again. Though he had a room of his own now, the boy never failed to see his sister to bed. Nine years without a true mother had created some habits in him that were proving difficult to break. But taking care of his sister? Isa was more than fine with that.

"Alright, you two. I think that should suffice. Genny, remember what Daddy said. He will be home as soon as he can. And Henri, how about I tuck you in now?" Henri nodded, so after a quick prayer and kiss for Genny, Isa walked with him to the next room over.

"How are *you* feeling tonight?" she asked him.

He shrugged. "Fine, I guess. My stomach hasn't hurt in a few days."

"Good. Let's keep it that way by getting some sleep." Isa waited as he climbed into bed. Just as she was about to blow out his candles, however, Henri sat back up.

"I have a question."

Curiosity sparked as Isa sat on the edge of the bed. "What would that be?"

Though Henri had seemed relieved and even a bit excited with his new title as Crown Prince of Destin, he was still finding it more difficult to open up than Genny. And that was to be expected, Isa knew, as he was much older than Genny and had seen far more rejection and danger than his sister had. Still, she yearned for him to talk to her as he seemed to want to do now.

"If you have ... if you and King—Father have a baby, will we still be..." He let the question die, but Isa drew him into a fierce hug.

"When your father and I swore to keep you, we meant that as long as we live and breathe, you will always be our first son, and Genny, our first daughter." She ruffled his hair. "Besides, I don't think there is much chance of that. It seems the Maker wanted me to have a boy and a girl, and I am overjoyed to have you both. I wouldn't change a thing about you if I could."

Henri nodded, seeming mollified. As Isa left his room, she wished to the Fortress that she could convince him of their commitment once and for all. But, she knew, it would take time. There were some truths that needed time rather than power. He would simply have to see that their love was faithful. And that was a gift she was more than willing to wait for.

Isa paused and rubbed her own sore stomach as the door of her chambers closed behind her. After Ever had left to chase down the remaining Fae, giving them the choice to either return to their world or die, the Fortress staff had returned. It had been a wonderful reunion until half of the Fortress occupants had fallen ill with some awful stomach sickness. Henri, Genny, and Isa had held off for a while, but three weeks before they had succumbed as well. It was strange, though, Isa thought as she began the weary walk to her bed. The sickness seemed to linger for a week or so in most, but she was taking far too long to recover. The healer was nearly beside himself with worry. She had taken quite a beating from Sacha and had been feeling ill since the curse had first fallen. Perhaps she would call for the healer again in the morning.

She paused before the full-length mirror, suddenly glad Ever wasn't there to see her. Not that he would have minded, but the bags beneath her eyes were nearly purple and her skin was still too white. And though she hadn't been able to keep much food down at all, her belly was still slightly swollen as well.

Isa frowned, stepping closer to the mirror, squinting in the evening light that shone through the balcony. She turned, pulling her gown tight to see better. Isa's gowns had been snug as of late, but that had been from the upset stomach. Hadn't it?

The nausea.

The constant exhaustion.

The stiff muscles.

Her small but undeniably round belly.

"Someone get Gigi!" Isa ran back to the door and shouted at the first servant she saw. "Get Gigi!"

Isa had never seen Gigi run so fast as she did when she burst into the room. When she took one look at Isa's face, however, and one glance at the way Isa clutched her belly, the old woman's face broke into a glorious smile.

"I don't understand!" Isa said as Gigi began to gently feel around her stomach.

"Oh, Isa," Gigi fussed as she stepped back and looked her up and down, "you're at least four months along!"

Isa stared back at her, her mouth falling open in shock. "But the curse! My cycles stopped when Sacha cursed me!"

For some reason, this made Gigi laugh. Isa frowned, trying to figure out what she had missed.

"Oh, me!" Gigi exclaimed between giggles. "You are not to blame, my dear, for you're the one with the muzzled mind of the expectant, but I've no excuse!" She grabbed Isa's hand. "Garin said the children's illnesses and injuries were deceptions, illusions, yes?"

Isa felt so foolish. Of course! The curse she had felt must have been an illusion as well!

"But why would the Fortress have allowed me to think I was cursed? I surely would have known much sooner than this!"

Gigi drew Isa in for a deep embrace, then patted Isa's tummy as she turned to leave the room, to boss the Fortress staff into preparing a nursery already, no doubt. "Would you have fought so desperately for Henri and Genny if you had?" And then she stepped out, leaving Isa to puzzle in wonderment at such a thought.

EVER SUCKED in a breath of air that smelled of roses, fresh grass, and his beloved mountain. Never had he guessed it would take three months to track down every Fae in the land.

"I was beginning to think you'd never find all the little buggers," Acelet called as he greeted Ever from the stables.

A sharp pain gripped Ever's heart as he remembered every time Garin had come to meet him in such a way. The three months had lessened the shock, but the hurt was still strong. And he wasn't sure if it would ever quite be gone. Not, at least, until he was in that blessed eternity as well.

"I didn't either," Ever admitted.

"It is done then?"

"Yes." Ever hopped off his horse and took a long swig of water from a nearby bucket. "Most of them were surprisingly ready to return. But the veil is finally sealed. I think we should hopefully have a moment to breathe before the next disaster befalls us."

"I certainly hope so," Acelet said, a sudden ornery gleam in his eye.

"Oh, and Acelet, please send for Eloy. I have a task for him before I go up and see everyone."

In just a few moments, the men Ever had brought with him had dispersed, and only Eloy stood before him in the stables.

"Walk with me." Ever clapped the young man on the shoulder as they slowly started for the Fortress. "So what did you think of guard duty?"

Eloy gave him a big grin. "It was an honor to keep your children safe..." he paused, "when I was able to keep up with them."

Ever snorted out a laugh. "Good then. Because I have a position I would like you to consider."

Eloy's eyes went wide, but he said nothing.

"I grew up under the watchful eye of my father," Ever said, his laughter quickly dying, "but I became a man under the guidance of Garin." His chest tightened as he said the steward's name. He drew in a deep breath. "If you are willing, I would be honored to have you continue on as the personal guardian for my children."

Eloy's mouth dropped open, and it was a moment before he could speak. When he did speak, he stuttered terribly. "Sure... surely ... y...y...you must have s...s...someone else more qualified than I, Your Majesty. I have only just begun—"

"You saved Genny's life when the cauldron exploded. In that, you have already proven your worth as a soldier. But if you must know more, the children trust you. And that is no small feat for Henri." Ever frowned. "He needs someone with a good heart who will help him see himself as he is, not who he fears himself to be." He turned a sharp eye on the young man beside him. "But I warn you, watching over them will age you, making you far older than your years."

Eloy's grin spread across his face once more. "You have been gone for some time, Your Majesty. How do you know that Henri is such a hooligan as you make him out to be?"

"Because I was a hooligan."

"Ah, I see." Eloy stopped and gave him a bow. "Then it would be an honor, Your Highness, to guard your most precious possessions." His face grew more serious as he looked back up at Ever. "I will keep them with my life." Then he looked slightly confused. "You do mean all of them, don't you?"

"Both of them, yes." What a strange thing to say.

"Oh, then ... of course, sire." Just as Acelet had left him with an ornery gleam in his eye, so did Eloy now. Ever shook his head as he continued to the Fortress alone. What had gotten into everyone?

As he drew closer to the Fortress's front steps, he could see the crowd waiting for him in the distance, and he couldn't help but marvel at how the Fortress had saved them one small miracle at a time.

To begin with, Henri's bird shouldn't have reached the army. He couldn't have known which one to send, nor did he know how to use his power to alter the animal's mind so that it might fly to the right destination. On top of that, Sacha's Fae had killed nearly every homing pigeon they owned. But somehow, Henri's bird had survived, and it had arrived at Launce's camp at just the right time. An hour later and none of them would have survived. It was a gift of the Maker, Father Lucien had told him.

They had found the holy man walking along the road between towns. Apparently, the priest had caught wind of the coming uprisings. He had taken the church's messenger birds and the church's holy writ to a larger town nearby, where he stayed with the priest there until he heard that all of the sick children had been healed. That, he'd told Ever, was when he realized Sacha had been defeated. As they traveled together after that, he and Ever had made plans to discuss Sansim's future once the kingdom was put to rights.

Ever was pulled from his reverie by the shrieks of a little girl. He barely had time to hold his arms out when Genny bounded into them. Ever laughed, hugging her close.

"I missed you too!" He put her on the ground. "Where are your brother and mother?"

"Henri's back there." Genny pointed behind her. "And Mummy—"

"Don't you say a word!" Henri darted up and clamped his hand over his sister's mouth. "She's in the tower." After he was done reprimanding his sister, Henri looked up at Ever and, to Ever's surprise, slipped him a small but genuine smile. Ever squeezed Henri's shoulder then set off for the tower. After a few steps alone, however, he turned. "Aren't you coming with me?"

"Yes!" Genny said, but Henri shook his head.

"I think Cook has some sweet bread for us to try." He looked at Genny. "Wouldn't you like some sweet bread?"

"No." Genny pouted. "I want to stay with Daddy."

"Oh, come on!" Henri took her by the arm and dragged her away. Ever watched them go, mystified, but finally shook his head and continued his walk to the tower. Perhaps now that he was home, he would eventually learn to somewhat understand those two.

He didn't see Isa at first when he entered the tower. Since the battle, new panes of glass had been fitted into the walls and balcony door, and the shelves, books, furniture, and rugs had been put to rights. All signs of the black magic were gone. It was a peaceful, sacred place once more.

Then he saw her. Standing out on the balcony, Isa wore a long flowing dress made of a lavender fabric that looked thin and cool, fitting for the late summer heat. He paused on the threshold and knocked on the glass of the open door. "May I have an audience with the queen?"

Then she turned, and all of Ever's teasing words fled him. "Is... Are you?" As though in a dream, he walked toward her. When he reached her, however, he stopped, unable to touch. For touching would make it real, and this could only be a dream.

Isa gave him the most beautiful, radiant smile he had ever seen. She reached down and took his hands in hers, then gently placed them on her belly. And though Ever had thought he couldn't be more amazed, he wanted to shout when he felt the slightest movement within her. Her baby.

His child.

Ever heard a shuffling sound behind him and smiled to himself. His *third* child.

"You can come out now." Isa smiled around him, and Genny and Henri crept out to stand beside Isa. Genny looked quite pleased with herself, but Henri seemed unsure.

"How?" Ever managed to whisper.

Isa shook her head and grinned again. "The Fortress does as it pleases." But that was as far as she got, for in a second, his lips were on hers. He wrapped his arms tightly about her, holding the world's most beautiful soul close, in awe again as her belly pressed against him.

"Ew." Genny made a gagging sound.

"Oh, you think it's disgusting when I kiss your mother?" Ever turned and raised his eyebrows. Before Genny could answer, though, he had fallen to his knees and pulled all of them into his arms. "Just wait until I kiss you all!"

Genny squealed and tried to wriggle free, while Henri groaned and tried to push himself away. Isa laughed, and Ever felt tears prick his eyes.

"Thank you!" He let his head fall back as the tears fell freely. "Thank you!"

All he had ever wanted was here in his arms. He had gone from a lonely, angry prince to a king, married to the most worthy woman in all the world. And in five months, they had gone from having no children to three.

"Will we be happy now?" Genny pulled back from his crushing hug to study him quizzically.

Ever laughed through his tears at her serious expression. "Yes."

"How do you know?"

"Because we have each other. And no matter what comes, the Fortress has us all."

Girl in the Red Hood
A Clean Fairy Tale Retelling of Little Red Riding Hood

LIESEL SAT PERFECTLY STILL for an immeasurable time, staring into her mother's ashen face. But deep inside, the part of her that dreamed couldn't be still. It couldn't accept that this was how it ended. Words began to echo in her head, some from her mother. There were other voices, too, however, and eventually there was one command that drowned out all of the rest.

Whatever you do, you must escape those woods! Her grandmother's voice commanded desperately. *Come back to me, no matter what!*

Grandmother had been right. They had come to this wicked village, and the healer was either completely incompetent, or she had just poisoned Amala purposefully. With all of the lies that had been told, all of the desperate looks the townspeople had been giving one another after seeing her, something in the town of Ward was very wrong.

Without knowing what she was doing, Liesel found herself out of her chair and running. Night darkness was beginning to cover everything, but it didn't matter. Liesel knew which direction the vineyard was in, and she wasn't stopping until she got there. It didn't matter that she could no longer see more than five feet in front of her, nor did she care that she had no supplies. All Liesel could think about was going home, running into her grandmother's arms, and leaving this wretched forest behind forever.

But soon it grew too dark, and Liesel's skirt caught on a low branch, causing her to trip. Her hands stung as they scraped against unseen sticks and dry pine needles, and she stubbed her toe on a rock. Wet earth stuck to her as she began to rise, but something made her freeze halfway up. Her breaths were ragged and heavy from her run, but she tried to quiet them as she strained to listen. She was almost sure she'd heard breathing that was not her own.

Turning slowly, still on her hands and knees, she nearly fainted.

The silhouette of a creature stood out against the shadows. A growl slipped out, so slight she wasn't even sure she'd heard it. Fear made her blood turn cold, and with all thoughts of the damp ground and her scratched palms forgotten, Liesel took off again, even faster this time. A tiny voice in her head wondered what she was doing, why she was even in the forest, and screamed at her that no sane girl of thirteen years would be where she was, but she ignored it completely.

She'd gone only little ways, however, before she was flat on her stomach, the creature crouching on her back. For the first time, Liesel found her voice, screaming as loudly as she could for help.

A heavy paw was shoved expertly onto the back of her neck,

shoving her face into the ground, cutting off her cry as a snout with gleaming white teeth lowered itself down beside her face to growl. It occurred to Liesel that she was going to die.

A part of her wondered if this was the Maker's way of secret mercy, saving her from a long, miserable life in that horrid village without her mother. The rest of her, however, was terrified. What kind of pain could a creature like this inflict upon a human, particularly one that wasn't yet fully grown? What kind of gruesome things could those teeth do?

In the brief second before the bite, Liesel wondered which side he would attack her from. The neck? Or perhaps a leg?

A warm pang from her right hand surprised her, however. She turned her head as best she could to look through the darkness at her hand as the warm blood trickled down it. It hurt, but it wasn't the killing lunge she had been expecting. And even stranger was that the animal wasn't continuing the attack. As soon as he had bitten her, he had moved a few feet away, a low growling still in his throat.

Despite the blackness of night, she could make out the contour of a wolf, the biggest she'd ever seen. His coat was silver, and it almost gleamed in the gray haze that filled the dark woods. Liesel had seen wolves before, but only from a distance, and with the comfort of her grandfather's expert crossbow nearby to protect her. This beast's claws were difficult to see, but they looked longer than anything Liesel could have imagined.

At that moment, she locked eyes with the beast, and as soon as she did, she began to shake. The eyes into which she gazed were unmistakably human.

She didn't have time to linger and ponder his unusual eyes, however. In one second, the wolf was watching her intently, as if surveying its strange work, and in the next moment, it was lying lifelessly on the ground, an arrow in its heart. Liesel watched in horror as the human eyes closed.

"Are you alright?" a man's voice called from a distance.

As heavy footsteps approached, Liesel found herself incapable of answering him. She couldn't even lift herself up off the ground. She could only lie there trembling uncontrollably, scrunching her eyes shut as though that would make the horror disappear.

"That's a nasty cut there," the deep voice said. Gently, Liesel felt herself lifted by strong arms and cradled like a child. "Do you live in Ward?" he asked.

Liesel racked her memory, trying to remember the village's name. Ward sounded right. Even if it wasn't, she didn't really care. She just did her best to nod.

"What are you doing out here all alone?" She could hear the frown in his voice.

Liesel finally opened her eyes and looked at him, but her chattering teeth made it impossible to answer.

His expression softened. "Well, no matter. We'd best get you home. I'm sure your mum's worried something awful. I know my wife would be." He didn't see, but Liesel felt a tear roll down her cheek. Yes, Mother would have worried.

As he carried her, he talked, and Liesel found his voice to be soothing. He was a hunter, he said, and his name was Paul. He didn't usually come this far east, but the buck he'd been chasing had led him outside of his normal grounds. He had a family back in higher country, including a daughter about her age, and he didn't like to leave them for long.

Liesel began to drift in and out of slumber as he carried her back and chatted away. It wasn't until they were at the edge of the village that she realized she'd fallen asleep.

"You, sir!" The hunter called out. "I have a girl here, and she's not well! Do you know where I might find her family?"

"I'm new here. I wouldn't know." Liesel's eyes were closed again, but she recognized the worn, rough tone of her father's voice. Instead of its usual arrogance, however, it was hoarse and broken. A small piece of Liesel's senses returned, enough to feel pity for the man. But with the pity came rage as well. It was he who had dragged them to this place of death, and he had been the one to hold her back when Amala still could have been saved. And he knew it, from the sound of his voice.

"If you please," the hunter said, shifting her weight in his arms, "I found this girl in the forest. She was being attacked by a wolf—"

"Girl?" Warin's voice lifted slightly. "I've been missin' mine since I came home and found her mother dead."

"I ... I'm sorry," the hunter said softly. "I found this child in the woods, like I said, bitten by a wolf. Perhaps the pain of losing her mother was just too much ..." He stepped forward again. "If you would just look and see if she's yours." Liesel heard her father rouse himself from the stoop slowly and walk towards them.

"Aye, she's mine. Don't know what the fool girl was thinkin', runnin' into the woods alone at night." Despite his harsh words, his voice was soft and gentle. Familiar arms lifted her from the hunter's. Liesel wished she could find her voice to thank the stranger for his kindness.

Her father didn't put her into the bed, and Liesel couldn't look to see if it was because her mother's body was still there. Instead, he simply carried her to a chair in the corner of the room and cradled her as he had done when she was young. The last sound Liesel heard that night was Warin's quiet sobbing as he held her close. Her last thought was a desperate one.

She still hadn't escaped the woods.

Continue Kurt and Liesel's tale in Girl in the Red Hood: A Clean Fairy Tale Retelling of Little Red Riding Hood.

Dear Reader,
I want to thank you for journeying with me through Before Beauty.

Writing the final installation of Ever and Isa's story was a treat, and I'm so glad you were along for the ride.

If you like free stories (including more about Isa and Ever) visit BrittanyFichterFiction.com. By joining my email list, you'll get free access to secret bonus stories (about Ever, Isa, Henri, and Jenny), sneaks peeks, book updates, exclusive coupons, and more!

And if you loved this book, please consider giving it a rating or review so other readers can find it to on your favorite retailer or Goodreads.com.

Sign me up!

ABOUT THE AUTHOR

Brittany lives with her Prince Charming, their little fairy, and their little prince in a ~~sparkling~~ (decently clean) castle in whatever kingdom the Air Force has most recently placed them. When she's not writing, Brittany can be found chasing her kids around with a DSLR and belting it in the church choir.

Subscribe: BrittanyFichterFiction.com
Email: BrittanyFichterFiction@gmail.com
Facebook: Facebook.com/BFichterFiction
Instagram: @BrittanyFichterFiction